Full Figured 5:

Carl Weber Presents

Full Figured 5:

Carl Weber Presents

Brenda Hampton
and Rose Jackson-Beavers

www.urbanbooks.net

Urban Books, LLC
78 East Industry Court
Deer Park, NY 11729

ISBN 13: 978-1-60162-352-2
ISBN 10: 1-60162-352-6

First Trade Paperback Printing September 2012
Printed in the United States of America

10 9 8 7 6 5 4 3 2 1

Distributed by Kensington Publishing Corp.
Submit Wholesale Orders to:
Kensington Publishing Corp.
C/O Penguin Group (USA) Inc.
Attention: Order Processing
405 Murray Hill Parkway
East Rutherford, NJ 07073-2316
Phone: 1-800-526-0275
Fax: 1-800-227-9604

WHO YA WIT' 3

by
Brenda Hampton

Chapter 1

I wasn't sure if I would ever get this thing called love right. Ever since I could remember, my relationships had been complicated. Divorcing Reggie was just the beginning, and even though we were high school sweethearts, once I found out he had cheated on me, he had to go. I started dating a few other men from time to time, but it was a complete waste because none of them tickled my fancy long enough for me to keep them. Then, I met Roc. Roc was nearly half my age. He was the only man who had brought out that fire in me. He made me smile and laugh again. He made me feel as if I could breathe again, but the drama that came along with him was unacceptable.

Roc could be classified as a thug to many, and being in the drug game for so many years really disturbed me. He'd done some jail time, all in the name of protecting his uncle Ronnie. Roc loved Ronnie with every fiber of his being, but only a few months ago some decisions had to be made after Ronnie had threatened to kill me and my daughter, Chassidy.

According to Roc, he made the decision to have Ronnie removed from this earth. I was stunned yet grateful at the same time, because I knew it was either Ronnie or me who would wind up dead. The sad thing was that Roc continued to make decisions to walk away and leave me high and dry. A few years ago, he went to jail by choice and took the blame for someone else. When he got out, he promised me he would never leave me and Chassidy, but after Ronnie was killed, Roc walked away from us again. He told me he was moving on and would never look back. That meant our relationship was history, until he showed up at my son Latrel's wedding. I was shocked. Roc professed his love for me that day, trying to represent Black Love. He claimed he was ready to be all that I needed him to be. I didn't believe him for one minute and I had no choice but to let him go.

That day, however, was something I couldn't erase from my mind. I kept seeing him standing in the rain in his dripping wet suit that melted on his muscles. His eyes stared into mine, as my friend Monica, who was driving the car, drove away. My heart was calling out to him, even though I didn't want it to. Days after, I kept asking myself if I had made a mistake by letting him go. Was there something with this relationship that I was missing, or missing out on? I couldn't stop thinking about Roc, but since he hadn't reached out to me, that made things easy.

I had to face the facts that our relationship had been very unstable. The drama with his baby mama, Vanessa, was too much. I was so sure she continued to play a big part in his life. At forty-three years old, I needed something solid. I needed someone I could depend on and Chassidy needed a father she could look up to, one who would be there for her. At this point, I wasn't convinced that Roc was the one.

Still, I missed him. A flash of his pearly whites when he smiled kept appearing before me. His dimples were put on display right before my eyes and I kept reaching out to touch his midnight muscular frame that made me attracted to him even more. His frame, however, wasn't there for me to touch, nor were his hooded, sexy eyes that showed much seriousness at times. I wanted to look into them, again, just to say those words he was probably dying to hear from me. Those words were that I'd made a mistake by letting him go. I wanted to know if we could reconcile our differences and start seeing each other again.

During my dream last night, I'd said those words to Roc and he was more than delighted to reconcile. He squeezed me in his arms and planted soft kisses on my lips. Right before we were about to indulge ourselves in hot and heavy sex, my alarm clock went off. I had to get up for work, so I rushed out of bed to take a cold shower.

Once I was dressed, I hurried to get Chassidy ready so I could drop her off at preschool. Every single morning she asked about Roc, and about seeing her little brother, Lil Roc, whom she'd gotten so close to. Removing them from our lives didn't seem like the sensible thing to do. Chassidy made it clear that she wanted to see her daddy, as well as her brother.

"When?" she asked as I pulled the purple shirt with Tinker Bell on it over her head. "When is he coming home, Mommy? You said it would be soon, but I haven't seen him in a long time."

I was too ashamed to tell Chassidy that Roc and I couldn't get our mess together. I told her he'd been on a long vacation, and once he got back, he and Lil Roc would come see us. It didn't seem as though that was going to happen anytime soon, and I didn't want to break Chassidy's heart.

"His phone number changed, sweetheart, and I've been unable to reach him. I'll do some searching. If I get his phone number, I'll tell him how much you miss him, okay?"

Chassidy displayed a wide grin while stepping into her jeans. She looked so much like Roc, chocolate with pretty round eyes and wavy hair. I figured Roc was probably upset with me, but I wondered if he'd even thought about his daughter. I had to be sure that bringing him back into our lives was a good thing to do, because it was evident that all the back and forth between us was starting to affect Chassidy.

Almost an hour later, I dropped Chassidy off at preschool and headed to work. While waiting in my car at a red light, I tapped my fingers on the steering wheel, contemplating my next move. I had called Roc's number several times, but his phone was disconnected. I'd even gone to his place, just to see if he had moved to Kansas City as he had said. I wasn't sure if Kansas City was his destination, but one thing was for sure . . . his place was empty. It was obvious that after what he'd done to Ronnie, Roc didn't want anyone, including me, to know where he was. Something inside told me to let go; then there was something encouraging me to pursue what I was feeling in my heart. In my heart I was still in love with the father of my child, and with the young man who made my life feel complete. We'd had our ups and downs, but there was no doubt in my mind that we still had love for each other.

Like always, work was hectic. I kept busy, and since Mr. Anderson knew my vacation started tomorrow he couldn't stop bugging me.

"Desa Rae!" he yelled from his office. My cubicle sat right outside his office, but yelling for me seemed very inappropriate. It was something I'd gotten used to, though, so I didn't trip. I rushed into his office, wearing a popping peach sheer blouse with ruffles around the collar and a fitted cream-colored skirt that cut above my knees. My outfit was accessorized with gold bangles at my wrist and a thick shimmering gold belt that I'd gotten at Ashley Stewart. I was proud of my curves. Mr.

Anderson shifted his eyes from my 40 double-Ds to my face, and all he could do was smile.

"I apologize for yelling, but my intercom is broken," he said, reaching out to hand me several papers. "Would you mind making copies of these reports for me?"

I took the papers from his hand. "Will do. And can I get you anything else while I'm away from my desk?"

His eyes shifted again, this time at my breasts. I wasn't sure if Mr. Anderson was intentionally flirting with me, or if he just couldn't help himself. I guess any man in his right mind would look at a beautiful woman, but as long as he didn't touch, or say anything inappropriate to me, I was cool.

"A Pepsi," he said, turning his attention to my eyes again. "Bring me a Pepsi with a cup of ice."

I nodded, and as I turned to walk away, I could feel Mr. Anderson's lustful eyes all over me. He was an older black man who cheated on his wife and simply did not give a damn. He was sloppy with his mess, too, with his out-of-control mistresses calling the office and showing up whenever they wanted to. His wife popped up at the office, several times, trying to catch him in the act. I'd heard them arguing over his actions, but after thirty-plus years together, his wife remained with him. That was their business, not mine. Even though she had questioned me about my involvement with him, I let it be known that I was only his administrative assistant. Nothing more, nothing less. She had much respect for me, and remained cordial each time she called or came into the office. Their daughter was the one I took issue with. She dated my son, Latrel, but seemed fake as ever. When I found out she'd had sex with Roc, when she'd told Latrel she was a virgin, she had to go. I was so glad that Latrel was now married to Angelique.

They still had another semester and a half of college to finish, but my daughter-in-law was a jewel.

I made copies of Mr. Anderson's reports, then stopped by the lunchroom to get his soda. I chatted for a few minutes with some of the ladies I'd known from other departments, then headed back to Mr. Anderson's office. As I swayed my wide hips from side to side, making my way down the carpeted hallway, I heard a whistle. I snapped my head to the right, seeing a man named Greg whom I'd dated a few times while Roc was in prison. Needless to say, things didn't work out. Greg was a nerd and nerds I could not do.

He stepped outside of his cubicle to check me out. "Looking good, Desa Rae. Sweetheart, you always look dynamite."

I stopped in my tracks, just to give him a forced smile. Too bad I couldn't say the same for Greg. His suits were always too big on him and he looked slouchy. He was a nice man, though. I didn't want to be disrespectful and not acknowledge him or his kind words. I walked over to his cubicle and stood inside to talk.

"Thanks for the compliment, Greg. You don't look bad yourself."

He blushed and dropped back in his swivel leather chair to take a seat. "Soooo, how have you been? I don't see your boyfriend around here anymore, so I suspect the two of you must have broken up."

"Just because he doesn't work here anymore, it doesn't mean we're not together."

Greg licked his lips and cleared his throat. "If you don't mind me saying . . . I think you can do a lot better than him. He's still wet behind the ears and you, Miss Thickety-thick, need a real man to handle you. I doubt that he can do it."

There he goes with that Thickety-thick mess again. Didn't men know that it was an insult to say that to a healthy woman with curves? True to the fact or not, Greg was out of line. "Well, Mr. Boney-Maroni, if it takes a man who is still wet behind the ears to please me, so be it. You had your chance, and don't discredit Roc for being all that I needed him to be."

"You said 'needed,' as in past tense. I guess that means the two of you aren't together anymore, so why don't you let me slide back in and take you to dinner? I can be everything you need me to be and then some."

I didn't want to hurt Greg's feelings, but Roc or no Roc, Greg was out of luck. "Sorry, Greg, I'm not interested anymore. Got other things on my mind right now and the last thing I need to be doing is going on dates. Besides, I'm still upset with you for telling Roc our business to begin with. Something about that whole thing rubbed me the wrong way, so I'd better leave well enough alone."

"Awww, come on, Desa Rae. All I did was answer the man's questions. I didn't think I was telling him something he should've already known."

"Well, he didn't know. I was left with a bad taste in my mouth. I'm sure you understand. Good day, Greg. I'll see you around."

Greg pursed his lips, but didn't say another word as I walked away. When I got back to Mr. Anderson's office, I stopped dead in my tracks at the doorway. Sitting in a chair in front of his desk was a young woman with long legs and eight-inch high heels. The tight skirt she wore barely covered her ass and the flowing weave down her back made her look like a stripper. She tossed her hair aside and scanned her eyes up and down me, from head to toe. Gold digger was written all over her, and even though Mr. Anderson was a handsome black man, I could tell this woman was interested in his money.

"Come in," he said to me. I stepped forward and reached out to give the copies, soda, and cup of ice to Mr. Anderson.

"Thank you," he said, then looked at his gold watch. "It's almost lunchtime, Desa Rae. Do you have any plans?"

"No, I'm going to sit at my desk and make some phone calls. I brought a tuna sandwich today anyway, so I'll be at my cubicle if you need me."

"I have a meeting with Ms. Avery and won't require your assistance for at least a few more hours. If you have some errands to run, go right ahead. Please close my door behind you."

"Sure," was all I said, without looking at Ms. Avery, who had her legs crossed, wanting to be seen. Mr. Anderson's so-called meeting wasn't on his calendar. I suspected that when I returned, his office would be lit up with the smell of sex. Like the last time, I hoped he had some air freshener to kill the smell, but I guessed he would leave that up to me too.

Before I had a chance to leave his office, Ms. Avery stood up, showing off her big butt and hourglass figure. She wanted me to see what Mr. Anderson was paying for, but little did she know I truly didn't care.

"I'm thirsty too," she said, looking at me, then at Mr. Anderson. "Maybe you can make your secretary get me a soda before she goes to lunch."

My eyes narrowed. Before any words escaped from my mouth, Mr. Anderson spoke up. "I . . . I will get you something to drink. Have a seat and watch your tone."

She smirked at him, but did as she was told. It was obvious who had the upper hand, and Mr. Anderson's scolding look told her to shut the hell up. I felt no need to comment. It was clear that some side hoes just didn't know their place or when to keep their mouths shut.

Excited that Mr. Anderson was allowing me to leave, I said good-bye to him and closed his door on my way out.

While sitting in my car, I took bites of my tuna sandwich and downed a strawberry Vess soda. The sodas were killing me, and if I could cut back on them, I knew my weight would drop tremendously. I was still wearing a size fourteen to sixteen, and the only thing my doctor encouraged me to do was take walks. He insisted that walking contributed to having a healthy heart, so on a regular basis I took walks with Chassidy at the park. I couldn't help but think about my conversation with her this morning, and my thoughts quickly turned to Roc again. Knowing that I would hear that his phone was disconnected, I still dialed out to see if anything had changed. It hadn't. I wasn't sure where else I should turn, but I always knew I could get good advice from my best friend, Monica.

Monica and I were supposed to go to Jamaica on my vacation, but since money was tight, she backed out on me. Yes, I was upset, but I understood her situation. She just didn't have the money, and quite frankly, I didn't have it to give. If I did, we would have been out of there tomorrow. Instead, I had planned to give my house an old-fashioned cleaning and get ready for the upcoming holidays—Thanksgiving and Christmas.

"I know you're still mad at me," Monica said over the phone. "I really needed a vacation, Dee, but these kids done borrowed so much money from me, I barely have money for myself. That along with my bills ain't no joke. This economy has to get better, and since the rich are the only ones getting richer, I may have to start looking for a rich man to throw in some help!"

I laughed, but was grateful that Monica and I both had been handling our finances on our own for years.

"I'm not mad, girl. Disappointed, yes, but we'll go somewhere next year. Maybe by then we'll both be married to wealthy men who can help get us out of these ruts!"

"I agree. Wealthy, sexy, and good in bed. Don't know if those kinds of men exist anymore, and you know the last man I went out with, Chance, was out of control. The way he carried on made me take a step back. I'm afraid to date again."

I giggled, thinking about what Monica had told me about her date. Chance was a man she'd met on a dating site. Monica had tried something different, but was disappointed when he showed up at a restaurant looking nothing like his profile picture. He was five feet four, had a bald head, and wore a round earring in his left ear. Monica said he looked like a mini pirate and I couldn't stop laughing that day as she gave me the horrific details of their evening together. "That was an awful experience," I said. "But don't give up on relationships. Somebody is out there for you. He'll come when you least expect it."

"I guess so, but I do get lonely sometimes. I'm not going to accept anybody, though, and you shouldn't either. Maybe we should go out this weekend and see what's happening at the comedy club. We haven't been out in a while and dancing, a good laugh, and drinking may be what we need."

"That may not be a bad idea. Besides, Chassidy is going to spend some time with Latrel and Angelique. They're coming to get her tomorrow, so I'll call you on Friday."

"I can't believe you've agreed to go out, but I'm glad you did. Who knows . . . you just may find another man like Roc. I can tell you miss him, Dee, and if you do, why don't you just call him?"

I wouldn't dare tell Monica that I had been calling him; I was too embarrassed. I told her it was over and I didn't want her to judge me for still having some hope in our relationship. "Girl, I'm not thinking about Roc. I hope he's somewhere living happily ever after. If he is, good for him."

"Uh-hmm," Monica said, knowing me all too well. "I can't see you not thinking about Roc, and I don't believe for one minute that he hasn't crossed your mind."

I bit into my nail, wanting to tell Monica the truth. "Maybe just a little. I've been thinking about him a little, because I think I made some mistakes."

"If you're having regrets, call him. What can it hurt? You said Chassidy wants to see him and it's obvious that you do too."

"I do want to see him, but I'm not sure what to say. I guess I'd have to find him first. It seems to me that the man has disappeared."

Monica was silent for a while; then she responded. "Go back to the first place you met him. It was at the carwash, wasn't it? If he's not there, I'm sure somebody there knows how to reach him. And, if you're lucky to catch up with him, good for you. What's meant to be will be."

I couldn't agree with Monica more. We talked for a few more minutes; then I took her advice and drove to the carwash I'd met Roc at on Lindbergh Boulevard. His uncle Ronnie used to own the place, and even though he was no longer alive, the carwash was still open for business. It was in no way as busy as it had been before, but I wasn't sure if that was because winter was just coming in, or business wasn't that great. Either way, I parked my car, and as the gusty wind slapped my face and blew open my trench coat, I hurried inside to see what I could find out.

"May I help you?" asked a white man with a wrinkly face. He definitely wasn't who I'd expected to be standing behind the counter, but what the hell.

"I hope you can help me. I'm looking for Rocky Dawson. He used to work here awhile back, and his uncle Ronnie owned this place. I'm an old friend and I'm trying to catch up with him."

"Ronnie no longer owns this place, I do. And I don't know who Mr. Dawson is. Sorry I couldn't help you."

I nodded, pretty much knowing that I wouldn't have much luck here. My luck, however, changed when I saw Roc's friend, Bud, standing in the back office with a black phone pressed up to his ear.

"Excuse me, but isn't his name Bud?" I asked the white man.

He turned to Bud, then back to me. "Yes, he's the manager. Would you like to speak to him?"

"If you don't mind," I said, smiling. "I hope it won't be a problem."

"Not at all."

The white man walked away. Shortly after, Bud came from the office and made his way to the front desk. He inquisitively looked at me, then smiled.

"Desa Rae," he said, coming from behind the counter. He reached out his hand to shake mine. I accepted.

"Hello, Bud. It's been a looong time. I'm so glad that you remember me."

"Of course I do. The last time I saw you was at the hospital when Roc had been shot. I'm glad it all turned out for the best, because he damn sure had all of us worried that day."

"Yes, he did. Very worried, as I am still worried about him right now. I haven't seen him in a while, and I heard that he'd moved to Kansas City. Have you heard from him at all?"

Bud nodded and tucked his dirty gloves into his back pocket. "We talk every now and then. When Ronnie was killed, so many things changed. Several of our partners went down, and a few came up missin'. We never found out who was responsible, but I know Roc won't rest until he finds out what really happened. The last time we spoke, he was on a mission to do just that."

"I can only imagine. I wouldn't want to disturb his mission, but I would like to talk to him. Do you have a number where I can reach him?"

Luckily, Bud did not hesitate. He pulled a business card from his pocket and scribbled Roc's number and address on the back. He gave the card to me. I looked at the card, noticing that it was a St. Louis number.

"I thought he was in Kansas City. Didn't he move?" I asked.

"I believe he has a place in Kansas City, but he has a place here too. Go holla at him. I'm sure he'll be glad to see you. I know he really cared for you, Desa Rae, and after losin' Ronnie, I'm sure seein' or hearin' from you would up his spirits."

"I hope so," I said, feeling the same way as Bud. I thanked him for the information and returned to my car. Once inside, I reached for my cell phone and dialed the number Bud had written on the card. My heart was racing a mile a minute. When I heard Roc's voice on the other end, my heart started slamming hard against my chest. My mouth was dry; I was barely able to speak.

"He . . . hello, Roc," I said with a stutter.

"Who dis?" he asked in a sharp tone.

"It's me. Desa Rae."

There was ongoing silence, then a deep sigh that was followed by a click.

Chapter 2

Nearly an hour later, I was back at my desk with a serious attitude because Roc had hung up on me. I couldn't believe he'd done it. I knew he wasn't that upset with me where he didn't even want to talk. I mean, after all the crazy mess he had done to me, I was always willing to listen to what he'd had to say. I may not have agreed with his decisions, but I always gave him every opportunity to express himself. Shame. Shame on him for dissing me like he did. In no way would I kiss his tail or try to get him to change his mind about us. I viewed it as his loss, not mine.

Mr. Anderson's door was shut, so I figured his meeting with Ms. Avery was still going on. I had no intention of interrupting him, but I surely couldn't wait for this day to be over. Even though my vacation plans to Jamaica were squashed, I was still looking forward to chilling around the house, doing nothing but resting, reading, cleaning, and catching up on reality TV shows. Monica's suggestion to go out this weekend seemed right up my alley, too, but I wasn't so sure about the club scene in St. Louis. The last time I'd gone out, drama ensued. Somebody started shooting and Roc and I got caught in the crossfire. I was thinking about changing my mind, but when I called Monica to renege, she tore into me.

"You had me hyped about going, now you done changed your mind that fast? I guess I'll just go by myself, and why must a little partying at a comedy club be considered a crime?"

"It's not and that's not what I'm saying. I was just thinking about the last time I went out with Roc. Things didn't go so well. I don't know if the club scene has changed."

"I don't know either, but I'm willing to go out and have a good time. We don't have to stay long, just for a few hours."

I sighed, but agreed to go because I hated to let Monica down. After all, we were both single, so what did we have to lose? "I'll go. But you're driving. Pick me up around nine o'clock on Saturday."

"Will do. Now, changing the subject for just a minute. Did you have any luck with getting in touch with Roc?"

"If you believe that him hanging up on me when I called was success, then I had it. Can you believe that? I want to call him back and cuss him out, but forget it."

Monica laughed. "See, you're better than me. I would call him back and get in his shit. What nerve does he have hanging up on you? I know he's not upset about how you walked away from him at Latrel's wedding, is he? What did Roc expect for you to do?"

"That's what I want to know. He keep disappearing, then showing back up, expecting me to be there for him no matter what. What kind of mess is that?"

"I'm with you this time. Forget him. If he wants to act like that, who needs him?"

I was so glad that Monica had taken my side and was seeing things my way. We kept talking about my unfortunate situation with Roc, but when I turned to the right and saw Mrs. Anderson coming my way, I whispered to Monica that I had to go.

"I'll call you later," I said, slamming the phone down and jumping to my feet. A wide grin covered my face, and I smiled as Mrs. Anderson approached my cubicle.

"Hello, Judy. You look lovely today," I complimented her. She did look nice in her winter-white pantsuit and black high heels. Her healthy gray hair was full of tight curls that hung past her shoulders. She was a beautiful black woman and Mr. Anderson knew better than to trade in class for trash who was in his office.

"Thank you, Desa Rae. It's always a delight seeing you. By any chance, is my husband here? I've called his cell phone several times and didn't get an answer."

I swallowed hard, then looked at his office door that was still closed. I couldn't hear anything coming from inside, but I was sure he hadn't left. "I . . . I just got back from lunch, but per his calendar, it looks as if he's been in meetings all day. Once he returns, I'll ask him to give you a call. I'm sure it'll be soon."

I hated to be put in the middle like this. Lying to Mrs. Anderson didn't feel right to me. I didn't want her to get her feelings hurt, nor did I want to find myself without a job.

"If he'll be back soon, I'll wait for him. I do need to go to the ladies' room, so I'll be right back."

I sighed from relief as Mrs. Anderson walked away. As she did, I quickly buzzed Mr. Anderson in his office. He didn't answer.

"Mr. Anderson," I said, raising my voice through gritted teeth. "Please pick up! This is urgent!"

Finally, he picked up the phone, sounding as if Ms. Avery had drained every ounce of semen from his dick. "Whaaaaat is it, Desa Rae? Didn't I tell you not to interrupt me?" he hissed.

His tone raised my brows, but now wasn't the time for me to show my ass. "Your wife is here to see you," was all I said and hung up.

I dropped back to my chair. My heart was racing for Mr. Anderson. I could hear a bunch of bumbling going on in his office. Minutes later, I could see Mrs. Anderson coming my way, causing me to sink into my chair. It was obvious that things were about to turn ugly, and as soon as she neared my cubicle, Mr. Anderson's door came open. His eyes connected with Mrs. Anderson's, but her eyes were glued to the Video Vixen. I immediately noticed that her weave was now a bit tangled, her makeup had disappeared, and her short skirt had wrinkles. The beads of sweat on Mr. Anderson's forehead were a dead giveaway and his white pressed shirt was barely tucked into his slacks. Why people chose the workplace to have sex, I didn't know. But Mr. Anderson was a risk taker. I wasn't so sure that it would pay off for him today.

He displayed a fake grin on his face, but when Mrs. Anderson's hand went up to her hip, it was obvious that his grin had not sold her. "I've been trying to reach you," she said in a sharp tone. "Looks like you've been tied up with this heifer and unable to answer your phone."

Ms. Avery pointed her finger near Mrs. Anderson's face, but before she could say anything, Mr. Anderson spoke up. "It's not what you think," he said to his wife. "Latrese just stopped by to let me know what was going on with our son at school. I transferred my calls to voice mail, and our meeting has only lasted thirty or forty minutes. You know I would've returned your call. Don't I always?"

His son! I thought. *Wow, he has a son by this woman?* That was something new to me, and I was all ears.

Mrs. Anderson shook her head and pursed her lips. "When are the lies going to stop? I've been trying to reach you for two hours, not thirty minutes. I told you that if you continue this thing with Latrese, you and I are over. Expect to hear from my attorney tomorrow, and since you can't find time for me, maybe you'll find time for your mother. She's been taken to the hospital. I don't know how serious it is, but if you weren't so busy playing house at work, maybe you would've learned of her condition faster than me."

Without saying another word, Mrs. Anderson walked away. She wasn't about to make a damn fool of herself, clowning over no man, and I didn't blame her. Ms. Avery stood with a grin on her face, and even though I had nothing to do with it, I surely wanted to slap the mess out of her. I despised women who interfered in people's marriages. And then to have a child by a married man was tacky. Apparently Mr. Anderson didn't give two cents about her, and all she was worth was a fuck in his office. He had gone back into his office to make some phone calls, I guessed to find out what was going on with his mother. Ms. Avery waited for him by the doorway, until I heard him tell her to leave.

She folded her arms, and tried to show a look of concern on her face. "Are you going to be okay?" she asked. "Let me know if you need anything. I'm just a phone call away."

He didn't even respond. I could hear him speaking to someone over the phone, so it was time for the trash to make way back to the Dumpster. She could see the scolding look in my eyes, but all she did was smile and walk away. Good for her, because I wasn't one who could hold my peace with women like her. The situation with my ex-husband, Reggie, left me bitter. We had been through some of the same mess, but eventually Reggie simply told me that he didn't love me anymore. He wanted to be with his mistress, but after we divorced, their relationship didn't last much longer. Reggie tried to come crawling back, but there wasn't a chance in hell that I would ever let him back into my life. I was at an age where I needed peace and stability in my relationships, and in no way did I want to find myself at the age of Mr. and Mrs. Anderson, still dealing with this kind of foolishness. When was enough, enough? The truth of the matter was, Mr. Anderson had been getting away with this crap for a long time. I hoped Mrs. Anderson was serious about taking action, but that was her decision to make.

I was so glad the day was over. I barely had a chance to say good-bye to Mr. Anderson because he had left to see about his mother. Also, he'd spent much of the afternoon trying to calm things with his wife over the phone, so there wasn't much for me to do. I packed it up early and left too. On my way to pick up Chassidy from preschool I made a quick detour. I still had at least an hour and a half to pick her up, and going against everything I had felt inside, I decided to see what was up with the address that was written on the card from Bud. If Roc had issues with anything I'd said or done to him, I wanted him to tell me face to face. It was ridiculous for him to hang up on me, and if the shoe were on the other foot, he would want some answers too. I had plenty of questions, so I pressed my foot on the accelerator and sped up.

When I arrived at the ranch-style home off New Halls Ferry Road, I became a bit nervous. Two SUVs were in the driveway and one had the hatch lifted. The front door was open, but the screen door was not. The house itself looked to be in good condition and the neighborhood was populated with Blacks. I wondered if Roc was living here with someone, or if the house belonged to him. I didn't think that Bud would give me another woman's address, but when I saw a young chick looking to be in her mid to late twenties or early thirties come outside with a bag in her hand, maybe he did. She was an attractive young woman, a bit healthy like me, but her hair was cut short. I was glad not to see Vanessa, but I wasn't happy to see that the woman was pregnant. She looked to be at least four or five months—she was definitely showing. I couldn't help but to think how long Roc and I had been apart, and if my calculations were correct, it had been, maybe, seven months. Also, I wasn't sure who the woman was, but when she saw me parked across the street, she waved. I didn't want to look as if I was checking out the scenery, so I proceeded out of my car, just to get the answers I came to get.

"Excuse me," I said, walking up the driveway with a smile. "Does Roc live here?"

Her seemingly nice demeanor changed and her face fell flat. "Who wants to know?" she asked. Her eyes were all over me and much attitude was written on her face.

I reached out my hand to shake hers. She looked at it, and hesitated before she shook it. "My name is Desa Rae. I'm just an old friend of Roc's. I'm not here to cause any trouble and all I want to do is speak to him about our daughter."

She pulled her hand away and attached it to her hip. "Desa Rae? Are you one of his babies' mamas?"

Well damn! That didn't even sound right to me, but I guessed I was, especially if she was one too. Thinking about it, I now wondered what the hell I was doing here. I started to walk away—run—but when I heard Roc's stern voice, my head snapped to the front door. Almost immediately, my heart slammed so hard against my chest, as if it wanted to get out. Roc looked fine as ever, and without a shirt on, his buffed chest was carved in all the right places. The blackness of his silky skin was a beautiful sight and the waves on his Caesar cut were flowing deeper than the ocean. His jeans hung low on his waist, showing his baby-blue boxers. He leaned against the doorway while holding the screen door open. I hadn't moved and neither had the other chick, so he called out again.

"Tiara, come here," he said. "Come back inside."

Tiara rolled her eyes and closed the hatch. She walked toward the front door, stopping before going inside. "See, this is what I was afraid of," she said to him. "I get tired of your hoes showing up at their leisure. I wish you would handle this."

Tiara pulled on the screen door and bumped Roc's shoulder as she walked into the house. He said not one word to her, but the smirk on his face showed that he really didn't give a damn. I'd seen that look plenty of times before. The one thing that I had known about Roc was he got a kick out of drama and could handle any woman who would bring it.

As I approached the door, the smirk on his face disappeared. His face was without a smile and seriousness was in his eyes. "What?" he said. "What do you want? Before you tell me, though, let me just say that you are awfully bold showin' up at my house and callin' me. This better be good, Dez, and you got two minutes to get to the point."

Yeah, he was working me, but I tried to remain calm, especially since he had a point about me being pretty bold. True to the fact or not, I was here and I needed to get some things off my chest. His chest, however, had me screaming inside and creaming where I didn't want to be. I started my conversation, lusting at his chest and his numerous tattoos that ran up and down his arms. "It's kind of cold outside, so you may want to go back inside to put a shirt on," I said.

Roc sighed and let go of the screen door to step outside. Keeping his shirt off, he crossed his arms across his chest, causing more muscles to bulge. *Damn!* I thought. This was so hard! My tongue was tied and I wondered if he could see all the lust I had in my eyes for him. I wasn't so sure how he felt about seeing me, but his stern look didn't appear down with my visit.

"A minute and a half, Desa Rae. Speak."

To stay warm and calm my trembling cold hands, I eased them into the pockets of my trench coat. "I . . . I just wanted to see how you were doing and tell you that Chassidy really misses you. I've been trying to get in touch with you and haven't had much success. It's obvious that you're still upset with me, but I think it's been so unfair to our daughter that you've made no attempts to be in her life. I've never asked you for much, Roc, but I never thought you would separate yourself from your daughter as you have. What's up with that?"

He sucked his teeth, staring at me as if I irritated him. "I told you what was up, and when I tried to make things right, you basically told me to go fuck myself. So, don't stand out here and make this all about Chassidy, because if it was, you would've thought about her when I gave you an opportunity to. I don't know why you've all of a sudden had a change of heart, but my heart don't get down like that. Using Chassidy ain't workin' for me either. If she misses me, you need to woman up and tell her why I'm not around anymore."

Roc's words and tone stung, but I did my best not to let my frustrations with him show. "I'm not making this all about Chassidy, and I'll be the first to admit that I miss you too. But you know better than I do, Roc, that your timing at Latrel's wedding was off. I hadn't seen you in months and—"

He quickly cut me off. "So fuckin' what!" he shouted. "I was tryin' to get my damn life together like you had asked me to. You were complainin' all the time about how I was livin' and when I attempted to do the right thing, it still wasn't good enough for you. I ain't havin' this conversation with you, Dez, 'cause life goes on. The shit that went down between us is a wrap and I ain't one to reflect or harp on the past. What could've been, will be no more. And as far as Chassidy is concerned, you work it out and get at me when you do."

Now, I was pissed. What in the hell did he mean by that? "Work it out? How? I don't understand the *slang* you're using and you need to simplify your choice of words," I said.

Roc uncrossed his arms and slowly inched forward. He stood face to face with me, so close that I could smell his peppermint breath and could see cold air coming from his mouth. "You can tell Chassidy that I miss her too, but you, Desa Rae Jenkins, can kiss my black ass. I hope that simplifies my words enough for you."

Without saying anything else, Roc turned and slammed the door after he went back inside. My feelings were bruised, but I took a hard swallow and left to go get Chassidy. I would never, ever put myself in a situation like this again. If Roc ever wanted to be a part of our lives, he would definitely have to make the next move.

Chapter 3

Latrel and Angelique came to pick up Chassidy on Friday. They were off from school for the next two weeks and had plans to spend Thanksgiving with Angelique's mother and stepfather at their resort in Florida. I had to get used to being without my children on the holidays, and even though I viewed it as them sharing time with Angelique's parents, I still didn't like it. I figured Chassidy would be bored staying here with me, and she probably preferred being with Latrel and Angelique. They had Chassidy spoiled rotten, and being with them would surely take her mind off Roc. I continued to tell her that I was unable to get in touch with him. I didn't know what else to say and my hope was that she'd stop asking. At this point, it looked as if we were on our own. When she was a little older, I would share the truth with her.

On Saturday, Monica was right on time picking me up. Now, I was excited about going out and had pushed what had happened with Roc to the back of my mind. That was until I sat at a two-seat table with Monica at the comedy club, waiting for the comedian, Fatz, to make his appearance. The club was crowded with people over the age of thirty-five and the environment was pretty nice. The waiters and waitresses were very polite and many of the partygoers around us seemed down to earth. We all joined in on a conversation about the last comedian who had us cracking up.

"He was hilarious," one lady said, who sat next to us at a different table. Her hand was on her chest and she was smiling while shaking her head. "I almost spit my drink out, laughing so hard. And when he started talking about the *Maury* show, I could have died!"

Monica agreed, and even though I'd never watched the *Maury* show, what the comedian had said about it made me want to tune in. I couldn't believe some women would lie about the father of their children. Didn't they know the only ones they would hurt were the kids? Either way, we were having a good time. I reminded myself to thank Monica for inviting me, especially when I saw an old flame from high school in my view. His name was Darrell. I'd dated Reggie throughout high school and college, but I'd had a crush on Darrell for years. Of course he looked much older, but with a shiny bald head and a physically fit body, he was doable.

"Isn't that Darrell over there?" I whispered to Monica.

She had known how I'd felt about Darrell in the past, so Monica almost broke her neck as she snapped it around to look behind her. She smiled and waved from afar, obviously realizing that it was him. I waved too, not knowing that he was looking in our direction.

"Oh, my," she said, turning to face me and speaking in a whisper. "It looks like he's headed over here."

"Yes, he is," I replied, as I, saw him coming to. I was always worried about my weight. I was proud of my curves, but I couldn't deny that I was a size ten in high school and college. Tonight, though, I looked good. My hair was full of tight curls that rested on my shoulders. Several tresses dangled in my face and my makeup was on light, but flawless. The turquoise dress I wore was loose at the top, but hugged my ass and hips. Dangling silver earrings hung from my lobes and silver-strapped heels adorned my feet. I could tell Darrell liked everything he saw and his wide smile displayed it.

When Darrell approached the table, he reached out to shake Monica's hand first. "What's going on, Miss Monica? How are you?"

She shook his hand, appearing to be happy to see him too. "I'm fine, Darrell, looks like you are as well."

We all laughed. Monica was a person you could always count on to somewhat tell the truth. Darrell did have it going on from afar, but his suit didn't quite fit him as I had hoped. His shoes looked a bit worn, and as he reached for my hand to shake it, his hand was a bit rough. Ashy, too, but maybe I was being too observant. I was sure he'd seen some of my flaws too, and he could've easily been thinking that I had put on some weight.

"Desa Rae Jenkins," he said. "Don't you look lovely . . . lovely as ever. I had to come over here to say hello. I'm so glad that I did."

His compliments were nice and so was he. I had to realize that not every man was capable of setting it out there like Roc, and to be honest, Darrell wasn't bad looking at all. He pulled up a chair to sit at the table with me and Monica. Before I knew it, we were all talking about back in the day and I'd forgotten about how ashy his hands were. It wasn't nothing a hint of lotion couldn't cure. The comedian, Fatz, was onstage and he had everyone cracking up. Darrell had lighter skin, and he was laughing so hard that his face was turning red. Monica's laugh was the loudest, but when a man behind us reached out for conversation, she turned to him and tuned us out.

"So," Darrell said after he paid the waiter for our drinks. "What are you doing these days? Are you still married to Reggie?"

"No, I'm not. We divorced several years ago, but we do have a son. I work for St. Louis Community College as an administrative assistant for one of the bigwigs. What about you? What have you been up to?"

"I work as a customer service manager at Express Scripts. Been in that position for the past seven years. Never married, but I do have two kids. One just finished college and the other is trying to start a business. I live in Maryland Heights. Are you close by or what?"

"I'm in O'Fallon. Not that close by, but this city is one big circle. You can get to any jurisdiction without long delays."

"I agree," Darrell said, looking at his watch. "It's getting pretty late. Would it be possible for us to continue this conversation in the car? I can take you home, if you'll let me."

Monica was still busy conversing with the other man, but when she'd heard Darrell ask to take me home, she turned her head. "Go ahead," she said giving me a suspicious eye. "I'll be fine and I think I may have something cooking." She winked and I figured that she wanted to get to know the man she had been talking to a little better. With that, Darrell stood up and so did I. I air kissed Monica's cheek and told her we'd talk tomorrow.

Darrell and I left together. He drove a 2012 GMC Terrain and politely opened the door for me to get in. Just by the conversation that we carried on in the car, and the memories that came back to me from high school, I started to feel better about Darrell. He parked his truck in my driveway, still laughing at me for bringing up his unattractive girlfriend in high school.

"Hey, she was the best I could do. The young lady I was interested in was in love with Reggie and I didn't stand a chance."

"Yes, I was in love, but I still had a teeny tiny crush on you too. But, a crush wasn't enough and here we are years later talking about what could've been."

"Or what should've been," he countered.

We sat quiet for a moment. I really didn't know where to go with this, because the last thing I needed was to start another relationship that I really didn't have time for. Then again, maybe I wasn't being fair to myself or to Darrell. I knew I didn't want to spend the rest of my life alone, and if that meant I had to open up and give somebody a chance, so be it.

"Would you like to come inside?" I asked Darrell. I hoped he didn't think that coming inside would lead to us having sex, because I wasn't feeling up to that right now. I did, however, enjoy his company and I wasn't quite ready to end my enjoyable night with him.

"Sure. I would love to."

Darrell followed me inside, and after I turned off the alarm, I stepped into the living room to join him on the couch.

"Would you like something else to drink? I don't have much, but I do have some beer and wine coolers in the fridge."

"A beer would be great. Thank you."

As I made my way to the fridge, I couldn't help but to think about how nice Darrell was. Actually, he was too nice. I was still in love and used to bad-boy Roc and the differences between them was apparent. When I returned to the living room, Darrell's head was slightly slumped to the side. It looked as if he was falling asleep, and the closer I got to him I could tell he was. I lightly shook his shoulder.

"Darrell," I whispered. "We can do this some other time. I don't want you falling asleep on my couch and if you need to go home—"

Darrell coughed and slowly sat up. "I need to use the bathroom," he said. "My head is spinning a little. I'm really, really tired."

I directed Darrell to the bathroom, and after I heard him urinate, I heard water running. I also heard him cough a few more times, and after several more minutes, he came out of the bathroom. He looked awfully weak. I wasn't sure if it was from drinking so much alcohol, but I offered to let him stay the night on the couch.

"Are you sure?" he said. "I really don't feel like driving and I promise to be out of your hair in the morning."

"It's no problem. Let me go get you a pillow and a blanket. Make yourself at home."

Darrell thanked me and sat back on the couch. He wiggled his tie away from his shirt and started to remove it. When I returned to the living room, his shirt, socks, and shoes were off. He'd kept his pants on, but the smell of his funky feet was nothing pretty. The musty smell permeated my entire living room causing my nose to wince a bit. I gave the blanket and pillow to Darrell, telling him again to make himself at home.

"I really appreciate this," he said. "I'm not used to being up this late . . . or should I say this early in the morning. My body is screaming for some rest, and thanks again, beautiful."

I smiled and left Darrell at peace. As soon as I got to my bedroom, I sat on the bed and checked my messages from earlier. Latrel and Chassidy had called to say hello and to check on me. After I listened to their calls, I couldn't believe that I'd had a message from Mrs. Anderson, telling me that she had a few questions to ask me. The last thing I wanted to do was get in the middle of her dispute with Mr. Anderson, so I deleted her message without taking down her number. I hated to be that way, but I was in no position to lose my job. I was sure that Mr. Anderson would have a fit if I spoke to his wife and provided her with any information about his whorish ways. To me, there really wasn't anything I could tell her. After being married to a man for thirty-something years, she should have known him like the back of her own hands. I fell asleep thinking about the two, and woke up to hard knocks on my door and the doorbell ringing. I also heard Darrell call my name, and as I squinted to look out the bay window in my bedroom, I couldn't believe my eyes. The same SUV that was in Roc's driveway was in mine, parked next to Darrell's truck. I couldn't see who was at the front door, but it was pretty obvious. I had fallen asleep in my dress, so I hurried to change into my passion purple silk robe. I also left my hair scattered over my head and my makeup was already smeared. Yes, it looked as if I'd had a rough night in the bedroom, but I didn't care. My only hope was that Roc didn't get his clown on when he set eyes on Darrell.

I walked toward the front door, and when I looked into the living room, Darrell was sitting up on the couch yawning. He was still in his pants, and I assumed the knocks and doorbell ringing had awakened him too.

"Sorry," I said to him. "I think this may be my daughter's father, but he doesn't know she's not here."

Darrell didn't say anything. He reached for his shirt and started to put it on. I opened the door, and on the other side stood Roc. He was dressed in a black leather jacket and heavy, starched jeans that showed a pointed crease. A black button-down shirt was underneath his jacket and a silver rope chain with a diamond cross on it barely dangled from his neck, as he cocked it from side to side. I tightened my robe, attempting to cover a sliver of my meaty breasts that I intended to show.

"May I help you?" I asked nonchalantly.

"Is my daughter here?"

"No."

He looked at Darrell's truck in my driveway, nudging his head toward it. "If she ain't, then who is?"

I took a few steps back in disbelief that he had the nerve to ask who was in my house. "A friend. Now, if you don't mind, I'd like to get back to entertaining my guest."

Roc's eyes narrowed and I could see his reluctance to leave. Little did I know, Darrell wasn't reluctant at all. He stepped up to me as I held the door open. "Thanks for letting me stay," he said. He kissed my cheek and made his way out the door. "I'll call you later."

Darrell barely looked at Roc, but Roc sure as hell checked him out. He smirked a bit as he watched Darrell get in his truck and drive off. Afterward, Roc turned his attention to me again.

"Now that you're done entertainin', do you mind if I come in?" he asked.

I couldn't lie . . . I was happy to see Roc, but I'd be damned if I let it show. I pulled the door open, allowing him to come inside. The first thing he saw was the blanket on the couch. The pillows on the couch were smashed and it looked as if Darrell and I had an eventful night.

Roc wiped underneath his nose, then placed his hands in his pockets. He sniffed. "What the hell is that musty-ass smell? I know you ain't up in here doin' it like that. You can do much, much better than that nigga, can't you?"

Okay, so I was a little embarrassed by the smell, but Roc referring to Darrell as a "nigga" was out of line. I still wasn't comfortable with the way Roc spoke, and it was something that I refused to get used to.

"He's not a nigga," I said. "And for your information, he's a very nice man. His feet may carry an odor, but it's something that I can live with."

Roc shrugged and skeptically walked to the couch to take a seat. He kept looking around; then his eyes met up with mine.

"So, what's up?" he said, resting his arms along the top of the couch. His sexiness had overtaken the room. I was sure he knew it. His legs were open and his twelve-inch hump that raised his jeans was on display. "I've been thinkin' about what you said the other day. I came here to apologize for tellin' you to kiss my ass. I didn't mean to come off so harsh, but seein' you brought out a li'l anger in me."

I tightened the belt on my robe, again, then went to the other side of the sectional couch to take a seat. I crossed my legs, just so the robe could slide open and show my smooth, thick legs. Roc took a glance, but he looked away, particularly at the blanket on the couch.

"Apology accepted, but why are you looking at my blanket?" I asked.

He picked it up and shook it in his hand. "I'm checkin' for stains. Tryin' to see if that muthafucka makes you shoot juices from that twat like I do."

I rolled my eyes, and tried to snatch the blanket from Roc. He pulled the blanket away from me, and as soon as I stood up, my robe fell apart. Roc could see my goodies underneath. He tightened the blanket in a ball and tossed it across the room. His arm reached out to my waist and he pulled me on top of him, leaning back. I grabbed his arm, trying to pull away, but he had a tight grip on me. I didn't bother to tussle with him, and all I did was look down into his eyes.

"Why are you really here?" I asked. "And I advise you not to use Chassidy as an excuse, as I had somewhat done when I came to see you."

"I'm here to see my daughter, but I'm also here to see if you want to get your groove back like Stella. Looks like I'm too late, especially since you got this other fool over here dippin' and divin' into the goods."

"He hasn't dipped or dived anywhere, but how can you be so interested in me getting my groove back when you are getting yours back with Tiara? She is pregnant with your child, isn't she?"

"Tiara is good people, and yes, she is pregnant with my child. I'ma do right by her, too, and I wasn't serious about comin' here to see what was up with us. While I miss the hell out of you, Dez, you hurt me like I'd never been hurt before. I did a whole lot of shit for you . . . made some changes that I hadn't made for no one. That doesn't even include what I'd had done to Ronnie and it still wasn't enough. I want us to be good friends, though, and I hope you'll be down with me comin' to see Chassidy again."

"She's your daughter and I have no problem with you being in her life. I hope you are serious about doing right by the woman you're with, and if you are, why do you have me wrapped in your arms like this?"

Roc loosened his grip and eased his hands over my ass. He squeezed a nice-sized chunk of it, then let out a deep sigh. I could feel every bit of his hardness pressing against me. I wanted to straddle my legs so badly to ride him, but I didn't want to appear anxious or desperate, especially since his intentions were to do right by another woman.

"You wrapped in my arms like this because I still got love for you," he admitted. "You ever hear of lovin' somebody who you just can't be with? Well, that's what's goin' down with me. I'm not turnin' back again, Dez. I don't think you want to either. With all that I have goin' on right now, it would be a big mistake. So, allow me to do what I need to do as Chassidy's father and let's keep all that other shit to the side."

I couldn't tell if Roc was serious, but it sure as hell sounded like it. I had no desire to persuade him to change his mind. It appeared that he had some feelings for the chick he was living with and wanted things to work out. I wasn't going to interfere, so it was wise for me to halt the drips from my coochie, remove myself from on top of him, and let him go. I did just that, and made my way to the door to open it.

"I couldn't agree with you more, Roc. Turning back does not seem like the sensible thing to do, but I am deeply sorry if you feel as if I was the one who hurt you. Maybe you'll have better luck with Tiara. I'm proud of you for wanting to do right by her. If it were me, you know I'd want you to do the same."

Roc rubbed the minimal, trimmed hair on his chin, and slowly got off the couch. He stretched his arms, then yawned. "When can I expect to see Chassidy?" he asked.

"She won't be back until after Thanksgiving. You can stop by to see her then, but please do me a favor and call before you come."

He nodded and made his way to the door. His eyes lowered to my lips, but as my mouth started to water, he walked out the door. I closed it, wondering if we would stick to the plan.

Chapter 4

The plan was in place, for now, and Roc and I seemed to be sticking to it. I hadn't heard from him since the day he'd left. Had I thought about him? Absolutely. But Roc was right. If he had that much going on in his life, I really didn't want to be a part of it. And the whole thing with him having another child on the way truly bothered me, but it didn't upset me enough where I wanted to inject myself into the madness. I had to leave well enough alone.

The day before Thanksgiving, Darrell called to see if he could come over to keep me company. I'd told him the kids were still away and I really didn't have much going on. In other words, he was welcome to come over. Monica had plans with her children, and even though she'd invited me over to join them, I just didn't feel like leaving my house. Instead, I put on some soothing music and got busy on the few items I had planned to cook. I put my ham in the oven and started to boil the water for my mac and cheese. My stuffing had to be made and so did the crust for my peach cobbler. I had all night and Darrell claimed that he would help me with the cobbler. Actually, he'd made a bet that his cobbler would be better than mine, so it was on.

I danced around the kitchen with my apron on while listening to my girl Mary J. I stopped to stir my noodles in the boiling pot on the stove, but when the doorbell rang, I wiped my hands on the apron and headed toward the door. My hair had a band around the front that pushed my curls to the back. I wore jeans and a Black Girls Rock T-shirt that Monica had purchased for me last week. When I opened the door, Darrell had a plastic bag in his hand. He was ready to throw down with me.

"I see you came prepared," I said, taking his brown leather coat and hanging it on a coat hanger.

Darrell laughed and pulled his pie crust from the bag. "Very prepared. Just point me in the direction of your kitchen and it's on."

I pointed toward the kitchen, following Darrell as he walked in front of me. He also had on a pair of jeans, with a tan and brown sweater that matched his square-toe leather shoes. His bald head had a shine and the beard on his face was neatly trimmed. What I liked about Darrell the most was his eyes. They were light brown and alluring.

Darrell placed the plastic bag on the kitchen table and pulled out a bottle of red wine. "I hope you like this wine. Let it chill for a while and we'll toast to new beginnings later."

New beginnings? I wasn't so sure about that. I took the wine from Darrell and put it over ice in the fridge. I then tossed him an apron, so he could get busy with me in the spacious kitchen that gave us plenty of room to cook.

"I don't need an apron," he said, pulling out his pie crust again. He rolled up his sleeves, like he was getting ready to throw down. "All I need is for you to move out of my way, beautiful, and let me do my thing."

"I heard that. But I can already tell my peach cobbler is going to turn out much, much better than yours. I make my crust from scratch and my peaches do not come from a can."

Darrell watched as I pulled out all of my ingredients and put them on the table. He folded his arms, insisting that I wouldn't be able to resist his cobbler once it was done.

For the next hour or so, Darrell and I got busy. Both of our cobblers were in the oven with the ham. The whole house was infused with the smell of cinnamon and cooking peaches. I couldn't wait to eat, but I was still in the midst of putting the finishing touches on my dressing. Darrell had gone to the bathroom and had taken two trash bags outside to the Dumpster. When he returned, he washed his hands and looked into the oven.

"My cobbler looks ready," he said. "The crust is golden brown, how I like it, but yours is still doing its thing."

I tossed Darrell a potholder and he removed his cobbler and my ham from the oven. He took the French vanilla ice cream that he'd purchased from the fridge and waited for the cobbler to cool, before he set it off with a scoop of ice cream. The slice he cut was put into a bowl and he topped the cobbler and ice cream with drizzled caramel. He couldn't wait for me to taste it. His spoon was already up to my mouth. I opened it and the cobbler melted in my mouth. I closed my eyes, allowing the taste to marinate.

"That is deeeelicious," I admitted. "Oh my God, Darrell, your cobbler does taste better than mine. What did you put in there?"

He was all smiles. "Wouldn't you like to know? It's my mother's recipe and I can't share it with no one. Not even you, beautiful, but I will make it for you anytime you want me to."

I had to have another piece of Darrell's cobbler, and I had a slice of ham to make sure it was cooked to perfection. We sat at the kitchen table while enjoying a pleasant conversation.

"I'm glad you let me come over to see you, Desa Rae. I didn't have much to do today either. I'll be going to my mother's house tomorrow and I'm anxious to see my sister, who I haven't seen in a long time. She's coming in tomorrow. I have to pick her up from the airport."

"I remember your sister. She was on the cheerleading squad wasn't she?"

"Yes, she was. When I told her I'd been talking to you, she couldn't believe it. She thought you and Reggie would be together forever. I think most people who you ask will probably say the same. The two of you seemed inseparable."

"At one point we were. But as we got older, he went in another direction. My heart was broken, but I've learned to cope with it. Our divorce was for the best, and there isn't much that you can do when a man says that he's fallen out of love with you."

"I feel you, but what about your daughter's father? I didn't get a real good look at him, but from what I saw, he looked real, real young. You don't have that cougar thing going on, do you?"

"I don't know what the cougar thing is, but I do know that I found a man whose company I enjoyed. We had a child together and the rest is history."

"Are you still seeing him? I mean, by his reaction, I sensed something still going on with the two of you, even though you told him you were entertaining."

"There is nothing going on between us. Prior to a few days before that I hadn't seen him in months. I am looking forward to him spending time with our daughter, but that's it."

Darrell sipped from his glass of wine, I guessed thinking over what I had implied. I got up from the table to check on my food. I didn't want to talk about Roc, as talking about him made me think about him. I stood, gazing at the pot of greens while stirring them. I wondered what Roc was doing for Thanksgiving. I figured he and his girlfriend was planning to have guests at their house. As I was in thought, Darrell crept up from behind me and put his arm around my waist. Honestly, I didn't like the feel of his touch, nor did I enjoy the feel of his dick poking me in the back. I tried to play it off by smiling, yet pushing him back with my elbow.

"Come on, Darrell. Let me get finished with cooking. I'm almost finished."

He kissed my cheek and asked if my cobbler was ready. I guessed my mind had been so preoccupied that I had forgotten about my cobbler. By the time I pulled it out of the oven, the edges of the crust were burnt. The inside still looked good enough to eat, but after eating Darrell's cobbler, I wasn't in a rush. I hurried to prepare the rest of my food, and after nibbling here and there, Darrell and I went to the family room to relax. I was kind of exhausted from cooking all day. I really wanted to take a shower and call it a night.

"You look tired," Darrell said while sitting next to me with a drink in his hand.

"Very."

Darrell got on his knees and started to remove my house shoes. I laughed as he tickled my feet and massaged them. The massage felt pretty good, but when he eased his hand up my legs, I stopped him.

"What's going on with you, Desa Rae? Every time I make an advancement toward you, you stop me. Are you not feeling me? If not, let me know. I don't want to waste my time."

"It's not that, Darrell. I do like you, but I'm not some oversexed woman who has to have sex with every man she meets. I know we've known each other for a long time, but I really don't know much about you, other than we went to school together. Besides, and to be honest, my heart is in another place right now. It may take some time for me to get over my previous relationship, so give me a little time, okay?"

"Well, at least I know I'm not doing anything wrong. I'm glad you told me your heart is elsewhere and I really don't want to waste much more of my time with this."

Darrell stood up. He went into the kitchen to gather some of his things. I felt terrible. I knew he was trying. Shame on me for acting as if he wasn't good enough. *I could very well let a decent man slip away.*

"Wait a minute," I said to Darrell as he made his way toward the door to get his coat. "I don't know why you're rushing out of here. All I asked was for you to give us a little time. Is it that important for us to jump in the bed right away? I assume that's why you're upset, but I don't normally get down like that, Darrell. It's not my style."

Darrell folded his coat across his arm. "I don't know about you, Desa Rae, but I'm not in high school anymore. We're grown folks who are capable of making grown folks' decisions. All I know is I like you, a lot. I've always liked you, and if I am given the opportunity to hook up with someone from my past whom I really cared for, then I'm going to take advantage of that. I guess your crush wasn't what I thought it was."

Was this fool trying to play a guilt trip on me? So what I'd had a crush on him? That was a long time ago. Yes, we were grown, but being grown didn't mean we couldn't get STDs and we didn't have to be careful about who our sexual partners were. I had no idea what Darrell had been doing for the past twenty years and I wasn't in a rush to sleep with him, period. The way some men think drove me nuts, and since Darrell had taken the initiative to get his coat, I felt like whatever.

"Call me when you feel as if you're old enough to have sex and your feelings for that young buck are intact. It's obvious that you have something going on with him and the look in your eyes the other day said it all. I should've gone about my business then and not wasted my time."

Darrell's true colors were starting to show. Instead of responding to his ignorance, I opened the door for him and let him leave. I watched as he pulled out of my driveway, feeling no gain and no pain.

After Darrell was gone, I cleaned up my kitchen and put the food away in the fridge. I was truly exhausted, ready to take my shower, get in bed, and read a book. My shower was so relaxing. As the water sprayed on my face, I scrubbed it with soap and water. My eyes were closed, but when I heard a noise, my eyes shot open. I stood for a moment, trying to see if I'd hear the noise again. I didn't, but as soon as I turned off the water, I heard the phone ringing. I figured it was probably the kids calling me back. I'd planned on calling them before I went to bed. I dried myself, moisturized my body, then changed into a cotton nightgown that made me comfortable. I tossed my body towel over my shoulder, just so I could take it to the washroom with the other towels to wash them. But as I made my way down the hallway, I was cut off by Darrell. He jumped out from my guestroom and stood in front of me. My heart dropped to my stomach. I was so nervous that I couldn't even scream.

"What are you doing in my house, Darrell? You scared the shit out of me! How did you . . ."

The weird look in his eyes didn't feel right as he stared at me. His face was that of a stone and he didn't blink. I didn't say another word, and when I attempted to rush back into my room, he grabbed me by the back of my hair. He pulled it so tight that I had to squeeze my watery eyes to cease the pain.

"What do you want?" I cried out as he shoved me into my bedroom. I reached up to pull at his hands, but they felt solid, like a rock that I couldn't move.

He spoke through gritted teeth. "I don't like how you tried to play me! I should take what I want, but it's going to suit me just fine to knock the shit out of you."

Darrell pushed me on the bed and like a raging madman he jumped on top of me. I swiftly kicked my legs and wiggled around like a flopping fish so he wouldn't be able to restrain me.

"Nooo!" I shouted. "Get the hell off meee!"

Darrell used the back of his hand to slap it across my face. My head jerked to the side and my left cheek burned. The blow was so powerful that it knocked me into reality. I wasn't sure if he was going to try to rape me, and I questioned my strength to get him off me.

"You're not going to get away with this!" I yelled. "Yo . . . you can't do this to meee!"

"Shut up!" he ordered, then head-butted me. My brain felt rattled, so I squeezed my eyes to help ease the pain.

Darrell pinned my hands down to the bed, holding them so tight that I thought my wrists would crack. He seemed to get heavier, and I was running out of breath trying to force him off me. My next move was to distract him, and when I spat a gob of saliva in his face, he jerked his head back. I watched my spit slide down his face, and as soon as he wiped it, I kneed him in his groin as hard as I could. His eyes opened wider and his mouth dropped open. "Fuuuuck!" he shouted. "You fucking biiiiitch!"

I knew he wanted to reach down to soothe his burning balls, and as he thought about doing it, I kneed him again. This time, he released my hands and rolled over on his back. He used both of his hands to cuff his nuts and swayed back and forth on the bed. I didn't have much time before he came after me again, so I had to think fast. It was either the phone, which was ringing again, or my gun that was tucked away in my closet. Calling 911, it would take the police time to get here. I didn't want to answer the phone, because I suspected it was my kids. I was already off the bed and in my closet. I knocked several of my shoeboxes off the shelves and reached for my pistol that was hidden behind them. By this time, Darrell was already standing at the door, staring at the trembling gun in my hand.

"Don't make me do this, Darrell!" I shouted with tears streaming down my face. My hair was sitting wildly on my head and my nightgown was ripped down the middle. Titties hanging out and all, I was now looking like the madwoman.

"Put the gun down, Desa Rae," Darrell said, inching forward. "I was just playing—"

I wanted Darrell out or dead . . . didn't matter either way. He wasn't exiting fast enough for me, so I cocked the gun, closed my eyes, and pulled the trigger. The loud pop scared the shit out of me! My body jerked back a bit and I almost lost my balance. I wasn't sure where the bullet went, but Darrell moved so fast that if you blinked, you missed him. He was gone. I rushed out of the closet, following him as he pulled on the front door, leaving it wide open. He peeled out of my driveway, tires screeching and burning rubber.

"Don't bring your ass back here again!" I yelled out to him. "Next time you may not be so lucky!"

I closed the door, thanking God that this situation didn't turn out in Darrell's favor. I was thankful that I'd had a gun, and the only reason I'd had one was because of the threats I'd gotten from Roc's uncle Ronnie. While I didn't have to use it for him, it disturbed me that I had to use it for somebody I thought I knew.

I walked away from the door to go turn on my alarm. I checked all of my doors and windows, realizing that Darrell must have left the back door unlocked when he'd taken out the trash. I knew there was something about him that I didn't like. What I felt inside didn't have much to do about my feelings for Roc. Being desperate for companionship was a dangerous thing. I realized that I had to be careful about the men I brought into my home. Chassidy could've been here. A man like Darrell proved that he was capable of doing anything.

I changed into another nightgown and reached for the phone to call the police. I wanted to report this incident and stop Darrell from doing this to another woman. He was straight-up crazy, and his charming ways were a bunch of bologna. I guessed it upset him when I didn't fall for it, and I felt deeply sorry for the women who had. The 911 operator said that she'd send a policeman right over, so I waited on the couch in the family room until he arrived. I also checked my phone to see who had been calling me. I didn't recognize the number and when I checked my messages, there were none. I dialed Latrel's cell phone number, just to see if the number was from Angelique's mother's resort.

"I called you earlier, Miss Lady, but you didn't call back," Latrel said. "What's up with you?"

I wouldn't dare tell Latrel what had happened. "Nothing, sweetheart. I left a message on your phone earlier. You should've checked it."

"Maybe so. We've been so busy, I hadn't done so. Angelique's mom wanted to see how you were doing too, and she wanted me to tell you that it's not too late for you to come to Florida and join us."

"Tell Jenay I will join you all next time. I've been trying to get some rest during my vacation. I'm sure you all have been all over Florida and haven't gotten much rest at all, especially with Chassidy."

"No, we didn't take a vacation to rest. Chassidy is having a good time. She wants to speak to you, so hold on."

Right now, there wasn't much to smile about, but when I heard Chassidy's voice, it brought a comforting smile to my face. "Mommy, I had so much fun today. I met Mickey Mouse in person and I bought you a pair of Mickey Mouse ears and a cookie jar for your cookies. I bought my daddy a Mickey Mouse watch and I hope to give it to him on Christmas. Have you spoken to him yet? I hope so because I really need to see him . . . and my brother. I got him some Mickey Mouse ears too."

This situation was starting to hurt. I didn't know what to tell Chassidy, because I wasn't so sure if Roc was serious about coming by to see her. My mind was all over the place, so I handled this as best as I could. "I haven't heard from him yet, sweetheart, but I'm so sure I'll be hearing from him soon. I know he'll love his watch. I bet he has something nice for you too. For now, enjoy yourself and Mommy will see you soon, okay?"

"Okay," she said. Without seeing her, I could still feel her happiness over the phone. Chassidy told me she loved me and gave the phone back to Latrel.

"Hold on a second," he said. I could hear Latrel moving around, and when he got back on the phone, he questioned me about Roc. "That's all Chassidy talks about is him. At first it was here and there, but now it's more often than usual. Have you heard from him? I tried to call him myself, but his number was disconnected."

"We've talked, Latrel, but I don't want to talk about Roc right now. I have some other things going on. I will deal with the situation when I can."

"Okay, Mama. I'm not going to get on you like you do me, but if I can do anything for you, let me know."

"You already do enough. All I want is for you to finish school, take care of your wife, and be happy. Seems like you're on the right path."

"I am. No doubt."

The doorbell rang and I told Latrel I had to go. We exchanged the love and ended the call. Hurrying to the door, I pulled it open, but forgot to turn off the alarm. It blasted loudly and startled me more than I was, after seeing Roc. He stepped inside and I ran to the kitchen to key in the code for the alarm. It went off as Roc came into the kitchen.

"I've been callin' you all day," he said with a frown on his face. "Why haven't you been answerin' yo' phone?"

Before I could say anything, I heard an officer's walkie-talkie. Roc heard it too, and we both made our way back to the front door. The officer had stepped inside with his hand on his holster. When he saw me and Roc, he gripped it tighter. I quickly spoke up.

"My name is Desa Rae Jenkins. I'm the one who called."

The officer looked past me, turning his attention to Roc. "Who is he?" the officer asked.

I could see the puzzled look on Roc's face. It was an angry yet serious look that alarmed the officer. "This is a friend of mine," I said, touching Roc's arm and looking at him. "If you don't mind, would you have a seat in the living room while I talk to the officer about what happened?"

I hoped that Roc wouldn't question me, or say anything to the officer. But he kept looking at me, then asked how I had gotten the red mark on my face.

"I promise to tell you in a minute. Let me talk to the officer first, okay?"

Roc nodded, but instead of sitting in the living room, he made his way back to my bedroom. The officer and I remained standing in the foyer. I told him everything that happened with Darrell and the officer took notes. While he took notes, I took him to my bedroom and let him see the inside of my closet where I'd shot at Darrell. He saw the bullet hole that had gone into the lower wall. My aim wasn't worth a damn. I also showed the officer my gun.

"Is it registered?" he asked.

"Yes," I said, then showed him my registration papers.

The officer stepped out of my closet and glanced at Roc, who was sitting on the bed with his arms folded and eyes focused on the TV. There was a little tension between the two, and on Roc's behalf, I certainly knew why. I was relieved when the officer made his way back down the hallway.

"We'll put a warrant out for Darrell's arrest. Feel free to call me if you need anything else. I will do the same if additional information is needed."

The officer gave me his card and left. I peeked through the window, looking as he sat in his car for about ten minutes, writing notes and looking at Roc's SUV. I was a bit nervous, but when the officer slowly pulled away, I felt better. I returned to my bedroom where Roc was still sitting on the bed. He couldn't wait to ask. "What in the hell happened?"

I sat next to him on the bed, telling him what had gone down between me and Darrell. Roc's eye kept twitching and he continued to suck in his bottom lip. After I finished telling him, he stood up and put his hands in his pockets.

"Why you let that funky-feet muthafucka up in here anyway, Dez? My daughter could've been here with that nigga. Don't you recognize a sly-ass fool when you see one? Are you that damn naïve and desperate?"

Roc's words shocked the hell out of me. I couldn't believe how angry he was, and he didn't have to diss me. I was the one who was about to be beat down by this fool, not him. "I had some eerie feelings about Darrell, but since I'd known him from high school, I didn't think he would do anything like that. The guy I'd known had always been a nice guy, but I guess people change."

Roc shook his head. He looked disgusted. "Nice guy from high school, huh? What kind of shit is that? You damn right people change, but my problem is women like you, Dez. Y'all always goin' for the men who dress nice, who talk a good game, and kiss y'all asses. If he got a li'l change in his pockets and got a nine-to-five job, he's the best thing since sliced bread. Y'all want somebody to cater to yo' every damn need and do what y'all tell him to do. A brotha like me, on the other hand, can't get no play."

"That's not so and you know it. I gave our relationship a chance, but you made a lot of mistakes too, Roc. Mistakes that—"

He quickly shot me down. "Mistakes? Naw, baby, I just wasn't perfect enough for you. Ya see, I'm looked down on, and because my English ain't that of a professor, I don't know shit. I'm too thuggish to be considered a 'real' man, and whether you know it or not, by my own people, I'm tossed into the category of a street nigga. One who don't know how to make a livin', always lookin' for handouts, and don't know shit about how to treat women. You damn right I'm a street nigga, with street smarts. I know how to make money and don't nobody give me shit. If I got love for my woman, I give her the respect she gives me. Unlike your high school lover, I don't have to take no pussy, because a woman who knows what I'm all about will willingly give it to me. But, like you, many think I'm not good enough. Keep on thinking that, and I guarantee you that many more of your so-called high school lovers will cross your path. Have your gun loaded with bullets, because you'll need it again. I'm out."

Roc turned to leave, but I tried to make light of the situation, even though I knew it was bad. "He wasn't trying to rape me, so get that out of your head. He was upset and wanted to fight. . . ."

I rushed up from my bed to stop him from leaving. I grabbed his arm and turned him to face me. "Look, forget about him. But, don't you dare put those words in my mouth about how I feel about you. I never said you wasn't good enough, Roc, and you know it. Perfect men don't exist and neither do perfect women. I've made some mistakes too, but you were the one who left me and Chassidy, time and time again. What was I supposed to do, Roc? When you came to Latrel's wedding, what did you expect for me to do?"

Roc peeled my tight fingers away from his arm and faced me. "You sound like a fool defendin' him. You don't know what he was capable of doin' to you. But, regardin' us, you were supposed to give us a chance. You knew what I had done for you, Dez, but you walked yo' ass away from me that day and hurt the shit out of me. That pain was worse than what I had done to Ronnie. To do that to him, then have you turn your back on me . . . it wasn't a good feelin'. You'll never understand what I'm sayin' to you, because you don't want to. It was all about you, but you know what, baby? Not anymore."

Roc walked off, again, but I refused to go after him. This was just too much; he was blaming me and a huge part of me was still blaming him. I was drained from all that had happened, and once I heard the front door shut, I got in bed. I tucked my body pillow between my legs, thinking about this long day that disgusted me. My throat ached so badly; it was hard for me to swallow. Maybe I had been desperate and naïve. Why else would I have let a man like Darrell come into my home? I didn't know, but one thing I was sure of was I felt so alone. The man I really did love was with another woman and they had a baby on the way. Roc had no clue how much I still loved him, and at this point, I would've taken a man like him over a man like Darrell any day of the week. As I was deep in thought, wiping my tears, I heard someone clear his throat. My breathing came to a halt as I quickly lifted my head to see who it was.

"You should've gotten up to lock the door," Roc said, coming farther into the room. "I can't believe after what happened today, you would lie there without makin' sure your door was locked."

I never liked for a man to see me cry, so I hurried to wipe my face and sat up in bed. "I was getting ready to get up and check it."

Roc stood silent in front of the bed while looking at me. "I regret bein' so hard on you and I'm sorry that you went through that bullshit today. If the police don't find that nigga, I guarantee you I will. He will never be given the opportunity to put his hands on you again and his ass will pay."

I was sure Roc wouldn't listen to my recommendation, and I figured he would do something to Darrell behind my back. "I'm sure the police will find him, so please stay out of this. I don't want you to get involved, and we both can agree that you've already done enough to protect me."

Roc stood silent again. After a few minutes, he pulled his shirt off and tossed it on a leather recliner that sat near my television. "I'm stayin' the night with you," he said. "You look like you could use some for real company and I don't want you up all night worried about what happened."

Now, what made him think I was going to get some sleep with him in my bed? I was glad that he was staying. He left the room, then came back with ice wrapped in a towel. When he lay next to me, I felt very protected. Roc wrapped his arms around my shoulders, then put the icepack on the side of my face. I rested my head on his solid chest, appreciating the nice gesture as well as his good-smelling cologne. His jeans were still on and his cell phone was ringing inside his pocket. He pulled it out and looked at the number.

"Do you mind if I answer this?" he asked.

I shrugged, feeling somewhat uneasy. I assumed it was a female.

"What up?" he asked. He paused and I could hear the sound of a female's voice on the other end. "I'm with T-Bone and Durk right now. Don't know how much longer I'll be, but I'll hit you back when I'm on my way." He paused again. I could hear her talking; then there was laughter. Roc laughed too. "Yo' ass is crazy than a mutha. I knew you was gon' say somethin' about that fool, and when he go off on you, don't come cryin' to me." She spoke up, then Roc did. "You know I will. But let me get at you in a minute. We need to make a move." I figured she told him she loved him, because he replied, "You'd better," and ended the call.

"Sorry 'bout that," he said. "I wasn't tryin' to be disrespectful, but when she calls I try to answer, especially with her bein' pregnant and all. She's had some complications and I want to make sure she's all right."

"Sure," was all I said. Lord knows the conversation didn't sit well with me, especially if Roc had found a woman he seemed genuinely happy with. It didn't seem like this chick brought the drama like Vanessa did, but there was one thing. He was willing to lie to her in order to be with me. If he cared so much about this woman, why was he not with her on the eve of Thanksgiving? I wasn't sure what his excuse was going to be in the morning, and as nice as she seemed right now, I was sure her tone would change.

As we lay in bed, I wiggled my fingers between Roc's and held his hand. I asked him to remove the towel because my face was starting to feel numb. He placed the towel on the nightstand, then secured me in his arms again. I rubbed his chest while his hand swayed up and down on my back. Being with him felt so right. I wondered if he was feeling what I was. He pecked my forehead a few times, trying to comfort me. "If that nigga would have hurt you tonight," he said, "I don't know what I would've done. I'm glad you had that gun, but I wish you would have blown his fuckin' brains out. I hate niggas who go out like that. If a woman don't want you, she just don't want you."

"I agree. But, when she does, you'll definitely know it," I said, looking up at him. My eyes lowered to his sexy lips.

"Don't even think about it," he said with a smile. "I told you we ain't gettin' down like that and I mean it."

"Well, I guess this means that I'm in trouble again. Deep, deep trouble . . . trouble that I'm always looking forward to."

"You are in trouble, but I'm not the one who is goin' to punish you. Now, get some sleep and erase those dirty thoughts from yo' mind. You ain't got jack comin', baby. Nothin'."

Roc was really standing his ground, and if he was trying to be all that he needed to be to another woman, I said that I wouldn't interfere. I dropped my thoughts and put my head back on his chest. Within minutes, I could hear myself, as well as Roc, snoring.

By morning I was still tired, and was awakened by the sound of grunting. Roc's phone ringing throughout the night drove me crazy and every time it rang, I jumped from my sleep. At some point he had turned it off and that allowed the both of us to get some sleep. I raised my head, only to see him on the floor doing sit-ups in his boxers.

"Morning," he strained to say. "Your bathwater ready, so get to it so I can get some breakfast."

I got out of bed and stepped over him. "Thanks for getting my bath ready for me, but you should be able to handle breakfast too, right?"

"Yeah, I can do that, so hurry."

As he continued with his quick workout, I kept thinking of Lance Gross in my mind. When I told Roc I thought he resembled Lance, he totally disagreed. That was funny, because they could be considered twins. To cool myself, I hurried to take my bath. While I was in the tub, Roc said he was going to the kitchen to make us some bacon and eggs. I thanked him again, and was delighted that he was prolonging his visit.

Within the hour, I wrapped up my bath and covered myself with a pink cotton robe. I'd washed my hair, and put it in a thick ponytail that had plenty of dangling, tight curls. My full face was free of makeup and my body lotion had me covered with the smell of sweet strawberries. I left my bedroom and as I reached the end of the hallway, I could see Roc in the kitchen cooking. He had a Bluetooth attached to his ear while talking to someone. I couldn't hear his conversation, but with his back facing me, I heard him laughing a few times.

My eyes scanned the back of him and I was unable to seal my thoughts. The back of him was just as spectacular as the front. Muscles looked perfectly carved by a butcher and his Calvin Klein cotton boxers hugged his meaty ass tight. His thighs and calves showed strength and I didn't know how much longer I would be able to keep my hands off another woman's man. I tried to put myself in her shoes, but damn! I justified what I was about to do by saying that at least he wasn't married.

With that thought on my mind, I rushed back to my bedroom and removed my robe. I changed into a two-piece sheer baby-doll negligee that was a soft mauve. The wire cups held up my healthy breasts, yet the sheer showed my nipples. A matching thong with strings that tied at my hips revealed my goodies that I knew Roc wouldn't be able to resist. I didn't want to seduce him like this, but then again, yes, I did. I removed the band from my hair and teased it wildly with my fingers. After taking a deep breath, I made my way toward the kitchen, hoping that Roc wouldn't reject me. He was still on the phone. Several pieces of crisp bacon were on a plate and he was in the process of scrambling some eggs. I inched my way forward, but always being observant of his surroundings, Roc heard the floor squeak and quickly turned around. His eyes narrowed and his conversation came to a halt. Before he could tell the caller to call him back, I removed the Bluetooth from his ear and placed it on the counter. I also turned off the burner on the stove.

"I'm not in the mood for breakfast," I softly said. "And I can show you what I'm in the mood for better than I can tell you."

Roc still had a look of shock on his face. His phone rang, but he ignored it. I took his hand and walked him over to the kitchen table. I invited him to take a seat, and after he did, I sat on top of the table, straddling my legs in front of him. Roc squinted and swallowed hard as he gazed between my legs and witnessed my moist folds. He still hadn't made a move, though, so I snatched up a napkin from the table, tying it around his neck. I then picked up a fork and twirled it in front of him.

"It's time for breakfast," I said. "I prefer that you use your tongue to eat, but if you have no use for me, then you can go stick this fork in those eggs and hope that they'll be to your satisfaction."

Continuing to hold a serious look on his face, Roc took the fork from my hand and held it. "So, since you settin' that shit out there like this for me, I assume that you're sayin' you want me and you don't give a damn about the other woman."

I slowly nodded, while looking into his eyes and trying to read him. "I do. I really do want you and you're the only one who should care about the other woman, not me."

"If you do want me, then you know there are certain things about me that you have to accept."

I shrugged and held my stare. "Things like what?"

"Like . . . I get high. Real high, sometimes, and I'm not givin' up my marijuana."

"And? So what. Next."

"I curse a lot and I will not refrain from callin' anyone that I want to a nigga."

"Speak what you wish. No problem here and I won't say another word."

Roc snickered a little, then smirked. "I'm capable of causin' major damage to anybody who hurts me or causes disrespect to the ones I love. In some cases, the consequences may be one's life."

"What I don't know won't hurt. A snitch I will never be."

Roc nodded and looked at the fork. This time, he twirled it. "I got some deep feelings for Tiara and I'm not tryin' to hurt her. She was down with me when you wasn't and she helped me somewhat heal from my situation. My back will not turn on her, no matter what."

I leaned forward and placed my arms on Roc's broad shoulders. "I'm not so sure about those feelings that you have for Tiara, and the only way you will hurt her is if you continue to deny your love for me. I'm the one who can help you truly heal from the hurt, and once I do, I hope you'll commit to never turning your back on me."

Roc gradually stood up. He tossed the fork over his shoulder and moved in closer to the table. My legs wrapped around his waist and I brought my body as close to his as I could.

"I don't want no bullshit out of you, Dez. I know you just said some of those things because you think that's what I want to hear, but you gon' have to accept a brotha for who he is."

I looked at his juicy lips and couldn't wait to suck on them. "I accept everything there is about you," I said with a crooked smile. "And don't you ever forget it."

"Bullshit," Roc said. At least he recognized that some of it was. He tugged at the string on my thong. The loose knot came apart and he cuffed his hand over my shaved pussy. Two of his fingers slipped inside and the sound of my juices stirring was like music to our ears. "Yeaaah, with a wet pussy like that, yo' ass is gonna be in some serious trouble. I can't dip into you like I want to on this table, so you gotta come down."

Roc was getting ready to remove his fingers, but I grabbed his hand to keep them in place. "You already know my motto. Be creative," I said. "And work with whatever space you have," we said in unison.

We laughed and I removed the napkin from Roc's neck. I placed it on my stomach to send him a clear message that it was time to eat good. He licked his tongue across his snow-white teeth, then stepped back to bury his face between my legs. While holding my legs far apart with his hands, Roc feasted upon my insides. I could barely keep still on the table, and dropped back on my elbows to keep from losing my balance.

"Damn, you . . . you make me feel so gooood," I strained to say. My heartbeat was increasing by the minute, and as Roc's tongue was swiftly circling my hard clitoris, it was about to burst. "I looove you!" I shouted with tightened fists, as I pounded them on the table. "God knows I love your ass! Don't ask me why I . . . I just do! Damn it I do!"

Roc didn't say anything, until my orgasm came and I filled his mouth with my cream. He licked his shiny lips, then wiped across them with the napkin. His arms caged around my waist and he picked me up from the table. My legs remained wrapped around his waist and my arms were secured around his neck as he carried me to my bedroom.

"Now all I need is for you to say that shit you said while on the table, when you ain't havin' no orgasm. You were tryin' to put it out there for a nigga, weren't you?"

"Not for a nigga, but surely for the man I love. I do love you, and I hope like hell that it matters."

Roc didn't respond until he laid me back on the bed and got on top of me. His dick entered me with ease, causing me to close my eyes and savor the moment I had waited so long for. "I love you too, Dez," came from his mouth, but that's not all he said. "Love you a whole lot, but love don't mean shit when you don't know how to show it and you don't know what it takes to keep a nigga in it."

I fired back. "Well, all I can say is I have you now. We'll see how long I can keep you."

For the record, it was three long days that Roc stayed with me. He not once answered his phone to see what was up with the other woman, but you'd better believe that his phone rang like he was the owner of a billion-dollar business.

Chapter 5

Chassidy had returned home. Latrel and Angelique had already made their way back to school, but they were due for another short break because of Christmas. This time, they were spending it with me. I was so excited. I had the entire house decked out with Christmas decorations, and with Roc's help, Chassidy and I put up a nine-foot Christmas tree with colorful ornaments. She was so happy that Roc had been to see her and he'd even brought Lil Roc over as well. It was just like old times, but like always, there was always something or someone between us.

I never thought I'd be in a position where I would willingly know that I was sharing a man. In the past, I figured Roc had been seeing other people, but what I didn't know didn't hurt. This time I knew it. I knew he had a baby on the way and I knew he was living with someone else. Thing was, I never understood how any woman could find herself in this situation, and I somewhat despised women who allowed a man to have his cake and eat it too. But, there I was going through the same thing. At times I was okay with it, but many times I was not. Roc and I never argued about it, and to be honest, we'd been getting along quite well. Tiara's name was never brought up during our conversations. It was as if she didn't exist, but deep inside I knew she did.

Then there was Lil Roc's mother, Vanessa. She was his ride or die chick for many years, but Lil Roc had mentioned that his mom was getting married. I assumed she had finally moved on, but there was something in Roc's eyes that didn't seem right when Lil Roc mentioned the marriage thing. All of this was starting to get to me, but I kept my cool, partially because of Chassidy. I also didn't want to find myself all alone again, but in a sense, I felt as if I was alone because Roc was living with someone else. I questioned if I was settling for whatever, but after what had happened with Darrell, I was sticking with the man I was used to.

The police had informed me that Darrell had been arrested. They were charging him with assault and that wasn't all. When I found out he'd had several molestation charges against him, I could have died. I didn't realize the danger I had put myself in, as well as my daughter. *Never again,* I thought. And that's why being with Roc made not much, but some, sense to me.

There was a full house on Christmas. Angelique and Latrel had spent the night in his room in the basement. Lil Roc had stayed the night in Chassidy's room, Monica had slept in the guestroom, and Chassidy and I slept in my room. Roc had left yesterday evening and said he'd be back a little after noon. Monica's new man, Shawn, had come over so I could meet him, and we all sat in the family room talking and eating. With Monica's help, dinner had been prepared yesterday. We had a full table and were thankful to God for our blessings.

"Yes, I'm grateful for all that God has done and will continue to do, but this has been a crazy year," Monica said, sitting next to Shawn and drinking eggnog. "2012 can't get here fast enough."

"I agree," Angelique added. She was a petite little thing and was sitting on Latrel's lap. He was putting together a die-cast model car that Roc had gotten for Lil Roc. "I'm so ready to graduate," Angelique continued. "And once we do, Latrel and I are moving out of Columbia, Missouri and right to Florida."

My eyes widened as she puckered to kiss Latrel. They kissed, but the move to Florida was news to me. I hated when somebody hit me with something that caught me off guard. Latrel and I had spoken at least twice a week and he never mentioned moving that far away. What about my grandkids? Would I have to travel that far to see them? I kept my mouth shut, but I was steaming inside. Then, maybe it wasn't the breaking news about Florida that upset me. It was almost six o'clock in the evening, and I still hadn't heard from Roc. He left yesterday, saying that he would be back no later than a little after noon. Lil Roc hadn't seen him all day, and neither had Chassidy. From what Lil Roc had said, Vanessa was getting ready to go on vacation with her fiancé. She hadn't even talked to her son today, and the least Roc could do was be there for him. Maybe I was the only one tripping, but things like that mattered to me.

My glass was empty, so I excused myself from the conversation and went into the kitchen. Monica followed. She could tell something was on my mind.

"Out with it," she said, taking a seat at the kitchen table. "What's going on in that thick head of yours?"

"Not much. Just a little irritated that I haven't heard from Roc. Don't get me wrong . . . I love the fact that Lil Roc is here with me and Chassidy, but don't you think it's unfair that he hasn't heard from either of his parents?"

"Honestly, I don't think he cares. He's having fun with Chassidy and I get a feeling that he enjoys being over here. You said yourself that he sometimes refers to you as his mother, didn't you?"

"Yes, but we both know that I'm not. I just don't think it's fair for people to have children, then dump them off on others all the time. Lil Roc spends a lot of time with his grandmother, more than he does with Roc and Vanessa put together."

"Is this all about Lil Roc, or the fact that you're pissed because you haven't heard from Roc?"

"It's both. I'm not going to call him either. I guess he'll get here whenever."

"I don't know what else to say to you about this relationship between you and Roc, Dee. I know how much you care for him, but you said yourself that you were looking for a stable relationship with a man you could trust. If you stick with Roc, I do not see that in your future. He's fine and all, and the sex is dynamic, but you need much more than that, don't you?"

"Of course I do. This has nothing to do with how fine Roc is or how he lays his pipe. I genuinely care for him and I love him a lot. I'm not happy about what is transpiring outside of my door, but as long as he doesn't bring his mess here, I guess I can deal with it."

"How long is that thought going to last? I know you, Dee, and this will not sit well with you for long."

"I agree. But if it doesn't, please tell me that Shawn has a single brother. He is a very nice-looking man who seems to have it together. Got a good job and everything. Kind of reminds me of Brian McKnight. Can he sing?"

Monica threw back her hand and laughed. "I can't vouch for his singing, but I can vouch for something else." She winked at me.

I gave Monica a high-five, as I knew exactly what she was talking about. We laughed and returned to join the others in the family room. Chassidy and Lil Roc had gone downstairs to play, while the rest of us stayed in the family room. Monica and I double-teamed Latrel, as we shared with Angelique how bad he was growing up.

"He was terrible," Monica said, laughing. "Girl, your husband almost burned my house down! I told Dee not to ever bring him back to visit me again!"

Latrel quickly spoke up in his defense. "Monica, that's a lie. You were the one who almost burned your house down that day, trying to cook me and your kids some flapjacks. As a matter of fact, you were on the phone with my mother, complaining about your outrageous kids. You laid your apron on the stove and it caught on fire. I was smart enough to grab the fire extinguisher and saved us all!"

I had gotten two sides of the story, so I wasn't sure who or what to believe. Monica said Latrel put the apron on the stove, but he said she did. Either way, it was good that we could now sit back and laugh about it.

As we continued, the doorbell rang. By now it was almost eight and my insides were boiling. I went to the door, opening it so Roc could come in. Without saying anything to him, I turned to walk away. He grabbed my hand to stop me.

"Damn. Merry Christmas to you too," he said, puckering for a kiss. I barely touched his lips with mine, and when he tried to hug me, I pulled away.

"I have company to get back to," I said dryly. "Merry Christmas."

Roc followed me as I made my way back into the family room. He already knew Monica and Latrel, but had never been officially introduced to Angelique. She shook his hand, and so did Monica's man, Shawn.

"What's up?" Roc said, sitting on the couch near Latrel and Angelique. He and Latrel kicked up a quick conversation before Lil Roc ran into the family room and jumped into his father's lap. He thanked him for the Christmas presents, and so did Chassidy, as she was all over him too. They all got along extremely well and that made me feel good. Angelique had gotten off Latrel's lap, and leaving the men in the family room, the ladies went to my bedroom so I could show them a dress I'd purchased last week.

"That is so sexy," Monica said as I turned the dress in circles so she could see it. "Where are you going to wear it to? Bed?"

I had to laugh, only because Monica was always on me about living a boring life. "That's not fair," Angelique said in my defense. "She may not go out often, but when she does, she sure in the heck be clean!"

I gave my daughter-in-law a high-five. She was probably trying to score some brownie points, but it worked.

Monica went into my closet, pulling out some outfits that still had tags on them. She was trying to make her point about me buying stuff and never having a chance to wear it. All the pieces were being sprawled out on my bed.

"Let's see," she said. "There's this and that. That dress and this one."

She kept at it until I agreed with her. After that, we left the room and joined the men back in the family room. Roc was in the kitchen preparing a plate while talking on his phone. He was so loud that everyone could hear his conversation in the family room.

"Man, that's what that nigga get! They tenderized his ass . . . beat the shit out of him." He laughed. "I wish I would've been there, 'cause you know I would've put my foot in that ass too."

Roc's conversation was a bit much. And when he started talking about some cracker-ass white man who almost tore up his car, I'd had enough. I went into the kitchen and tapped his shoulder as his back was turned. He turned, looking as if I'd startled him.

"Can you please lower your voice? These kids don't need to hear you cursing like that, and neither do my guests."

Roc cut his eyes at me, then got back to his conversation. He did lower his voice, a little, but a few more "niggas" and "muthafuckas" did come out. Finally, he ended his call and sat at the kitchen table to eat. When he asked for some salt, I reached for it on the counter and then placed it on the table in front of him. Before I could pull back, he slammed his hand on top of mine, gripping it tight.

"Don't you ever speak to me in that tone around other people, nor when I'm on the phone, a'ight? You haven't said two muthafuckin' words to me since I entered this house, and how dare you get at me over some bullshit?"

I tried to move my hand, but he squeezed it. "Let it go," I said in a sharp tone. "We'll discuss this later."

"Not on my watch we won't. And just in case you don't understand what I'm sayin', this a done deal."

He let go of my hand and shook the salt over his food.

My brows rose. I was clearly irritated. "I don't understand, and to hell with your watch. Obviously it doesn't have the right time, because if it did, you would've been here at noon like you said, instead of at eight."

Roc ignored me and continued to eat his food. When I turned to walk away, he called my name. I turned and he pointed his fork at me. "If you want respect, you'd better give it. And if you don't want to get embarrassed, you'd better walk yo' ass out of here and not say shit else to me. That, I hope you do understand."

Now, this was my house and he was in no way calling the shots. As far as I was concerned, he had already embarrassed me with his loud and obnoxious talking. All I asked was for him to hold it down. He acted as if

I'd told him to shut the fuck up. I was getting ready to open my mouth, but the doorbell ringing stopped me. I hadn't invited anyone else to come over, but I wasn't sure if Latrel or Angelique had. I hoped Latrel hadn't invited Reggie. I feared opening the door and it would be him. Thank God that wasn't the case, but when I looked out the peephole, standing on my porch was Tiara. Her face looked a little fatter than the last time I'd seen her, her nose was pug and her eyes were puffy. I could tell she'd been crying. Her hair was now in long braids. She wore a heavy winter coat, but her belly was poking through it. I wasn't sure if I should open the door, or if I should go get Roc to deal with his woman. But like I said, this was my house and it only made sense that I was the one to open my door. She reached out to knock and I pulled the door open.

"May I help you?" I asked.

"Is Roc here?" she asked with a little snap in her voice.

"Yes, but please do me a favor and call him on his phone to speak to him. I have guests and I really do not want things to get heated around here."

Her neck started to roll. "Well, I'm sorry for the intrusion, but as I see it, to hell with your guests. I need to speak to Roc, right now, face to face. Tell him to bring his ass out here!"

I hated arguing with women over men, truly I did. But this fool was standing on my porch telling me to hell with my guests and ordering me around. Either way, I refused to respond to her, so all I did was shut the door. She rang the doorbell, again, but I was already in the kitchen where Roc was. Everybody in the family room was looking at me to see what was up, and even Roc questioned who was at the door.

"Tiara," I said with steam shooting from my ears. "She wants to speak to you. *Now.*"

Roc got up from the table and made his way to the door. Latrel asked me if everything was okay and I told him to chill out and take Angelique and the kids to the basement. I wasn't sure how heated things were going to get, but Latrel hesitated on doing what I'd asked. I had to pull him aside and tell him that Roc's girlfriend was outside. It was only then that he told everyone to follow him downstairs, with the exception of Monica and Shawn. He remained seated, but Monica was up on her feet like me.

"No, this heifer didn't," Monica whispered while looking out the living room window. She could hear Roc and his girlfriend going at it. "It's some bold-ass women in this world. How in the hell are you going to come to another woman's house and clown on her property?"

I kept quiet, because I had gone to their house too. It wasn't that I was upset with Tiara, even though she had disrespected me by what she'd said. My issue was with Roc. Period. We could hear almost everything that was being said.

"Fuck you, Roc," she yelled. "You told me you were coming over here to see your damn daughter, but Durk told me you've been over here fucking this bitch! Then, you got that tramp Vanessa blowing up my damn phone saying the same shit! So I came here to see what the fuck is up. Are you or aren't you sticking your dick in this bitch? When you claimed that you were out of town for three days, were you with her or not? If you don't tell me the truth, I'm going to ask her! Come clean, or else!"

"You need to calm your ass the fuck down! To hell with what Vanessa said! She also said that you told her that baby wasn't mine! Now what?"

"Now what my ass! I'ma call Vanessa right now and we can settle all of this shit once and for all! You's a lying-ass fool, Roc, and . . ."

Monica looked at me, shook her head, and chuckled. "Sounds like somebody may need to call Maury. You said that as long as this mess didn't come to your home you could deal with it. It's here, so what are you going to do now?"

"Be careful what you say, because you can speak it into existence, right? Please go entertain Shawn. Let me take care of this, okay?"

Monica cocked her head back, surprised. "Are you going outside?"

"Yes."

"Then I'm staying right here. Shawn can wait. If this chick starts acting a fool with you, she'll have you and me to deal with."

I opened the front door, but by this time Tiara and Roc were in my driveway arguing. She looked over his shoulder at me since I was heading their way. He turned around.

"Roc, if you need to leave, please go ahead and do so. It's getting pretty darn loud out here and the two of you are causing quite a scene."

Roc ignored me. He told Tiara to get in her car to go, but she refused to do it. He held her back, as she moved toward me. "So tell me, Desa Rae. What's up with you and Roc? Is he your man or what? If ain't nothing going on with the two of you, Roc, confront this bitch in front of me! If it's all about your motherfucking daughter say so, *nigga!*"

This was just sad and sickening at the same time. First Vanessa, now her. No, I had no right messing with a man who was seeing someone else, but why was she coming after me? Why bring my daughter up in this mess and call me out of my name? Hell, we all knew Roc's ass had told some lies, but I was anxious to hear the lie for myself. I folded my arms and looked at him.

"Tell me, Roc. I'd love for you to confront me. I'm also surprised to hear that Tiara really doesn't know what's up. Should I tell her, or will you?"

Roc was about to lose it, but ask me if I cared. These were the consequences of wanting to have your cake and eat it, too, and one could always find oneself being put on the spot. "I'm not tellin' nobody shit!" Roc shouted. "Tiara, I'm gon' tell you one more damn time to get in your car and go home! If you don't, I'm gon' put you in there my damn self and you won't like it if I have to put my hands on you!"

She was a feisty chick. Roc's threat in no way moved her. She continued to shout at him, and only a few minutes later, another car came screeching down the street. Out of the car hopped Vanessa. "Where my muthafuckin' son at? I don't know why you got this ho callin' me about some shit I supposedly had said! That muthafuckin' baby ain't yours and you know damn well that you and Desa Rae still fuckin'!" She looked at Tiara. "I'm gettin' married next week so stop callin' my phone, 'cause I ain't got shit to do with this triflin' nigga no more!"

"Who you callin' a ho?" Tiara yelled. "And when in the hell did I tell you this baby wasn't Roc's? You's a lying bitch, and if it wasn't his baby, why in the fuck would I tell you something like that?"

By now, Monica had rushed outside to add her two cents. I was trying to hold her back, especially from Vanessa, who had the biggest mouth of all. "Slut, I will stomp your hoodrat tail to the ground," Monica shouted. "Both of you nappy-head tricks need to take this dumb crap somewhere else and get the hell out of here!"

As I was pushing Monica away from Vanessa, Tiara reached out and struck her in the back of her head with a tightened fist. Roc grabbed Tiara around her waist, but not before Vanessa took her foot and kicked Tiara dead in her stomach. I felt the pain, but I guess she didn't. She reached over Roc and pulled at Vanessa's hair. Roc was between the both of them, but they were swinging so wildly that he was getting punched too. I was getting ready to go inside to call the police, but within minutes, they were already flying down the street. The sirens were loud, causing several of my neighbors to come outside. Shawn was standing in the doorway looking too, and I assumed that Angelique and Latrel were still downstairs with the kids. This was embarrassing and downright ridiculous. To find myself dealing with some crap like this was a disappointment.

The police rushed out of their cars, aiming their guns everywhere. "Down on the ground!" they shouted. "Everybody get down on the ground!"

Vanessa and Tiara pulled away from each other and slowly kneeled to the ground. So did Roc, and when one of the officers aimed his gun at me and Monica, he yelled for us to do the same. "Down!" he shouted. "Now!"

I couldn't believe it. There I was, kneeling to the ground with a gun covering me. The same officer yelled for Shawn to move away from the doorway, and yes, he was ordered to get down too!

"We didn't have anything to do with this," Shawn said in our defense. "Why are you asking for us to get on the ground?"

The white officer's eyes cut Shawn like a sharpened knife. "Because I said so! Now down! If I have to say it again, you will be arrested!"

None of us wanted to get arrested, so all the way down on the ground we went. Handcuffs were immediately placed on Roc, Tiara, and Vanessa. When one officer asked whose house it was, I told him it was mine.

"Stand up," he said. When I did, he asked me what had happened. I told him and several other officers the truth. Afterward, they told Monica and Shawn to get up and go back into the house. One of the officers removed the cuffs from Roc, but left them on Vanessa and Tiara, who were sitting on the ground less than a few feet away from each other. A few other officers questioned Roc.

"If your truck is registered in North County, what are you doing out here?" an officer asked.

Roc folded his arms and leaned against his truck. "So in other words, if I live in the hood, I don't have no business out here in O'Fallon, right? Is that what you're sayin'?"

"I didn't say that. I'm just asking why you're at Ms. Jenkins's house."

"Because she invited me over here for Christmas, that's why."

"Any weapons or drugs in your truck?"

Roc shrugged. "Don't know. But you'll need a search warrant to search my truck, and I will not give you permission to do it unless you have one."

The two officers kept at it, while the others were running the license plates on everyone's cars. The officers were doing their best to irritate Roc. I could tell it was working, so I walked over closer to them to intervene. "Have you ever been arrested before?" the officer asked Roc.

"Yep. Plenty of times," he said with a crooked smile.

"Why is all of this relevant?" I said to the officers. "All I want is these two uninvited young ladies to get off my property. They were asked to leave, but refused to do so."

"You didn't ask me shit, bitch!" Tiara shouted as she remained on the ground. I guessed she was upset because I was standing close to Roc. "This is fucked up. But what's more fucked up is this baby might not be yours, nigga. See, I can play like you do too. So, now what, sucker?" She laughed. "What yo' ass got to say about that?"

Before Roc could say anything, while sitting on the ground Vanessa reached out her foot and karate kicked Tiara right in her face. Her head snapped to the side. I felt that hard kick in my stomach and I cringed from all that was happening.

Roc smiled, then shouted at Tiara, "What I got to say about that? Nothin'! I didn't have to say shit! Her foot said it, baby! It said it all." He laughed.

Frankly, I didn't see a darn thing funny. Neither did the police as they grabbed Tiara and threw her in the police car, after she tried to charge Vanessa. Vanessa was put in the police car too, but she had the audacity to shout out for her son. "My son is in that muthafuckin' house! I want my son!"

"Yeah, well, you should've thought about your son a long time ago. Tonight, you're going to jail." The officer lowered Vanessa's head and put her into the back seat of the police car. I couldn't have agreed with him more. She didn't give a care about her son, and if she had, he would've been her priority, not Tiara and Roc. I guessed Tiara was now regretting that she'd called Vanessa to come set the record straight. This was pure deep madness and the one in the center of all of this was the man himself . . . Mr. Roc. This was definitely the downside of dating a man who was much younger than I was and who brought a bunch of immature women right along with him.

Chapter 6

Just like last Christmas, when I had gone to Roc's place and saw him having sex with Vanessa, my Christmas was ruined again. After Vanessa and Tiara went to jail that night, Roc came inside apologizing to everyone and trying to explain. I didn't buy it. While I was aware that he was seeing someone else, never did I think his mess would be placed at my front door. I was as embarrassed as ever. Humiliated, more like it, and the effects of dealing with a man in his late twenties, who seemed to get a kick out of the drama, was wearing on me. After everyone had left that night, the only thing Roc could do was throw up the respect thing. He claimed that I had continued to disrespect him and it started with when he'd come into my house on Christmas. He complained about my attitude and had the nerve to call out Tiara for showing up as well. It was all her fault and she should have never come over, griping. Then there was Vanessa, who he claimed he didn't give a damn about anymore. She was out of line too, and the both of them were stupid, immature bitches. According to him, he had suspected that Tiara wasn't pregnant with his child. But he didn't want to tell me until he was sure. The baby was due the week of my birthday and that's when he would know for sure.

Either way, after all that had happened, he was the one bitter. The best he could do was pay the bail money to get Vanessa and Tiara out of jail, and after that, he wanted nothing to do with them. As for me, I bitched too much, complained too loud, belittled him, disrespected him, and made him feel less than a man. I hadn't "accepted" nothing about him, so he had been keeping his distance from me. While he didn't exactly say those things, I suspected that's what he was thinking. But at this point, my main concern was his relationship with Chassidy. That was still going well, and all this other nonsense was placed at Roc's feet to deal with.

The New Year was over and it was back to work for me. Not only was I walking around with a bad attitude, but so was Mr. Anderson. He had been clowning all week, and on Friday, he called me in his office to apologize.

"As you know . . ." he said as he sat behind his desk. I kept my distance by standing near his doorway. "My wife and I are getting a divorce. I'm a bit on edge, because I definitely didn't see this coming. Our kids are devastated behind this, and I'm pretty darn upset about what this will do to me financially."

I really and truly had no sympathy whatsoever for Mr. Anderson. Some men just didn't realize all that was at stake until it was too late. His pitiful tail sounded like Reggie, and if Mr. Anderson thought he was going to get any comforting words from me, he was sadly mistaken. My mouth was shut. All I did was listen, and kept it short when I responded.

"I accept your apology. I hope everything works out for you. I'm dealing with some things right now too, and I would appreciate if we would keep our personal business out of the workplace and respect each other."

"I agree," he said, reaching out to give me a piece of paper. "Will you type that up for me before you go to lunch? That's if you can get around to it. If not, you can e-mail it to me later today."

"I should be finished with it before lunch. I don't really have much else going on, but I am having lunch with Monica. We're not meeting up until two o'clock, so I'll be taking a late lunch."

Mr. Anderson nodded. He asked me to close his door on the way out, so I did. I got busy typing his letter, but was interrupted by a telephone call on my personal line.

"Desa Rae Jenkins," I said. "How may I help you?"

"Desa Rae, this is the nurse, Sandy, at Chassidy's preschool. She's running a slight fever and we wondered if you could come pick her up?"

"Of course," I said. "I'm on my way."

I hurried out of my cubicle and knocked on Mr. Anderson's door. When I opened it, I saw that he had his head on his desk. He looked to be upset and he quickly blinked away the tears that appeared to be held up in his eyes. Funny, because I never knew he cared that much to cry about his situation. "Yes, Desa Rae," he said, trying to choke back his emotions.

"I just got a phone call from my daughter's school. She's running a fever and I need to go pick her up. Do you mind if I type your letter from home and e-mail it to you later?"

"No, I don't mind. Go ahead and see about your daughter. I'm sure she needs you."

"Thanks," I said before saying good-bye.

When I arrived at Chassidy's preschool, I was surprised to see Roc's truck parked outside. I went inside, and saw him holding her. Her arms were wrapped around his neck and her head was slumped on his shoulder. Her eyes were fluttering as he spoke to the nurse, while he rubbed up and down her back. I walked up and reached out for Chassidy. She climbed from Roc's arms to mine. I could feel how hot her body was.

"She is awfully warm," I said. "What's her temperature?"

"Close to one hundred," the nurse said. "There's some type of bug going around. Some of the other kids have gone home sick with the flu. I'm sure she'll be okay, but we had to call you to come pick her up."

"I appreciate it," I said. "Thanks for calling and we'll see you all when she gets better."

The teacher and nurse waved at Chassidy as she left. She was too ill to wave back. When we got outside, Roc told me to get in his truck so we could take her to the emergency room. As hot as she was, I agreed.

For the next three hours, we sat in the emergency room, waiting for the doctors to tell us what was wrong and what was needed. Chassidy did have the flu and she was given some medicine for her fever as well. After getting a shot, she cried herself to sleep. We left the hospital, and by the time we went back to get my car and made it home, Chassidy was still knocked out. I felt so bad for my baby. I wanted to trade places with her and I hated when she got sick. I helped her change into her nightgown, and stayed in the room with her until she fell back to sleep. The medicine had her so drowsy that it wasn't long before she was out.

It had been a long day, and I was pretty sleepy myself. When I went into my bedroom, I thought Roc would be there, but he wasn't. I went to the family room and that's where I saw him lying on the couch, watching a basketball game.

"How's she doin'? Is she asleep?" he asked.

"I think her fever has gone down, but I'm not going to take her temperature again until the morning. She's knocked out right now. I can only imagine how terrible she must feel."

"She'll be okay. Don't stress yourself, a'ight?"

"I'm not. I need to type up a quick letter for Mr. Anderson and e-mail it to him. After that, I think I'm going to shut it down myself. Are you staying the night or going home?"

"I'm staying. Want to make sure Chassidy will be okay in the mornin'. Tomorrow, though, I have to jet out of town to take care of some business for a couple of days. I'll be back late Sunday night."

I shrugged, and instead of inquiring about his "business" trip, I sat at my desk in the family room and scooted my chair up to the computer. As I started to type, Roc called my name. I turned around in my swivel chair.

"Yes."

"Can we talk about some things? I want to clear the air. Been sensin' a li'l friction between us since Christmas and I don't like where things are headed. You know what I'm sayin'?"

I really wanted to get Mr. Anderson's letter typed, but I was sure that if I told Roc the letter was more important, he would accuse me of not caring. Instead of typing, I got up and joined him on the couch. He sat up and rubbed his hands together.

"I'm not gon' keep pointin' the finger at you and tellin' you why I think this relationship keeps takin' turns for the worse, but I need to hit you with some facts. First and foremost, I never hid my relationship with Tiara or her pregnancy from you. You seem to think that I want to have my cake and eat it, too, but the fact is you gave me the cake, so why shouldn't I eat it? Two, I do not know if the child Tiara is carryin' is mine. I have suspected some shit with her for a long time, but I don't like to come over here talkin' about my madness with other women. I felt that we were gettin' along fine, and tellin' you about what I had suspected would have brought about questions that I won't have an answer to until she has this baby. Three, Vanessa and I are over. Done. It's been a wrap with us for some time now, and I hope you ain't around here speculatin' about somethin' goin' on between us because it ain't." He paused, then continued, "I apologize for what happened on Christmas, but that shit was beyond my control. I didn't mean to embarrass you in front of yo' friends and family, but the damage has already been done. You think I'm a cold nigga who enjoys the madness with women, but what you witnessed from me that day is a man who don't give a fuck about women who dog me out, call me a nigga, and treat me like I'm a punk. You may think I get a kick out of that shit, but fact is, I don't. That's why I feel differently about you. That mouth of yours can get real slick at times, but I appreciate that you don't always cross the line."

Roc said a mouthful. I wasn't going to dispute any of his facts, because all I wanted to do was finish Mr. Anderson's letter. I kept my response short. "Thanks for sharing and your apology is accepted."

I got up and returned to my desk. As I typed Mr. Anderson's letter, Roc got up and went downstairs. I heard the stereo blasting music, but I tuned it out. After I finished Mr. Anderson's letter, I e-mailed it to him and told him to have a good evening. I then went downstairs to ask Roc to turn the stereo down a bit, but when I got there, I saw him lying on Latrel's bed with his arm resting on his forehead. He was staring up at the ceiling, deep in thought. His shirt was off and the sheets covered his bottom half. I walked over to the stereo, turning it down.

"Are you sleeping down here tonight?" I asked.

"Yes."

"Why?"

"Because I want to. Besides, you actin' all funny and shit, so I'ma stay out of your way."

"I'm not acting funny. I'm just tired of the same old stuff, Roc. Tired of the same excuses, tired of dealing with your women, or should I say your Bad Girls Fan Club, and some of your facts didn't sit well with me."

"Nothin' I say sits well with you, Dez, and day by day you're pushin' me away. I get that a lot of this shit is on me right now, but I'm tryin' to show you that I care, ma. The last thing I want is for you to walk away from this with harsh and hurt feelings."

"The last thing I want to do is push you away, and I'm sure if I continue to express myself, that'll give you a chance to run like you always do. So, for the sake of not hurting our daughter, I'll keep my mouth shut. I'm not mad anymore, just concerned. Get some rest and good night."

I went back upstairs to my room, leaving Roc with his thoughts of how I was the one who had been badly screwing things up. He just didn't get it. I didn't know what else to say to make him understand.

I tossed and turned all night long, and hadn't slept well since my incident with Darrell. Every little noise caused me to jump in my sleep, and since it was thundering outside, that really made it difficult for me to rest. I did, however, feel safe because I knew Roc was still downstairs in the basement. I got out of bed several times throughout the night to check on Chassidy. It felt like her fever had gone down, and the medicine she'd taken still had her knocked out. I was glad she was resting well, because I knew if she'd heard the thunder roaring, she would be right in bed with me. I quietly closed her bedroom door and tiptoed back down the dark hallway to my room. I jumped a bit when I heard the crackling sound of thunder, and instead of going to my room, I made my way toward the kitchen to get something to drink. As I neared the kitchen, my nostrils filled with the smell of burnt leaves. When I looked in the family room, I saw Roc lying back on the couch in the dark, smoking a joint. The windows were open, bringing in the whistling wind and a cool breeze from the rain that was beating down hard on the pavement. The weed smell was potent. Roc knew better than to be firing it up in my house.

"Would you mind putting that out?" I asked as I moved closer to him.

He sat up, but took a long drag from the joint before smashing the tip of it with his finger. Afterward, he laid the bud in an ashtray. "There," he said, swiping his hands together. "Are you satisfied?"

"Yes. Thank you."

I turned to walk away, but Roc reached out for my hand to keep me in front of him. "Why you so cold, baby?" he asked. "You are colder than a muthafucker, wit' yo' fine, sexy-ass self."

"And you're high as hell, wit' your words that only make me blush a little."

"That's 'cause you're stone cold like I said." Roc reached out to my waist to put me on his lap. "I am a li'l high, but that's because I couldn't get no sleep."

"Why is that? Are you worried about something?"

"Nah, not really. I . . . I never told you this before, but I'm afraid of thunder and lightnin'. I couldn't sleep, and bein' in the basement made me feel like this damn house was gon' crash down on me."

I reached up my hand and rubbed Roc's flowing waves. "Now, you know I don't believe that, right? I don't think you're afraid of anything, Roc, not you."

"Everybody has fears, trust me. When I was a little boy, and it would thunder outside, I used to go hide in the closet and cry myself to sleep. That shit lasted for a long time, and to this day, I still take issue with bad weather."

"I hate it too, but are you going to go into one of my closets and hide? If so, I'll go with you."

He laughed and squeezed his arm around my waist. We could still hear it clowning outside. "Nah, I don't want to go in no closet. I want to stay right here with you, so you can hold me."

"I can do more than just hold you," I said. I stood up and pulled my nightgown over my head. I then reached for one of the pillows on the couch, dropping it on the floor. I kneeled and eased my body between Roc's legs. As he leaned back, I removed his package from the slit on his boxers. To me, there was nothing on any other man's body more pleasing to look at than Roc's long and thick, shiny black dick that I was about to swallow. I opened my mouth wide, covering his shaft and taking it all in, until it shaved the back of my throat. My jaws tightened and my tongue went into action. Roc's stomach started to vibrate and his hand roamed in my hair.

"Now that's what I'm talkin' about, baby. Do that shit, Dez, you got skills!"

At Roc's request, I continued. Actually, we continued for quite some time, and had made our way over to the opened window that was still bringing in the breeze. Roc held my legs wide like a V, as he maneuvered back and forth with deep strokes. The feel of his meat pushing in my folds made me creamier with each thrust. My legs were getting weak, especially when I reached down to tickle my own clit.

Roc smiled. "Oooo, you nasty. But thanks for helpin' me overcome my fear. The weather outside can't fuck with this."

I released my hand from my clit, trying to calm my explosion. "I agree the weather can't and won't interrupt this. And since I've helped you overcome your fear, pleeease help me overcome mine."

Roc halted his smooth strokes. "Wha . . . what are you afraid of?"

"Losing you. I don't want to lose you. Ever."

Roc turned his hips, again, and then tightened his muscular ass as we released the results of our ongoing sexual efforts together. He leaned over me and whispered in my ear, "You won't lose me, unless you choose to. I'm down with this, and whether you're down depends on you."

I nodded, and after a lengthy kiss, we headed to the shower to wash up.

Roc stayed until midmorning, and after he saw that Chassidy was feeling much better, he left. Since he mentioned that he'd be going out of town, I expected not to hear from him for a few days. Actually, several days had passed and it wasn't until the following Sunday that he picked up the phone to call.

"How has Chassidy been doin'?" he asked. I could hear noise in the background; kind of sounded like someone speaking over an intercom.

"She's doing fine. She's much better. I'm getting ready to take one of her friends home. She spent the night."

"Did they have a good time?"

"Of course they did. They kept me up all night playing games and watching movies. I'm definitely not looking forward to returning to work tomorrow, but gotta make my money." I heard the intercom again and asked Roc where he was at.

"I'm at the hospital. Tiara had a miscarriage earlier today. She'd been havin' some issues for quite some time and the baby didn't make it."

"I'm sure she's probably upset right now, and by the sound of your voice, I can tell you may be disappointed too. I appreciate you calling us. It's always good hearing from you."

Roc paused for a moment; then he spoke up. "I told you what was up with this baby, but either way, I feel guilty about all the shit that went down. A nigga do have a heart, you know? Tiara was under a lot of stress, and some of it was from dealin' with me. At the end of the day, she good people and I hate when shit like this happens to the ones who don't deserve it."

"I feel you, but don't be so hard on yourself. Do you really believe that the child was yours?"

"Deep down, I don't. But that don't even matter right now. I just want her to get well." Roc sighed, then spoke up again. "I'm talkin' too much about things that you don't care nothin' about, so I'ma let you go. Tell Chassidy I'll see her over the weekend. Maybe I'll take her and Lil Roc to the movies."

"I'm sure she'll enjoy that. We'll see you next week, and whether you realize it or not, I do care."

Roc didn't reply. He just hung up. I couldn't believe that he'd had me pegged so wrong. I did care, and the person he was trying to make me out to be, I wasn't. I didn't think much of it and chalked it up as him being upset about the baby. If he was blaming himself, I was sure Tiara had him eating from the palm of her hand. For now anyway.

When next week rolled around, Roc came by to pick up Chassidy so she could go to the movies with him and Lil Roc. A 3-D kiddy movie was showing at St. Louis Mills and the kids were anxious to see it. As I put on Chassidy's hat and gloves, then zipped her coat, Lil Roc tapped my shoulder.

"After the movie is over, can Chassidy come over to my dad's house with me and spend the night? She's never been over there and I want to show her all the stuff I have to play with."

I wasn't sure if Roc had put Lil Roc up to asking me that question or not, but either way, my answer would be the same. "I don't think so, sweetheart. Chassidy needs to come home after the movies. Maybe some other time."

While standing in the foyer with us, Roc cleared his throat. "Why you askin' Dez if Chassidy can spend the night? You should've asked me, 'cause I would've given you the answer you wanted to hear."

I crossed my arms, rubbing up and down them. Wasn't quite sure what Roc meant, so I asked him. "He asked me because I'm Chassidy's mother. We've never been invited to your house, and I think it's fair to say that if I'm not welcome, neither is she. Please bring her home once the movie is over. I don't want any trouble, Roc, and all I'm doing is asking, not telling."

Roc's eyes narrowed and he told the kids to go out to his truck. Before they did, both of them gave me big hugs and kissed my cheeks. "Have a good time," I said to them. "I'll see the two of you later."

The kids ran outside, but played in the snow that was less than three inches high. Roc looked at me, shaking his head. "I was gon' say somethin' to you, but you know what? Fuck it. Forget it, Dez . . . Sleep tight."

He walked out and I yelled after him. "What is that supposed to mean? If you don't bring her back tonight, you will never be allowed to leave with her again. I can promise you that, so have fun too."

Roc kept it moving. He opened the doors to his truck so the kids could get in. They were strapped in tight and Roc turned to look away as he drove off.

I went back inside, and on a Saturday night I found myself slumped down in my leather recliner with a soft throw covering my body. A good book was in my hands and I was very much into it. So into it, that by the time

I looked up, it was almost nine o'clock. Roc and the kids had left a little after three, and I figured the movie was over by now. I reached for my cordless phone and dialed out to call Roc. His voice mail came on.

"Where are you?" I asked. "Hope you all had a good time, but please call to let me know where you are. I'm getting a little worried."

I got back to my book, but this time I kept watching the clock. It ticked away, and not only was I worrying, but I had started to get mad. I hoped that Roc wouldn't go against what I'd said earlier. Yes, he was Chassidy's father, but from what I had witnessed with Roc, some of his family, and with his ghettofied women, Chassidy didn't need to be anywhere near that mess. Too much drama ensued, and I was sure Tiara was still living with him. If she didn't like me, I was sure she wouldn't like having my child around. Then, Roc was always talking to his friends on the phone and not paying attention to the kids. He got off into heavy, vulgar conversations that caused him to lose focus. Chassidy and Lil Roc were capable of getting into a lot of things if no one was paying attention. Taking them to the movies was one thing, but Roc's supervision wasn't quite up to par with me yet.

Another hour had passed. I placed the book on my lap and sighed. When I dialed his number again, as expected, he didn't answer.

"Roc, I'm trying to be as nice and patient about this as I can. And if something has happened, please just call to tell me. It's after ten o'clock now and I'm feeling sick to my stomach. I need to hear from you, soon."

I ended the call and almost twenty minutes later, he called back. "What up?" he asked.

"Where is Chassidy?"

"She's with me."

"I know she's with you, but I asked you to bring her home once the movie was over."

"And I told you that we were goin' to the movies. Afterward, we went to dinner and we're now at my house playin' video games. The kids are gettin' a bit restless, so I'ma lay them down for bed in a minute."

My mouth dropped open and I clenched my teeth together. "Once they're done playing video games, would you please bring Chassidy home?"

"I'm gon' make this simple for you. No. Hell, no. See you tomorrow and sleep tight like I said earlier."

I was in disbelief when Roc hung up on me. The steam from my ears was as thick as steam shooting from a locomotive. I quickly called him back, but this time, his phone went straight to voice mail. I sure as hell hated to go there with him, but I couldn't help myself. I hurried to put on my jeans, a thick sweater, and Ugg boots to tackle the snow. My hair was pulled back into a ponytail that was in no way sleek. I snatched my keys from my dresser and jetted to Roc's house off New Halls Ferry Road.

When I arrived, like the last time, there were two trucks in the driveway. I didn't give a damn who was there. I marched straight to the door and knocked. Within a few minutes, someone opened the door and it was Roc. The look of madness was in his eyes and he shook his head from side to side.

"I . . . I can't believe you're here," he said. "Then again, yes, I can."

"I don't know why you can't believe it. I came to get Chassidy. Please put on her coat so she can go."

"She's asleep, Dez. I told you I would bring her home tomorrow. What in the hell is the big fuckin' deal? Damn!"

I darted my finger at him. "The deal is I asked you to bring her home. I didn't want her coming over here.

I don't know what you have going on up in there, and from past experiences, it hasn't been good."

Roc walked away from the door and I widened the screen door to follow him inside. He turned to face me, while holding out his arms. "Since you're inside, why don't you look around, Dez? If you look hard enough, maybe you'll find my stash of cocaine or heroin needles somewhere. Maybe you'll see loaded guns on my tables and buck-naked hoes with pussies on display. You damn sure gon' find a bunch of lowlife niggas up in here parlayin' around, and the ashtrays you see may be overflowin' with smoked blunts. So," he said, walking over to the horseshoe-shaped black leather sofa and taking a seat, "take your time, ma. Let me know what you find when you get finished. Then tell me if my place is anything like you imagined—or should I say suspected—it to be."

I stared at Roc without saying a word. I did, however, glance at two ashtrays that were on his end tables, but they were empty. As far as I could see, his house was spotless, creatively decorated with contemporary furniture, and quiet. I wasn't going to leave the living room to check elsewhere, as all I'd come over for was to get my daughter.

"If you wouldn't mind going to get Chassidy for me, I would really appreciate it. I'm not here to argue with you, Roc. I just came to get my daughter."

He jumped up from the couch and charged toward me. Stopping right in front of me, he yelled out loudly and dotted my face with sprinkles of spit, as he darted his finger in anger. "She's my fuckin' daughter too! You didn't make her by your damn self! My muthafuckin' dick made her! Got it? You don't control everything that she can and cannot do! What the hell is wrong with you? What you're sayin' to me . . . basically been sayin' to me all along is the only thing I'm good for is stickin' my dick in you and suckin' yo' pussy! I'm no good at bein' a father, no damn good at shit I do, but when it comes to sex . . . I'm on fuckin' fire, right!"

I backed away from Roc. His face was twisted in pure, deep anger and his chest was heaving in and out. I hadn't seen him this upset in a very long time, and I knew that taking myself to his level would only make matters worse. I wiped my face, trying to clear his sprinkles of spit. "I . . . I was just worried, that's all. You don't understand—"

He quickly cut me off. "You damn right I don't understand! I don't understand why you think I'm some lowlife, low class ass nigga who can't even take care of his kids. You treat me like your fuckin' son, thinkin' you can tell me how to walk, talk, eat . . . look. You complain about every goddamn thing, and I bet you that even when I shit, you gripe 'cause it don't smell like roses! You fucked up in the head, Dez, and you ain't the only one tired of this bullshit. I am too!"

Roc stormed off into another room. A few minutes later, he came back with Chassidy sleeping on his shoulder. Her coat was already on, but it wasn't zipped. Roc handed her over to me, then kissed her forehead. Without saying anything else, I walked to the door and left. Roc slammed the door so hard that it rattled the huge picture windows. I kept it moving, figuring that it would be awhile before Roc and I settled our differences.

Chapter 7

I was right. It had been two weeks since I'd talked to Roc, but he had spoken to Chassidy on several occasions. She had invited him and Lil Roc to come to her school play, which was on a Friday at four in the afternoon. The teachers had made a really big deal about the play, and so had I. Chassidy was going to be a talking sunflower, and we had worked hard at rehearsing her lines over and over again. Latrel was supposed to drive in to see her too, but at the last minute he told me something came up and he couldn't make it.

"Is everything okay?" I asked him over the phone, while changing into something more comfortable for the play. I had left work early, just so I could make it. I didn't feel like being suited up, so I was dressed down in black pinstriped pants and a fuchsia cardigan sweater with ruffles.

"Everything is going okay. I didn't do so well on my finals last semester, so I have some catching up to do."

"Why didn't you do well on your finals?"

"I'm not sure. I guess I just didn't make enough time to study. But I will this time around for sure."

"I hope so. And I hope being married isn't too much. I still think you and Angelique rushed into this thing too quickly. I wish you would've waited until you graduated. That would've made much more sense to me."

"Well, it didn't make sense to me. My marriage has nothing to do with my grades. I told you I hadn't made time to study and that's all there is to it."

Latrel's tone had raised and I didn't like it one bit. "Why every time I open my mouth to say something, everybody catches an attitude? Whether you realize it or not, marriage is a big responsibility. It takes time and effort. Time that could be put into you finishing school, and effort that you need to put forth to bring up your grades. That's what's important to me. I don't want you flunking out your last year in school, so excuse me for caring so much."

"It's the way you say things to people, Mama, and Roc is right. Your tone is shitty. You have a nasty attitude and you're always trying to tell me what I should or could have done. I get that marriage is a big responsibility, and if I wasn't ready to take on those responsibilities, I never would've gotten married. Just back off. You've been doing good for a while, but here you go, again, with a bunch of nonsense."

My eyes widened as he spoke. He must've been talking to Roc, because he sounded just like him. I was on the verge on telling Latrel off, but I decided against it. "Latrel, at the end of the day, I am your mother. I will always offer you advice, take it or leave it. When you get snippy with me, I have every right to get snippy with you. I have not told you to do anything, but now that you mentioned it, I am telling you this. I took out a twenty-five thousand dollar loan, just so you could have some extra things in college that your scholarships didn't cover. My money will not be wasted, so you had better get your act together and get to studying for your finals. I love you and I will see you soon."

I ended our call, furious because everyone was trying to tell me that my attitude stunk. I guessed menopause would be the next excuse, or I was getting too old and didn't understand "young" people like I should. I got it very well, and I also knew more about my son than he thought I knew. He and Angelique had been having some problems and he was unable to focus because of their middle-of-the-night arguments. Arguments about stupid stuff that newly married couples could find themselves in. It was hard living with someone, and since they had never lived together, the new experience was driving both of them nuts. She'd been complaining about him not cleaning up, and he'd been complaining about her not cooking. Their final year in school was already stressful enough, and what they did by getting married was add more burdens. I suspected that they would get over this hump, because at the end of the day, I knew they loved each other. Then again, loving each other wasn't enough to make it work, so that's why I was somewhat worried.

My information about Latrel came straight from someone Latrel had trusted over the years, more than he'd trusted me. Someone who Latrel had counted on for every single thing, and felt his secrets were safe with: Reggie. Reggie told me what was going on, and while we didn't converse on a regular basis, he felt it was important for me to know what was going on with our son. I was always thankful to Reggie for sharing.

Chassidy's play took place in North High School's auditorium that was across the street from her preschool. School had already let out, but many of the students stayed to watch the play. I was so proud of my daughter. She had been rehearsing her lines in the car and knew all of them like the back of her hand. The teacher had given her at least ten long sentences to practice. I kept my fingers crossed that she wouldn't forget any.

As the auditorium filled in with people, I wondered if Roc was still going to show. I'd saved seats for him and Lil Roc, because I wanted Chassidy to see us sitting together. But as my head was turned, watching the door, I got the shock of my life. Roc came into the door with a young lady trailing closely behind him. Not only was it disrespectful, but it was damn disrespectful. I bit down on my lip and quickly turned in my seat. I hoped that he hadn't seen me, and I figured he wouldn't have the nerve to come sit by me. I was wrong. He excused himself as he stepped over four people who were sitting in my row, and took a seat right next to me. The chick who was with him sat next to him.

Roc leaned forward and removed his puffy cream-colored leather jacket with a hood. It looked like something a rapper would wear and so did his platinum chain. He laid the jacket across his lap, then turned his head toward me. "Dez, this is Raven," he said and left it there. With her arms folded across her chest and her long dark chocolate legs crossed, she leaned slightly forward.

"Hello," she said with a forced smile.

Trying to be polite, I spoke back. I swallowed the baseball-sized lump in my throat and kept my eyes on the burgundy curtains on stage, waiting for them to open. My thoughts, however, were all over the place. Roc had to know that this would infuriate me, but he obviously didn't care. My blood was boiling over, and I'd be the first to admit that I was very, very jealous. Raven was an attractive and fit woman. In order to compete, I had to work out more often. She looked like a Victoria's Secret model, yet had curves in all the right places. Her adorable, round eyes were hard to look into and she presented herself to be a classy young lady. Roc's look was stellar too, even though I wasn't down with the hip hop look. His cream cashmere sweater melted on his muscles and his black jeans went well with his leather Timberlands. There was a diamond ring that I had never seen on his finger, and the diamond in his earlobe was glistening too. His masculine cologne infused the space around us, but I could also smell Raven's perfume. I kept envisioning their near-perfect chocolate bodies pressed together while having sex. The thought of it hurt me, but what else was I to do but sit there and pretend that it didn't bother me?

Roc looked at his watch. "I thought the play started at four?" he inquired.

I was mad, so I didn't respond. Raven looked at her watch, then lifted his wrist to look at his. "Now, you know you always set your watch ten minutes early. It's only five minutes after four, and nothing that I have ever attended started on time."

Roc reached out to pat her leg; then he rubbed it. She put her hand over his, squeezing it together with hers. He turned his head to look at her, and that's when she puckered for a kiss. He leaned in to peck her lips, then looked straight ahead at the curtains.

Now, would I be wrong to get up and go sit somewhere else? Nope, that's what Roc wanted me to do. He was trying to get underneath my skin, but I wouldn't let it be known that he was. I sat there listening to them talk about going to dinner afterward and him staying the night with her. She giggled and he laughed. He touched her leg and she rubbed his. It was sickening. I was thankful when the curtains finally opened. Everybody clapped and so did we.

The play took my mind off Roc and his woman. Chassidy, as well as the other preschoolers, put on quite a show. So many of them had forgotten their lines, even Chassidy. That's what made it so much more entertaining. The audience laughed as one of the teachers whispered the lines to them, and the preschoolers yelled them out loudly. Chassidy had even scratched her head a few times, and walked over to the teacher so she could hear what she'd said. She bent down, trying to whisper to the teacher as if no one saw her. It was one of those memorable moments, and when I looked at Roc, he couldn't stop smiling. I hadn't seen him hold a smile on his face for this long in a very long time. I guess the same could be said for me.

When the play was over, Chassidy and the other students ran to their parents. Chassidy ran right into Roc's arms, and after not seeing him for the past two weeks, she was delighted.

"Daddy!" she said as he picked her up, rocking her back and forth in his arms.

"You did your thing, girl. And you made yo' daddy real proud."

Chassidy was smiling hard. She reached out for me and I took her from Roc. "I forgot my lines, Mommy, but I remembered them after the teacher told me what they were."

"Yes, you did. And you couldn't have done any better," I said with enthusiasm. With Chassidy in my arms, we all moved toward the door to exit. Roc's hand was on the small of Raven's back and I couldn't help but notice her perfect, heart-shaped butt. I heard her tell Roc that Chassidy was so cute, but when Chassidy knew Raven by her name, and thanked her for coming, I was taken aback. I wondered how Chassidy had known her and I didn't.

When we got outside, Roc told Raven that he was going to walk us to our car and go get his. In other words, stay put. She stood inside of the double doors, watching as we walked to my car together.

"That was a nice play," he said to Chassidy. "Thanks for invitin' me. I want you to come to my truck with me, because I got somethin' I want to give you."

Instead of going to my car, we went to his truck. There was a balloon inside, and a small brown teddy bear holding a red rose. Chassidy switched from my arms to his again. She was still smiling as Roc gave the balloon and teddy bear to her.

"Thank you, Daddy. You rock!"

He laughed and so did I. "I'd like to think so too," he said. "If only *some* other people thought that way."

Doing the norm, I didn't comment. Besides, I was still worked up from him coming to the play with Raven. Roc drove us to my car and told Chassidy he would see her soon. He then drove to pick Raven up at the door and they left.

On the drive home, Chassidy sat in the back seat, playing with her teddy bear. I watched her through the rearview mirror. I had a lot on my mind . . . her play, my conversation with Latrel, and Roc and his woman. I turned down the music and asked Chassidy how she'd known Raven's name.

"She was with us at the movies that day. I remembered her name from then," she said.

"Did Daddy pick her up so she could go with you, or was that his first time meeting her at the movies?"

Chassidy scratched her head. "I . . . I think she met us at the movies."

"Did she go to dinner with you all and was she at his house that night?"

"No, but I think she's his girlfriend, because they kissed. I thought you were his girlfriend, Mommy, because the two of you are always kissing each other too."

I didn't know what to say. And shame on me for trying to pump information from my daughter. "He's not my boyfriend. We were just a couple."

I was surprised when Chassidy took my comment further. "If he's not your boyfriend then how did the two of you make me? I thought a girl had to have a boyfriend to make a baby."

Honestly, I got tongue-tied. Chassidy had been paying way more attention to us than I thought she was. I didn't want her to believe that it was okay for boy- and girlfriends to make babies, nor that it was okay for a boy to have two girlfriends. But that's how she viewed my situation with Roc. How was I to tell her that it really wasn't the right way, even though I had been representing that it was? "Sweetheart, sometimes people have children out of wedlock, which me and your daddy did. Truth is, you should be married to a man before you have children with him and he shouldn't be allowed to have two women. We'll talk more about that as you get older, but right now, all I want you to think about is being in more awesome plays like you were just in, learning new things, and maybe even modeling again. You used to love having your picture taken and I couldn't keep you away from the camera. What happened?"

Chassidy shrugged her shoulders. "I broke my camera and didn't want to tell you. I do like taking pictures and I want to be in more plays too!"

I was glad the subject had changed. I guess my asking questions brought out something I hadn't prepared myself for. It was a wake-up call that I had to be real careful about the messages I was sending to my daughter about relationships.

That night, however, I tossed and turned, thinking about Roc and Raven. I couldn't get the thoughts of what they were doing out of my head. Why did she have to be so pretty and petite? Tiara or Vanessa never made me feel this insecure. Even though I'd known how strongly Roc and Vanessa had bonded over the years, I'd never felt threatened by her. I knew he would always be searching for something better, and that's why he'd kept coming back to me. But now, Raven appeared to have her stuff together. I didn't know much about her, but I figured I would soon know more.

The next day, Chassidy and I went to Monica's house to spend the day with her. Chassidy was playing with Monica's niece, Brea, and the two of them were in one of the guestrooms. We, however, were up to no good. I told Monica about Roc's new chick, Raven, and after the description that I had given Monica, she was dying to see who had been getting a piece of the Roc. Those were her words.

The one thing we could count on was Facebook. If Raven was on there, hopefully she wouldn't have her privacy settings blocked where we couldn't see her wall. I didn't know her last name, but if Roc was on Facebook, I was sure she was one of his friends. Under my login, Monica went to Roc's profile. Ninety-five percent of his friends were females, and you'd better believe they had been setting it out there for him. He hadn't commented much, but he did have plenty of sexy pictures out there that showed his physique, tattoos, and charming smile.

"Look at this hoochie here," Monica said, reading a comment from a picture of a female who had her back turned. Most of her ass covered the photo. I could barely see her face, but she was definitely putting her assets on display. She told Roc to check his inbox and his reply was "got it."

"I wonder what that was all about?" I asked. But as we scrolled down his wall, there was much, much more. Again, Roc had only responded to a few, particularly to the pretty ones who had been showing much skin. Monica clicked on the link to his friends and we searched through them. Many of the pictures caused us to shake our heads, and how in the hell could any man be faithful when the women were making themselves so available?

Finally, we came across a photo of Raven. Monica clicked on it and it allowed us to look through her pictures and read her wall. Her personal information was available too. In a matter of minutes, we found out that Raven's birthday was in April and she was twenty-nine years old. Her last name was Smith and she worked at Ameristar Casino as a blackjack dealer. She'd graduated from the University of Missouri and was also a model. She had numerous pictures of her in seductive positions, as well as simple ones that looked as if they belonged in magazines. Did she have to look that spectacular in a white swim suit, where she was sitting on Roc's lap? Her favorite activities included traveling, which she often did, and cooking was a favorite too. There was so much more about her available, but what stung the most were the numerous pictures of her and Roc. He was all over her wall. Friends complimented her "fine-ass man" and they seriously looked like a happy couple. From the outside looking in, it appeared that they'd been together for quite some time. At this point, I was speechless and so was Monica.

She took a deep breath. I figured she had been thinking the same thing I had been thinking. Roc and Raven looked good together. "How long has he been seeing this chick?" she asked.

I shrugged my shoulders, regretting, again, that I was snooping. The saying "what you don't know won't hurt" was fitting. "I'm not sure. But with all of these pictures of him on her wall, it seems as if it's been a long time."

Monica started looking at the dates on the pictures, pointing them out to me. I had walked away from the computer, because I'd gotten my feelings hurt. Monica turned around, telling me that most of the pictures were recent, but there were are few that dated back to the summer of last year, when Roc claimed to be in Kansas City, getting his life together.

"It doesn't appear that he's known her for that long. And you know darn well that Roc would drop her in a heartbeat if the two of you would get your act together."

I sighed. "You're just trying to make me feel better. Raven has Roc wrapped around her finger, and he has a thing for shapely women. I've been thinking about joining Weight Watchers anyway, and every time I see all that weight Jennifer Hudson has lost, I get hyped."

"She looks spectacular, but why are you always going there with the weight thing? I thought you were happy with how you looked, and from what I can tell, Roc couldn't care less about a woman's weight. He's been down with you no matter what and you know that. And as for Raven having him wrapped around her finger, that's bull and you know it."

"I . . . I know, but Raven looks so perfect. I'm sure he appreciates a woman with a figure like that. I hate to talk like I'm so insecure, but you know how critical men are about healthy women."

"Some men, not all. But that's because those men have their own insecurities. A decent man would look at a woman as a whole, and I have to defend Roc this time. He has never said one thing about your weight and it's obvious that size is no concern of his."

I had to agree with Monica. Roc accepted me "as is" and even though I had been hard on myself after seeing Raven, I felt good about myself too. I scrapped the idea of Weight Watchers, because the thought of losing weight for someone else didn't make sense. If I was happy with me, so be it. I chuckled and pulled Monica up from the chair.

"You know what? I'm not going to do this to myself. I'm well aware that Roc has no issues with my appearance, but I also need to accept the fact that he has too many issues with women. He's not the man I see in my future. I don't want to spend my Saturday cooped up in your house, looking at pictures on Facebook, and discussing Roc. Let's go shopping, and take our butts to the Cheesecake Factory. We can take the girls with us. Reggie sent me some back pay money on my child support. Since my bills are paid up, I have nothing to do with the money."

Monica shut down her computer and jumped up from her seat. "You don't have to ask me twice about going shopping and eating. I'm all for it, girl. Let's get going!"

Monica hurried to change clothes and we headed to the Galleria to shop. Being with Monica and Chassidy took my mind off all that I was feeling inside, and I couldn't help but thank God for my best friend who was helping me cope.

Chapter 8

I needed to get away, even if it meant going to Columbia, Missouri to be with Latrel and Angelique. This time, Latrel had invited me and Reggie to come to one of his basketball games. He hadn't played in several seasons, because his second year in college he had torn ligaments and his leg hadn't healed. He was on the bench more than anything, but Reggie sometimes visited to show his support. I was more excited about Latrel getting a degree in engineering. Angelique was getting a journalism degree and they seemed to have a bright future ahead of them.

Monica had agreed to watch Chassidy for me, and as soon as I dropped her off, I made my way to Columbia. It was only a two-hour drive from where I lived, but the ride was very peaceful. Gave me time to think and take in the soothing music on the radio. The last time I'd seen Reggie was about six or seven months ago. I promised Latrel that I would be on my best behavior. He didn't know that Reggie and I had occasionally talked on the phone, nor was Latrel aware that we had been discussing him. I told myself that I wouldn't confront Latrel with anything Reggie had told me, and I would definitely keep that promise.

Angelique and Latrel had moved into an apartment that was off campus, but nearby. After their wedding, I drove to Columbia on several weekends to help Angelique dccorate. She said that she not only liked the decorations, but that she also appreciated my help. It wasn't until I stood in their apartment, giving them hugs, that I realized she'd changed every single thing around.

"The place still looks nice," I said as I looked around at the now tacky-ass furniture and non-matching décor. Where did brown, orange, and gray match? It didn't. I didn't know if Angelique really wanted my help or if she was just being fake. She didn't come across as being that way, but every single thing that I'd purchased, and my décor suggestions, were done away with. How was I not to take it personal?

"We're so glad you're here," Angelique said. "Will you be staying with us for the next few days, or at a hotel?"

"I'm staying at the Hampton Inn on Fellows Place. I know the game is tonight and I'm sure the two of you are anxious to get out of here. I just wanted to stop by to let Latrel know I'd made it."

Latrel sat on the couch, tying his tennis shoes. "I'm leaving in about fifteen minutes. You do know where the arena is, don't you?"

"Yes, I do. I'm going to take my luggage to the hotel, then I'll meet the two of you at the game."

Angelique nodded and Latrel stood up. "I wish I had time to help you with your luggage, but the coach wants us to be on time. This will be my first time actually playing since I hurt myself."

I could tell that Latrel was a bit nervous. I gave him a hug and told him not to worry. "You'll do fine," I said, trying to encourage him. "And I'll be in my seat rooting for you."

Latrel walked me to my car, and kissed my cheek before I drove off and made my way to the hotel. As soon as I got to the Hampton Inn, I saw Reggie at the counter, waiting for the reservationist to finish with a man in front of him. I knew we'd bump into each other, but I didn't expect to be at the same hotel with him. The last time I'd seen him was at Latrel's wedding and he was with another woman. Since then, he looked as if he'd picked up a few pounds, but not where it affected him in any way. Reggie had always had a thick build, and was approximately six foot five. That's where Latrel had gotten his height from and he was even taller. Reggie played football in college and basketball as well, but neither panned out for him. It didn't matter because he was good at business. Even though his realty company had suffered a significant loss last year because of the economy, it had since recovered. He was back to giving me a little more money and I was happy about that.

So, in a nutshell, our relationship was . . . okay. In the past, he'd been upset with me about Roc and was devastated when he found out I was pregnant with Roc's child. But after a while, he seemed to get over it. Since we'd been divorced, he had been running from one woman to the next. He had also remarried, but got divorced less than a year later. Stability didn't seem to be working for him either, but we were here to support Latrel, and the both of us had to make the best of it.

I stepped up next to Reggie as he waited by the counter. He was just as surprised to see me, and reached out to give me a hug. "Hello, Dee," he said. "I didn't know you were staying at this hotel."

"They have some of the most affordable rates and I like their rooms. Called around and couldn't beat it. How long have you been waiting?"

"Not long. She's wrapping it up now."

Reggie and I waited together. When we stepped up to the desk, he told the reservationist to put both of the rooms in his name and he took care of the bill. He then asked for a bellboy to help me with my luggage and we made our way up to the third floor together. His room was directly across from mine. I thanked him for the generosity, and after he told me to knock on his door before I left, I went into my room to change for the game.

Almost forty-five minutes later, I had changed into a gold ribbed turtleneck and black denim jeans. I wanted to represent Mizzou's colors, just as the other fans would be doing.

Like Reggie had asked, I knocked on his door to see if he was ready. He was, and was dressed in a Mizzou sweatshirt and jeans. A Mizzou cap was on his head and it looked as if he had trimmed his beard. As we walked to the elevator together, it felt so awkward. I had been married to Reggie for almost twenty-something years, yet felt uncomfortable around him. Maybe it was because of the bitterness I still carried inside of me for how badly he'd done me. But I was so sure that I had put all of that behind me. When somebody did me wrong, it was hard for me to let go. I had to work on that, because it seemed to be doing more harm than good.

Mizzou Arena was packed with basketball fans. I felt like I was at an NBA game, the place was so alive and rocking. Mizzou was winning the game and Latrel had scored six points. He was a great rebounder, too, and it was another one of those moments where I felt so proud of my children.

Angelique seemed happy when Latrel scored too, and I watched her as she watched him. I could tell when a woman was genuinely in love; she definitely was. Her eyes lit up, and she was on her feet way more times than me and Reggie were. That made me feel good, and my concerns with the decorating disaster were no longer an issue.

Finally, the game was over and Mizzou had won. The noise in the arena was so loud that I shielded my ears with my hands. It was a very good game and the players, including Latrel, were hyped about their win. They were still on the floor congratulating each other, and as I saw several cheerleaders crowding around Latrel and whispering in his ear, I watched Angelique. Her face went flat and she had stopped cheering to pout. She had no clue that I was watching her, and when the same cheerleader who kept on hugging Latrel kissed his cheek, Angelique dropped back in her seat. Her eyes watered, and she blinked her tears away. I surely wondered what the hell that was about. To me, Latrel acted as if he were a single man, and instead of keeping it moving, he continued to stand there for a while, lollygagging with the women around him. After a while, Angelique got up from her seat and walked off. A few minutes later, I got out of my seat to go follow her. Reggie grabbed my hand.

"Stay out of it, Dee. I know where you're going with this and it's none of your business."

I politely moved my hand away from his. "Like hell it's not. His tail is out of line."

I walked away and saw Angelique as she went into the bathroom. She had already gone into one of the stalls and I waited by the sinks for her to come out. When she did, she was blowing her nose and her eyes were slightly red. She was surprised to see me.

"I guess you have to use the bathroom too," she said, putting on a fake smile as if everything were okay.

In no way would I be considered fake, so I spoke my piece whether she liked it or not. "What's going on with you and Latrel? I know there is something, Angelique, and you weren't in that stall crying for nothing. Is he cheating on you?"

Just with me saying it, she busted out in tears. I knew exactly how she felt . . . been there, done that. I reached out to embrace her. "I'm not sure what he's doing," she said. "He's always leaving and doesn't come back until late sometimes. When I question him, he acts as if I don't deserve an answer. Says that I'm trying to keep tabs on him. Girls are always hanging around him and I don't know what is up with him and that cheerleader. Every time I see her, she's whispering something in his ear and laughing. They have several classes together and it drives me nuts!"

"Well, the last thing you need to be doing is standing in here crying. Latrel is your husband and you should not stand back and let other women have at him. I have a lot of faith in my son, and I don't believe that he would've married you just to cheat on you. As for you, don't go around acting like a wimp. Get a backbone and stand up for yourself. Show Latrel who the real boss lady is, and if he comes in late, send him right on back out the door. Don't let him come lie in bed with you without giving you an explanation. Make him live up to his vows and call him on his mess when he doesn't do it."

Angelique backed away from me and wiped her tears. "I just don't like arguing with him. I keep a lot of things inside because I don't want to—"

"No," I said, cutting her off. "Always tell him how you feel. Make him listen to you and don't you hold anything inside. All you're doing is building up your frustrations. I would hate for you to bust him upside his head one day because you're so mad you couldn't control yourself."

Angelique smiled, then we both laughed. "Splatter some water on your face to clear it up. Then, let's go out there and congratulate your husband on a good game."

Angelique cleared her face; then we left the bathroom to go find Latrel. Like many others, we waited outside near the locker rooms until the players came out. Standing close by was the cheerleader who couldn't keep her hands off Latrel. She smiled at me from afar, but I turned my head. I wasn't trying to be ugly, but she knew better carrying on as she had with a married man. I noticed as she kept looking over one of her friend's shoulders at Angelique. She, too, was playing the sneak-peak game. There was no doubt . . . I was going to hurt Latrel if my suspicions about what he was doing were correct.

Some of the players started to exit; then out came Latrel. Angelique and I didn't have time to rush up to him before some of the other students did, including the cheerleader. She hadn't given him room to breathe, and it wasn't as if she didn't know he was married, because he had on a ring. Angelique just stood there, taking tiny steps through the crowd. I wanted to snatch her ass up and throw her right by Latrel's side. Instead, I pushed her back and whispered . . . well, gritted my teeth as I spoke in her ear.

"Go up to him and hug him. Kiss him on the lips, then put his arm around your neck. Tell him his mother is waiting over there to congratulate him and pull his hand in my direction. Go!" I said, shoving her forward.

She swallowed, then pushed through the crowd to get to Latrel. By the time she got there, the cheerleader was standing next to Latrel as if she were the prize winner. Angelique did exactly what I told her to do, except the kiss she gave him was on his cheek. She held his hand, pulling him with her through the crowd. I saw the cheerleader purse her lips; then she turned away to talk to some friends. Latrel walked up to me, smiling.

"So, I guess you liked the game," he said to me.

"The game was fine. But my son was off the chain." I hugged him and patted his back. I didn't care how old Latrel was, he always wanted my approval. I was very proud of him.

"Where's Dad?" he asked while looking around. I wanted to say "he's probably around here chasing ass," but I decided not to go there.

"He was sitting with me, but we went to the ladies' room. I'm sure he'll find us."

"I wanted to say what's up to him before I get out of here. The fellas and me going out tonight."

I looked at Angelique, waiting for her to say something. She didn't, so I addressed Latrel. "Where are you all going?"

"To a party."

My eyes shifted to Angelique. I hoped she was able to read me. Unfortunately not. "Are you going?" I said to her. "If so, have a good time. It's so good to see the two of you hanging out together after the game, and y'all be careful."

Latrel looked at Angelique. "She doesn't want to go, do you?"

She just stood there. At this point, I could have punched her in her face! I had to speak up again. "Of course she wants to go. What woman wouldn't want to celebrate with her husband after playing the game you just played? I'm sure she'd be delighted."

Latrel waited for Angelique to speak up. "I would like to go, if you don't mind," she said skeptically.

"You know I don't mind," Latrel said. He lifted her chin and gave her a kiss. I sighed, thinking about how much Angelique reminded me of myself when I was in college. Reggie meant everything to me, like what Latrel means to her. I kind of just went with the flow, but going with the flow and being timid didn't pay off. There were too many cutthroat women in the world, willing to take my place. Unfortunately, I'd let them win, but never again.

We walked off to go look for Reggie, but I snapped my fingers, pretending as if I'd lost something. "Doggone it," I said, touching my earlobe. "I lost one of my earrings. Why don't the two of you go ahead? Let me go back to look for it."

Holding hands, Latrel and Angelique walked away. I made my way back over to the cheerleader who was still cutting her eyes and talking to her friends. I walked up and tapped her shoulder. She turned her head and smiled. "Hello," I said, smiling back at her. "I'm Latrel's mother, Desa Rae. May I speak to you for a minute?"

"Sure," she said, moving away from her friends. She tucked her pompoms underneath her arm and tugged at her tiny top that barely covered her perfectly sized breasts. Of course she was pretty, but pretty or not, she wasn't cut out for my son.

"I don't mean to inject myself in my son's affairs, but are you aware that he's married to Angelique?"

"Yes. And Latrel and I are just friends. We have a few classes together and sometimes we help each other with homework."

I nodded. "That's good. I truly hope that's all it is, because if I ever find out that the two of you are doing more than homework together, you're going to hear from me. And trust me when I say you wouldn't like me when I'm angry, because bad things happen when I am. So do yourself a favor and stay away from my son. Stop hanging all over him as if he's yours. He belongs to me, and to the woman I happily released him to. That woman is not you."

I turned to walk away, but heard her speak up. "If that's a threat, I assume you would like to know my name so you can come after me?"

I swung back around. "Your name doesn't matter, and just so we're on the same page, soon, neither will you."

I caught up with Latrel and Angelique. They found Reggie at the snack stand finishing his nachos and we all left together. Angelique and Latrel said they were getting ready to go back home to get ready and go out, so Reggie and I left them at peace.

Not ready to call it a night, we drove to a nearby bar to have a drink. The bar was kind of crowded with many people who had just come from the game, but we found a cozy booth in the corner. The bar was more like a wooden shack, and country music was playing. Many of the waitresses wore cowboy hats and boots. The food smelled pretty good, so we ordered hot wings and two beers. Before I could take a sip from my mug, my cell phone rang. I answered and it was Roc. I really couldn't hear because of the music, so I excused myself from the table and went into the bathroom.

"I'm sorry, I couldn't hear you. What did you say?" I asked.

"I stopped by your house, twice, but no one was there."

"Chassidy's with Monica. I came to Columbia to spend some time with Latrel. I'll be back Sunday night, so if you want to stop by then, that's fine. Just call before you come to make sure we're home."

"Will do. Tell Latrel I said what's up and I'll get at you Sunday."

Roc hung up and so did I. I hadn't thought much about him today, and after seeing those hurtful pictures on Facebook, I pushed the thoughts of Roc to the back of my mind. Being with Latrel and Reggie was helping me cope with my feelings for Roc, so I left the bathroom to go join Reggie again. After two plates of hot wings, several margaritas, and six or seven beers, we were laughing and talking as if our lives hadn't missed a beat.

Reggie held up his frothy beer mug that was filled to the rim. "What are we going to drink to now?"

I held up my margarita glass. "Let's drink to Latrel and Angelique staying together. Lord knows they are going to need all the prayer they can get!"

"Amen," Reggie said, clinking his glass with mine. We laughed, and when several people started doing a country western step dance, Reggie got up. I did my best to talk him out of it. Not only because he was half drunk, but because he looked stiff as ever when he danced.

As expected, he made a complete fool of himself. The people in the room stood back and clapped their hands as he tried to do everything from the Stanky Legg to the bump to the Jerk. I covered my face in shame, but laughed my ass off. It was just like old times, when things were going pretty good in our marriage.

"Reggie," I said in a whisper as he came close to me. "Sit down and stop clowning."

He took my hand, pulling me up from the booth. Yes, I was pretty messed up too, and after he twirled me around, I really got dizzy. I didn't know what the hell the bartender had put in our drinks, but it sure had me feeling good. So good, that after the dancing wrapped up, Reggie and I found ourselves back in his hotel room, ripping each other's clothes off. We couldn't stop laughing and feeling each other up.

Reggie gripped my ass as I straddled him with no clothes on. "Yo . . . you don't know how long I've wanted to feel you like this again, Dee. Daaaaamn you feel good."

I was pleased by the feel of his hard meat between my legs too, and when I lifted myself to ease down on his thick pipe, we both let out a sigh of relief. Reggie had always been a decent lover, but I took control of what was transpiring tonight. I fell back on my hands, and worked my hips and ass like a pro. He couldn't keep up with me, but he used his hands to reach out and massage my wobbling breasts. "Ahhhhh," he groaned. "Right there, baby. Keep letting me hit it right there."

Reggie was hitting it all right. And when I got on my hands and knees, he really hit it. He was hitting it so well that I couldn't help but think of Roc. Only because Reggie's dick was a few . . . several inches shy of Roc's mammoth-sized penis. I closed my eyes, imagining that Reggie was Roc and he was giving me all that he could. Lord knows I wanted to scream his name, but all I did was bite down on my lip and close my eyes in deep thought of him.

By morning, Reggie and I were knocked out. We were awakened by hard knocks on the door, and both of our heads snapped up from the plush pillows. My head was banging, my body felt like I'd been in a heavyweight fight and I was wet, as well as sticky between my legs. We'd had a long night, but too bad I couldn't remember all of it. I reached for a sheet to cover up, while Reggie went to the door. He looked out the peephole, then cracked the door. "I'm still sleeping," he said. "I'll put on some clothes and be out in a minute."

"Can I come in?" I heard Latrel ask. I surely didn't want him to know that I was in the room with Reggie. I whispered for Reggie not to let him in. I hoped he'd heard me.

"I . . . I'm kind of in the middle of something. Give me about thirty minutes or so. Is everything okay?"

"Not really. But I'll be in Mom's room waiting. Let me know when you're done."

"I will. Give me a sec. Then we can talk."

Reggie closed the door and I scrambled around the room to hurry and put on my clothes. So did Reggie. He didn't want Latrel to know what had gone down either. I looked through the peephole and saw Latrel standing in front of my door, knocking on it. A few minutes later, he knocked on Reggie's door again. I stood behind Reggie as he cracked the door again.

"What's up, Latrel?"

"Look, I know if Mama isn't in her room, she's with you. Please tell her to come out here so we can talk."

I rolled my eyes to the back of my head, accepting the fact that we were busted. My hair was a wretched mess, my clothes were wrinkled as ever and they reeked of alcohol. Without saying anything, Reggie stepped away from the door and I walked out. Latrel looked me over, then folded his arms.

"Do you mind if we go inside of your room to talk?" he asked.

"Su . . . sure," I said, feeling uneasy because, as far as Latrel knew, Reggie and I were supposed to dislike each other. I used the keycard to open the door. As soon as we entered the room, Latrel stood by the door, displaying much attitude.

"Why are you always in my business? Why, Mama? When will the bullshit with you stop?"

"Before I answer any of your questions, let me remind you to watch your tone with me. I may be forty-four years old, and shorter than you, but I can still knock you on your butt."

"You're forty-three and won't be forty-four until March, so don't make yourself sound as if this craziness is beneath you. As for knocking me on my ass, that's not going to happen. I don't want to argue with you, but I'm damn mad right now. Just who do you think you are, coming to my school and threatening people? What you said to Jordan was way out of line. You went too damn far and you really hurt her feelings."

I folded my arms and pursed my lips. "Don't be so sure about what I can't do to you. You'd be foolish to underestimate me. As for Miss Jordan, I figured she couldn't wait to call and tell you about what I'd said. I meant every single word of it, and if your ass don't wake up, you're going to mess up a good thing with Angelique. She really loves you, and you're running around here like you're a single man. To allow another woman to hang all on you like that, knowing that your wife may be somewhere looking, was very disrespectful. You should've told Jordan to back the hell up. But all you did was stand there with glee in your eyes. Shame on you, Latrel, shame on you! I found Angelique in the bathroom, in tears. Crying 'cause her feelings were hurt, and you and I both know that there is more to it. All I'm asking you is to get your act together, before it's too late. Don't be like your father, running around at forty-five, still chasing ass. Build a lifetime of happiness with somebody. Have something to show for it and do not let another woman's sloppy-ass free pussy ruin your dreams for you. If you do, you'd be one big fool."

Latrel licked his dry lips, then wiped them with his hands. "You know, you sure know how to give advice, but damn sure don't know how to apply it or take it from others. You can stand there and dog Daddy out, but I bet you wasn't saying that when you were fucking him, were you? Not only him, but Roc too, right, Mother? How can you stand there and criticize my life, and your life is so fucked up? Whatever Angelique and me are going through we will deal with it. Stay the hell out of my business, or you're going to find yourself without a son!"

Latrel turned around to open the door, but I reached up and grabbed him by the back of his collar. I pulled tight, almost choking him. "You're darn right I may be without a son. And if you ever speak to me like that again, you will find yourself six feet under. Now, this isn't about me or who I'm screwing. It's about you. Grow the hell up and be the man you told me you were ready to be. Stick to your vows and do right by your wife. As for me, I'm not married to anyone. I will screw any man I wish to, and if you don't like it, too darn bad. Now, good-bye, Latrel. I'll keep you in my prayers, and as always, Mama loves you."

I opened the door for Latrel to leave, and he stormed out of my room. Having nothing else to say, I slammed the door, packed my clothes, and headed for home early. I was mad as hell at Latrel for disrespecting me. He made me seem like some tramp who was running from one man to the next. *Is that really how he views me? Or, did he say those things just to get underneath my skin?* I hoped that was the case because, as much as I didn't want to admit it, I didn't want him to view me as some type of confused whore who was torn between two men. That wasn't the case. Either way, I felt a need to put some space between us. All I was trying to do was help him. He'd need me before I would ever need him. And at the rate he was going, I was sure he'd be calling soon.

Chapter 9

Traveling back down memory lane always had repercussions. Reggie was trying to ease his way back in, but I had already regretted having sex with him, especially without using a condom. He'd been jumping from one woman to the next. I should've known better, but when he called to talk about us, and about Latrel, I tried to be cordial.

"We're not going to discuss Latrel anymore, Reggie, because you always take his side. He was out of line by saying those things to me. He was lucky that he left my room alive."

"I'm not taking nobody's side. I do agree with him when he says that you need to stay out of his business, though. You're too controlling, Dee, and you get upset with people when you don't get your way. Whether he's messing around with Jordan or not, it wasn't your place to confront her. Angelique needs to get a backbone. If she can't stand up now, Latrel is going to run over her. No man wants a weak woman, and we definitely don't want women with big mouths, either."

"Big mouth, little mouth, weak or strong . . . Men will always find an excuse for cheating. I'm no puppet, so take me or leave me. I guess you made your choice. Bottom line is Angelique shouldn't be put in a position where she has to stand up to no one. Latrel is getting his advice from you and I don't think that's a good thing. You say that what I'm doing and saying is wrong, but look at you. He's going to follow in your footsteps, and eventually, he'll regret it."

"That was an insult. You act like I'm the worst person ever, Dee. If I'm that bad, then why did you have sex with me? There must be something about me that's pretty damn good."

"Don't flatter yourself, Reggie. Your sex wasn't all that great. I was thinking about someone else the whole time. Besides, I don't really remember much about that night, the alcohol had me tripping."

I had to go there, because whether Reggie admitted it or not, he had taken Latrel's side. He never saw things my way, and it was because of Reggie that Latrel kept a wall between us. I had done some things to make him uneasy with me too, but Latrel had always been closer to Reggie.

"Woman, please. The way you were hollering and screaming my name that night, I doubt that another man was on your mind. And you're always tripping. Like you're tripping right now. I called to have a civil conversation with you, but you're always going on the attack. All you do is sit back and judge people, trying to make them feel bad so you can feel good."

My mouth dropped open. I couldn't believe he had said that. If being factual about someone was judging them, then I guess I was. I was so done with this conversation, but Reggie wasn't.

"You'll never keep a man, because you don't know what is required to keep him. I don't see how Roc puts up with you and I'm surprised that you've kept your hood Negro for this long. Especially since you were the one who used to cringe all the time and hold your nose in the air when I took you to my relatives' houses. You looked down on all of them, as if they weren't good enough. You went to the same schools as many of them did, but now you see yourself on a much higher level. Their skin color is the same as yours . . . Some have had struggles just like you, but moving on up to the suburbs made you think you were so much better. There is so much about you, Dee, that you need to correct. The last thing you should be worried about is Latrel. He's still young and he's in the process of living and learning. You, on the other hand, will be forty-four in a few more weeks. Look in the mirror and ask yourself if you're content with who you see. Personally, I think if you open your eyes wide enough, you'll start to get the picture."

Reggie waited for me to respond, but I couldn't. His words had taken the breath out of me, and it was interesting to know how he'd felt. I slowly put the phone down and hung up on him. There was much hurt inside of me, only because I couldn't accept the person the men in my life were making me out to be. I accepted that men and women viewed things differently, but what was so wrong with me wanting my son to do right by his wife? What was wrong with being bitter at an ex-husband who had treated me as Reggie had? Was it a crime that I didn't want the man in my life smoking weed, cursing all the time, seeing numerous women, and making a living by shaking and moving? I truly didn't get it. Maybe my approach wasn't the best, though, and did I really need to change my way? But then again, why change for people who weren't willing to change for me? If I died today or tomorrow, Roc would still be doing Roc. Reggie would be doing Reggie, and Latrel . . . I wasn't so sure about Latrel, but I hoped like hell that he wouldn't keep his father on a pedestal and aim to be like him.

***

The big day had finally arrived—my birthday. There was nothing really spectacular about it, but I was thankful to God for blessing me with another year. It seemed as if the holidays or special occasions always brought out the negative, so I decided to do the smart thing for my birthday this year and share it with my best friend. Monica's daughter was here from California and she had taken the girls, Brea and Chassidy, out with her. Monica and I, however, were at a spa, getting a pedicure and manicure. She sat next to me in one of the comfy white plush leather chairs, paging through a magazine while an Asian woman worked her feet. I was on the phone with Latrel, who had called to wish me a happy birthday.

"You haven't said much since we last talked, and I hope you've accepted my apology for speaking to you the way I did," he said. "I won't elaborate more, because I'm sure you don't feel like going there with me on your birthday. I hope you and Monica are having a good time. Tell her I said hello."

I forced out the negative thoughts of my disrespectful son, and proceeded on a positive note, because life was too short to hold grudges. "We are having a wonderful time. I'll tell her you said hello and you tell Angelique the same."

"Hold on. She wants to speak to you."

Angelique started to speak. She sounded way more enthused than Latrel did. "Happy Birthday, Mama," she said. "I hope you got the present we sent you. It should be there today, but if not, Monday for sure."

"Thanks. I'll be sure to look out for it. How's everything going? Is Latrel behaving himself?"

"Yes," she said, laughing. "He's better. We're doing good."

"Are you sure?"

"Positive, and thanks for asking. I . . . I think that little thing you did helped. And when I grow up, I want to be just like you."

I paused, thinking that was the nicest thing anyone had ever said to me. But, we all knew that I had my issues. "That's sweet, but know that you can do you much better than you can ever do me. Tell Latrel that I love him and I love you too."

"Same here. Have fun and we'll talk soon."

We ended the call and I couldn't help but to think how sweet Angelique was. Some men just didn't know or didn't recognize a blessing.

Monica interrupted my train of thought when she started complaining to the Asian woman about how hard she was massaging her calves. "Do you have to press so hard?" Monica asked. "Be gentle with these old calves. They've had years of wear and tear. Not as much as my dear old friend next to me, but they've had enough."

We laughed and so did the Asian woman. She put more lotion on Monica's feet and legs, rubbing softly. Monica dropped her head back on the contoured pillow. "Awww, that's much better. Thanks."

I shook my head and cut my eyes at Monica. She was a clown. "So, since you're going out with Shawn tonight, what else am I supposed to do?" I asked her.

"That's up to you. But I'm sure you'll be in bed making love to one of your books. My suggestion, however, would be for you to call Roc and see what he's been up to. I know he's still on your shit list for bringing his woman to Chassidy's play, but get over it. At the end of the day, the two of you always have a good time and you need to have a good time on your birthday."

"What I need is not to be dealing with any drama. That's Roc's middle name, and around this time last year, we were dealing with what had happened to Ronnie. And look how Christmas turned out. Last Christmas I caught him on the couch with Vanessa. This Christmas you got Tiara and Vanessa fighting at my house. I'm for peace, and you'd better believe I'm going to have it today. Me and my daughter. I may wind up in bed with a book, but that sounds pretty darn good to me."

"Well, you can keep Chassidy out of it, because I doubt that she's going to want to leave my house. She and Brea be having a ball and they've become really good friends. I'm glad Jade is home to watch them, because I'm looking forward to my date with Shawn tonight. I thought we scared him off after what had happened at Christmas, because he was in awe. We both agree that you may need a reality show dealing with Roc and his rats. I couldn't believe how they were going at it. I didn't know women could fight like that, and as mad as I may get sometimes, I could never see myself kicking a pregnant woman in her stomach, or in her face. That heifer Vanessa is ruthless."

"I agree, and as I told you before, Tiara lost her baby. Not right after that incident, but several weeks later. You know she's not seeing Roc anymore, but it seems to me that Miss Raven is keeping him pretty darn busy. He's real short with me when he comes by to see Chassidy. We barely say anything to each other. Most of the time, I go in my bedroom and close the door. I haven't said a word to him about Raven, and one time he came over to drop off a DVD for Chassidy, Raven was in his truck. I suspect he wants a reaction from me, but he's not going to get one."

"I wouldn't react either, but don't be so uptight about the situation. When he comes over, laugh with him, talk to him, and show him that him being with her does not bother you. Even if it does, he doesn't have to know it."

I agreed. Monica and I spent the next few hours yakking and getting pampered. Afterward, we went back to her house, and she was right . . . Chassidy didn't want to go home with me. The girls had made me a birthday cake, though, and we sat around eating cake and pizza that Monica had ordered.

It was getting late. I knew Monica was anxious to get ready for her date and go. I told Chassidy I would be back late tomorrow to pick her up and Monica walked me to the door.

"Thanks for sharing my birthday with me. Have a good time tonight with Shawn. Don't do anything I wouldn't do and call me tomorrow."

Monica gave me a squeezing hug. "I will, but unfortunately, I've already done everything and there is nothing else left for me to do."

She winked and I threw my hand back at her, shaking my head as I left. While in the car, I'd thought about calling Roc to see what he was up to. I was quite surprised that I hadn't heard from him today. Maybe he'd forgotten about my birthday. I suspected that Raven had his mind in another place.

As soon as I got home, I showered and changed into my nightgown. I tied a paisley-print headscarf around my head, but left several curls hanging in the back. It was almost eight o'clock and I couldn't wait to finish the last few pages of Silhouette's book, *Street Soldier*. The main character reminded me of a younger Roc, as the character described his struggles with growing up in the hood. I got comfy in bed, propped my plush pillow behind me and sat against the headboard. No sooner had I started to get into my book than my phone rang. I looked to see who it was, and it was Roc.

"Hello," I said.

"Just checkin' to see if you were home. I'm comin' over."

"You mean . . . may I come over? You do have to ask."

He hung up, and even though I was annoyed by his actions, I did want to see him. I didn't bother to call him back to tell him not to come, but I tried my best to finish the book before he got here. It didn't take long, because twenty to thirty minutes later, the doorbell rang. I got out of bed to go open the door. Roc came inside with a sly smile on his face. "Why you lookin' all hood and shit with that do-rag on your head?" he asked.

"It's a scarf, but I'm sure a woman with a do-rag on her head would suit you better."

He shrugged. "She most likely would. But, uh, happy birthday. Is Chassidy here?"

"No. She's at Monica's house."

"Then go get your coat on so I can take you out to dinner."

"Dinner? I'm not going to dinner this late, and if I was, I wouldn't be going dressed like this."

He sighed. "Okay. Then go put your coat on anyway. I want to show you something outside and it's cold."

I hesitated, but went to the closet to get my coat. I hoped Roc hadn't purchased anything for me, because I still wasn't so sure where he was getting his money from. I never accepted any of his money, nor did I ask him for money to take care of Chassidy.

Shivering a bit, I followed him to his truck, which was parked across the street from my house. My house was near a dead-end street, and Roc's truck was close to it. The hatch was flipped up in the back, and when I looked to see what was inside, the back seats were pushed down and two pillows were against the front seats. A wool blanket covered the carpet and a wine bottle was chilling in an ice bucket with two flute glasses beside it. Pink and red rose petals were spread throughout, and the smell of hickory barbecue was coming from two white foam containers. I smiled, even though I was freezing my butt off.

"I already know what you're thinkin'," Roc said. "But just so you know, thug men can represent romance too." He helped me climb into the truck. I sat Indian style, and after he lowered the hatch, he put the heat on full blast and lay sideways with the pillow propping up his neck.

"I never discredited what a thuggish man could do," I said. "And I'm sorry that you see yourself that way. Either way, this was a real nice thing for you to do. I guess you figured you wouldn't be able to get me to go out for dinner, right?"

"Let's just say I know you pretty well by now. Gettin' you to go to dinner with me would've been impossible. So, I had to bring the dinner to you. I love the beef brisket sandwiches at Lil' Mickey's and I wanted you to try it."

I opened the foam container and was hit with a sweet-smelling smoky brisket sandwich that I couldn't wait to dive into. The meat was hanging over the bun and I knew things were going to get messy. Roc gave me a plastic fork for me to dive into it.

"This was so sweet of you," I said, forking up a piece of the brisket to put into my mouth. It was delicious. "Mmmm, good. But you didn't have to do this. I wonder how your girlfriend would feel if she knew you were over here, going all out like this for another woman."

"I'm not sure how she would feel, but since you brought her up, I have to ask. Are you jealous?"

I looked at Roc with a straight face, but lied. "Not hardly. If she's what you want, so be it. I wish you well, and as long as you're happy, I'm good. Besides, she's a beautiful girl. I'm sure her assets work in your favor and most men would agree."

Roc cocked his head back. "Her assets? You think it's all about a woman's assets for me? Baby, you got me all fucked up. I couldn't care less about a big ass and succulent titties. While that shit makes my dick hard, it don't do much for my heart."

"Then, what is it, Roc? What attracts you to Miss Raven? How long have you known her and what's up with the two of you?"

I was surprised that he didn't hesitate to tell me. "She good people. I met her while I was in Kansas City for those few months, but when I came back to the Lou, we went our separate ways. I kicked it with Tiara for a while, and you already know how that shit turned out with her. Surprisingly, when I took the kids to the movie that day, I saw Raven and we hooked back up. You and me had been havin' our problems, so I moved in her direction. I like her, a lot, but she ain't no Dez. But Dez be trippin' too much for me and I realized that I will never be the man you want me to be. So, as far as acceptance goes, I'm down with the one who loves and appreciates Roc for bein' Roc. Her fat ass has little to do with it."

"So, if her ass was flat, you'd feel the same way?"

"I don't do flat, but you know what I'm sayin'. You're tryin' to skip over all that I said and bring up what's not important."

"Look, I get what you're sayin', but there is too much about you that drives me nuts. We've known each other for quite some time now and I'm still not comfortable with who you are. You keep too many secrets. You don't tell me anything about your friends, family . . . work. How do you survive?"

"I don't tell you because you don't ask. You couldn't give a damn about my friends and family, Dez, and breakin' news, baby, I do work. On my time, I do. I also don't say much because you are very judgmental. You have a cut-and-dry way of thinkin' and you believe your assumptions are always correct."

"Ninety-nine percent of the time, they are. And the only time that I've known you to do any work was when I got you a job. I'm not talking about the kind of work you're talking about, so tell me . . . where do you work?"

"I'm glad you finally asked," Roc said. "It's about damn time." He sat up and opened the armrest to get something out of the compartment. He also removed a small cake box that was sitting on the front seat. He tossed a business card to me. I picked it up to read what was on it. I saw Roc's Auto Body Shop and Car Maintenance on the card, along with an address and phone number.

"The shop that I own is near Kossuth and North Taylor. You might have to bring your pistol if you ever come see me, but with it being dead smack in North City, I'm not sure your face, nor your purse, will be found anywhere near the vicinity."

Well, at least he was right about one thing . . . he definitely knew me well. I wouldn't be caught dead at an auto body shop in North City, and Roc was brave to set up shop in that neighborhood. "I can't argue with you there. Thanks for telling me. It's good to know that you're doing something productive with your time."

Roc cut his eyes at me. "More than you know."

He opened the cake box, pulling out two medium-sized cupcakes with chocolate icing stacked high. A candle was in one cupcake and he used a lighter to light it. Once it was lit, he moved closer to me. He pecked my lips, then backed away. "Happy." He pecked them again, then back away again. "Birthday." Peck. "To." Peck. "You. Now, blow out the candle and make a wish."

I closed my eyes, making my wish. After I blew out the candle, Roc asked what I had wished for.

I held the cupcake in my hand. "Nothing spectacular. Just wished that when I smash this cupcake in your face, you don't get mad."

Roc tried to duck, but I smashed the cupcake in his face, getting him back for chasing me around the kitchen with my birthday cake last year to throw it at me. The chocolate icing was all over his face. He didn't smile at all, until I leaned forward to lick off the icing. I twirled my tongue on his cheeks and then stuck it into his mouth. As we kissed, and put icing into each other's mouths with our tongues, I felt the other cupcake smash at the side of my face. He rubbed it in good, all on my scarf, hair, and then some.

"Now, you know we're going to have to go inside and clean all of this up, don't you?" I said.

"Nah, let's stay right here and clean it up. Per Dez, I've learned to be creative and work with the minimal space that I have."

I lay back and Roc lay over me. "Well, you can't be in trouble for that. Smart man."

"I can't be in trouble, but you definitely can be."

There was no doubt about that. I found myself sitting between the front seats and holding on tight to them, as Roc was down low making sweet love to my pussy.

His tongue was so fierce that when I screamed from satisfaction, I was so sure I had awakened my neighbors. Neither one of us cared. I turned on my stomach, enjoying the feel of Roc's twelve inches disappearing inside of me, as he held my cheeks apart. His thrusts were always to a rhythm that kept me on my toes, and the way he rotated his hips, while digging deep into me, was on point.

"I don't care what you say," he said, guiding my hips and pulling me back to him. "This juicy pussy was made for me. Specifically for me, baby, and you need to do what it takes to keep this shit between you and me together."

At the moment, that's what I thought I was doing. My body felt so heated that I had a desire to cool off. I forced Roc backward, until we both were halfway out of the truck with our feet on the ground. I remained bent over, while taking in all that Roc was giving to me. The cold air was cooling down our naked asses and it prevented us from sweating so much. We were definitely getting it in; had the back of his truck rocking for a while. There wasn't a man on this earth who could make me feel like Roc did. I wasn't sure if anyone was watching, but it was yet another memorable day that left me loving him more and more.

"I love the way you do this to me," I grunted while Roc played my clitoris like a violin and pushed in my folds with the force of his big dick. My wetness glazed his shaft, and he was in so deep that I could feel his balls smack my ass cheeks. It wasn't long before I felt his liquids and my hot lava flowing down my legs. Roc's body went limp. He laid his head on my back, then pecked his soft lips down my spine. I closed my eyes, savoring the moment.

"I love you," I mumbled while trying to catch my breath.

He continued to peck my back. "You always do, especially during times like this."

I slowly opened my eyes, staring in front of me and thinking about what he'd said. He was right, but I didn't want to admit it. Maybe I was wrong for not expressing my love for him more often, but it was so hard for me to do, under the circumstances. I didn't want to appear desperate for this relationship, especially since he was with someone else. So, for now, I had no reply. Not even when he pulled me into the truck and locked the hatch. We cuddled our cold bodies together and wrapped them in the warm blankets. Something about all of this felt good, and as Roc had quickly fallen asleep, I lay there awake. I played back many of the things he had said to me over the last several months, realizing that it was time for me to take a clearer look at myself.

Chapter 10

The past month and a half had been very busy. Latrel and Angelique were due to graduate from college and we were all running around like crazy, trying to make sure everything went well for them. The things you do for your children . . . I don't think any of them quite understood. Latrel was my priority and so was Chassidy.

I was so busy that I hadn't made much time at all for Roc, but to be truthful, he hadn't made much time for us either. He'd only been to see Chassidy about three or four times, and when I asked him what was going on with him, he replied "nothing." I didn't have time to seek further for the truth, but I knew it was something. That something was answered for me when Monica called me while I was at work and told me to go to Raven's Facebook page. Monica stayed on Facebook more than I ever did, only because she had been networking to let people know about her event planning.

My face twisted with a bit of anger. "I couldn't care less about her Facebook page. I need to make some phone calls about the menu for Latrel's graduation party. I thought you were supposed to be helping me, but you're too busy on Facebook looking at pictures of Raven. Come on, Monica. Please."

"Dee, you know darn well that I wouldn't call you about this unless I thought it was important. If you don't care that she and Roc are engaged, then don't worry about it. I'm just telling you what I saw. Take my information and do what you wish with it."

Monica hung up, leaving me in complete, utter shock. Engaged? Really? Not Roc. Had he lied to me in the truck that day? He made it seem as if his feelings for Raven weren't all that. I knew those pictures I had seen revealed more than what he was willing to say. I was damn mad at myself for accepting his lies and it drove me crazy that I could never really tell what a man was really thinking. *Damn him. His ass can go to hell.*

I quickly called Monica back to apologize. She and I rarely had any disputes and I knew she was only looking out for me. Her phone went straight to voice mail. "I'm sorry. You know I've had a lot on my plate, but that doesn't excuse the way I spoke to you. I love you so much and I appreciate you for making sure I have a heads-up on everything. Call me back when you can, and don't stay mad at me for too long, because I'd have to hurt you if you do."

Mr. Anderson was calling for me, so I hung up the phone to go see what he needed. "Two things," he said, seeming more upbeat this week. "My file cabinet is a mess. When you get a chance, would you please go through it to make sure everything is in alphabetical order? Also, I need to make some changes to my calendar. I'm going on a two-week vacation with my wife. I need to move some of my meetings to other days."

Wow. I was surprised to hear that he and his wife had worked it out. I scooted a chair next to his file cabinet and started to organize his folders. As he was doing something on his computer, I couldn't stop thinking about him and his wife. I wondered how they were able to work things out, as Reggie and I couldn't. What made their marriage so different from ours? I was no dummy . . . I knew there had to be something, but I wanted specifics. I cleared my throat, then questioned Mr. Anderson.

"Mr. Anderson, do you mind if I ask you something personal? If you don't wish to answer, you don't have to." All he did was look my way, so I continued. "What makes your marriage work? I mean, and no offense, but after your numerous affairs, and the fact that you have a child with another woman, why did your wife choose to stay with you?"

He swallowed hard, and the look on his face implied that my questions surprised him or he was insulted by what I'd said. He crossed his legs and leaned back in his chair. "There are many things that make my marriage work . . . Basically, so many good things that outweigh the bad. There is no doubt that I've had my share of women during my marriage, but I believe that my wife made her decision to stay because she knows that my issues with cheating don't define me as a whole, and they are a small part of who I am. Now, many people don't get this, but I do love my wife. I don't do things to intentionally hurt her, but my flesh is very weak. I have so many good and positive things going on, but then there are my struggles with women. My wife was able to appreciate all the good things about me, and not give up on us based on that issue alone. I'm not saying cheating is no big deal, it is. But if I were an all-around no-good fool, then I would've suggested that she go on her merry way. I consider myself a decent man, Desa Rae. I'm not perfect . . . nowhere near perfect, and the woman I've been married to for thirty-four years knows this. There's no way I intend to live my life without her, and I'm willing to get some help so I don't lose out for good."

That was his answer and I had to leave it there. Mrs. Anderson was the one who had committed herself to loving and living with him for the rest of her life. If it was good for her, I was in no position to dispute it. I did, however, regret judging him. I thought I'd had him all figured out, but there was so much more about my boss. He had a genuine side to him that I completely overlooked. I began to think about my marriage to Reggie and my relationship with Roc. And even though Reggie had some good qualities, he was still a no-good fool who left me with a bad taste in my mouth about men period. Roc, like Latrel, was young and still learning. I didn't know what kind of man he would ultimately become, but if he was engaged, I suspected that I wouldn't be the woman to see his destiny. That was unfortunate, too, because no matter what, I still loved Roc.

Right before Latrel's graduation, so many things came to the light. My past conversations with Latrel, Reggie, Roc, and Mr. Anderson caused me to stand before the mirror and take a good look at myself. I saw a beautiful, full-figured woman with flaws that were affecting me in so many ways. I was never one to accept the negative things that were said about me, and most of the time, I pushed those comments to the back of my mind. I had a serious problem listening, and compromising with anyone was always out of the question. The reason that Monica and I remained good friends was because I liked the fact that she agreed with me 95 percent of the time. As my friend, she didn't want to be real with me, because she loved me so much that she wanted to protect my feelings. I got that, but I also knew that it was vital for me to hear others out as well. While I in no way held myself totally responsible for my failed marriage or relationships, I did start to hold myself accountable for a lot of things that had happened. In doing so, I was able to release that hint of bitterness that I held inside of me. I was able to see Reggie in a different light, and I realized that he'd made many of his choices because he felt as if he was doing what was best for him. At this point, I had to do what was best for me too.

That started with my relationship with Latrel. I had to limit my involvement in his life, as well as in his marriage. For so long, I had been a "hands-on" mother and it was so hard for me to let go. By not doing so, the only thing I was doing was hurting him more, and not allowing him to be the man I truly wanted him to be. Whether his marriage worked or not, it wasn't up to me. It was up to him and Angelique, and of course, their relationship with God.

I felt so good about reforming myself. My attitude was better and I was starting to enjoy life even more. And even though Roc hadn't found the words to tell me that he was getting married, I, too, never shared with him that I knew. I truly believed that when a man wanted you to know something, he would tell you. However, that wasn't always easy for them to do. And when they couldn't do it, it always took a woman like me who was willing to call them on their shit. There was definitely a time and place for everything, but that time wasn't going to come until after Latrel had his diploma in his hand. For now, he was my priority.

The graduation was long, especially with Chassidy moving around and unable to keep still. There were minimal tickets available to the students, so even though Latrel had invited Roc, he was unable to come. I had also invited him to Latrel and Angelique's graduation party, but since Roc and Reggie didn't get along, Roc declined. I was kind of glad that he did, because the last thing I wanted was for anyone to ruin my son and his wife's special day. They were so happy. The plan was to move to Texas, not Florida, and get to work. Latrel had already been offered a job in engineering and his career in basketball didn't seem to be going much further. Angelique was planning to go back to school to get her master's degree, but she had interviews set up for a few positions in journalism. I sure regretted that they were moving so far away, but like I said, it was beyond the time for my son to move on and live his life how he wished to do it.

After the graduation was over, we headed to Boshee's, where the dinner and dance took place. The room was real elegant and the food on the buffet looked delightful. Angelique and Latrel had invited plenty of their friends, along with lots of family. We had a blast and I was cheesing so hard when Latrel called me over to take a picture with him and Angelique. I stood in the middle as they proudly held their diplomas up high, cheesing right along with me.

"Let me hurry up and get this picture," Reggie said, snapping the photo with his camera. "We all know that Desa Rae won't be cheesing that hard for long."

Everybody laughed, but you see, Reggie didn't have to go there. I promised myself that I'd be good, and when he asked me to dance, I didn't hesitate. The DJ had some hip hop mess playing, but I did my best to work with it. On the crowded dance floor, I moved side to side, while Reggie held back his suit jacket, trying to break it down to the floor. Latrel, his friends, and Angelique were cracking up at us. I ignored them because they had no clue what real dancing was all about.

"I see you still can't dance," Reggie said, snapping his fingers while looking at me.

"And too bad you still don't know how to fuck."

I rolled my eyes and walked away. Good thing Reggie was laughing, because so was I. Monica was cracking up. "Oooo, the two of you are vicious. Just nasty to each other, but I think that's because neither of you want to admit that y'all still care."

Of course we cared for each other, but Reggie was not the man I wanted. Roc was. Latrel and his frat brothers were so outdone with the way we danced, they got on the floor and started stepping. Everybody crowded around to watch, but I sat back in my chair thinking about how glad I was this day was behind me. Monday couldn't get here soon enough and it was time to do me.

On Monday, I dropped Chassidy off at preschool around noon and went to Roc's house. When I got there, his SUVs weren't in the driveway. I knocked on the door and no one came. The only other place that I suspected him to be was at his auto body shop. Lord knows I didn't want to go there. I debated with myself if I should just wait to talk to him. I wanted to get so much off my chest, so I headed to his shop off Newstead. I took Highway 70 to the Kingshighway/ Union Boulevard exit, and as soon as I got off, I double-checked my doors to make sure they were locked. I know it was considered a booshie move, but I just wanted to make sure I was safe.

At the corner of Kingshighway and Natural Bridge, a man was selling candy. He lowered his head to my window, knocking on it as I looked straight ahead and waited for the light to change. It did, but I was stopped again near a PX Liquor Store. Several men were hanging outside of the liquor store with brown paper bags in their hands. I wasn't trying to go there, but drinking on a parking lot couldn't be considered work. Looking at it from another point of view, maybe they did have jobs. What did I know? As I continued to look at them, I saw a dull gold Regal pull beside me. The music inside the car was so loud that it vibrated my car. The youngster behind the wheel had thick braids that ran past his shoulders. He glanced over at me, sucking his teeth, and then he winked. I quickly turned my head, trying to ignore him and doing my best not to show fear. I knew that the way I felt inside was stereotypical, but I couldn't deny that St. Louis was considered a high-crime area. True to the fact or not, I wasn't running through the city like I was Superwoman, and anyone expecting me to was out of their minds. I couldn't wait for the light to change, but when it did, my GPS tracking system kept sending me in the wrong direction. I couldn't find Roc's shop for nothing, but I knew I was close. Unfortunately for me, I had to pull over and ask an older gentleman for directions.

"Are you from out of town?" he asked. "Everybody around here knows where that place is. If you go about two . . . maybe three blocks down, make a left. Keep straight, then at the first street make a right. You should see Roc's place on yo' left."

I thanked the old man for giving me directions. I did as he'd told me, and as soon as I made a right, there was Roc's Auto Body Shop on my left. I could see the red brick building from afar, as well as the sign with his name on it. There were numerous black men, young and old, standing outside. Some were talking, some looking to be working. Cars were parked everywhere, and car parts were on the side of the building and in front of it. It looked more like a nightclub than it did an auto body shop. And I wasn't going to lie . . . I was very nervous and tense. I prayed that Roc would be inside.

As I made my way toward the door, I regretted that I put forth so much effort to look nice. I wore an off-the-shoulder royal grape top with gray wide-legged pants. My hair was full with tight-hanging curls and my peep-toe heels made me look taller than what I was. One man who was power-washing tires stopped to open the door for me. The other men's eyes stayed glued to me, as if I had dirt on my face.

"Damn, shorty," one of the men said. "How can a nigga like me help you?"

I clipped my lip tight, wanting so badly to respond, but didn't want to find myself in trouble. Instead, I smiled at the man and kept it moving. I found more men inside, and a few women were standing around, too. All eyes shifted to me, and a hefty man behind the counter with rotten teeth asked if he could help me.

I lightly scratched across my forehead, trying not to make it obvious that I was wiping my sweat. "Is, uh, Roc here?"

"Yep," the man said, coming from behind the counter. "Follow me."

I followed the man as he walked me through a hallway stacked high with chrome rims and tires. He was stopped by another man who asked where another person was. "That nigga somewhere outside. I saw him about an hour ago with Romo and Gage. Check outside."

The other man nodded, then moved aside to check me out as I passed by him. "Umph, umph, umph. What a pleasure, what a pleasure. Today may be my lucky day."

Not quite. I forced out another smile and kept moving to the back. We walked through another area where several customers were sitting. Small flat-screen TVs were on the walls, and comfortable blue chairs circled the room. There were two offices to the right, but the man walked me back to a huge shop area that was lined with numerous cars being painted and some being worked on. The man held the door open for me. He looked around at several men working, and plenty of them standing around talking and laughing.

"Roc-kay," the man shouted. "You in here?"

"Yeah!" I heard Roc say. "I'm over here!"

The man and I followed Roc's voice, which was near an old-school Cadillac that was being painted a shiny black. Roc was underneath the car doing something, and the only thing I could see was his blue work pants that were covered with paint as well as grease stains. His black boots were busted up and his shoestrings were untied.

"I'm not tryin' to interrupt you, but somebody is here to see you," the man said.

"I'm real busy right now, Craig, so handle that shit for me. Tell whoever it is I'm not here."

Craig was getting ready to say something, but I placed my finger on my lip, asking him to shush. I kneeled on the ground, poking my head underneath the car. Roc's head was turned in the other direction.

I cleared my throat. "I know you're busy, but I came all this way . . ."

His head snapped to the side and his eyes bugged as he looked at me as if he'd seen a ghost. He quickly rolled from underneath the car on a creeper with wheels on it and stood up. I swear I had never seen Roc look so sexy. The white V-neck T-shirt he wore had grease stains on it and revealed the numerous tattoos that covered his arms. The tee stretched across his muscles and he used it to wipe the sheen of sweat from his forehead. A smudge of oil was on his left cheek and his hands were blackened with oil. He looked embarrassed, but little did he know what I was thinking. An orange rag was in his back pocket, so he used it to wipe his oily hands.

"Damn, Dez. I didn't know you were comin' down here. You know I don't like for you to see me like this."

"Why not?" I said, looking him over. If I could have pulled my clothes off and screwed him right then and there, I would have. "You . . . you look nice."

"I'm not sure about all that," Roc said, continuing to wipe his hands on the rag. The rag wasn't doing a good job, so he walked over to a huge stainless steel deep sink to wash his hands. I followed him. "So, what brings you down here in the neck of my hoods?" he asked.

"I wanted to talk to you about something important. Didn't want to wait until you stopped by the house, because Chassidy would be around."

Roc nodded, then pulled down a few paper towels to dry his hands. He told me to follow him and we went back to the offices I'd seen by the second waiting area. He reached for a set of jiggling keys that were in his pocket and unlocked the door. "Who the fuck turned off the air in here?" he said, walking into the junky office you could see through the glass windows. Papers were piled high on his desk and so were many auto books. A calculator was on there, too, and so was a phone. There was also a picture of Lil Roc and Chassidy hanging crookedly on the wall, and a picture of him and Raven. He saw my eyes on the picture, but he yelled out to one of the men in the waiting area standing at a soda machine.

"Keith!" he yelled again. Keith headed toward Roc's office, poking his head inside. "Find out who the muthafucka is who keep playin' with my air. It's hot as hell in here and y'all got my customers and me in here burnin' the fuck up!"

It was rather hot in the whole place, so I understood his concerns. Obviously Keith did too, because he got on the intercom and said, "Roc said whoever it is messin' with the goddamn air, leave that shit alone. If not, he gon' cut off yo' greasy, fat, crusty fingers! Troy!"

Everybody around us laughed. Personally, I thought it was very unprofessional, but what did I know? I sat in one of the metal chairs in Roc's office. He moved some of the books aside and partially sat on the edge of his desk. Before I could say a word, another man came in. He was chubby and had a scraggly beard. The name TROY was on his work shirt.

"Sorry 'bout that, boss. Just tryin' to save you some dollars, that's all."

"I dig that, but, man, you don't want us to die up in the mutha from heat exhaustion, do you? Leave my damn air conditioner alone and close my door. Tell these niggas to let me be for a while, a'ight?"

Troy nodded and closed Roc's door. He pushed the intercom button, shouting as well. "Roc said get to work and stop lollygaggin' around! Anybody caught slippin' will not be paid! He also said don't bother him for a while, unless it's in regard to m-o-n-e-y!"

Roc shook his head and you could hear laughter again. "These fools are crazy. But, uh, what's up, ma? I still can't believe you're here. You gon' have to pinch me 'cause I feel like I'm in a dream."

I crossed my legs and playfully cut my eyes at him. "You're not in a dream, okay? I'm just concerned about a few things and I really need to talk to you about us. But first, I want you to be honest with me about something."

"Shoot," he said, touching the hair on his chin. "What is it?"

I glanced at the concrete floor, then looked up at him and sighed. "Are you engaged?"

Roc licked his dry lips while holding his stare. "Who told you that?"

"It doesn't matter. Are you?"

I held my breath as he swallowed, looked out the window, then turned his eyes to me. "Yep. I am."

Hearing him say "yes" caused me to tighten my stomach. My heart had dropped somewhere below it. "When were you planning on telling me?"

"I was gon' tell you, Dez. I just didn't think it was important right now."

My eyes bugged. "Really? What would make you think that?"

"Because we really haven't been seein' much of each other since yo' birthday. You've been busy, I've been busy, and it never seemed like the right time."

"I get a feeling that you were never going to tell me. I think you were going to string me along and take all that you could from me until you couldn't take no more. And if I by chance found out, you were going to happily walk away and do your best to do right by your wife."

"See, there you go, again, tellin' me how you think I do things. You don't know what I was plannin' to do, Dez. I told you that I was goin' to tell you, whether it hurt you or not."

"Seems to me that it doesn't bother you to hurt me. You told me on my birthday that Raven was cool people. How does being cool people turn into the woman you're going to marry? Out of all the things I've had to deal with, never did I think that I would be faced with you marrying anyone. You don't seem like the marrying type. I am stunned that after all we've shared you feel as if you've found a woman who you want to share your life with."

Roc scratched his head and sighed. "You know what I found, Dez? I found the complete opposite of you. Like all of these niggas you see runnin' around here, I found a woman who loves me like they do. Who appreciates everything that I do and who does not make me feel as if I'm some little boy with no direction. A woman who ain't afraid to come to my place of business and shoot the breeze with me and my friends. Who can walk into my family members' houses and kick game with them as if they just like her. Basically, one who prefers not to tear me down, and don't mind liftin' me up. I can go on and on, but the last thing I want to do is hurt your feelings. You and I both know that we've been tryin' to do this shit for a few years now. I got to shake and move, baby, and too bad you didn't think I was capable of settlin' down. Thugs do that too, just in case you didn't know."

As Roc spoke, tears rushed to the brim of my eyes. Had I really been that darn hard on him? I wasn't tearing him down, was I? All that I'd been holding inside for months . . . maybe even years was starting to flood me. This news about him getting married would've been less painful if he would've pulled one of the daggers off his wall and sliced me in half. My breathing started to increase and he could tell that I was about to lose it. He squatted in front of me as I dropped my head and closed my eyes to fight back my tears.

"Maybe I should've said somethin' sooner," he said. "But I don't know if it would've made a difference, or prevented what you're feelin' right now. We tried, baby, and we both know this thing between us ain't possible. Let's stop foolin' ourselves."

I swear I was about to break down right then and there. And in a matter of seconds, things turned from bad to worse. I opened my eyes and saw Raven playfully pushing the shoulder of one of Roc's workers as she made her way toward his office. Unlike me, she had a big, bright smile on her face that seemed very genuine. She said hello to everyone who passed by her and she rushed into Roc's office as if she was delighted to see him. Her steps halted when she saw him squatted in front of me. Roc slowly stood up. My watered-down eyes were blinded by the diamond that glistened on her finger.

"Di . . . did I interrupt something?" she asked in a calm manner.

"Nah, baby. Dez was just leavin'. She was tellin' me somethin' about Chassidy that has her a bit upset."

"Awww," Raven said, looking at me. "I hope everything will be okay."

I couldn't even look at her, and I knew Roc was trying to spare me the embarrassment. Raven turned Roc's face, giving him a juicy but short kiss. "I'm going to let the two of you talk. I'll be—"

I stood up, but left the tresses of hair that dangled over my right eye in place. I needed them there to shield all the hurt that could be seen in my eyes a mile away. "You don't have to leave. We're done here," I said.

I walked by Raven and Roc without even looking at them. As I hurried through his shop, my legs felt so weak, as if I had just run a marathon. It felt like everybody had their eyes on me and that's because they did. I couldn't get out of there fast enough, and for whatever reason, I surely thought Roc would come after me. He didn't.

By the time I reached my car, I was in a mess. I was so choked up, because I knew this thing between us would never be. I felt like a failure. I thought that if he saw how much I loved him, things would be different. I thought that coming down here would prove to him that I did want to know more about the man behind my madness. *Why can't he see that? Why?* I thought as I sat full of emotions in my car. Then it hit me. Maybe he didn't see it and I had to tell him. The only time I told him I loved him was during, before, or after sex. Maybe he needed to hear me say it just because. I wasn't sure if it would make a difference like he'd said, but I had an urge to lay it all on the line. I didn't come this far to turn away or to let another woman have the man I was still in love with. I took a few minutes in the car to gather myself; then I got out to go back inside. I walked with my head up and ignored the many stares from those who just didn't understand. Troy, however, attempted to stop me by putting his arm up to block my passage as I made my way down the hall.

"Everything gon' be cool in there, ain't it? If not, I can't let you go by me."

Yeah, these men definitely had Roc's back, but they didn't have to worry about me. "Everything is fine. I just forgot to tell Roc something."

Troy moved his arm, allowing me to go back to Roc's office. Through the glass windows, I could see him sitting at his desk with Raven sitting sideways across his lap. Her arms were wrapped around his neck and she loosened them when she saw me come through the door.

I looked past her and gazed directly at Roc. "Yes. To truthfully answer the question that you asked on my birthday, yes, I am very jealous of your relationship with Raven. An . . . and right now, all I can do is take you back to this thing you once referred to as Black Love. Do you remember Black Love, Roc? If you don't, I do. Because Black Love makes what others may see as impossible relationships, possible. Black Love makes a woman living with too high standards jump back to reality. The reality is I love the hell out of you, Roc, and I am willing to accept who you are. I will grow to love your family and friends as you do, because Black Love is about acceptance, not judging. I will not make you feel like my son; rather, I will make you feel like my king and not tear you down anymore. I hope you understand that, sometimes, Black Love can make you so bitter when you don't get it right. An . . . and when it shows up again, one may find themselves unprepared. I was unprepared for the man who had the courage to show me what Black Love is really about. That man is you, baby, only you. If, and only if you have ever loved me, I want you to give us our final chance to get this right. Only if you can promise me no more heartbreaks and headaches, and that you can be a faithful man, I want you to take that ring off her finger and put a new one where it belongs. If you can't, allow me to shed my tears and leave me at peace. Keep that ring on her finger and always be thankful that we at least gave Black Love a chance. Neither of us can be mad about that." I paused for a moment to wipe the tears from my face and dripping from my chin. Roc sat in awe and so did Raven. The whole place was quiet, and you could definitely hear a pin drop. But having nothing else to say, I walked away.

Nearly everyone inside was looking at me, and when I walked by one man, he held up his fist. "Let's hear it for Black Love, ma. That's what's up."

I smiled, feeling good that I had gotten all that off my chest. My emotions were still running high, but I couldn't help it. I wasn't sure what Roc was going to do, but the ball was now in his court. I started my car and drove down the street. Just as I was passing by Roc's shop, he rushed outside. He flagged me down to stop, causing me to slam on the brakes.

"Open the door," he said, walking up to my car. Raven rushed outside too, calling his name, but he ignored her.

"Roc, please come here," she pleaded. "Don't do this!"

I opened the car door and he squatted beside me. "Let me deal with this right now," he said. "I'll stop by to see you later. Calm down. You gotta trust me when I say everything gon' be straight."

I couldn't believe when he leaned in to kiss my trembling lips, but I damn sure kissed him back. Raven called his name, again, and that's when he backed away from me. I reached for the door to close it, but watched as he pounded his chest and kept his eyes connected with mine.

"Black Love, a'ight, baby? You and me." He pointed his finger at me. "You." Then he pointed his finger at his chest. "Me."

I nodded, and with that, I drove off.

Later that day, I waited for Roc in the doorway, after he called to tell me he was around the corner from my house and would be pulling up soon. I bit my nails, nervous as ever about what he was going to say. I wasn't sure if he had broken Raven down gently, or if he was coming to give me his final good-byes. Minutes later, he pulled in the driveway with a blank expression on his face. He got out of his truck and I slowly walked up to him with my arms folded across my chest. My eyes showed worry, and Roc was well aware that I didn't want to come out on the losing end of this long battle.

"Who ya wit', Roc?" I hurried to say. "Tell me now, who is it?"

He blinked his eyes and lowered his head to look down at the ground. A sigh followed; then he eased his hand into his pocket. I reached out and threw my arms around his neck, squeezing it tight.

"Yes," I said, kissing him and sucking his lips into mine. "Hell, yes!"

He pulled his head back and had a playful smirk on his face. "Wha . . . what are you sayin' yes to me for?"

I moved my head from side to side. "Don't play with me because I know. I can feel it."

"Feel what?"

I paused and looked into his eyes. "Us. I can feel us."

Roc narrowed his eyes, then dug into his pocket, again, pulling out a suede black box. I was hyped and I was on the tips of my toes, as if the ground were too hot to touch. When Roc popped the box open, I looked at the ring, making sure it wasn't one I had seen before. Thank God, it wasn't. I threw my arms around him, again, and he hugged my waist. He nibbled on my ear and squeezed my side.

"You better make sure that you keep yo' promise on every last thing that you said to me," he demanded. "And tomorrow, you, me, and Chassidy gon' go to some of my people's houses so y'all can meet them. I don't want you gettin' all tense, either, and if you gon' be my wife, you gotta be down with my folks."

I leaned my head back to look at him. "I guess we have to start somewhere, right? I got you, fasho."

"I got you too."

Roc and I hugged as we walked inside of my house together. I hadn't seen him this happy in a long time. I guessed the same could be said for me. Because after all of this, the one thing that I realized the most was that Black Love wasn't about him having his way or about me having mine. No matter what age we were, it was about compromising and doing things that I was now able to do for the betterment of myself, and for the man I would soon call my husband.

CHOCOLATE TEMPTATION

by
Rose Jackson-Beavers

To all husbands and wives who fight to remain faithful to each other, and to the friends who encourage them to be true.

Chapter 1

Drained of My Energy

I was so tired. I noticed that it was becoming more and more difficult to work through an entire day. It wasn't the work that was so exhausting, it was my subordinates. They thought they had some dirt on me. They wanted to believe that I was doing the unthinkable. I heard the rumors and saw the looks on the faces of those who worked for me. One rumor I heard was that Travis Ingram and I had taken to leaving the office to go to cheap hotels. This particular rumor really angered me. It was said that Travis and I, along with one of my workers, had left the building to go to a five-dollar hotel to have a threesome. Travis was handsome and whenever he walked in a room, he had a smile that could make your heart skip a beat. His eyes were light hazel and they sparkled with an energy that radiated throughout the room, knocking lonely women to their knees. He wasn't arrogant or conceited, just good-looking. It was not his intention to make women swarm like bees to honey, but he was a successful young African American male who was hired to do a job for our agency. He couldn't help that the women in this office craved him like a pregnant woman craves pickles. Thinking about it, that was exactly what they wanted from him: his pickle.

It was a brisk October day when I first heard the rumor. One of my subordinates, whom I had a certain level of trust in, shared with me that she had heard her coworkers discussing the day I went to lunch with Travis. Felicia was a hard worker and she admired me. She spent many hours helping me by running errands as well as handling her own primary duties. She was loyal, acting as a protector and a friend, which I often discouraged between management and subordinates. I was the administrator and had been taught through books and experience that management should not mingle with those they managed. But Felicia was different. She drew everyone into her world. I wasn't sure what Felicia's world entailed, but I knew I would eventually find out.

I remembered the conversation about the *ménage à trois* as clear as a blue sky on a beautiful sunny day. When I walked into my office, Felicia appeared.

"Malika, you are not going to believe the stuff that happened today."

"Come in and talk to me." I lifted my finger and beckoned her. Her high heels click-clacked on the hardwood floor in my office. I was not prepared for what I heard next.

Felicia's chest heaved in and out as she took a deep breath. She drummed her fingers on my desk and I could tell by her hesitation and constant shifting in her seat that she was uncomfortable. She was probably hoping I wouldn't become angry and go for her coworkers' jugular veins. Looking at me, she whispered, "Please don't get mad, but Sarah and Frances were gossiping about you, Travis, and me yesterday. They said we went to this hotel on the south side. It's one of those garage-type sex places, where you can drive up to the garage and spend less than five dollars for each hour you use the room."

Rubbing my hands together in a circular motion, I asked, "What did you say? Please come again."

"See, Malika, you're getting mad. They are never going to allow me to sit around them if they think that I am telling you stuff."

"I can't believe them. Why in the hell do I have to take you with us? If I were fucking him, I wouldn't take you. They are so stupid." I smacked the stack of papers on my desk, sending them swirling through the air. I was indeed angry.

Felicia stood up from her chair and gathered some of the papers that had fallen near her. "See, I'm sorry I said anything. I just wanted you to know what people were saying, because you are married and those scandalous women could try to hurt you with vicious rumors."

As I collected the papers from Felicia's hand and placed them back on my desk, I responded a bit more calmly. "You're right. I am very angry, but I will figure out a way to clear this mess up."

Felicia leaned over and whispered, "You know that I wouldn't tell you anything unless I thought it was important."

I bent my head down and looked at my hands, which were folded like I was about to pray. I felt defeated.

"I will handle this later. Thank you for sharing that information with me, even though it is so hard to believe. I do feel that there is too much gossiping and negative talk happening in this small office. I have the right to go to lunch with anyone I choose and I don't have to answer to anyone. This is really unusual because Travis is an entrepreneur and I guess that makes him bankable and that's too bad. He's a nice person and he shouldn't have to feel uncomfortable coming to this office to repair the network just because he is a good-looking, successful black man. But I will figure this out. Thanks again."

I wasn't dumb and certainly wasn't slow. I had noticed Travis on the fifth visit to my small but elegantly decorated office. I was standing there face to face with him, discussing the possibility of extending his contract, when I looked at his lips. They were supple, with a slightly fuller bottom lip, which made him look like he was pouting. I thought he had the cutest mouth I had ever seen. I had to shake myself out of the trance I was in. He was six foot four with broad shoulders and a slim, sexy waist. His light golden-brown skin was smooth and the only sign of hair on his face was a thin, barely there mustache. In other words, he was a fine specimen. I was only five foot four, but tilting my head up and looking in his face took me on a pleasurable journey up his body. Looking at his eyes for that contact, I noticed their color. I said to him, "Your eyes are beautiful. I didn't realize they were hazel."

"Thank you," Travis said with that beautiful smile.

As we continued talking, he reached out and gently touched my arm. My heart beat like a drum. That was the first time I wished the rumors were true. Only we certainly wouldn't be with another woman, just Travis and I. It was a thought worth entertaining.

In fact, I wasn't looking for love. I had long since found it, almost twenty years ago, when I met and fell in love with my husband, Dexter. He was an excellent provider and lover. He was considerate and helped me with the chores in our home. He was a vice president at Bank of the USA, which was a large, distinguished banking and finance company. He was also handsome with strong shoulders, but he was not as tall as Travis.

In twenty years, I never dreamed that I would ever look at another man. Occasionally, I glanced when there was someone who was exceptionally good-looking heading in my direction. But I had never met any man who made me imagine him buried deep inside of me until I met Travis Ingram.

Travis was ten years younger than me and I wasn't about to teach a young man no grown-up tricks. However, when he was around, I noticed that I too was admiring his stately physique.

Travis had never done anything inappropriate to my staff or me. He was a professional who came to do his job and left when he was finished. But he had spent a lot of time at the office, because a virus had attacked the network system. He was good at what he did, but he had been unable to detect the virus. The more he came to the office, the more the workers salivated after him.

Travis and I spent a lot of time together creating a new computer program. We even shared lunch together in our office lounge. Then the rumors about Travis and me increased to an all-time high, probably because we had something in common. We both desired success and wanted to achieve our goals. Our conversations centered on our jobs, training my staff, and basic life issues. I never dreamed that a thirty-year-old young man would ever be interested in an overweight forty-year-old woman. We were turning into friends, nothing more. I loved listening to him talk about his dreams and formulating his big deals. Listening to him was intoxicating. Our friendship was blossoming. We both wanted to conquer our dreams and we both had big aspirations. There were not supposed to be any feelings involved, but something changed that one day in September.

It happened so fast. The staff had planned an educational workshop for some local residents. The workshop was "Handling Aggressive Children." It was to be held at the local community center, which was approximately five miles from our office. To present the information to the parents in attendance, we would need a television with a DVD player. All the staff had left the building earlier to decorate and pick up last-minute items. I was preparing to leave when Travis arrived. I informed him that there was a problem with the computers and explained that I needed to leave for the activity. He understood. He had worked more than four months with us as a contractor and knew our program.

On this particular day, I asked him if he could help with the television and DVD equipment. Agreeing to do so, he proceeded toward the kitchen. When he turned in the direction of the television, I admired his physique. His little butt sat up high and his long legs looked strong and sturdy. The back of his arms showed muscles. He was "well-built." He was wearing a pair of black jeans and a yellow cotton long-sleeved polo shirt. He was also wearing a pair of black leather shoes. He looked so good in those black jeans, which were not too tight or too loose, but showed the right stuff in the right places.

Damn, I thought, *I wish I were his wife tonight.*

As I turned to go back into my office to answer the ringing phone, he came in and stood in the doorway. Watching me with that beautiful, 100-watt smile, I put up one finger to acknowledge that I would be with him in a minute. When I hung the phone up, he asked, "Ms. Williamson, would you mind if I look at the system before you leave?"

"All right, but I need to leave within the next forty minutes," I said.

"No problem, I'll be finished with what I have to do within thirty."

I turned to make a phone call and watched as Travis inched his body slowly to the ground and lay on his back. After sliding under the table that held the computer networking system, he began working on the system. I looked down where he lay and watched his long, well-proportioned legs and thighs. Taking a deep breath, I let my mind take me to a place that was hidden in my subconscious.

I imagined walking slowly toward Travis. *I unzipped his pants, unbuckled his leather belt, and then slid my hand carefully into his boxers. I expertly gripped his penis, releasing it from his pants. Travis moaned lightly.*

He took my hand and pressed it down harder. As I took control, his penis grew harder and bigger. It was much bigger than my husband's. This only made me want him more. Finally, I bent my head down because I had to taste him. As I licked the head, he moaned louder. I inched his penis deeper and deeper inside my mouth. Then I slipped out of my panties because I wanted to feel his penis buried deep inside of me. I helped him ease into the condom that I had taken out of my desk drawer.

Once he had the condom on, I straddled him. Painful at first, I grinded my hips to help him enter my moist bush. He clutched my hips as I gyrated on his penis. I screamed, "Fuck me hard!"

He slid from under the table and gently laid me flat on my back on the plush, clean carpet. "I want you so bad. Girl, I am going to fuck you good."

"Then fuck me now!"

Travis lifted my legs up and placed them gently on his shoulders. He entered me and pounded his hard tool into my wet, waiting pussy. He rode me like a jockey rides his horse. Finally, unable to hold back, he whispered, "Damn, you feel so good!" His body stiffened as he came inside of me.

Exhilarated, Travis stood up and helped me to my feet. After kissing me for several minutes, he said, "Thank you. I really wanted you."

Unable to move, the phone rang, jogging me out of my daydream. "Thank you for calling the Pal Project, how may I help you?"

"Malika, where are you?" asked Felicia.

"I guess you know I'm still at the office, since you called my number."

"I guess I do. When are you leaving? We have about forty people already here." Felicia inhaled slowly. "Is he there?"

"Is who here?"

"Travis, 'cause he always comes when you have something to do," she said with a nervous giggle.

"I will be there in ten minutes." I hung up the phone and grabbed my purse and a pack of Johnson's Baby Wipes. Before I walked out of my office, I grabbed a large manila envelope that was lying on the desk. Travis grabbed the television and my office keys, and we proceeded to the elevator.

I remembered the first day I met Travis. I was in a business meeting with the chief executive officer of our parent company. We had scheduled a meeting with two large computer firms to design software for our new pilot program. The first company had completed their part of the project and was now bringing in a young company with a strong track record to finalize the project. Two CEOs were sitting at the table when Samantha Connors and I walked in. We all shook hands and sat at the long cherry wood conference table. Samantha started off the dialogue.

"I understand that you, Travis . . . I'm sorry, is it okay that I call you by your first name?"

"No problem," he said, while giving her a magnificent smile.

"Malika and I have gone over the original contract and the newly drafted replacement. We find no problem with the transfer of this contract to Enterprise Network Systems. So, once we set up a schedule of activities, we can begin the work with you, Travis."

"I can get the schedule back to you by tomorrow," he replied.

"Malika, do you have any questions?" asked Samantha.

"Yes. Mr. Travis, by accepting this contract, you realize that you will be responsible for correcting errors which would include episodic bugs or other problems?"

"I don't have any problem with that. As a matter of fact, Mr. Chen and I have worked together for several years and will continue to work together to clear up any issues."

"Well, that's great," I said, handing him a copy of the signed contract.

That was the first time I had ever laid eyes on Travis Ingram. I didn't feel a thing for him except I was proud to be handing over my business to an African American. That was so important to me to help African American businesses grow. But the drama hadn't started in my life yet. Yeah, I was a happy-go-lucky bitch. Walking around with my head in the air like the world owed my ass something. I was a smart-ass chick. I could analyze a brick, break that motherfucker down, and then put it back together in my mind. I could tell you what you were thinking before you thought it. But I wasn't conceited. I knew I was smart, but it wasn't like a bragging thing for me. I just liked me, all 180 pounds of me.

So I wasn't looking for anything, except for ways to please my husband. However, I was finding that hard to do. But I kept trying. I wasn't about to give up my man. He was fine, knew how to save a dollar, and was a great provider. Plus, the brother had that staying power. He knew how long it took for me to have an orgasm and knew how to pace himself—nice and slow, and he wouldn't stop sexing me until I got mine, before he got his. I wasn't about to take the time to let another brother learn my rhythm.

Who in the hell would give up a man like that? Not me. No sister or other woman would get my man. Hell, I was trying to keep him enticed. I tried hard to lose weight, but hell that shit was hard to do. I also wanted to try some stuff in bed with him that shocked even me. After twenty years, you ought to be trying to develop some other techniques to liven up your sex life. But no! He wanted me to be his wife, but deep down I kept thinking he would want a whore to do what I wanted to do for him. But he wouldn't let me. Stupid! A woman who wants to experiment will do just that. But for me, it was going to take time. I had morals. So I did what I couldn't do to my husband to Travis in my mind. I fucked the shit out of him, twice a day, sometimes three times a day, depending on my mood. My husband was really benefiting from this action, because I needed his dick inside of me to make my orgasms more intense. Don't get me wrong I really loved my husband, but I was bored. I needed much more than he was willing to give. It seemed at work I had all these things going on with putting out fires, dealing with conflicts between staff, handling budgets, and seeking new funding. Yet at home, it was almost too peaceful for my liking. I needed conversation to stimulate me, to feel alive. While my dear husband was a quiet man who felt that being a good provider was a man's job, I felt like we were two people crossing each other in the dark.

Chapter 2

Breaking My Heart

I kept trying to engage my husband into a civil conversation. I would come home from work and find him in the same chair that he had occupied for over fifteen years. It was an old chair, but we worked hard, bought nice things, and didn't tear them up. Our home was a clean home. We took pride in having a nice dwelling to come to. My husband said it was his castle and he was the king. Well, I said that king better pay more attention to his subjects, because it was easy to become bored in this kingdom.

On one particular day, I had had a hard day at work. I had to watch my back because Mr. Travis Ingram worked at the office most of the day.

The women at the office tried to get his attention. Every time he walked into my office, one of them showed up. Each had a question to ask. Yeah, right! What happened to the chain of command? I mean, we had procedures in place for the staff to get assistance. But somehow, when Travis was onsite, everybody forgot the proper damn office protocol. Sometimes, I even noticed the women would linger around my door, trying to hear what we were discussing. Travis even noticed it.

"Have you noticed the staff around your door? That kind of makes me uncomfortable, especially since I'm discussing my business and contracts with you."

"You're right. I did notice the traffic and I was trying to figure out what my staff was doing. As a director, it's difficult to make accusations, so I have to be absolutely sure that they are indeed spying on me."

"You have a very nice business here. I think it is wonderful that you guys help so many people in the community who need your services."

"You are right. In many of the African American communities, the unemployment rate is so high. Women are having a difficult time finding employment that will take care of their families plus pay for daycare. We work with families, trying to help link them to available resources throughout the communities that will help enhance their lives. What we do here is educate the family about effective job search techniques. We teach them resume writing, how to interview successfully, and how to dress for success. It is a task because there are so few jobs available that pay enough to pay bills and daycare. It is especially difficult for our clients because almost none of them have college degrees."

"I'm proud of you," Travis said. "I notice how your staff interacts with you and the way you respond to their questions. You really do give them excellent advice, especially when you send them right back to their immediate supervisors. I used to have that same problem, but had to deal with it straight on."

"I understand, but sometimes it can be so stressful."

Travis leaned over and took my right hand and gently caressed it like he was trying to soothe away my stress. "You're smart, Malika."

I looked into his eyes while sliding my hand out of his. Shifting my eyes away from his intensive gaze, I almost lost my concentration as I responded quickly, "Thank you."

That was how my day started.

He went back to the computer area to complete his work. Travis was working hard and he received so many interruptions.

“Mr. Ingram, would you like some water?”

“Mr. Ingram, would you like some coffee?”

“Mr. Ingram we are going to lunch, can we pick up something for you?”

Would these women ever learn? The brother had never accepted any of their offers. They were really asking him, “Mr. Ingram, could I suck your dick? ’Cause I could suck a mean one.” I thought if they came straight with the man he might’ve worked with them. I could see it now:

“Mr. Ingram, I think you are so fine. If you go to my car, I will suck your dick.”

“For real, let’s do it then.”

After Travis left my office, another one of my staff members walked into my office, and said, “Mrs. Williamson, can I ask you a question?”

“Sure. Please have a seat.”

“Is Mr. Travis married?”

“I’m not sure. Maybe you need to ask him that question. “

“Well, I feel uncomfortable asking him that. I’m not interested in him. I just see him in our office all the time. Is he attracted to someone here? After all, no computer needs that much work.”

I couldn’t believe that little bitch had the gall to walk in my office and insinuate that Travis had an ulterior motive for being in our building. I thought about reaching over and bitch-slapping that whore, instead I said, “Maybe you should get back to work. Try not to be critical of others when you don’t have any information to back it up. You are doing a fine job in your specialty, which doesn't call for much education or expertise, but computer folks have to have degrees and years of experience to maintain an entire network and troubleshoot problems. I would advise you that in the future you keep your opinions to yourself."

"Oh, I'm so sorry, Mrs. Williamson. I didn't mean anything by it. The brother is fine. I think he is attracted to you. That's all."

"Well, as I said, keep your opinions to yourself. As a matter of fact, Mr. Ingram is a professional and I'm sure he didn't build his company by going to agencies looking for a woman."

"Well, I think you should be flattered that he likes you."

Standing up to indicate the conversation was over, I walked to the door. "What part of 'keep your opinions to yourself' do you not understand?" I was pissed off. This, skinny legs, Humpty-Dumpty-built heifer had the nerve to stand in my office and try to have a personal conversation with me. I knew she was probing. I had to get her straight.

"I'd rather you not discuss Mr. Travis with me, and please refrain from interrupting him while he is working for this company. Further, it would really be in your best interest to go do what you were hired to do."

Sarah pushed her seat back, causing the legs to rake across my hardwood floor, and pivoted around, facing the door. She actually huffed and puffed her way out of my office. I knew one thing and it was this: the women were bold in St. Louis. When I took this job two years ago, after working in East St. Louis for fifteen years, I was in for a shock. People always said East St. Louis people were crazy. All they did was fight and accept handouts. I hadn't met any women from St. Louis who could hold a candle to the women in East Saint, as we called it. When I worked over there I found the people friendly, down to earth, and hard working. They were not sitting around, talking about and putting St. Louis women down. I had found them to be intelligent, very beautiful, spirited people. I never could figure out where the negative reputation about East St. Louis came from. Rumors spread for a variety of reasons, but that one was not true. In my fifteen years of working over there, with more than 200 employees to supervise, not one ever graced my door to discuss a man who was providing us a service. But here we were in the middle of St. Louis and already these bold-ass bitches were probing all up in my business.

While sitting in my office during the late evening, I overheard a peculiar conversation.

"She knows they are fucking or that motherfucker don't know shit about no computers. They always need work and I know more than him. I think that brother just coming up in here because he wants that wanna-be so-called professional bitch."

"Damn," I heard Felicia say. "Sarah, you act like you want to fuck him."

"If she get her fat ass out of his face, maybe I can."

"Sarah, you better be careful; I heard she was called Hitler on one of her former jobs and I know she will fire you for making those kinds of statements."

"She ain't gon' do shit to me because I will tell everybody what her ass is doing up here."

"Girl," Felicia interjected, "you better be careful 'cause now you are making serious accusations and you can get sued. If I were you, I would be real careful about running my mouth if you want to keep your job."

"Fuck her."

"Sarah, girl, I didn't know you hated Malika like that. She is so cool."

"That bitch thinks she is all that. She walks around here in those suits like she running stuff, but that bitch is not running me."

"Well, if you feel like that maybe you should leave."

"I ain't going anywhere."

"Well, maybe you should ask Mr. Ingram for some of that dick, since you seem to want it so bad."

"Girl, I ain't into his ass. I just don't care for her."

"Well, I'm through with this conversation. Watch your steps or you will be unemployed."

I walked away from my desk, laughing. I couldn't believe that shit. That little-legged bitch had the audacity to diss me to my employees. Okay, I let her have that one, but you better believe Sarah Lee Gee was on notice. *She had better make sure her work is top quality*. I had her on my list to fuck her up before I sent her ass packing. Wrong move! Dissing me and calling me a so-called wanna-be professional. Well, I was going to put my so-called all the way up her ass. This homie didn't play that shit.

When I walked through the door after my difficult workday, I said, "Hi, honey."

You know what that brother said? Nothing, zilch, nada. That's right; brother man sat in that chair and didn't bat an eyelash, just kept watching television like I was a ghost. I looked at his ass, and said, "Did you hear me speak? I'll be damned if I'm ignored in my own home. You know, there is no way I'm going to take shit at work and then walk into my home and be disrespected. What does it hurt to say hi?"

I wasn't trying to interrupt his time. I know how important it is to have quiet time. All I wanted was for us to acknowledge each other after we both had had long days at our jobs.

I said, "did you hear me speak?"

He just sat there for a second, and then nodded his head. You know, like they do in the South when they greet someone. So I walked up to him and slapped him across the back of his head, which was what I really wanted to do to Sarah. He looked stunned.

Finally, he said, "It looks as if someone had a bad day, but don't bring that stuff here."

Hunching my shoulders and walking by him to head up to the second floor, I turned to look at him. "You know you want this ass, I saw you staring at it."

"You need to get ready to cook."

"Well, you might as well get it started because I need about thirty minutes to myself."

"I'll wait then."

That's how our evening started. Since he couldn't recognize me for the fine, intelligent woman I was, I walked right up the staircase and changed clothes. I lay across the bed and thought about nothing. I awoke two hours later. He had cooked dinner and was watching the news. As soon as I walked into the room, he wanted to talk to me. That really pissed me off, but I decided to let it ride.

So you know what I did? The same thing he did to me, day after day: I ignored his ass. He was running his mouth, telling me about something on his job and I acted like a ghost—invisible. See, I didn't appreciate that shit, having a man who wanted to talk only when he felt like it. That shit didn't work here, not with this chick.

He was just running off at the mouth. It was easy to ignore him, and then he suddenly started asking me questions. That pissed the shit out of me. I turned to face him in slow motion like I was that girl Linda Blair's character, in *The Exorcist*, and sounding as if I was talking in double words. I said, "Are you talking to me, motherfucker?"

I don't know what came over me. Maybe Sarah really had gotten my goat at work or maybe hearing my husband act like we were having this great conversation was too much for me.

"I wish the people at church could see you now," he said. "You curse too damn much."

"I curse because of you. I don't curse at work or anywhere else. I only curse at you. You know why? You piss me off when I try to talk to you. You don't want to be bothered, but when you want to talk, I'm supposed to become Chatty Cathy. I'm not a robot, I can't turn from steel to soft like you."

He had the gall to tell me, "I'm the king and this is my castle."

I looked at that fool like he was crazy. I walked my ass right in front of him, making sure he got a look at my jiggly butt as I made my way into the kitchen. He got up and followed me, only stopping briefly to wash his hands as he passed the bathroom. When he entered the kitchen I heard him pull out the kitchen chair and sit down. I grabbed my plate and quickly exited the kitchen. I was too hungry to throw my plate at him and too angry to sit at the table with him, so I booked.

That night, when brother came to bed, I was waiting. I had lain in the bed ten minutes, thinking about that fine Travis Ingram. I was all ready to get laid.

He entered the bed naked as that statue in Forest Park. I pretended to be asleep, but when brother man slipped his arm around my waist and kissed my neck, and I felt that warm heat from his body mingle with my cold attitude, sparks began to fly all over that bed.

He entered me from the back, lifted my leg up, held it in midair, and put all his ten inches in me. At least that's the way it felt. I had never measured it with a ruler, but brother was packing. He put those slow, intense moves on me and all I could think was, *Work it, Travis. Work all that dick in me.* I was too angry to let him fuck me, so I imagined it was Travis. That shit felt so good. He was stroking and gently massaging my body in all the right places. I was so turned on I could feel my orgasm starting at my feet and moving slowly up my body. I was trying hard not to scream out Travis's name, but I was shouting in my head, "Oh, Travis! Oh, Travis!" Then I saw stars, and red and blue streaks, and my heart was beating fast and furious as if I were about to have a heart attack. But this one wasn't going to kill me. Then I felt his dick grow harder and he started pumping deep and fast. Then he exploded. That even felt good. See, I loved it when he came, because that quick exertion of energy flowing through him to me was like a burst of energy in my pussy.

Yes, I could always have an intense orgasm, because no matter how angry I got, I was still getting mine.

Chapter 3

The Green-Eyed Monster Reappears

Tuesday morning when I walked into the office, I could've sworn I saw Sarah roll her eyes at me. I figured she knew I'd gotten some last night. It was the way she kept looking at me sideways, like she was sneaking a glance. She really made me feel uncomfortable. There was something so sinister about her. I just couldn't understand why this young lady hated me so. After all, I gave her a job when she couldn't find anything else. She lacked skills and education, and I gave her a chance. Now, she was mad because even though we were about the same age, I had two degrees and many years of experience. She should have seen me as a role model, not as someone she wanted to kick into a roll.

I walked up to Sarah. "Did you finish the statistical report on the children in childcare?"

"I don't recall you asking me for a report, Malika. If you had you know I would have completed it."

"No, I specifically asked you for the report when you were meeting with your supervisor." Picking up the phone on Sarah's desk, I called her supervisor and requested her to come to Sarah's area. Jennifer trotted to the office.

"Jennifer, when you and Sarah were meeting yesterday, I came in and asked for what?"

"You asked Sarah to give you a statistical report on childcare and she said she would have it ready by 8:00 A.M. She also asked if you wanted the report in Microsoft Access or Excel."

Sarah quickly jumped in. "I'm sorry, Malika, now I do recall that conversation. I don't know how I forgot that."

I glared at Sarah. "I need that report in one hour." I turned and hastily walked back to my office.

I was working in my office when I heard Felicia speak to someone. Apparently, someone knocked at the door and she opened it. It was Travis. He was there to install a new network virus program. He was working on the network when I looked up and saw that he was smiling at me. I waved and continued my work.

"Excuse me, Malika, can I speak with you?" asked Bridgett, the health instructor. "Do you know who I can refer this young lady to for some resources? I met her while doing a presentation. She is about to get evicted and she has two children."

"Why is she being evicted?" I asked. "Did she lose a job and could no longer afford her rent? Is she on drugs? What exactly is her situation?"

"She is a former crack user. She has gotten her life together, but apparently, because she used so many people and told so many lies, no one trusts her. Her landlord said he wanted her out. He lost too much money messing with her."

"You can refer her to the House of Shelter. They will evaluate her situation and assist her." I jotted the number down and handed it to her. "Ask for Barbara Meyers."

"Thanks so much."

As Bridgett exited my office, Travis walked in.

"How are you today?" he asked.

"I'm fine. What about you?" I walked from behind my desk and stood directly in front of him. He looked down into my cleavage area. I smiled, knowing I had received the reaction I wanted.

"Everything is cool. I'm going to come back tomorrow, because I need to divide your hard drive. Because of the amount of data your staff enters, we need to separate your hard drive into four areas."

"What will that do?" I asked.

"For one thing, it will save space on your C drive, which you could use for other data."

"Is this going to cost me anything?"

"Only your time. Will you be here tomorrow?"

"Yes."

"Well, I'll come back tomorrow."

I sat down on my desk, directly in front of him. I crossed my legs so that he could view my well-toned thighs. Looking down, he suddenly moved backward with his eyes pointing directly at my thighs. That quick movement caused a tingle to resonate in my vaginal area. I squeezed my thighs together. He reached down, grabbed his crotch, and jerked his hand off as if he realized what he'd just done.

As Travis was talking, I found myself staring at his lips. They looked so soft and smooth. I wanted to feel them. Slowly, I slid my tongue from one side of my mouth to the other. What in the hell was wrong with me? Just last week I was minding my own fucking business. I wasn't thinking about anything but doing a good job. I didn't have my eyes on anyone. I was just doing what I always did, which was work hard and train my staff to do the same. Here this " powerful" man came and within a split second, my desires changed. Why now? Why him? I didn't know, but I had to get myself together.

Travis was smiling at me like I was taking a picture of him in a studio. Well, hell, I was not a photographer, so what was he smiling at me for? Maybe he could somehow tell I found him attractive. He licked his lips, leaving a trail of moisture as if he was returning the sentiment. Maybe he knew I fucked the shit out of him last night. *Could he feel me fucking him?*

"Malika, have you had lunch?" he inquired.

"No."

"Come on and let me take you to my favorite restaurant." He reached out and pulled me off the desk and with the quick movement my breasts disappeared into his chest. He grabbed me in a hug. "Are you okay?"

"Yes," I said, pulling out of his embrace. I looked at that man. Lord, what was he trying to do to me? Was this a friendly lunch or was he making a move on me? Hell, I had been married so long that I didn't know if a man was interested in me as a beautiful, sexy woman or if he was just trying to be friendly. Maybe he was trying to butter me up, so he could increase his contract on me. I hoped he didn't think I was stupid. I would leave this job before I did anything illegal or inappropriate. When it came to honesty, that was me; I didn't steal. It wasn't me. I was what some called the real deal. I would tell you what I meant without biting my tongue. I hoped this lunch date was platonic. Nah, I needed to stop lying. I wanted that boy and I wanted him to want me.

You know life is funny because of the way things happen. I was the oldest girl out of three children. I had one brother who was twenty-eight and a sister who happened to be only one year younger than I was. I had always been the leader of the pack. Not only was I a thinker, but I was also a doer. Whenever I put my mind to something, I could get it done. I never panicked. Nothing scared me, except dying violently.

I know you may be thinking that it is odd to be worrying about dying violently, but that was me. I feared knives, cars, and airplanes. I saw those three ways of dying to be awfully painful. I couldn't imagine anyone cutting me slowly as if I were a piece of meat. A girl I once knew was jumped by seven female gang members. They stabbed her and left her in the hot sun to bleed to death. I became violently ill, imagining how I would have felt if that had been me.

Cars frightened me because of the noise they made and the fact that they were made out of hard steel. I couldn't stand the sound of cars smashing against each other. I feared being trapped in a car and it catching on fire or submerging in water. I always kept scissors in my car to cut the seatbelt off me should it lock. I had something to break the car window should the car careen into the river. This would help me to safely get out of the car. At least, that was what I hoped it would do.

I was terrified of flying. I had this belief that if something happened while the plane was in the air, there was nothing I could do but die. In a plane, you lose your control. You can't use a parachute because you are too high. You can't jump out because you would die from a lack of oxygen. You can't help yourself. You'd only have prayer, but I couldn't imagine seeing and knowing that I was going to die. I would be absolutely terrified. Those were my quirks. I was a control freak. I enjoyed directing my path and my life.

I had a lot of associates and my two best friends had been in my life forever. Pamela and I had been friends since we were eleven years old, almost thirty years now. Zandra and I had been friends for fifteen years.

Whenever I needed my buddies, they were there for me. Likewise, I would do whatever I could to help both of them. But my family, on the other hand, was my burden.

My sister, Karen, was a beauty queen. She worried about nothing except how she looked. I couldn't reason with her about anything. Her best friend was a mirror. She didn't want girlfriends. She felt that they slowed her down with jealousy and backstabbing. Maybe she was right about that, but I had always told her that good friends were like wine: the longer you had them, the better they'd become. "You have to nurture friends," I told her. She thought I was silly.

Although I had two degrees and had been considering going back for my PhD in management, Karen thought I was an educated fool. She went to secretarial school and met her rich husband when she was sent out on a job referral. She married Tim Duncan and he let her get away with murder. But I still loved her, even though I couldn't stay in the same room with her for more than an hour without arguing with her.

My brother, Kurt, was a true fool. He couldn't hold a job because he was a mama's boy. My parents taught their daughters to wash, clean, and cook, and pressured us to seek higher education. They didn't do shit with Kurt. He had a ten-year-old daughter named Olivia who he did nothing for, so we all pitched in to buy clothes for her and pay for her school activities. He was twenty-eight and had never worked a job, but he drove a late-model car and kept money in his pocket. He gossiped like a bitch and spread lies to anyone who would listen. He thought that was the way to get people in his pocket. He was even known to tell folks' spouses that they were having an affair. This boy was beyond trifling. Every time I saw him, he asked me for a dollar.

Whenever I told him I didn't have any money, he tried to make me feel bad. Plus, he couldn't even pronounce the word "dollar." He called it "dolla'." He was just too cool. But if everyone he met gave him one dollar, he could become wealthy.

He made sure he mingled with people because that was how he got his information to gossip. I loved him, but I hated him, too. I wanted him to try to be something and to stop worrying my parents, but when you had never been taught to survive legally, you would do whatever you had to do to survive. So if you wanted to stay married, you had to stay away from my brother. Plus, we knew that he was using drugs. He was spending a lot of money and rumor had it that he was stealing things from my mother.

Why am I telling you about my background? You need to know this because as you read about my experiences, you may think I didn't have any morals. But I did! I was raised in a two-parent home, which was a feat in itself. My parents had good jobs and were excellent providers for their children. We didn't want for anything. Whatever I wanted, I got.

That was until I met Travis. He was the one thing I wanted that I hadn't been able to get. The more I realized I couldn't have him, the more I wanted him. The more I realized all he wanted was a friend, the more vivid my dreams became. Or shall I say, my wet dreams? Plus, his actions were confusing me. One minute he was touching me and romancing me with his eyes dancing at me. The next minute he was all business. I was confused enough about my own life and marriage, so I didn't need anyone else to confuse me more.

The best thing about my life was that my parents were great communicators. We could discuss anything—sex, politics, and life—and our parents would sit there, listen, and talk to us. So that was probably how I ended up in the helping relations field. I loved to talk and share my experiences.

See, I, Malika Williamson, really believed that adage, "Each one, teach one." If I knew something that could enhance someone else's life, I was going to share it. You could do two things with the information I was sharing. You could use it or lose it. That was right. Take what I had learned and save yourself some pain or file it away until later and use it when you really needed it. Otherwise, what were you going to lose by listening?

Even though I had never had an affair or slept with any man other than my husband, my knowledge in the sex department was extensive because of the information I had learned from clients who had come through the agency. No, I didn't do these things in the bed with my husband; they happened in my imagination. There was only one man who I had ever wanted to have sex with other than my boo, but he was only trying to be a friend.

When Travis and I arrived at the Lemp Mansion restaurant, which was located on the south side, I was impressed. I had never been to this restaurant theatre nor even knew of its existence. I opened the door to get out of the car, but Travis rushed around and held the door open. He reached for my hand and helped me out of the car. We walked into the restaurant, and with his hand on my back he guided me to the table, where he pulled out my seat and waited for me to sit down. How many men do you know who still do shit like that? Not many! You can count them on one hand. Whenever supply was more than demand, the value dropped and that was how I saw this man/woman issue.

Men think they don't have to do much to keep you, because they can find any woman to do what they want as quickly as you can say no. So they treat us any way they want, because they know we are going to allow them to get away with it. That is until a woman has had enough. Have you ever been around a woman who is fed up? Mark my words, you don't want to be. Remember what I said about knives and how I feared them; well, try dogging me out and watch what'll happen when I'm thoroughly pissed off.

After we were seated in the restaurant, he really talked to my soul and he listened to me. He wanted to hear what I had to say. He made me feel as if I were the only one in the room. I felt so special.

"Malika, I want to know all about you. I know you are married. How's that? Are you happy?"

Initially, I wasn't going to discuss my marriage, but changed my mind. "My marriage is fine. But anything could always become better. I'm happy. What about you? Are you happy?"

"Yes. But like it or not, sometimes to keep your marriage stimulated you have to provide a stimuli. You understand what I'm saying?"

"No, tell me more. I'm not sure I understand where you're going."

"Where do you want me to go?"

Just as I was about to answer, the waiter walked up. I gave my order and waited as Travis spoke to the waiter. We both ordered the baked chicken entrees with salads.

The Lemp Mansion had a unique story of its own. It was a story about a wealthy family from St. Louis in which all its members committed suicide. Unbelievable but true! They were rich people who couldn't find a way to live happily. If only I had that money, I would have done things differently.

The Lemp family once lived in this mansion. The new owners turned it into a museum and allowed people to take a tour of the entire house. You could see the rooms where some of the members in the family killed themselves. Supposedly, there was still blood on the wall in one of the rooms.

"Sir, while we prepare your lunch please feel free to take our tour of the mansion," the waiter said as he wrote down the orders. "Once you return I'll bring out your lunch. Enjoy yourself." He trotted away and we walked through the mansion, touring every room. It was really creepy in that house.

After the tour, we retreated to the restaurant area and had a great time just chatting. The more time I spent with Travis, the more I really wanted him. He was so attentive and a great talker. I enjoyed how well he spoke. He had a great command of the English language. I was falling for him, but not for his heart. I wanted his body. I wanted to lie in his arms and listen to him talk to me.

When we'd returned to the table, his phone buzzed and he took a call. While I sat there, listening to him talk, I imagined his tongue on every part of my body. I wished I could close my eyes. I felt so sexy.

"Malika, where was I?" he asked as he completed his call.

"You were telling me about a deal you made with a large federal agency."

"Yes, indeed. It's going to bring me a lot of business and I'll have to hire some more people." His eyes were beaming, and the words were tumbling out of his mouth with excitement. The more excited he became, the more I wanted to fuck him.

I moved my knee closer to his and gently caressed it against his. I imagined myself taking him by the hand and walking him to one of those empty bedrooms. Not the one with the blood on the walls, but the elegantly decorated one that was near the beautiful white staircase. I saw myself pushing him onto the bed. I wanted to climb on top of him, straddle myself over his chest, and kiss him hard. I wanted him to know that I wanted and needed him inside of me now.

I unbuckled his belt and pulled his shirt out of his pants. I gently massaged his chest. Then I seductively licked and sucked his nipples, making them hard as pebbles. His breathing became rapid. His chest heaved in and out. Sliding my hands into his pants, I stroked his penis. Travis was lying on his back. He reached up and massaged my breasts. He raised his head to kiss my neck and nipples. "Let me put it in you, Malika, I want you so bad!" I wouldn't have that yet, so I continued teasing him with my hands and mouth. I wanted to fuck him until he couldn't fuck anymore, but not just yet. I wanted him to remember this day. When he thought about me, I wanted his dick to become hard regardless of where he was.

So I slipped his penis out and sucked and licked it until it almost burst. At that moment, I was thinking how could people kill themselves in this room when they had so much to live for? Then I released his penis and quickly put it back in toward the back of my throat. Travis began moaning. "Oh, baby, I need you." He was trying to pull me off, because he wanted desperately to be inside of me. I guess with someone's dick in your mouth, you can't feel anything but close. *That man pulled me off him and tore my underwear off. He lifted my leg up and entered me in one forceful thrust. Rhythmically moving in and out of me had both of us moaning as he was stroking my pussy like a painter stroked his canvas, with long straight up and down strokes. I did something that I had never done before. I came twice. I actually had two mind-blowing orgasms. Once he released himself in me, we heard a knock at the door. "Are you guys okay?"*

It was the tour guide we had lost at the beginning of the tour. "The door is stuck," I said as we put ourselves back together. We quickly smoothed out the bed and I used my fingers to brush through my hair. I found my torn panties and slipped them into my purse. We waited until the tour guide rescued us. That was the best sex I had imagined since that day in my office.

I must have been looking strange because Travis asked, "Are you okay?" He had to ask me several times, because I was a goner.

"I'm sorry, did you say something?" I asked.

"Yes. Are you okay? I was talking to you and you blanked out on me. You were moaning."

"I'm sorry. I was thinking about the Lemp family tragedy. Moaning, no, I wasn't."

"I thought I heard you moaning. Maybe I was mistaken. It's a trip hearing about how their entire family killed themselves."

"They had to be depressed," I said as I pressed my thighs together to stop the throbbing.

"Depression must run in families," he replied.

"I guess so, but I really don't know much about that."

We continued to eat and talked about everything. As we finished our meals, it became very quiet.

Travis looked at me and winked his eye. Giggling, I bent my head down to hide my big ol' smile. When I looked up I found that we were staring into each other's eyes. It was a very intimate moment that felt so right. But as usual, he must have remembered that this was not a date because he shifted his eyes as if he was looking over my head and his tone changed from sexy to businesslike. "Did you enjoy your food?"

"Yes, it was wonderful. Thank you so much for getting me out of the office." I wanted to tell him that it was not the food that was wonderful, but my imagination. Just spending time with him had made me a victim of my imagination and him the object of my daydreams.

"My pleasure. I enjoyed your company," Travis stated. As we walked back to the car, we continued to talk. We talked all the way from the south side to North County. When we arrived at the office, we sat in the car and talked for thirty more minutes. As we walked into the building, we continued to talk for an additional thirty minutes in the hall. We spent over four hours together, just talking. We sat on the brick bench near the elevator. His shoulder touched mine and his hand lingered on my thigh. I leaned into him to respond to his touches. I wanted him to know it was okay. I half listened to him and thought about our situation.

If he didn't like me or find me attractive, why did I feel like he was dating me? I sometimes felt as if he was playing with my feelings, and that was wrong. Why would he do that to me? Was he like these other crazy men who would do anything to get in your panties, just to toss you to the side later? Even though I was a plus-size, beautiful woman, I still wondered why I felt he was interested in me.

I was the kind of woman who loved hard. When I made a decision to be with a man, I took it seriously. I had never wanted to sleep with a guy other than my husband, even though I suspected once during our marriage that my husband had had an affair.

I was in graduate school, trying to get my master's degree. My son, Little Dexter, as we called him, was only two at the time. We decided if I was to make more money, graduate school would be a great investment. At that time, we had to complete quarters instead of semesters. I wanted to graduate in a year and a half, rather than the normal two years, so I took accelerated courses. I would often leave my baby with my best friend, because I felt she was better equipped to care for him. She also had a son, who was the same age as Dexter, and I felt that our children would benefit from each other's company.

One day, I left class early to come home to spend time with my family. School had my undivided attention and since I was also trying to complete it quickly, I knew my family had been neglected. I picked up my son and arrived at our home that we had built two years earlier. I pulled our brand-new Volvo into the garage, removed my baby from his car seat, and walked toward the door of the house.

I entered the code on the security keypad and quietly entered the house. After putting Dexter in his swing in the kitchen, I went to look for my husband. Hearing nothing and thinking he was asleep, I decided to check our answering machine for messages. I picked up the phone and heard a woman ask, "Are you coming over today?"

"I'm not sure," Dexter said.

"I want to see you. Isn't she still in class?" the woman asked.

"Yeah, but I have to pick up my baby."

"She spends too much time away from you and your baby. I think she is stupid."

Now you know me. I wasn't going to let some bitch call me out of my name. She didn't know me. She didn't know that I would put my size-eight boot in her ass. I felt disrespected and insulted by this unknown bitch.

"Little bitch, I will knock my fist upside your head and knock your ass stupid," I rudely and insanely interjected.

There was complete silence. I said, "Is this your bitch, Dexter? Did you tell her that she is not the first and that you are HIV positive?"

"Malika, hang the phone up, please," my cheating husband responded.

"You wish I would, don't you, you bad-blood, disease-ridden motherfucker."

I wasn't even mad at him, but I was furious with her. I didn't understand why. Did I suspect him? No. I trusted him. I thought because I heard her ask if I was in school, which let me know that she knew he was married. In my mind, I knew men would always try to cheat if they could, but a woman who knowingly knew he was married and still tried to have a relationship pissed me off.

"Do you have HIV?" asked the young woman.

"You are fucked, bitch!" I screamed. "I don't care about you fucking this punk, 'cause neither of you will live to see my stupid ass graduate." I was hot and bothered with her, but I wanted Dexter to understand my sting. I wanted him to know that I would ruin him if he stepped out. My heart told me that he hadn't stepped out on me yet, but he was heading in that direction.

With that, the woman hung the phone up. Dexter walked into the kitchen, and said, "You do some stupid shit. She was a friend I work with."

"You and your friend can both kiss my ass. I am taking your ass to the cleaners. I'm sure your little friend will admit that you all had sex to a judge."

"You need to get out of school and spend time with your family. School is fucking you up and making you think stupid. I am not having an affair on you and when I do, I'll personally let you know."

Dexter picked up Little Dexter and started kissing on him and talking to him in baby talk. He then walked up to me and kissed me. "I love you and I am not having an affair on you. I'm always here and you know it."

"From now on you will be home, watching your son. If you are going to mess around on me while I'm trying to better myself for this family, you will have a toddler on your hip while you are doing it."

After that, I never had another problem with Dexter. I never suspected him again. Since that time, I had threatened him with God and how He felt about infidelity. Dexter had been a great provider and friend since that time. If he had had an affair, he did it without me finding out.

I always thought most men would cheat. Almost all the ones I knew from my brother to my friends' husbands were cheating on women they proclaimed to love. Some men who had tried to take me out on a date had admitted to being married.

When I asked these men why they cheated, they always said they loved their wives. But I couldn't understand that. If they loved their wives so much, why in the hell were they trying to sleep with someone else?

That was the old me. This was the new me. I understood now. Travis once said something to me that made perfect sense. He said, "After you have been married for a period of time, you become to your spouse just like that coat hanger. You're there. It's taken for granted that you would always be there". I just sat in my office and stared at that coat hanger. Maybe that's why I wanted to be with Travis so bad. He was paying attention to me. My husband was paying attention to building his bank account. He was leaving me vulnerable and unattended.

I started thinking. Did Travis see me as an attractive woman? Or did he see me as a professional woman who he could have an intelligent conversation with while just being my friend? I was so conflicted.

What was the hold this young brother was having on me? I had to find out, so I called my sister, Karen, the mirror lover. "Karen," I asked, "have you ever had an affair on your husband?"

"Why do you want to know?"

"I just want to know."

"Are you thinking about crossing that line?" Karen asked.

"I asked you a question. Just talk to me, girl, please."

"Yes, I have. But I love my husband and I will never leave Tim for anyone."

"Well, if that's so, why did you see another man?" Hell, what she said didn't make any damn sense to me. She loved Tim and would never leave him. Come on now, what kind of sense did that make? "I don't understand. If you love him so much, why cheat?" I asked.

"Dan, my boyfriend, is my true soul mate. When I'm with him, I feel satisfied. We are a perfect match in sex, love, hobbies, and everything in between. My husband is great. He loves me dearly and he loves our daughter. But we are as different as night and day."

"So what are you getting from Dan?"

"I'm getting straight-up passion, baby," she said with excitement as her voice went up to another level.

"Do you love him?"

"Hell yes!"

"How could you love two men at the same time?"

"I love them for two different reasons. Both have something totally different to offer. My husband will never know that I am seeing someone else. I would never hurt him like that. I respect him too much. With Dan, he satisfies the passion in me. What my husband won't do, he will. He loves to suck on every part of my body, everywhere. My husband won't do that. He is old fashioned. He is straight up a missionary man. I couldn't be happy with him sexually if Dan was not in my life."

"Have you ever asked Tim to do freaky stuff with you?"

"Hell yes. But as always, he is too tired or he doesn't think he will like that. Girl, as fine as my ass is he should be eating this all up. I work out, keep myself in shape, and I still look like I'm a teenager. By the way, you need to work out and lose some of that weight. Girl, what are you, about 180 pounds? That is too big. Your husband didn't marry a big woman and I'm sure he doesn't want one now. So you need to get off your ass and do something about your weight."

"Karen, I think I better go. You have a great day." I slammed the phone down in Karen's ear so hard; I was hoping to blow out one of her eardrums. See, that's what I meant about her. We could be having a conversation and really bonding with each other, and then all of a sudden she would start addressing my faults. She was the one having an affair, but she couldn't see that as doing wrong. But she could see a size-sixteen, too-tight dress was not attractive in her eyes.

The way my sister treated me always bothered Dexter. But I always found myself justifying her behavior and why I allowed her to hurt me.

"She is my sister," I'd say to Dexter. "That's why I let her get away with hurting my feelings."

"I've seen you chop folks up like a food processor and toss them like a pizza, but she is the one who breaks you down," Dexter would respond.

"She is my sister and I'm trying to keep us together for my mother's sake. She wants her family to stay close. I can't help that my sister is heartless and shallow."

"How can you be close with someone who doesn't care about your feelings? She always puts you down. She breaks your spirit and whenever she leaves, I have to deal with what's left of your self-esteem after every encounter you have with her and I'm sick of it!"

"You are right, Dexter, but until I figure out how to tell her off without dividing our family, I will continue turning the other cheek. Plus, I love her. She is just different, that's all."

"Do what you want, but don't come crying on my shoulder when she hurts your feelings again."

That was how my husband and I argued every time I had a conversation with my sister. He was the only person I generally screamed at without thinking. Others got the professional bitch, the one who could break you down like a fraction to the lowest common denominator. I was meticulous, slow to anger, generous to a fault, and one of the best friends one could ever hope for.

But I didn't play. If you hurt or insulted me, you would never get another chance to hurt me again. If you disappointed me by sharing something I told you in confidence, I would quickly forget your phone number and help you to forget mine. I didn't really hate people, I hated their actions. My mother, Barbara, called me true blue, which pissed me off. She and my dad, Sidney, put me on a pedestal that held me hostage. To them, I was their good child and that was how they wanted me to stay.

Every time I thought of doing something that was unbecoming of me, I thought about my family. My friends, Zandra and Pamela, said that was why I couldn't get Travis out of my mind. They were the only ones I told what was happening with me. They never judged me. They just listened, though I could tell by their words they didn't want me to have an affair. Even though I believed that they both had had affairs. But as usual, I was the one who should stay faithful. Living up to everyone's expectations was too difficult. I wanted to venture out and do things that I had never done before. I wanted to experience life to the fullest. But if I continued to live my life for others, I knew I was going to die a lonely, miserable death. Zandra told me the other day that I was an undercover freak. One thing about it though, only one man besides my husband could blow my cover, if only he tried.

Chapter 4

The Eyes Are the Windows to Your Soul

One week after I overheard Sarah dissing me, she appeared in my office, wanting to chat. I guessed she thought I was a Sammy Sausage Head or something. She thought she was so smooth. But I knew her like I knew the back of my hand. She wasn't the only woman who was jealous of me for whatever reason. I had been in this situation before at another job. The difference was it didn't go this far with negative words or insults being slung around the place.

The last person who tried to accuse me of having an affair actually came to me after finding out I was happily married and apologized to me. Initially, she had told all my employees that I was having sex with a worker whom she had a serious crush on. After weeks of rolling her eyes at me and going through a performance plan I had prepared for her to work on, she called a truce. I was actually preparing to fire her, because her work was suffering and she was spending all her time trying to tear my reputation down.

Gail walked into my office and told me she was totally jealous of me. She said she had graduated from high school with me and I acted like I didn't know her. I told her I didn't remember her. She said she had six children, no husband, and working for me as a recruiter was not exactly paying her bills. She told me I made her sick because I had made it and she didn't. It took me weeks to counsel her and convince her she was worthy and all she had to do was to go back to school. She finally enrolled in the local community college and ended up doing much better, but she was the only woman who actually told me to my face that she envied me.

Sarah wanted to chat. "Chat about what?" I asked her, while looking into her eyes suspiciously.

"Well, we haven't talked in a while."

She was smiling sweetly and her eyes had that happy glow. They were wide open and her pupils danced around. If you knew what I knew about her, you would know that this act was another one of her smoke-screens. Her eyes looked like the devil was inside of them. They were actually glaring and shining.

"If you can remember we spoke last week about making assumptions," I stated.

"You are right. I didn't mean any harm when I said Travis was attracted to you. Really, everyone can tell that he likes you more than as a boss. But as I said, I'm sorry for bringing his name to you like that."

Putting my guard down slightly, and I mean slightly, I looked at that bitch because that was what she was and reminded her of the program goals. She had the nerve to raise her voice to me. "I know what our goals are! You act like you can't talk to me on a personal level!"

I was sitting there thinking how easy it would be for me to cuss her ass out since I didn't have any witnesses, when she had the audacity to ask me, "Are you okay? Because it seems as if you are ignoring me."

"I often ignore people when they try to get in my personal business. For you, I just expect you to do what I hired you to do. Nothing else," I elaborated. I was not going to let this girl, who thought she was smarter than me, get into my business and try to use it against me later. I had to remain cool, calm, and collected. This heifer was actually testing me to see how far she could go.

"So did you and Travis go to lunch when you left earlier?"

I wanted to make her more envious. "Yes, we did and we had a great time. You know Travis is a very successful businessman." I leaned closer to whisper, so she would think I was confiding in only her. "He is also very rich." Pushing a newspaper to her, I said, "Read this article about him. It should answer all the questions you want to know."

As she read the article with deep interest, I saw her smile fade and wrinkles appear on her forehead. "This article says he received eight million dollars in contracts last year. That's good," she said. She dragged her raggedy, chewed-off nails across my desk and bounced her skinny legs up and down. I couldn't tell if she was happy or what because so much was happening with her facial and body movements.

"That's damn good!" I replied. Now I was egging her on. "Can you imagine being so young and so talented with the world in your hands and everybody wanting you, but even though you are so successful, you only want one thing and you can't have it? All the money in the world and you can't touch it."

"So what are you saying, that he can't have you?"

"Well, in your mind you think that's what he wants, but I'm not for sale."

"You're crazy, Malika. That man is fine and everyone knows he likes you."

"Sorry to disappoint you. Mr. Ingram is here to do a job and that is all. Now I have work to do. I can't entertain this mess any longer."

Looking deep into my eyes, she said, “If you don’t want him, someone else will.”

“Good luck taking him from his family. Oh, by the way, I’m sure he is not worrying about anyone from here taking him. See, men like him are not looking for someone who is beautiful and super skinny to hold on to. They are looking for someone who can enhance them, bring something to their lives like smarts, opinions, and bold ideas. You know what I mean? Travis needs not only someone who is accomplished, has skills and experience and who could run his company if need be, but smart enough not to want to because they have their own goals and desires.”

“That’s what you think. Men like him want sex.”

“I’m sure he does. But when it’s over he is going right back home to his wife and children. Anybody can be a whore.”

That heifer jumped up and said she had work to do. I was feeling too good. I had just called her a whore and sister girl knew it, but couldn’t do a damn thing about it. Today was going to be a good day because I was on a roll.

It didn’t take long for someone else to come along and try to ruin my mood. I was working hard on the budget when I heard some commotion. I got up and went to the area that the noise was coming from. Felicia and Sarah were arguing.

Felicia’s voice was raised and the tone was harsh. I could tell she was angry because her face was scrunched up and she displayed that look I’d seen before when she was in an argument. “I didn’t say anything to her,” I heard her say.

“The bitch was acting like she had a chip on her shoulder. She acts like she wants to fuck him.”

I rushed over to their cubicles. “Excuse me,” I asked, “what seems to be the problem?”

“Nothing,” Felicia said.

“No!” I said. “Something is wrong. Who are we talking about, me?”

Sarah quickly said, “We were talking about one of my clients. She is messing around with a married man and I told her she shouldn’t do that. I was asking Felicia her opinion and we disagreed with each other.”

“Well, I suggest that you two get back to work and if you want to discuss a client’s business do so with your supervisor.” I knew she was lying. She was on that Travis stuff again. Travis was going to give either her or me some dick or all hell was going to break loose on the second floor. As it was, he was causing a serious disruption in my office. I couldn’t keep dealing with my staff having arguments and disagreements on who was fucking him. Quiet as it was kept, any woman in her right mind would’ve wanted to, but only those with class would resist him with every fiber of their beings. I should have known because I was wishing he would walk through that door. Wishes must come true because when I turned, I bumped into him. Looking up into those beautiful light hazel eyes, I smiled. “I’m sorry,” I cooed.

“No problem. How are you, Malika?” he inquired.

“I’m fine.”

“I know that,” he said, “but how is the rest of your day going?”

I was staring dead into that man’s eyes. I wanted him to kiss my lips or something. I needed to touch him. So I took his hand and pulled him toward the computer. “Something is wrong with the computer,” I said.

“What is it doing?” he asked. He held my hand tightly.

"We seem to be offline," I said as I removed my hand from his and walked to the network area.

"Let me check it out."

I walked back to my desk, where I had a bird's eye view of him working. As I worked on the budget, I felt his piercing eyes. When I looked up, he was looking at me, smiling. Maybe he was attracted to me after all.

As I sat there working, he walked into my office and asked if he could check something on my computer. I said yes and attempted to move. "You're okay, baby." As he leaned over me, I could feel his warm breath on my neck. I felt comfortable and safe near him. He was standing behind my desk chair, leaning over my shoulders.

Suddenly, my mind went totally freaky. I imagined he had sat down on my desk with his front directly in line with my mouth. *I was sitting there in the chair. I unzipped his pants and pulled his penis out. Bending down, I kissed and licked the bead of moisture from the tip of the head of his penis. It was so beautiful to me. Finally, I put his throbbing dick in my mouth and sucked it like it was a baby's bottle. The poor man was moaning and rubbing my head as it went up and down his shaft. I could tell he had never had anything like this done to him before because he was actually shaking. He probably thought someone was going to walk in on us, but I didn't care. Like I said, I wanted that dick by any means necessary and this was one way to get it.*

I licked and sucked him until he couldn't take it anymore. He started shaking and trying to push his dick down my throat. When I felt him beginning to release I pushed him away and grabbed some Kleenex. I helped him come in the Kleenex. He lifted my head up and put his tongue into my mouth as I zipped up his zipper.

Travis asked, "Malika, what are you thinking about?"

"You don't want to know," I said. I realized that I was holding his arm that was hanging over my shoulder.

"Tell me about it."

"I wasn't thinking about much of anything."

"Something had you going. I called your name, but you were in a trance or something." He stood up and slowly massaged my shoulders.

"I was just thinking about all the work I have to complete today."

He kneeled and pressed on all my pressure points. "Relax, baby. Your neck has knots in it."

"I have a lot of work to do." I took his hands and removed them from my shoulders and hopped out of my seat.

"Is that all? Are you sure?"

Now we stood toe to toe, with our faces inches from each other. I looked this man in his eyes and you know what I saw? I saw the truth. He was attracted to me. Was it because of my position? A woman knows when a man is smitten and he really was. His eyes told me so. Eyes are the windows to one's soul. Eyes don't lie. I hoped he could see in my eyes what I saw in his. I wanted to fuck him and lie in bed next to those long legs, and I wanted him to want me too. I wanted to see if he was as good in bed as he looked and if he was, I wouldn't mind having mind-blowing sex every now and then.

"Travis, really, I'm okay."

He knew that there was more to what I was thinking. But I was afraid to share what I was feeling for two reasons. First, I thought he would reject me. It wasn't that I didn't have any self-confidence, because I did. I worked in a building where many handsome men, in all types of occupations, worked or visited every day to go to the doctor or the pharmacy. In one year, more than ten men, both young and old, had asked me out. I always turned them down, but I knew that I was attractive even though I was overweight.

I was afraid he would think I was too old because I was almost eleven years older than him. Initially, I never looked his way, but because of the office banter and chattering, I became drawn to him. After I noticed how fine and attractive he was, I began to find it difficult to be around him without thinking about sexing him. I never expected to have a close relationship with him. We could talk about anything. That's how I fell for him; he was a breath of fresh air. When I went home in the evening, I couldn't talk to my own husband, so I told Travis everything about my dreams and my goals. He even listened to my job issues. Dexter wasn't interested in office politics. He often reminded me he didn't want to hear about my job.

Secondly, I was scared to come clean with him because people were lawsuit happy. They would sue you for anything. Just the other day, I took my Pekingese outside to tend to her personal needs. Every morning for over six months we would go outside and I would wait until she did her business before going back into the house. A week ago, a new family moved into our neighborhood with two full-grown mutts. Since they had moved into the neighborhood, I noticed that they kept their dogs in the house, because we never saw them outside.

On this particular morning, I took Missy outside to walk her. She immediately walked toward the back of our house. I started calling her. "Missy, get back around here!" She turned to run to me and just as she did, the two huge mutts charged her. They were on long chains, but one broke. I was so scared. I ran, screaming, "Run, Missy, run!" One of the dogs was running so fast that his long legs outran my eight-pound dog, leaving Missy a brief moment to escape. In the process of screaming for her to run, I turned, twisted my ankle, and had to crawl up on the porch. I was wearing high-heeled boots and a business suit. I could not move. My ankle was throbbing and I was crying. Grabbing the front door, I pulled it open and screamed for Missy to run. She turned, jumped over me, and then ran into the house. The large mutt tried to catch her, so much so that when I slammed the door to secure her on the inside, the mutt stood there watching me. I screamed, "Get away!" and he did.

Granted, I left myself vulnerable to possibly being mauled to death, but my baby girl was safe. After I crawled into the house, I called my husband, crying. He said, "Call the police."

I called the office and told one of the supervisors what had happened and that I may not be in. She told me to go next door and let my neighbors know what happened. Then she told me to go to the hospital, so I could file a police report; then I could file a lawsuit.

Three weeks later, even after I was no longer limping due to a sprained ankle, people kept telling me to sue when they heard what had happened. I had no intention of suing those people. They had lived in Missouri for one week after moving from Florida when this occurred. There was no way I was going to welcome a new family into the neighborhood with a lawsuit. However, another neighbor had already told them they had sought an attorney and had filed to sue them because their dog had dug huge holes in their lawn. I also knew that on Zandra's job a supervisor was being sued by a worker for touching her and making her feel uncomfortable. Although there were many who would sue people in a New York minute, I wasn't a person looking to do that for trivial matters.

Here I was, falling for a person I hired as a contractor and all I was thinking about was him suing me. I didn't want to be sued for sexual harassment, a serious workplace issue, even though I had enough witnesses to support me. I mean, everyone was telling me that he was pursuing me.

Case in point, my supervisor, Samantha, came to visit from one of our satellite locations and saw that Travis was working on the computer. She briefly spoke to him. We worked together for several hours that day, giving her an opportunity to view the people in the office as well as Travis. She eventually asked me if Travis and I were messing around.

"Malika, can I ask you something personal?"

"Sure, what's up?"

"Are you and Travis messing around?" She dropped her bombshell just like that.

"Why would you think that?" I asked.

"It's obvious. He looks at you as if he's attracted to you. He smiles a lot while staring at you even when someone else is talking to him."

"I have never noticed that. He and I work well together," I replied nonchalantly.

"I bet. Look at him. He keeps staring at you."

"Samantha, he has never approached me in any way except professionally. He's a nice person, very professional, and I must be honest, he is fine."

"Malika, he is very handsome. But you guys be careful. If I can read his feelings so easily, others can too."

"He's never made a pass at me or done anything inappropriate to me."

"Malika, mark my words, he will. He is trying to gauge you first. You know, figure out the best approach. But eventually, he will let you know his feelings."

"I don't think so. We are just professional friends who can talk to each other."

"Just be careful, okay?"

"I will. You don't have to worry," I reassured Samantha. That was how it was. Others thought they could see his feelings. I felt his desires, though it was hard to admit it. But I could've been wrong. It wouldn't be the first time I was wrong about something.

Why did others think they could see the attraction? Or why hadn't he approached me? What was he afraid of? Was he afraid I might cancel his contract? If only Travis knew how infatuated I was.

I was beginning to see him in my mind. His body, his eyes, and now I could almost feel his hands roaming over my body. Why was I becoming so obsessed with having sex with him? It wasn't like I didn't get mine. My husband, Dexter, reached for me at least five nights out of the week. My shit was magic or potent or something. Dexter couldn't stay away from me. He was also good in bed, but maybe I was getting bored. After all, Dexter was so routine and most of the time I knew he used sex to make him fall asleep.

He was a gentle lover, but he didn't kiss much. That was it. Dexter was fucking the shit out of me and he was taking me for granted. I was missing the passion. I wanted that heated passion that made you tear clothes off and have sex in unusual places. I wanted the newness of a man wanting me, kissing me all over my body, across my face, sucking my nipples, and licking me down my stomach. I wanted him to tenderly spread my legs and kiss and suck on my clit. Yeah, that shit felt good. But it only felt good when the man liked going down on a woman. Dexter did it once and it was humiliating to him. He was licking it, but I could tell he was having a hard time. Eating pussy, as they say, was certainly not his forte, but he was doing it for me. But you should never do something that you are uncomfortable doing, because that could lead to some problems.

Since he didn't eat pussy, I didn't suck dick. It had been like that for years. Then I heard about all these young teenagers eating pussy and sucking dick, because the girls don't want to get pregnant. Hell, they were doing more than I was in the bedroom, and I was married and grown. That shit wasn't right and you know it definitely wasn't fair. These kids needed to have their little asses in class, trying to learn and get their minds out of the gutter. They needed to leave that gutter shit to us adults and get their education.

So I ask you this question: what was a forty-year-old, still highly sexual, beautiful, but somewhat overweight woman to do when her husband wouldn't talk to her and would not suck her pussy? Well, that's an easy answer. She should have gone and found someone who would give her what she wanted and then take her ass back home. But this sister was too scared.

I had been taught that I had to remain faithful and committed or I would surely burn in hell if I had sex with another man while I was married. But I was going to burn anyway, because I was lusting daily for this man. I had been praying and crying, but I was getting no answers.

I knew what some people would think if they knew: why was this heifer praying when all she thought about was fucking? But sinners need help too. I wouldn't have minded fucking him and marrying him, too, but we both were already married to other people. So I settled for fucking him once, but when I told Zandra, she freaked.

"Zandra, I really like this man."

"Leave that shit alone. That could be a lot of trouble and getting that dick ain't worth it."

"I want more than his dick. I like him," I muttered.

"Let it go. You got a good man. You don't need to fuck that up."

"Who said I was trying to fuck my marriage up? I just want to try another man. Hell, I've only been with two in my life."

"Well, you should have thought about that shit before you got married. You are married. Tell your man what you need."

"And when he doesn't give me what I need, then what?"

"Keep asking."

"Hell, I'm not begging anybody to give me what I need. I asked him, and he said, 'No. I'm happy with our sex life.' Besides, why should I suffer?"

"Girl, whatever your ass decides to do, just be careful. Don't tell anyone if you mess around. Not even me!"

"Why not?" I asked.

"Because you can't trust anyone. You have too much to lose."

"I can't do anything that he won't allow me to do with him. He hasn't made a pass at me."

"Let that shit go, girl, before you get hurt. You are not a street girl, you don't know how to play. Let it go."

"I can't."

I struggled with my feelings. I wanted this man because he talked to me. He showed an interest in my work. He stimulated me. He made me feel sexy. I loved my husband, but he made me feel sad. Alone. Unloved.

What would you do? Would you just lie down and play dead or would you try your hand at feeling loved again?

I wanted to feel that. I wanted to see a man become excited when I walked through the door. I wanted him to grab me, kiss me thoroughly, and tear my underwear completely off, while simultaneously sliding his finger in and out of my hot, steamy pussy. So why should I have settled for dry, dead emotions when I could have had fire, heat, and steam? Wasn't that what we all wanted?

In my opinion, I didn't believe this life was for living unhappily. I thought we had to seek what made us happy, even when it hurt others. *Must I live in this world desperately wanting to be held, touched, and needed? Should I lay in the bed, begging my husband to do what I need him to do to make me feel stimulated, by forcing him to do something he doesn't want to do? Must he give up his own comfort level and perform an act he thinks is gross?* Or would it make much more sense to find what I needed to make me happy?

A prudent person would agree that Dexter should have done whatever it took to make me happy, right? But how many men try to actually please their women or make them truly happy? Sure, Dexter was a good father and an excellent provider, but he was not a freak. He was a mild-mannered man, who was not into anything he thought was abnormal. So I suffered. I suffered because I was too scared to find happiness. So I sat in my world and fantasized about what would really make me happy.

You know what? Travis made me happy even though he was not supposed to. He was supposed to make his wife happy. Did she need what I needed and was not getting it? Was she going through the same thing

I was going through? Or did she lie in her bed at night, dreaming and fantasizing about another man? One who stimulated her and would give her what she needed to feel alive. Or was Travis sexing her so much she wished he would feed off someone else?

All too often, I realized the grass sometimes seemed greener on the other side. I knew some of these men walked around, looking good and acting like they were tender and loving, but were motherfucking hell raisers when they were with their families. They showed us compassion and made us feel like we had to have them. Some of us went all the way, sleeping with other women's husbands, not intentionally to make them unhappy, but to get that one ounce of happiness that we continued to look for in familiar places.

I knew these men were probably at home, pissing on the toilet and leaving the seat up. I knew they were sitting on the couch, watching sports and screaming for a beer while farting all over the place. Additionally, they were probably clipping their big-ass toenails and popping them all over. But as long as I didn't see that shit, I could dream and think they were sexy, fine, and smart. I would continue to think that Travis had more positive attributes than Dexter, because I couldn't see Travis's faults.

Chapter 5

The Bitch in Me

Last night when I went to bed, I waited until Dexter decided to join me before turning off the television. I was looking at one of my favorite television shows, *Law & Order*. I could look at that show every day of the week and still not get bored. I waited until Dexter finished cutting his hair because I was horny and I wanted that dick. It was a long Sunday. I had spent too much time sitting around thinking about Travis. I wasn't sure what was wrong with me. I couldn't stop thinking about this man. I could feel him sucking my breasts and kissing me. Most of the day, my panties were sticking to me because I was wet from my body automatically lubricating itself. My mind was glued to Travis sexing me. I could feel his hands playing with my clit. I wasn't crazy. I just wanted him.

When Dexter entered the bed, I grabbed his ass and began playing with his dick. I even decided to give him a little head. As I sucked and slurped he put his hand on top of my head and tried to control my movements. "Oh, baby, what the hell are you doing? This feels so good."

He was so excited, he almost climaxed too soon. But I helped him slow down his rhythm. I knew he was shocked and, truth be told, this was a once-in-a-lifetime gift and he would not experience my mouth on his dick again anytime soon. If he didn't kiss mine, I would never kiss his again and that shit you could count on. So I tried to make him go crazy and I succeeded. His dick was so hard when he entered me I started screaming from the minute he was inside of me. Shit was feeling good. He was moving in and out, up and down in me, and we were both going crazy with desire. But I still didn't get my pussy sucked.

I also knew that Travis started that shit because it was really him I wanted. All that passion that came from deep inside my heart was for another man. I had to have him. I was going to burst with emotion and lust unless that man gave me his body. I wasn't sure if I just wanted him to fuck me or if I wanted him to love me. This shit was becoming more and more cloudy.

When I awoke Monday morning, I was in a foul mood. I decided to wear my black wool two-piece sweater suit to face this cold October morning. I also grabbed a pair of black boots. I had to take pictures of my shoes and put them on the front of their boxes, so I would know which pair was in each box. I loved shoes, and I purchased so many in the same color from the same shoe store. I had to figure out a way to identify each pair before going through so many boxes and wasting my time and energy by picking the wrong shoes.

My girlfriend, Pamela, swore that when I wore the color black and boots I was feeling blue. She said that in theory I was setting myself up to kick ass. I wasn't sure where she got her theory, but she swore that when I wore that combination, heads would roll.

When I strutted into the office, the first person I saw was Travis. He smiled and stared straight at me.

"Malika, you look nice today."

"Thank you," I said as my blood rushed to my cheeks. What was I going to do with this man? *Must I cancel his contract to stop my heart from pining for him? Then again, why should he lose part of his income because of my weakness for him?* Even though he was here in this office on legitimate business, I couldn't stop my desires. I was fantasizing more each passing day. This was getting unhealthy. I guessed I was going to have to call my mama again and tell her my heart was betraying me.

Travis grabbed my briefcase and walked me into my office. From the corner of my eye, I saw Sarah at her desk. She was slamming stuff around and she snapped at Frances as she created a lot of noise. Her actions reflected someone who was upset. She had a little time with him before I arrived and now she was pissed because I had made my grand entrance.

She strutted to my office. "Malika, Samantha called you this morning."

After I thanked her, she stood in my doorway, staring at Travis. This girl acted worse than I did. She was more struck by love than I was. She was looking at him like he was a barbequed rib. I interrupted that dreamy look in her eye by saying, "You can leave now."

"Are you in a bad mood today?" she inquired.

"Excuse me?"

"You walked in this morning with your lips poked out and your heels slamming against the hardwood floor as if you were angry. I'm not trying to make you mad, but I can tell you seem out of sorts."

By now I was steaming. I could see that Travis was stunned by this conversation. I felt disrespected. I felt like striking her. No, I felt like kicking her in her pussy with the pointed toe of my boot, because she was acting like one. But I had to remain calm and professional. I could not allow her to make me look like an ass in front of the man I adored. So I did what I knew how to do well. I asked her, "Did you complete the report that I requested on Friday?"

"I am working on it today."

"I need it by ten, so I really don't have time to argue with you this morning."

She stuck her skinny leg out and smiled. "I didn't mean to interrupt you and Travis. I will get right on the report."

She turned and walked her funny-shaped ass out of my office. *I'm the fucking boss and this bitch had the audacity to walk her ass into my office and confront me.* The more I thought about that shit, the madder I became. "Travis, I'll be right back." I walked to Sarah's office and closed the door.

"Look, you trifling bitch," I began, "I have had all that I am going to take from you. The next time you walk your black ass into my office and question me, I will fire your ass. Who in the fuck do you think you are? You have one more time and your ass is mine."

"You are just jealous of me," she replied. "I can't believe you cursed me out. I'm calling headquarters on you."

I picked up the phone and told her I would dial the number. "I didn't curse your ass out. You can't complete the assignments that I give you. This is the fifth report that I have asked you for, and I gave you timelines to have them written and completed and each time, you failed. You will get a written warning from me today and the next time you walk your unprofessional, uneducated, wanna-be ass into my office and disrespect me, consider yourself terminated."

I turned to walk out of her office and suddenly turned around. "Jealous of you, why? You don't have shit on me, bitch."

Swinging the door open with force brought a shift of wind in the room and that shit felt good. Yes, it was bold and unprofessional. I knew she wasn't going to hit me, because if she did I would have had her arrested. I was smart enough to curse her out without witnesses. I also would never risk my professional career by hitting someone. I was willing to allow her to hit me because I would press charges and fire her. She knew I was not afraid of her, but she hated me with a passion and was willing to make my life miserable, because she thought I couldn't get rid of her. I also knew she wasn't taping the conversation, because the whole interaction wasn't planned and she didn't have time to do anything.

I walked out of her office and almost bumped into Felicia.

"Good morning, Malika, I didn't know that you were in. You had two calls this morning," she said while handing me my messages.

"Thank you. Please hold my calls, I will be in a meeting."

"Okay. After your meeting, I would like to talk to you about one of my clients."

"I will see you after I meet with Travis about the computers."

I walked back into my office and pulled the door closed. "Travis, I can't believe Sarah."

"I'm not trying to tell you how to run your office, but you may want to consider firing that girl. She constantly disrespects you and you don't have to take that."

"I know, but I am trying to do it as professionally as possible. I cannot make a mistake. I want to make sure that she doesn't have legal ground to stand on."

"I don't think she does."

"If I do this right, she won't be able to waste my time in court. She is so lawsuit happy. All she talks about is suing people. Right now, I have enough documentation to get rid of her. But I have to go through the steps to make sure it sticks. I have one more step before I fire her. I'm sure she is very close to doing something, so I can let her go."

"I trust your judgment. I just don't want anything to happen to you. These women are so treacherous these days. Be careful, okay?"

"I will."

"Hey, I care about you and the actions of Sarah are irritating to say the least. I'm used to women throwing themselves at me, but her actions are different. It's as if she knows that I am interested in someone else and she is trying to thwart us from coming together."

Okay. Let's analyze this shit. Did he just say what I think? Did this man like me or what? Was he playing with my emotions or did he really care what happened to me? I was even more confused. He always listened to me and he was concerned about my life, unlike Dexter who always said he didn't want to hear that shit about my workers. But Travis and I could discuss anything.

This woman, Sarah, really despised me. I had never done anything to hurt her. In fact, I let her get away with too much. She had left work undone. I had received complaints from her clients about the way she responded to their needs. I had sat with her to help her work on her files to assure the information was accurate and placed in the right places. I had given her time off to tend to the needs of her six babies. Yes, she was the prime example of a welfare mom; someone tried to help her and this was how she repaid her.

I didn't think I was better than anyone. I would give my last to help someone in need, but I had one pet peeve. I hated it when I tried to help someone achieve at a higher level and they repaid me by being a total ass. How many people do you think would take this much mouth from a person they had tried to inspire to achieve? Not many. As a matter of fact, with her mouth and innuendos, she wouldn't have lasted this long anywhere else. But I was too nice. I cared too much. Not this time. I had a reputation to uphold, plus she was after the same man I wanted. This was war!

Chapter 6

A Cry for Help

"Mama, what are you doing?"

"I'm watching *The Young and the Restless.* You know this is what I do every day at four o'clock."

"I don't want to interrupt your television show, so I'll call you back later."

"What is it, Malika?"

"I need to talk to you about Dexter. What am I going to do? I am unhappy in my marriage."

"You have a good husband. Talk to him about your needs. I'm sure he will listen and do what he has to do to please you."

"You have it all wrong. You know what, he is a good provider, but I can find that somewhere else. He is not the only one who can provide. I take care of myself. I work every day. I am sick and tired of trying to talk to him. I want a man who respects me and cares about my life. I would like for him to treat me like Travis, the man I told you about from my job. He's the one with the crush on me who I enjoy talking to."

"Like you, he is married too. Nothing good can come out of the two of you spending so much time together. You need to work on your marriage."

"I don't want to work on it," I responded. "I'm doing all the work now to no avail. Mama, why can't I see Travis? You know I like him."

"That's the problem. You like him too much. He is not your husband. You are not that kind of person. Your sister is, but not you. I can't see you risking everything for a romp in the hay."

"I want more than a romp. I want to spend time with him. I'm not trying to marry him, I just want to be with him sometimes."

"That's not you. I'm not trying to act holier than thou. I have messed around before, but you are different. You are classier. You don't have to do anything like that."

"I don't, but I want to."

"Does this man know that you are attracted to him?"

"I'm not sure. I think so."

"Why don't you talk to him?"

"I'm not ready for that."

"If you can't talk to him, then you are not ready to have a relationship with him or anyone else."

"Mama, I just like being around him."

"Be careful with your heart," she provided. "It's easy to fall in love with someone you can't have. It's best to try to work on your marriage because you won't find happiness messing with someone else's husband."

"Maybe you are right."

"Things will work out."

"I'll talk to you later. But I can't promise that I'm not going to pursue this man."

"Call me tomorrow. Talk to your husband and try to work this problem out. You'll do what is right. You always do."

"We'll see. Bye now."

I was not working shit out. I tried to but Dexter just ignored my pleas. He was not trying to work with me and I wasn't going to beg. He could have this pussy, but you had better believe it belonged to me, even though I wanted to loan it to Travis. As I said, all I wanted from him was sex and a little romance on the side. He wasn't someone I was trying to marry. I was already married and if this shit didn't last, I wasn't trying to do it again.

Marriage was so hard. I had done more than my share of trying to keep this shit together. I had caressed his body with my soft, sexy, well-shaped frame. I had kissed his ears and lips and sucked the nipples on his chest. I had even tried to suck his dick for a second time. It was so funny. I was going to surprise him one night. I got my candles and lit each of them. I placed them in strategic places around our bedroom, so I could freak him good by candlelight. I was going to make this motherfucker love me like he did when we first got married.

I soaked in a nice, hot bath with my favorite sweet vanilla bath oil from Bath & Body Works. I was preparing my mind to give my husband the night of his life. Once I dried off, I went to the kitchen, opened the refrigerator, and took out the chocolate syrup. I was looking for some whipped cream, but we were all out, so I had to find something to work with that was sweet. I also grabbed a banana Popsicle and walked up the twenty or so steps to work some love magic on my man. I eased into the bed and kissed him slowly as I slid next to him. Kissing his lips, I walked my fingers lightly down his leg until I reached his manhood. Gripping it gently and massaging him, using my thumb and index finger to guide his penis tenderly, I slid down to lick him. He moaned. He lifted his body, so I could accept his dick into my mouth. I sucked him. He moaned in ecstasy.

I sucked long and hard, pulling his dick all the way near the back of my throat. He grabbed my head and pumped his penis into my mouth. It tasted so sweet.

He was my husband and I truly loved him. I was willing to save our marriage. I was willing to do whatever it took to give him pleasure. Maybe if I did a good job on him, he would do one on me.

With his dick in my mouth, I reached for the chocolate syrup. Pulling the top up, I removed my mouth from him long enough to squirt the syrup on him. It was thick and sticky, and when I put my mouth back on him, it was too damn sweet. Chocolate syrup is good on vanilla ice cream, but on my husband's dick, it was extremely sweet. What was I thinking? His body was a sticky mess. We both burst into laughter. "Malika, where did you get this idea?" He was laughing and caressing my arm.

"I wanted to try something different. That's all. Heck I thought it would work."

"Baby, you know I love you. You're funny."

Reaching up, I kissed him. I allowed our tongues to mingle and dance together. "I love you too. I just want things to work with us."

"Hey, didn't I tell you I was happy?"

"I need more from you."

"More of this?" He pulled his body up over mine and entered me. He plunged hard into me. "Is this what you need, Malika? Talk to me, baby, do you need me to do this more?" He thrust into me harder with each question.

This was turning me on. I liked how he was taking control. "Yes, baby, this is what I need. Give it to me, baby. Fuck me like you mean it." With that all you could hear were our bodies slapping against each other.

"Oh, baby, this feels so damn good." Lifting my leg up and putting it over his shoulder, he pounded into me like a man on a mission.

Reaching up, I grabbed his head, bringing it down to my lips, and kissed him as my body began to tingle and come to an amazing head. "Oh, I'm coming." With that, both of us increased our speed, him pumping and plunging his penis deeper inside of me, and me circling my hips and gripping his penis with every muscle in my vagina. Finally, we lay there holding each other with our bodies throbbing from the intense orgasms we'd just experienced.

See, I told you I was not a dick sucker. I only did that shit in my mind. I was the ultimate head whore, a superhead, but when it came down to the real thing, having the real dick in my mouth, I was just like a virgin. This was my second attempt at trying to suck my husband's dick in two months so in my own mind, I was still a dick-sucking virgin, having yet to achieve what I wanted. But tonight was a good try.

That night brought us closer together. We discussed the incident and laughed because the act was nice, but highlighting it with that syrup was a disaster. My husband said, "I know you don't suck dick." I simply laughed because he didn't eat pussy. We were going to try to work on this marriage and try to do things to satisfy each other. At least, that's the promise we made that night. In the past, both of us had attempted oral sex, but it wasn't something we participated in regularly. As a matter of fact, we had tried less than the number of fingers on one hand.

Although we fucked that night, or shall I say, made love, I never got a chance to use that banana Popsicle. That shit melted in its wrapper and I tossed it out later. Next time, I planned on using a Popsicle and showing him how a cold mouth felt on his dick. I wondered if it would be sexy. Maybe the coldness would keep him hard. Tomorrow, I was going to buy some whipped cream. Next time, I was getting this shit right.

But Dexter simply reverted to his old, tired ways. I was trying hard to live right. I had done everything in my power to get Travis out of my head. But that shit was a bitch. You could get a man out of your head, but you sure in the fuck couldn't get him out of your heart. My head said, *stop thinking about him and think of your husband*. But my heart said, *I love him and I want him*. Why was my heart trying to betray me? I loved my husband and I wanted to sleep with Travis, but something kept pushing me to that threshold and I knew it wasn't love. It felt like love, but I knew it was lust.

Sometimes, when you want something so bad and it is denied for whatever reason, the desire to obtain it becomes stronger. Deep down, I knew I didn't love this man, but I wanted him because he was making himself unobtainable. Even though he was there to share my feelings and my concerns, he was withholding his emotions from me. I felt something for him. But I wasn't sure if he felt anything for me. Sure, he touched me, caressed my arms, touched my thighs, and smiled and teased me, but he still never voiced his feelings or his interests.

I knew exactly what I was going to do. The next time I saw Travis, I was going to gently brush this big ass up against his dick and see if I could get it to rise. If it did, I knew it was mine. When I saw him, I was going for the gold. No more wondering for me; I had to know if he was attracted to me. So rather than ask him how he felt and get hurt, I was going to let my body do the questioning and let his dick do the answering.

Chapter 7

Cold Vibes in the Fall Air

One week before Halloween, my staff and I planned a party for the families in the program. We scheduled the party for October Twenty-eighth. Our program worked with women who lacked parenting skills. Our goal was to teach them how to parent their children in every area of each child's life. Our parents were put through a series of workshops and training sessions on issues such as disciplining children, child development, social play, and positive reinforcement.

We decided not to have a "Halloween" party, as most of us did not believe in celebrating the devil's day, as it had been called. A fall festival and workshop were more suitable. We were sitting in the conference room, planning the activities to make sure they were age appropriate, when I looked up and saw Sarah staring at me. I looked back down and raised my head quickly to see if she was still staring. She was. I asked, "You need something?"

"No!" she stated quickly.

Everyone at the table looked up almost simultaneously to see what was going on. Felicia laughed while everyone else looked to see how I would respond. Today, I did not feel like being bothered, so I continued to write down the goals of the workshop we were planning. The room became quiet. I ignored it and asked

Felicia what she thought about giving small children candy.

"Malika, I think we should give fruit. That candy could slip down the children's throats and choke them."

Sarah jumped in. "You are right, Felicia. Giving children candy is like giving them matches."

"How so, Sarah? I don't get the comparison."

Frances put her two cents in. "Sarah, what in the world are you talking about? What you just said did not make sense."

"Never mind, y'all just don't get it."

"Get what?" asked Frances.

"Let Sarah share her opinions with us," I said.

"I said that it was okay, Malika."

I was getting sick and tired of that bitch. I had to count to ten and take deep breaths to keep from reaching over and punching her upside her hard-ass head. She really did test my professionalism. I knew she was trying to break me. I wasn't about to allow her to do that. So I moved the meeting right along. Our parent educator discussed the food that would be served. "We can serve fruit for the older children and applesauce to the young. We can also give out soft candy bars. Kids can eat candy as long as they are older than five. But I wouldn't want to give that to them because it is not nutritious."

"I agree," I said.

Felicia said, "I will organize and pick up the food."

"Who will supervise games?" I asked.

"I will," said Bridgett, the health instructor.

I wrote all the information down. Finally, turning to Sarah, I asked, "What activity will you supervise?"

"Whatever!"

"What do you mean?"

"Whatever you need me to do."

"I need you to make sure the place is cleaned up when we leave. Some of the workers will help you, but make sure the building is spotless. I will check to assure that it is since we want to make sure we can use the Jensen Center again."

Sarah's face scrunched up and her eyes tightened almost like little slits and she kept kicking the table legs like she was angry, but she didn't say anything. She knew she had asked for this poor assignment by trying to outsmart me. Now she had the worst chore of the day and she couldn't blame anyone but herself.

"I will type everything up and pass out the assignment sheet to you all later. Felicia, please make sure everyone signs off on the original memo once they receive it. I want to ensure everyone knows exactly what they are supposed to do and that there is no room for a breakdown in communication." I smiled at Sarah. She rolled her eyes up to the ceiling and kept smacking her lips while slamming her papers on the table. She mumbled something to Frances. Sweat beads had emerged on her forehead. She was showing in her gestures that she wasn't too pleased with her assignment. She was frowning, but the staff ignored her.

When I adjourned the meeting, we all walked to our assigned offices to finish our work.

I felt good. I didn't have time to play with Sarah. I had the budget to complete and a new grant to write. As I walked toward my office, the outside door swung open. It was Travis.

"Good morning," he said.

"Good morning," I returned.

"You are having network problems. I came by to find out what is happening with the system."

I asked him, "How do you know we are having problems? We haven't even used the Internet today."

"I can tell from my office. I have a code that I use. I checked it this morning, and then came right over."

"I'm glad you came by because we have a lot of work to do and we need the system up to complete it."

"How was your weekend?" he asked.

"It was fine," I said as I walked into my office. He followed me.

When I turned around, I noticed that he was staring at the picture of my husband that was sitting on my desk. When I looked at him, he smiled.

"Is that him?" he asked.

"Is that who?" I asked.

"Your husband!"

"Yes, why?"

"Just wondering."

He stood there staring at Dexter's picture with a smile on his face. Finally, he turned and said to me, "He looks mean."

"No, he is a good guy, maybe a little stuffy, but a very good husband, father, and provider."

He looked at that picture again and turned to look at me. I saw him take a couple more looks at the picture and then it seemed that his mind had settled to the fact that I was married. We stood in my office, smiling like two Cheshire cats. Then, after a while, we started talking about life in general. I found him to be extremely intelligent and knowledgeable about many subjects. We discussed politics, African American issues, and office problems. Finally, we discussed our goals and dreams. "Did you see the *St. Louis American* newspaper?"

"No. Why? What's in it?"

"One of my mentors won a national award for having one of the largest computer firms in the country. He's the one who helped me get started. "

"I'll definitely pick the paper up. It's amazing how mentors can really help people. We all need them."

"That's true. I try to give back whenever I can. I volunteer as a big brother in the Big Brother program."

"That's so good of you."

We continued to talk for two hours until a worker walked into the office to ask a question. That was how it was whenever we got together. We enjoyed talking to each other so much we lost time when we were together. It wasn't until that worker needed help that he finally stood to go check the network system. I stared at him while he worked on the system. When he looked at me, I twirled my hair around my fingers and leaned my head to the side. It occurred to me that he just wanted to see me and I demonstrated I knew. He sat in my office for two hours and not one worker complained about not having computer access. I was starting to see the light. Travis was interested in me.

While Travis tackled the network, I tackled my budget and completed the assignment sheet. Finally, I e-mailed the assignment sheet to the entire staff. Occasionally, I would glance up and find him staring at me. I would smile back and complete the work I was doing. Then I would feel his eyes on me again. I would look up and he would smile at me. It was so obvious to me that he was attracted to me. It was too difficult to try to hide our feelings. Funny thing though, I knew in my heart he would never make a pass at me. I believed he was a faithful husband to his wife and a good father, but like me, he was having difficulty getting his spouse to buy into his dreams and to be supportive.

It was easy to fall in love, since we were both idealists. It was also easy to fall in love since I had someone I could share my dreams with. I felt very close to him because he knew how to listen and support me. There were times when we would be talking and I would close my eyes and visualize his lips gently kissing my face. Sometimes, he would stand close to me, almost kissing me. He was so close, I wanted to tell him how I felt. But I was so scared of losing him. I didn't want to frighten him. I knew one thing and that was that he was as attracted to me as I was to him. We just needed to either get together and fuck or decide to remain just friends. I had to find out which one he wanted, because I knew exactly which one I was trying to make happen.

While sitting at my desk deep in thought, Felicia interrupted me on the intercom. "Malika, you have a call on line two."

Shaking my head to put on my work hat, I pressed the button for line two. "This is Malika Williamson, how may I help you?" I asked.

"Hi, young lady, this is Samantha."

"Hey, Samantha, how is it going?"

"Everything is going well on this end, how about at your office?"

"Things are great. I'm glad you called because I wanted to discuss a couple of grants that I think we should apply for to enhance our program. But first, since you called, what can I do to help you?"

"I was calling to see if you could put me down as a guest presenter at the advisory board meeting next month, so I can discuss Project MASK. I think people should know we are working with men, trying to instill positive self-esteem in them."

"What does MASK stand for?" I asked.

"It stands for Men Acquiring Skills and Knowledge for their families."

"Hey, that's a great name. I will definitely put you down. How much time would you need to discuss the program?"

Samantha hesitated as if she were deep in thought. “Thirty minutes should be more than enough time for me to make the presentation to the board.”

“Okay, you got it!” I said excitedly.

“Malika, have you seen Mr. Ingram lately?”

“Sure. He was here working on the network not too long ago. Did you need him?”

“Yes. I want to offer him an opportunity to work with MASK. I tried calling his office number, but it was disconnected.”

“It is not disconnected; he moved to a new location and the phone company did not transfer his services when he requested. You should be able to reach him now at his new office. In the meantime, I will give you his cell phone number. Do you have a pen?”

“Yes, what is the number?”

After giving her the number, I said, “I’m sure he will be happy to receive additional business. He is a very prompt and professional person.”

“Has he asked you out yet?”

“I don’t know why you think he is interested in me. He has never approached me like that.”

“Trust me, he will.”

“I don’t think so. We are both married.”

“What does that mean? I’m a woman and when I see you two together, you can see it all in your face. You both are attracted to each other.”

“Sorry, boss, but we are just business associates.”

“All right then. I will get back to you, but remember I’m a woman and I know what I see and if I see it, others do too.”

Laughing to ease the mood, I said, “I will talk to you later, bye now.”

That’s how it was with my boss, Samantha. We could discuss anything because she was so cool. I knew she wanted me to step out of the box and see what she saw. But I didn't want anyone to know that I had such an attraction for this man. I couldn't let her know that I would be willing to cross those boundaries. Otherwise, how could she trust me to do a professional job with her subsidiary company?

My girl, Zandra, was worried about me. She thought I would leave my husband or mess up a perfectly good marriage for a romp in the bed with Travis. She wanted me to stop this nonsense and get my head out of the clouds. Our last conversation earlier this week really pissed me off. I could still remember it.

"Have you given up on the thought of fucking your employee?" she asked.

"It is not that simple. It's not that I want to just fuck him. I care about him."

Laughing, she said, "Shit, girl, you want that dick and you need to forget about it before you ruin everything."

"I am not ruining anything. I care about him."

"Who your ass trying to fool? Your ass just wants to fuck him. You need to talk to Dexter and ask him to give it to you like you like it, because it's not cool to fuck another woman's husband. You wouldn't want anyone fucking yours, now would you?"

"Earlier this year, I would have put my foot in a woman's ass for trying to mack my man. Now, I see how that shit happens. I want another woman's husband and I have no guilt. I would be willing to trade."

"If you don't want his ass, what makes you think someone else does?"

This bitch who was supposed to be one of my best friends was about to make me mad. She was slipping on thin ice and one more stupid comment from her mouth would cause me to knock her ass out. I was so angry that I said, "I never told you I didn't want my husband. Don't you worry your fat ass about my life! If your ass can't understand my dilemma, then you better get your ass out of my life. I came to you because I'm scared. I love Dexter. I have never messed around on him and I never intend to. I like Travis and I am very attracted to both his body and his mind. For this to happen, he had to get me with his mind first before I noticed his body. But I would never leave my husband because I want to experiment with another man's dick."

"I'm not trying to make you angry. I want you to see that what you are thinking about doing could change your life. I know I tell you too rough, but you need to hear what I am saying. Once you cross that line, you can't go back. Can you handle that?"

"I think I can. But if I never did what I'm thinking, how would I know?"

"Just know this, you could fall in love. There are too many consequences if your husband finds out. You know that these men can go out and get as much booty as their hearts desire, but the minute that you do and they find out, your ass is in the streets."

"I know that. I wouldn't let him find out."

"Well, as I said before, if you mess with that man, don't tell me or anyone else. You have to keep that shit a secret. You can't trust anybody. It is too risky."

"You must have done this before."

"Don't worry about me. Just make sure you don't tell anyone. Get your dick and go home. Leave your heart with Dexter. Travis is married and he ain't leaving his wife."

"I wouldn't want him to. I'm no fool. If he leaves her for me, he will do the same to me later."

"You got that right."

That's how our conversation ended. At first, I was so upset with her, but when I realized she was trying to make sure I saw the picture from all angles, I understood. She was my friend and she was worried about me, plus I still believed her ass had already done what I wanted to do, or she was doing that shit now. I was glad my girl had my back, but she best have been careful how she came at me. I was about to tell her to kiss my ass for good.

Travis returned and prepared to leave, he stepped into my office and shut the door. "Malika, I need to leave. You had a virus. I secured the firewall, so that should stop any other virus attempts."

"Did we do something wrong here?"

"No, it's possible someone opened a bad attachment, but that could happen to anyone. As people create different types of viruses we just have to step up our game to protect the systems."

"I'm glad that you were able to clean it up."

"Hey, lady, I got you, you know that, don't you?" His voice lowered a half octave and his eyes were shining and had this romantic look.

"Before you go, Samantha called. She wants to talk to you about something. I gave her your cell number, but, here, take her number." I sauntered over to my desk and bent over with my butt directly in front of his crotch. He moved into me and leaned over to see what I was writing and I did it. I backed my ass into his dick and began to grind in a circular motion. His dick stood up to attention and to prevent me from seeing just how that one little action turned him on, he plopped down into the chair. Bingo, I had the answer clearly. Now it was his move.

"Do you know what Samantha wants?"

"Something about participating in a project."

"That should be interesting."

"Malika, line two. It's your husband," Frances said.

I jumped up and went around my desk, turned my back, and briefly talked to Dexter, and when I hung the phone up Travis was gone.

I was mad all week because everybody thought Travis was into me, including me, but ever since I backed my ass into him earlier in the week, I hadn't heard from him. Maybe it was best I didn't see him because I probably would have asked if he was interested in a relationship with me. If he said yes, I was prepared to go to a hotel with him. Then I would have fucked his brains out and sent him back home. I wondered if I would ever get that privilege.

Chapter 8

If Loving You Is Wrong, I Don't Want to Be Right

Lately, I had been listening to a lot of old-school music. Music from back in the day never died, because its lyrics were so soulful and deep. I mean those songs were about real shit that really happened. The young people of today sing about shit like "she took my man and I'm gon' kick her ass." But old-school music taught about the heart, why it was hurting and how to stop the pain. It was about love. No fighting. No killing, just plain, good-time love that was explained through the music.

Every time I heard old-school music, I started to cry. That was how you knew you had it bad, when you heard a song and it made you weep. I was crying because I wanted Travis. He made me feel good inside. He pushed me to be successful.

Dexter used to do the same. He was so sweet and caring back in the day. He wanted me to be successful and would do whatever it took to make it happen. I was only forty, but he acted like our life in the fast lane had come and gone. I was still ready to live, play, and enjoy this life. I was equally as ready to achieve at a different level during this phase of my life. It was not over for me. My life was just beginning. It shouldn't have taken a young man to spark those dormant feelings inside of me. It should have been my husband.

Yet, here I sat, lingering on the words of a young man who seemed to have his shit together. For all I knew he could be a wife beater or gay. But all I could see was a man who was so fine and who presented himself as an intelligent professional who seemed to have my back and I was infatuated with him. I wanted that man. I wanted him. I wanted him.

Funny thing though, I still wanted my husband. I really loved his ass. Even though when we were in the bed, right before we were about to get intimate, he let out this loud-ass fart. This shit was so loud that it shook the bed and the house. It was a major sexual turn-off. He lifted the covers off and fanned the scent away from me. That made me laugh.

I was a little bothered that he thought that after I had heard something like that I could still open my legs and let his stinky ass partake of my pussy. It was at this time that I saw Travis. I saw that bright smile and those pretty hazel eyes and I didn't smell anything funky. All I saw was a man I wanted to touch and feel. I didn't smell funky socks and I didn't smell morning breath. Even though I knew in my heart that his wife was probably wishing someone would take his trifling ass away from her, because she was maybe feeling the same way I felt.

We all think the grass is greener on the other side, but it isn't. We are just on the outside looking in or we think this person can do no wrong. Each of us has the ability to show people what we want them to see. It is because of not seeing the truth about the person at the beginning of the relationship that we end up getting hurt.

The only difference when you were messing around with someone else is that you got the good stuff—the love and romance. People don't start off showing you the bad things about their characters. They have to make you fall in love with them and then you won't care about the ugly stuff when it happens.

In my case, I could see this fine man who appeared to be every woman's dream. He was kind, sexy, attentive, and successful. But this was not my man. I had decided that I wanted him just for a moment. Then I would send him back to his family. Even if I found out later that he was not all that he portrayed, I needed to know if he could love me like I needed.

That brought me to this dilemma: how in the world would I ever strip down naked and get into the bed with another man? I really didn't think I could follow through on that part. I really liked Travis, but I needed to lose about fifty pounds before I got naked around him. I had my nerve because I acted like this was a done deal when it was not.

I must admit that I was self-conscious about my body. I had never ever been this big in my life, but being overweight didn't stop my need to be desired. It only made my desire to be held, to be kissed, and touched stronger. I wanted to know that I could still have that fairy tale kind of love.

I was trying to lose this weight so I could fuck Travis. I knew that was kinda stupid. Even though I hadn't really noticed what others seemed to think he felt about me, my heart said he wanted me, even now, while I was overweight. But I wanted to look and feel sexy when I slept with him. I wanted a slim, beautiful body when I fucked him. I could remember my mother always said that when folks start telling you stuff, you tend to start believing it. Losing the weight was my issue, not his. He had never treated me less than beautiful. Even though I loved me, before I allowed anyone other than my husband to see my naked body I wanted to lose a little weight. I was thick, but I was overweight by my doctor's medical standards. But hell, fat girls needed love too.

We all have idiosyncrasies. We are who we need to be when it is important to make a positive impression. We grin and bear it to reach our goals. We change the way we do things to be accepted, even in love.

But sometimes in love, you have to do things you wouldn't normally do. You close the door when you go to the bathroom. You try to make everything smell good and fresh, because you don't want to offend the person you love. You keep everything neat and clean, because you want that man to believe he has a good catch. So you do everything decent and in order. That is new love. That was what I wanted.

I wanted my man to want me every night because I made him feel good. I wanted him to be happy to see me because he missed me when I was gone. I wanted him to send flowers to me at my job just because he was thinking about me. I wanted him to take me on a shopping spree because he enjoyed doing things to make me feel special. That was what I wanted—that fresh, new love.

But all I got was, "I don't have time." Every time I asked Dexter to do something as a family, I got, "Maybe next time." That shit was for the birds. I wanted something different. Travis presented that for me. He seemed to be together. Don't get me wrong, I knew I was looking through rose-colored glasses, but this was the way I needed to see things. Otherwise, I didn't have anything to look forward to.

I knew it was wrong to want this married man. I was a married woman. We were in the same position. Both of us were probably not getting what we needed to stimulate our souls and our hearts. We were both struggling with our feelings. We were trying to remain professional. But I saw his eyes and I knew in my heart that for now, this very minute, if loving Travis was wrong, shit, I didn't want to be right. Be still my heart.

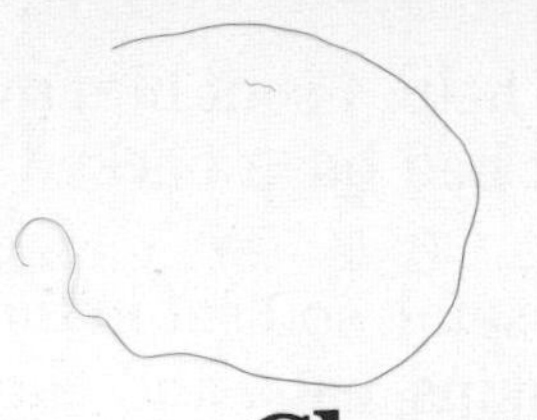

Chapter 9

Party Like It's 1999

I watched over ninety mothers and their babies parade through the door of the community center. Some decided to wear costumes even though we were not celebrating Halloween. The children were dressed as pumpkins and famous actors. Thank goodness there were no witches, goblins, or devils. We had enough of those in the daily newspapers and in the news without our children trying to mimic those thugs.

I walked over to Felicia, who was organizing the gift table and giving the parents instructions. Sarah was standing in the corner, talking to one of the parents on her caseload. She glanced at me with a half-cocked smile. I smiled at her and she turned her head. I laughed. The other staff members were working and talking to the parents while manning their stations. I noticed Frances kissing an infant.

Some of the parents were playing Pin the Tail on the Cat, while others were helping their children bob for apples. Music was blasting and the air was full of beats and happiness. The smaller children were dancing, some in circles, and others were jumping up and down. I even saw babies gently trying to clap their hands.

Mothers were socializing and eating. There were several fathers walking around, trying to make themselves useful. One walked up to me, smiling like a slick cat, asking if I needed his help. I sent him over to help serve the goody bags that had been packed for all the children.

I tried to make myself useful, so I sat in the corner in my booth, painting pumpkins, cats, and ghosts on the children's faces. I really had no idea what I was doing, but the children were so excited and it gave me such joy to work some magic with my hands. My artwork was quite impressive. Everything was going well until Travis walked in. Apparently, Felicia had invited him to come by; he took her up on her offer. I noticed Sarah's face immediately as Travis made his way to me. Suddenly, I wasn't having any fun.

See, I was okay when I wasn't standing in his presence, but something happened inside of me whenever he was near. I got nervous. The palms of my hands became sweaty and I lost my confidence. I knew my staff was watching my reaction to his being there. I wasn't sure if I could pull off hiding my feelings. I was trying, but the more I saw him, the stronger this thing was. I was so conflicted inside. What was going on with me? Why was I so bottled up inside? I had to get my cool and control back with quickness.

When I walked into the kitchen area of the community center, Felicia was sticking her head into the refrigerator. Walking toward her, I said as professionally as I could, "Why did you invite Mr. Ingram to this activity?"

"Oh, he heard us talking about it and I told him if he wanted to stop by he could. Did I do something wrong?"

"No," I said quickly. "I just wanted to know why he was here."

"Malika, girl, it is common knowledge around here that Mr. Ingram is attracted to you. I don't care how you two try to hide it, we can all still see it. Good or bad, that's just how it is. Otherwise, why is he here?"

"Could it be that he came because you invited him?" I stated sarcastically.

"Are you upset with me?"

"No! I'm just tired of the rumors around, I don't need to start new ones."

"I wouldn't worry about rumors. These women here are very jealous and vindictive. They will start rumors on anybody. Just don't buy into that crap."

"I'm not, but sometimes conflict and confusion can be so exhausting. I have too much work to get done. I don't have time to deal with things that have nothing to do with our work. At least this shouldn't have anything to do with it, but because he is a contractor it seems that his coming around does or should cause me some concern."

"I know that things like gossip and backtalk can cause problems, but only if you let them."

"I realize that, but I am spending too much time defending my honor when I should be trying to improve on the services that we give to our parents. I just don't have the energy to fight office conflicts and politics."

"Then don't worry about that stuff. Be who you are. Enjoy your life. Don't let others dictate how you feel."

"Are you sure that you didn't go to school to be a counselor? Because you have some serious skills."

"That's what I have been trying to tell you. Now, when are you going to give me that raise?"

"Oh, you are going to get a raise when I raise my hand to give you some assignments to complete."

"So you think you have jokes?" Felicia said as she grabbed me by the elbow and pulled me back into the atrium.

We both entered the atrium, laughing. As I walked back over to my booth to join Frances in painting faces, Travis grabbed my arm and asked, "Hey, Malika, how have you been doing?"

"I'm fine, Travis. How are you?"

"I couldn't be better. I just signed a huge deal, so things are really looking up for me."

"That's great."

"Yeah. I'm interviewing network administrators, so if you know anyone, feel free to refer them to me."

"I'll do that."

"What are you doing this weekend?" he asked.

"Nothing much. I plan on going to church and visiting my folks."

He stood there, staring at me as if he had more to say. He looked as if he was trying to find the words to use, but as soon as he said, "Have you seen that movie—" Sarah butted into our conversation.

"Hi, Travis," she said, with the weirdest smirk on her face.

"Hi," he replied.

He quickly turned back to me. But that fool grabbed his arm and pulled him toward her. "I have a question to ask you."

"What is it?" he asked as if he was agitated.

"It's my computer. I can't open up my homepage. I'm not sure what's happening, but when I turned it on to type in my password, it gave this message that my password is not valid. When I request to change it, it won't allow me to."

"Well, I'll look at it the next time I visit the office." He started walking back toward me when she again grabbed his arm and asked, "Do you want to try to pin the dick on the cat? I mean, the tail on the cat?"

Travis looked at that bitch in disgust. I didn't have to say a word. His face told how he felt about the comment she had just made.

She hung her head and walked away in shame. Bitch was thinking about his dick. That was why she said that shit. I knew her ass was embarrassed.

He smiled at me. "I love to see little kids having a good time." He turned his head and watched the children. A huge beach ball bounced in his direction and he giggled as he hit it back to the kids.

"I know. I love throwing parties for the kids."

"That's why I like you so much, Malika. I know you care."

I took his hand into mine and squeezed it. "Thank you."

We resumed talking about people, the happy children, and politics. He never finished asking me about the movie. I wasn't sure if he was going to ask me to go with him. Sarah messed that one up for me. I had to remember that I owed her for that. It was going to take me a couple of days to come up with the assignment from hell to pay her ass back for interrupting Travis and me. Now I would probably never know whether he wanted to make me his mistress. For that, Ms. Sarah would pay dearly.

Just as I turned to walk toward the food and beverage table, Felicia took the microphone and announced the Soul Train Line was forming. "For all the pumpkins, Jay Leno, and Michael Jackson wanna-bes, put on your dancing shoes and get ready to take a trip on the S-o-u-l T-r-a-i-n." Felicia announced that like she was Don Cornelius himself. Suddenly, there was a stampede as the children and their parents ran toward the area where Felicia was standing. The music was turned up and the kids were dancing all over the place.

After the kids and their parents had gone down the line once, my staff took their turns. I looked around and saw Travis. He was standing to the side, laughing and smiling, when one of the kids left the line and pulled him over. He was embarrassed, so he basically did something like a walk-dance down the aisle. He was just walking and stepping to the beat and every step or so he would bounce. The kids cracked up. Travis couldn't dance.

Felicia with her smart ass decided I needed to participate and get off the sidelines. She pulled me and asked me to go down the line with her. So we did the old-fashioned bump all the way down to the clapping and laughing of everyone. We had a ball.

Finally, it was time for the day to end. We started cleaning up as the cabs returned to pick up their passengers. Travis stayed and helped us clean up the place. He stayed there until every family was gone. Sarah never did come around us again. She stayed away; I assumed she was too embarrassed to be in our presence. Who could blame her, because she actually made an ass out of herself.

After I returned home, I started thinking about the evening with Travis. I thought about what he meant to me. It was strange he knew more about my job than my own husband and that made me sad. How could I not be attracted to a man who paid so much attention to me? My own husband didn't even want to hear about my day, but here was this man, taking an interest in my life. Why wouldn't Dexter try to act like he was interested in what I did? Yet I was falling for this guy and no matter how hard I tried to get my own husband to pay more attention to me, it was not working.

I tried again to engage him in conversation when I returned home. “Hi, honey, what are you watching on television?” I asked in my sweetest voice.

“What are you begging for now?” he asked sarcastically. “Some money?”

“Every time I try to talk to you, it’s like pulling teeth.”

“Well, don’t try to talk to me. Every time you say something, it’s about spending money and the answer is no.”

Just that fast I was angry. Who in the hell did this bastard think he was? I worked every day and if I wanted something, you best believe I was going to get it. So brother man was wasting his time making a statement like that to me. “Your ass don’t rule me. Until you are taking care of me, you don’t tell me what I can and can’t do. If I want to spend some money, I will. You ain’t running shit up in here.”

I stormed out of the living room and ran up the stairs to our bedroom. I lay face down on the bed and cried like a baby. “How come I can’t make this marriage work?” I whispered to myself.

Li’l Dex walked into my bedroom and asked me what was wrong. I told him I was just upset about some things.

“Anything that I can help you with?” he asked with concern in his voice.

“No. I’ll be okay.” I sat up and hugged him tightly to my chest. “Don’t worry about me. I’m okay,” I said.

He walked out of my bedroom, looking perplexed. He was such a good child. He played football and basketball and was very good at both. He brought home good grades.

I was afraid he would end up like his father. I didn’t want that to happen. I was teaching him to communicate. All his young life, I had spent time telling him to talk about his issues, to share himself with his family and me. He was doing just that. He often expressed his feelings about girls and questioned his dad about math and biology. He had a good relationship with both his father and me. We were very proud of him. I certainly had no complaints. Dexter always attended his basketball and football games, as a proud father should.

Dexter was taking advantage of me. He stopped taking me out as much as he used to. We went to a movie once every three or four months. We rarely did much of anything else. Thinking about it, our life together was very boring. His main goal was to save as much money as he could for the future. Whose future did he mean? Certainly not ours because he wouldn't even talk to me.

I had to keep trying to make my marriage work. I had to make him see that he was the one pushing me out of his life. So I jumped out of the bed and walked quickly to the stairs. Taking my time and trying to relax, I took some deep breaths. I walked slowly down the steps to make sure I wouldn't trip. I had to keep my composure. I didn't want him to burst out laughing.

I sat on the couch next to him. "We need to talk."

"About what?"

"About us. I'm trying hard to keep this marriage strong, but you won't help."

"Malika, I don't understand you. You have a man who is home every day and who takes care of his home by paying the bills and you are still not satisfied. I don't know what else I can do to show you that I love you."

"You can take an interest in my life. You can act like you are interested in me and what I do."

"Why should I pretend? I am not interested in what you do on your job. But that doesn't mean that I don't care about you. If I didn't care, I wouldn't be here."

"Marriage is more than just being here. It is about sharing, communication, and respect. Half of the problem is I can't count on you to listen to me. I need you to be interested in me and my job, or whatever makes me happy. I want you to be a part of everything in my life."

Dexter was getting frustrated. "You know me or you should. I love you. You know that a man who doesn't love his family will not provide for them. I'm here and not running the streets. If you want to throw away our marriage on something stupid, then that's on you."

"I am not trying to throw anything away. I just want you to spend time with me."

"I'm here, aren't I?"

I was not getting anywhere with this conversation. Either my husband didn't understand or he didn't care. I needed to find out and soon, because I couldn't take much more of this. I got up and walked into the kitchen. He followed.

"Malika, how many men do you know who cook almost daily for their family?"

"Not many. I admit that."

"Isn't that love? Am I showing my family how much they mean to me?"

"I guess so. But why can't we do things together?"

"We go to the movies."

"Every three months," I said.

"But we go, don't we?"

"There's more to entertainment than attending a movie every three months."

"You want to travel, go out of town?"

"How far?" Hell, I wanted to know. Ever since the 9/11 tragedy, I was fearful of flying. So to take me away from St. Louis would be like pulling teeth.

"That's what I'm saying. What's in St. Louis that we haven't done?"

"Theater, mystery dinner theatre, concerts, and parties."

"We've done all that. Why keep doing it?"

"To be together and enjoy each other's company."

"Okay, just plan something and I will go," he stated. "I have no problem with that. Just let me know when."

I walked away, unsure of how I should've felt. Sure, he would go with me if I planned something. But rarely would he come up with an idea. I wanted more. Did I want passion and a listening ear? I thought that was what my heart was missing. I needed something else. I needed someone to desire me in the worst way. Or was I just bent out of shape and not sure what I wanted or needed because another man was paying attention to me? I was so confused.

I wanted my husband to take an interest in my life. I needed him to understand my needs. I wanted him to love me like he did when we first got married. I wanted my husband to need me and if he couldn't do that, Travis could. At least that is what I wanted to believe. But if I really looked deep inside of me, I wasn't sure what the fuck I wanted.

Chapter 10

Daydreaming and I'm Thinking of You

The weekend came and went. I spent it mostly hot and moist between the legs. Who would have ever thought you could want a man so bad that when you thought about him, you became wet? Well, that's what happened to me the whole damn weekend. I thought about Travis's dick. Was I obsessed with having some of that man or was I so hard up for love that I couldn't let go of wanting him inside of me? It was just like I was walking around with a hard dick in my pussy. Otherwise, how was I staying so horny for him all day?

If Travis knew my obsession with him, would he visit me at the office as much as he did or would he have simply sent one of his technicians? Better yet, maybe he knew I desperately wanted to fuck him and suck on his earlobes, his nose, and whatever part of him that I could have. Mmm, I could imagine tasting him right now. His skin would taste so good like hot chocolate, supple and smooth. I had to get this boy out of my head. He made me constantly think of sexing him to death. This was not me, not the person I knew. I had enough work to do than to sit here day in and day out, thinking about sucking another man's dick, especially when I didn't want to do my own husband's.

Monday morning, I walked into the office with a plan to do research via the Internet on single working women making low salaries, so I could write a grant. As I typed in the subject on the address line of the Internet, my phone rang. It was Dexter. "Hey, babe, would you pick up my clothes from the cleaners? I have to work late tonight, so you will have to cook dinner, too."

"No problem. I'll leave work early today."

Just as I hung up the phone, Sarah walked in, took a seat, and asked, "How was your weekend?"

"It was great. What about yours?" I asked, not really wanting to know.

"It was fine. I cooked a big meal. Some collard greens, fried chicken, yams, macaroni, cheese casserole, and cornbread."

"I know all six of your kids came for dinner. That sounds like a wonderful, delicious meal. Sounds like you slaved over the stove the entire weekend."

"Not really. I enjoy cooking for my family."

I started to say something negative, but decided to continue to remain professional. I wanted to ask her if all six of her children's daddies came, but decided that since she was being pleasant, I should be too. Just as we began to have a decent conversation—and don't think for one second I let my guard down—Sarah asked, "You talked to Travis over the weekend?"

"I don't get you, Sarah. Why in the world would you think that I talked to Travis over the weekend?"

"I just asked because I thought you all were friends," she said, as she rolled her eyes to the top.

If I was not careful, this girl was going to catch me off guard and make me cuss her ass out in front of witnesses. But I kept my cool. "Travis and I are not friends. We are business associates. Please let me explain what that means, since you have never worked in management. It simply means that we only communicate about the work he was hired to do in the office.

This means that I have no reason to talk to him outside of the office unless it is about something involving his work under that contract. For your information, I would not hire a friend to work for me unless I was absolutely sure that they could handle such a feat. I would never lose a friend over work issues. So to make a long explanation short enough for you to understand, Travis is not my friend. He is a contractor who bid on work and won a contract."

"Oh, I see. I understand." Sarah sat in that chair as if she were glued to the seat. She did not budge.

"Do you have anything else you would like to say?" *Damn,* I thought. *I should slap my own face for engaging her further.*

Crossing her legs at the knees, this heifer thought she was getting ready to get me to gossip with her. "Did you hear what Felicia did?"

"No, what did she do?"

"She was getting all in Frances's face about something she didn't want to do. Did you hear about that, since you hear about everything else?"

"So what are you trying to say?"

"Well, you know everyone around here thinks that you and Felicia are too close. But like I say, these people around here are a major trip. They are always talking behind each other's backs. Be careful, Malika. All they do is sit around and talk about Travis. Everybody wants him, you know."

"No, I didn't know that. The people here should concentrate on helping our mothers find jobs that pay more than minimum wage. They should work on their files and other things that they need to do rather than harass a contractor."

"But, Malika, sometimes it is hard to work when he is around because he is so fine."

"Well, maybe you all need to think about whether or not you can work around here, because we need contractors for various jobs and we have so much work to do that we don't have time to gawk at men doing work to support this office."

"I know what you mean, but sometimes it's hard. Malika, you know he is fine."

"You can't run a business getting involved because of how someone looks."

"Malika, how do you keep it so together? I feel like no matter how hard I try, I just can't seem to make my life work. I want what everybody else has: a happy family, a man who loves me, and peace at home."

"Remember, you can't look at people's lives through rose-colored glasses. The grass really isn't always greener on the other side. You must find your own peace. What makes you happy?" I suddenly felt sorry for Sarah. Her eyes seemed to have a cast over them, like a cloud had just covered up her sun. Here she was, looking pitiful and lost. She was seeking solace from me—the person she hated and despised the most. I felt good, but not proud that here, the troublemaker in the office, was crying on my shoulder. All I kept thinking was this bitch was trying again to set me up. I shrugged off my attitude to embrace this lost sister. "You have your health," I said. "Your children are happy and seem to be doing well. They are not in jail, on drugs, or preg . . ." I tried to take that one back, because Felicia told me Sarah's twelve-year-old daughter was pregnant.

"Well, I'm healthy, but things can be better. See, you have everything together."

"You can too. If you know what you want."

"Do you find Travis attractive?" she asked.

See, that was what pissed me off. First, she walked in my door, tried to get in my business, and I impeded that, only to be given enough information to make me feel sorry for her, then she came up with this shit about Travis. Now I was boiling. But I did what Pamela had told me to do when we were ten years old—take deep breaths and exhale. This was supposed to make me feel better. I needed my best friend to talk to me now, so I could calm myself down; you know, remain professional.

Finally, after much deliberation, I said, "I'm not going to discuss Travis with you, because it is not professional to discuss the business of workers, contractors, or anyone unless there are problems that I need to address. Please don't discuss your personal feelings about workers with me. It is unprofessional and out of line."

"How come every time I bring his name up you get an attitude? Maybe, Malika, you need to check yourself too, because you get so angry at the mention of his name."

I tried to figure out how I could respond to that question, remain the sweet person I was, and put her in check. This sister just didn't get it. I mean, was she that desperate or what? I wasn't going there with her today. I would not let this girl bring me down.

"You hear me, Malika? What about you and Travis?"

"Sorry, I'm really late for an appointment. I'll talk to you later."

Just like that, I got up and grabbed my purse. So far, my day had been ruined. As I prepared to leave, Sarah got up and walked to her desk. I locked my office door, told Felicia I would see her after lunch, and then walked out the door. Just like that. I didn't look back. Not once.

As I walked, I was thinking that I needed to quiet this girl, but how? As I pondered this thought, I hit the elevator's down button. As the doors opened, Travis walked out. My eyes lit up and he smiled.

"Hey, where are you going?" he asked.

Before I could respond, he said, "I came to spend the morning working on the computer system and then take you to lunch."

"I was leaving to get some air. But I am free right this moment and forever," I said.

"Right!" he said, looking at me with those beautiful, hypnotic eyes, as if he didn't believe I was actually free forever. "Come on, let's ride." He gently grabbed my hand and led me onto the elevator. As we stepped on, the doors closed. I moved to the corner and he scooted close to me, looking into my eyes. This man was so close that all I had to do was snap my fingers and the air between us would hit him in the face. As he looked down at me, our faces were so close that all I had to do was turn my face upward and our lips would touch. I wanted to turn. I wanted him to kiss me. We stared at each other until the door opened.

I knew it finally: our attraction was real. He wanted me like I wanted him. All I had to do was make that move. But I was scared. This was not me! I was not fast like my mother used to say about girls who did it with the neighborhood boys. I was not a whore. I was married. Or was I? The way I felt, I wasn't sure if I was married or what, because if I was, why was I feeling like this about another man?

We exited the elevator and walked toward his Benz. He walked to my side of the car and opened the door. I entered the car. *Just ask me, I will go with you anywhere.* "Ask me," I said out loud, not meaning to.

"Ask you what?" he asked, while turning to face me.

"I was just thinking out loud."

"You had a bad day I gather."

"Yes," I said.

"Let's see if I can make you forget it."

"I'm sure that you can. Make my day."

Travis looked at me, perplexed. I could tell he was confused. Finally, he said, "I know the perfect place to take you."

I smiled. *He's taking me to a hotel. Yeah! Yeah!* Just my damn luck, he turned into a Dierdorf & Hart's restaurant. Was this supposed to be what I needed? Now I was depressed. A fat girl's anthem, to take me to a restaurant!

When we walked into the restaurant, all heads turned. I was proud to be with this man. He was a man who knew exactly what to say to a woman to make her heart sing. He was very smart and his baritone voice was mesmerizing and soothing. As I sat at the table, staring at him, he searched the menu. I thought again about his wife. Was he this tender and in touch with her feelings? Did he make her toes curl when he touched her? Did he know when her heart was lonely and needed to be fed? I wondered what kind of woman was she. After all, she had him. She must've been someone who was very special to have such an attentive man.

"A penny for your thoughts." He surprised me.

"I was just thinking," I quickly began. "I was wondering; people who have a nice person to share their lives with, do they know?"

"Do they know what?" he asked.

"Do they know they have someone special to share their lives with and a person who will listen and treat them with kindness?"

He looked at me and smiled. "Most people don't know how to treat their spouses because they take them for granted."

"What do you mean?"

"You become just like that." He pointed to the coat rack and I stared.

"The coat rack?"

"You see," he continued, "when people have been together for a while, they stop doing the very things that attracted them to each other in the first place. They stop talking to each other and they basically lose touch with the other person's feelings. They become stuck."

"The coat rack is there. Its duty is to hold coats and umbrellas." I saw where he was going with the analogy.

"Right! It's going to be right there in that same position. Unless, that is, someone decides to move it. To change its position. Or even to get rid of it."

"That's good."

"If people are having problems they have to do something different. Make changes and agree to work it out. But people become accustomed to standing in one spot, like the coat rack. People forget whatever it took to get a person is the same thing it is going to take to keep them." He looked at me and winked his left eye.

"That's great food for thought. Thank you!"

I sat there wanting to tell him that if he would have me, I wouldn't forget. Every day, I would make every effort to make him feel loved. I wanted to say it, but I lost my nerve. So I said, "It's too bad that people lose that special connection. I have a friend who is going through that now. She goes home every day and her husband doesn't talk to her. She said that she feels unloved and lonely. What do you think she should do?"

"She should try to talk to her husband," he responded. "Explain her feelings and if he loves her, maybe he will make the effort to improve."

"What if he doesn't?" I asked.

"If he doesn't, she should try to find out why he won't talk. Maybe he doesn't feel that a problem exists. Maybe it's her pressuring him."

"You know what, Travis, my friend has told her husband, but he won't change. She said she is getting frustrated because everyone keeps telling her the same thing."

Travis picked up his glass and took a swallow of water. He picked up his napkin and dried the water droplets from his hand.

As I sat there I became angry because I had talked to my husband. I had asked him to work with me, but he didn't feel there was a problem. I was getting sick and tired of folks telling me the same shit, and everything I tried gave me no results. Frustration snaked across my face. I picked up the napkin and wiped my forehead and nose because I felt they were shining because my body temperature was increasing.

"You know, Malika, I am going through something similar. I love my wife, but we are slowly being pulled apart. I've spoken to her about it, but she doesn't see a problem. When I reach for her at night she pulls away because she is so tired from running with the kids and working. But I have my needs and she doesn't feel she needs to address them. We're talking about it. You have to decide if your marriage is worth saving. For me, I want it to work, but it's hard when you know someone else would be willing to love you and meet your needs."

"So what you are saying is, fight for your marriage?" Now I was pissed. I thought we were heading somewhere as a couple together but he was just like my friends and my mother. Talk to your husband, tell him, keep talking. Damn I was more frustrated now than ever. So now I needed to know what he wanted from me. Soon I would find out. This was getting tiresome.

If he wanted me, he wouldn't tell me to work things out with my husband. I believed he knew it was me and not some friend. But I could play that game too.

"Travis, I will tell my friend what you said. I'm sure that will help her."

The waiter returned and we ordered lobster, crab cakes, and shrimp. We stared at each other as if we were looking into each other's soul. Both of us were wondering what was next and then his cell phone vibrated. He pulled it out of the holder that was hooked to his waist and looked at the number on the phone. He pushed end on the phone and put it back on his waist. He looked back at me. "What happened at work today? You looked like it was rough."

"It was rough. It was Sarah. Sometimes she can be sweet, easy to get along with, then just like Samantha on *Bewitched,* she changes. Within a finger snap, she goes from sweet and lovely to the most deadly and doggish person I've ever seen. This happens in a split second. It's like she has a split personality."

Travis said, "Please be careful around her. You don't know her intentions. People can be so devious. I worry about you being there with some of the women you employ. Just be careful. People are so cold and easy to turn violent out of jealousy, hatred, and misery."

"I don't think she is that bad. I mean, I don't think she would stoop so low as to try to hurt me. At least, I don't think so." I smiled.

I couldn't help thinking, *if only he knew how carefully I would be unbuttoning his shirt, gently kissing his eyelids, lightly sucking his earlobes, as I move down his throat to his chest and nipples*. Shit, just thinking about him naked made me press my thighs together to stop the throbbing.

Why did this man have so much power over my feelings? Why didn't he know he had the power to make me his love slave? After all, here I was, salivating over him, wanting to lick his body like a kid licking an ice cream cone. If I didn't get myself together, I was going to fall apart. Already I had crossed the boundaries of professionalism, because I was having lunch in the middle of the morning with my contractor. But I wasn't thinking about business, I was thinking about sex.

"You always seem so deep in thought. Is everything all right with you? I mean, I realize that you go through so much with the women on your job, but you can't let them get you down. Hold your head up high. It is nothing but jealousy."

I looked at him and wondered if he was a blind fool. I was thinking about putting his dick in my mouth and he was thinking I was thinking about some women. What the fuck was on his mind? I looked him in his face and was just about to say, "I want to suck your d . . . d . . . d . . ." but instead I said, "I really want to taste the lobster. When are they bringing out our lunch?"

We sat in the restaurant, laughing and talking about his business. He and I shared so much information with each other. We talked about our desires.

"You know what I want, Malika? I want to grow my company like World Wide Computers. I want to be big in this industry. I know I'm on the way."

"You can do it too. I know you can."

"What do you want, Malika?"

"I want to accomplish a lot, but I really want to become a bestselling author and start a small, independent publishing company."

"Really! I didn't know you liked to write."

"I love the art of writing stories."

"Have you written anything?"

"Some short stories."

"I would love to read them."

"Okay. I'd like that!" This is why I really had affections for him. Dexter thought my writing was insignificant, not important. He had never read anything I had written. Travis wanted to.

He encouraged me to get busy and to write to my heart's content. He told me I could do anything because I was smart, talented, and very attractive. I smiled and thought about the two of us lying in bed, talking business.

Then I felt my eyes close. I was slowly getting ready to seduce him, and then I shook myself. I informed him we needed to leave. As we walked out of the restaurant, we stood on the sidewalk and chatted. We talked in the car and he walked me back into the building, rode up the elevator with me, and we sat on the bench in front of the doors and chatted some more. Sitting on that hard bench was becoming a habit! We couldn't get enough of each other.

Chapter 11

Another Day's Journey

I didn't know how I made it safely home. I was thinking about my lunch meeting with Travis. I was singing and humming all over the place. The next thing I knew, I was pulling up in the driveway. When I got out of the car and bent down to pick up the newspaper lying in the yard, I saw my good friend, Zena. We had been neighbors and friends for about twelve years. It was funny thinking about our relationship. For twelve years, she and I had been walking, trying to lose weight. Funny thing though, we were still the same size we were when we started walking twelve years earlier. All those long years of walking and talking, and dreaming and hoping and still, well, you know what I mean.

"Hey, girl. What have you been up to lately?" I asked.

"Nothing much. You know I am back in school, studying to become a nurse."

"How do you like that? It's so much different than what you are doing. I mean, how do you go from being a certified public accountant to a nurse?"

"Bad high school counseling. Girl, as much as my ass talk, they should have called me Ann Landers and counseled me to become a reporter, nurse, social worker, journalist, or anything else. They put me at a table with a damn calculator and told me to shut my mouth and add. I haven't been happy in my job since I graduated from college."

"Finally, girl," I said, "it is now or never."

"I am going back to school to get a bachelor's in nursing, and hopefully, later a master's in nursing."

"I'm proud of you, Zena. Girl, you know it is wrong for those high school counselors to misguide folks. They either lead you the right way or misjudge your abilities. Either way, you have to fight for what you want. For instance, my high school counselor told me to major in social work. She noted how everyone came to talk to me about their problems and how some of my friends told her I helped them with some pretty deep issues. She thought I should be a social worker because I was a natural with people. But she missed one thing: I needed to live. Social workers do not make any money unless they get into management, and that takes a master's degree plus ground-level experience. Even though I like what I do, hell, I need more money."

"You got that right, my Nubian sister." Zena was just standing there as if she was in great thought.

Finally, I asked her, "Is everything all right?"

"Not really, girl. I think I am depressed."

"Have you been to the doctor?"

"No. I don't need a doctor to tell me that I am depressed. I feel like I don't have any energy."

I wondered if I should say something to her about what the signs of depression were. I wasn't a doctor, but I did know about depression and stress. I didn't know about depression and heredity issues, but I knew the symptoms. I decided to tell her the real signs of depression, but just as I was about to explain the symptoms, her husband called her.

"That's my ticket. My man is calling me. I'll holler at you later."

"Okay, girl, if you need me, call me."

"I will," she said as she quickly rushed across the street. I put a note in my head to remember to discuss depression with her and to try to encourage her to see a doctor.

As I walked through the garage to enter the kitchen, Li'l Dexter walked up and hugged me. "We won our soccer match."

Li'l Dexter had recently started playing soccer. "Sweetheart, that is wonderful. How many goals did you score?"

"Only three. But Coach said we are getting better every game. Plus, Dad was so happy we won. He was shouting in the bleachers. I saw him."

I looked up at Dexter. He was so fine. I knew those women at the game couldn't keep their eyes off him. He was a well-built man, with strong muscular arms and legs. He had a thick mustache and really long, thick eyelashes. He was handsome. If Dexter was willing to put in more time and energy in reigniting our marriage I wouldn't be so confused. Suddenly, I felt jealous even though I was lusting after another man. It pissed me off, thinking someone was doing the same thing I was doing, wanting my man. If only he would work on his behavior and our relationship.

"Hey, how ya doing?" Big Dexter asked.

"I'm doing fine, Dexter. Thanks for taking Li'l D to the game."

"You didn't think I wouldn't go support my son, did you?"

"No, that is not what I was saying. I am just glad that you take such an interest in our child."

"You know you say some stupid things," he responded in jest.

"Whatever." See, that was what I was talking about. He always found a way to piss me off. I decided I was not going to argue with Li'l D in the room. So I asked my son, whom I affectionately nicknamed Li'l D, what he wanted to eat. That was the best I could do to diffuse the situation. I walked toward the kitchen and walked up to the sink to wash my hands. I then opened the oak wood cabinet next to the stove and pulled out a large pot and two small ones. I was going to cook some green beans, corn, and spaghetti. Then I looked for the deep fryer to fry some tilapia fish. Reaching for the lemon-pepper seasoning, my mind floated to Travis. I felt the pit of my stomach weaken. Was I falling in love with this man? I couldn't go an hour without thinking about him. This was a setup. Those little bitches at the office had poisoned my mind. I never thought of Travis like this until they started that mess at the office. Shaking myself as if I was shaking that man right out of my hair, I smiled. Then I started singing, "I'm going to shake that man right outta my head. I'm going to shake that man right outta my head." Seasoning the fish, I laughed. That's exactly what I was going to have to do.

"Malika, did you get the mail?" Dexter hollered.

"No!"

"At least you could have done that. Especially since you don't do much here. What I need you for? My secretary said that you don't do anything."

"You tell that bitch to kiss my ass," I angrily replied. "I told you to stop discussing me with that dumb ass. She would love to be your woman and you just sit there telling her my business. Stop talking to your damn secretary about me. You don't want me to fire that yellow-teeth bitch, do you?"

"She doesn't mean anything by what she says. She's impressed with you. When I talk to her she just gets a little hyped, that's all."

"Well, you need to stop talking with her about me. You're just making her think she has a chance with you."

"I'm not interested in her. You should see her. She has gained a lot of weight and she is really fat. Plus, she has this acne all over her face. I think she is picking the bumps, because she has little dots of blood all over her face."

"That does it. You are going to have to move her to the back and move someone else from the secretary pool to the front."

"She is going to be so upset."

"Either that or you will lose business. You can't have someone meeting your customers looking like that."

"I know." Dexter looked so concerned. He hated dealing with personnel issues that had more to deal with appearance than performance. He would do it, but it pained him. He cared a lot about others. Maybe what Travis said about that coat rack applied to me and Dexter. He didn't worry that much about me. At least, he never said anything to make me think he did.

"Is dinner almost ready?" Li'l D was back in the kitchen, ready to eat. He had showered and changed out of his soccer uniform.

"Give me about ten more minutes. I'm almost done. Why don't you sit down and do your spelling while I finish up."

"Okay, Mom," Li'l Dexter said as he walked to the living room to work on his spelling words.

While his dad sorted through the mail, it occurred to me that I was tingling between the legs. I was thinking about Travis again. This was going to have to stop because I couldn't continue to desire this man the way that I was. So I shook him off the second time since I had been home and prepared the table for dinner.

We had a quiet dinner. Everyone seemed to enjoy what I had pulled together. Then Big Dexter decided we needed some jokes.

"That was some nasty food," he said as he stood up to stretch and rub his stomach.

"Yeah! That's why you ate it all up, every morsel."

I knew he enjoyed my meals. Whenever he did, he would always say the food was nasty. That was his way and most of the time I would just laugh at him, because really, my man was really funny.

Finally, I cleaned the kitchen and then went upstairs, showered, and changed into something more comfortable. I was feeling more vibrant than ever before. Did young men make you feel so much life? I actually felt young and horny. I sat next to my husband and kissed him softly on the cheek. He didn't say anything. He just sat there like a bump on a log. I would take care of him in bed. We watched television. Then around eight, I put Li'l D in the bed. After I read him a bedtime story, he was knocked out. As I closed the door, I smiled. Li'l D was down for the count.

In bed that night, I did all kinds of things to my hubby. I tried to turn his ass out. It was easy to do because my mind was being constantly bombarded with images of that fine-ass Travis. The more he smiled, the harder I rolled my hips. I could feel his hardness inside of my vaginal walls. He finally turned me over and pushed my legs together tightly as he entered my vagina from the backside. This was a great feeling. It was also one of my favorite positions, one that I had visualized Travis doing to me. As my mind quickly rambled, tingles shot through my body. Dexter was putting that thang on me. I lifted my body up about an inch off the bed. This made him slide deeper into me. As I gently rolled my hips, I whispered breathlessly, "I'm coming."

Upon hearing me moan those words, Dexter's body went into speed mode. He was rolling his hips, thrusting deeper into me. It was feeling so good. I finally scooted to another position almost on my knees. I was so weak. I was confused, too, because I couldn't remember who I was having sex with. Was it Dexter or Travis? Why was he playing with my mind? I had to shift gears and think about something else, but just like a record player with a skipping needle on a scratched album, my mind was stuck. Suddenly, my body shook and Dexter let out a long groan. As he pumped faster and faster into me, both of us released ourselves into a feeling of passion and paradise. That was a first for me. Having two orgasms back to back was basically unheard of for me. Dexter fell on top of me and my body crashed gently into the bed. After kissing my forehead and neck, he rolled off me and cuddled my body up against his in a spoon-like fashion. While I lay there, he held me until I heard him snoring in my ear. Then I gently pushed him away from me.

As I lay in bed, waiting for sleep to come, I thought about how much I really loved my husband. Was it possible to be in love with two men? Nah! I didn't think so, but why couldn't I release Travis from my mind? Before I could get the answer I was seeking, I fell fast asleep. I was so spent sexually that I slept for more than five hours, which was a major feat for me.

Chapter 12

The Commitment is Sacred

Friday morning, I dropped Li'l Dexter off at his school. As I walked him into the building, Principal Morgan stopped to speak to me. "Your son is playing well on the soccer team. He is also performing well in all his classes. He is such a well-mannered young man."

"Why thank you. Knowing that will start my day off great. I appreciate you telling me that. You know most of the time when administrators and teachers talk to a parent it is usually about something negative the child has done. I'm grateful to know you notice the good things our children do and you are so willing to let us parents know. By the way, I will be attending the PTA meeting on Monday."

"I look forward to seeing you there." Mr. Morgan shook my hand and then walked down the hall. I stood there smiling, looking around the building, which was so nice and clean. The students were rushing to class. While I was talking to the principal, Dexter had rushed to his classroom. Before leaving the building, I peeked into Dexter's classroom; he was looking through his book.

I waved at his teacher and then left the building.

Once in the car, I heard my cell ringing and pulled it out from deep inside of my purse. I answered the phone with a smile, because my caller ID informed me it was Pamela. I hadn't spoken to her in days. I wanted to share my feelings with her. I wanted her to understand how I was feeling. I needed my best friend to help me sort through this confusion and, mostly, I needed her to convince me not to kick Sarah's narrow ass.

"What's going on, girl?" Pamela always spoke with so much confidence.

"Hi, lady. I don't want to fight with you. I need my friend to be here for me. I am so confused. Don't abandon me, Pamela, because of what I am going through."

"Malika, I am not abandoning you. You know I love you, but I really want you to think about how your actions might affect your family, your workers, and also, our relationship."

"What do you mean our relationship? How can my fucking someone else affect us?"

"Think about it, girl. We are like family. Our husbands are friends too. It is not just about you. What about the rest of us? Have you once thought about that?"

"Hell no! I am thinking about my needs. Not yours, not Dexter's, not anyone's. What about me and how I am feeling?"

"Let's talk about this over lunch. Would you meet me at the Salad Bowl at eleven-thirty? I have a meeting near Lindell around ten A.M. The meeting is scheduled to end before eleven. Isn't that close to your office, too?"

"Yes, I can meet you there. Don't come talking no shit, okay? I just want you to listen to me."

Pamela asked, "Malika, don't I always listen to you? Even when I don't like what you are saying, I'm still listening."

"I guess you are right. Well, I'll see you at eleven-thirty. Have a great morning."

"You do the same, girly."

"See you later."

"Later, Malika."

As I walked into the office, I felt a sense of doom. It seemed that ever since I found out Sarah had feelings for Travis and hated me the office had that dry, stale feeling. It was as if the air had this maddening, confusing state. Like any minute, something negative was going to happen. I just didn't have the energy. I was exhausted. I wasn't sleeping well at night because Travis was sexing me to death in my dreams. It was as if I could feel every touch. Sometimes, I found myself waiting for him to appear.

Was I falling so hard that I was losing my mind? Was this why Zandra and Pamela were fighting to stop me from doing something so stupid? I felt sorry that they couldn't save me, but I couldn't help myself. I had to live for me and find my own happiness. I decided I was going to ask Dexter to go to counseling with me. Without help I wasn't about to let my girls stop me from experiencing something I felt would be absolutely passionate for me. Plus, I knew those heifers had strayed. Hell, all the signs were there. Like the time Pamela's daughter called and asked me if her mom was still at the house with me, and I hadn't even seen her. I had to call her butt and tell her to call home. Was she being scandalous that day too? She wouldn't tell me a thing about her whereabouts. I knew she was up to something.

Zandra knew she needed to quit. I almost caught her coming out of a hotel room on Lindbergh Boulevard, where I was attending a seminar. I left the meeting room to go to the restroom and spotted her coming off the elevator. When I called her name, she practically ran out of the building. She was coming down the elevator from the rooms located on the upper floors. The hotel conference areas were only on the bottom floor. So she was definitely doing something. When I confronted her later, she acted as if she did not know what the hell I was talking about. So I knew what that trick was up to. So why in the hell were they out here getting dick, but didn't want me to?

After speaking to my staff and briefing them on activities we had planned for the day, I opened my office door, turned the light on, and opened my briefcase to pull out my agenda. Turning quickly toward the left, I hit the button on my computer to turn it on. I was going to read my e-mail first, something I did most days before returning calls. E-mails for me were the way I communicated with mostly everyone—business associates, family, politicians, and even staff. I preferred e-mails because I could easily save files without having to use so much ink printing, then taxing my secretary to file, organize, and label everything. Yes, e-mails were certainly a great documentation tool for me. I also backed up my computer and saved the files to my data disk. No information could escape me. The staff knew I was a stickler for organization and I kept everything in order. So I knew they too were careful about what they sent me.

My first e-mail of the day was from Samantha. She wanted to know if we could meet for lunch later that week. I e-mailed her a list of my available days and times. As I scrolled down I read other messages, deleting some that slipped through our firewall, like "grow a larger penis in five days" or "I give the best oral sex."

I stopped at an e-mail from Travis. It read:

> Good morning, Malika!
> I was wondering if you want to go to lunch today.

Wanted to discuss with you some server problems you are having. Let me know. I will check my e-mails again by 11:00 or just call me on my cell.
Travis

I could not stop that smile from stretching across my face. I could feel it. It suddenly felt as if I was liberated. I didn't know. I could only explain it like this: My day was sorta gloomy, like a black-and-white movie. When I read his e-mail, I suddenly felt gleeful and cheerful, which made me feel like I was in living colors. I could feel myself becoming more vibrant and happy, even though I wasn't sad. This man brought stuff out of me. Not only did I see it and feel it, so did some of my staff.

As I looked up, Felicia walked in. "Malika, you must have heard from Mr. Travis," she said with a huge smile on her face. I simply laughed. She knew me better than I thought. But I couldn't let on.

"What can I do for you today?"

"I was wondering if you wanted me to go shopping at the dollar store to find some decent gifts like lotions, books, and things for the kitchen that our parents could use. We are having that activity next week with the parents and we need door prizes."

"That's fine. Take the corporate American Express and spend about three hundred dollars. You can also go to one of the other stores like Kmart, Walmart, or Target and purchase some nice gifts like pots and pans, telephones, lotion and cologne gift sets, bedding for the babies, and other baby gifts."

"That sounds like a winner. Do you want Bridgett to go with me?"

"You will have to ask her. She may have a scheduled health workshop in the community."

"Okay, I will check with her. Thanks, Malika."

"Oh, here is the card. Make sure you take your staff ID and driver's license."

"I'm covered. I got this. You know me."

Smiling, I laughed. "You are right. I do know you." Felicia walked out of the office. Then I returned to my e-mail. I already had a lunch date. I wanted to cancel it badly to be with Travis, but I couldn't. Pamela was going to be sitting at the Salad Bowl at 11:30 A.M. and I could not disappoint her. So I e-mailed Travis back.

> Hi, Travis,
>
> I can't make it today. I already have a lunch appointment. Maybe you can stop by later.

I hit the send button. Within five minutes, the phone at my extension rang. It was him. He simply said, "I will be there around four o'clock today."

"Okay, I'll see you then. Have a great day," I said.

Smiling to myself, I wondered if he could feel how happy he made me. As a matter of fact, I was glowing and I felt it. You know how old folks say they can tell you are pregnant because your eyes are glowing? Well, if anyone saw me now, they would be dead wrong about me being pregnant, unless I could get pregnant having hot passionate sex in my dreams. In that case, I would be nine months pregnant by now—ready to deliver.

Chapter 13

Two Friends, Two Views

I rushed out of the office, trying to get to the Salad Bowl by 11:30 A.M. If I got there late, Pamela would have a fit. She was always prompt. I was too, most of the time. But I had an unexpected encounter with silly-ass Sarah.

Sarah saw me leaving and she decided she needed help with a client.

"Malika, I need to discuss a case with you. Do you have time or do you want me to wait until you come back? You seem so excited, like you are about to meet Travis."

"What do you need?"

"Are you meeting Travis? Because if you are, like I said, I will wait until you return."

"What part of this do you not understand, Sarah? I asked you politely to stay out of my business." Looking around to make sure that no witnesses were present, I turned back to Sarah and hissed, "Do your job or you are history!"

"All I did was ask you a question. I'm sorry. I didn't mean to get into your business. Plus, I thought Travis was a contractor and not someone you personally dated."

I didn't respond to her statement. "Upon my return, Sarah, I will be auditing your record files." I walked quickly but calmly to my secretary. "Please pull Sarah's files and lock them in my office, right now."

"Right away, Malika." Ingrid got up and strutted to the file cabinets and began removing Sarah's file.

Turning swiftly to Sarah, I smiled. I saw her fear. She had played the wrong card with me at the wrong time and payback was going to be a motherfucker. I hummed my favorite song as I walked out the door. I could feel the hatred from her hitting me in the back like darts on a dartboard. But I felt nothing but happiness, because I knew that the ball was back in my court.

As I drove to the Salad Bowl, I thought hard about my life and how I got into my current situation. I was a Christian, though I knew sometimes I cussed too much. But believe me I was pushed to say things I normally wouldn't say. Plus, when I became overly stressed, I might have said anything. But I prayed often to God to clean my filthy mouth and to help me to control my anger. There were many times when I felt people were trying to use me because of my position in management. Often, people who befriended me thought they knew me and they began to think that I was soft and they could do anything to me. Usually, they were fired because they overplayed their hand too soon. What these employees failed to understand was that there was always at least one person on the job who had my back. It never failed, because not everybody was out to malign, cause problems, or backstab. Most reasonable folks knew they needed a letter of reference to get another job and that they had to explain any gap in their employment history, so they tried to stay on my good side. I hated that Sarah and I were having problems, especially over a man who wasn't ours.

Once I arrived at the Salad Bowl, I parked and walked into the restaurant where I sought out Pamela.

I found her sitting at a table, looking out of the window, facing Lindell Boulevard. I walked over and she stood up and hugged me.

"You look so good, Malika. Are you losing weight?"

"It's possible. I tend to lose weight when I am stressed out."

"Well, you are simply going to have to let that stress go. It is much more harmful to hold on to that stuff."

"That's easier said than done. Let's go through the line and select our food."

As we walked toward the line, I stopped briefly to speak to two ladies I knew from the social service industry. We chatted briefly, and then I continued to the line and selected a raisin and carrot salad, a side vegetable salad, and some baked codfish. Returning to our seats, Pamela and I bowed our heads and prayed over our meals. Tasting the codfish, I informed Pamela that it was quite tasty while pushing it toward her to sample.

"Wow! That is very good. I should have selected that. Now back to you, my friend. What are we going to do with you and this man?"

"You know it is not that simple. After all, something like this doesn't happen every day. How often does a married woman fall for another married man?"

"Well, who's to say that you are in love and not just infatuated?"

"I know the difference between lust and love, and to be honest, I am in love with two men."

"Malika, get over that man. If you start seeing him, your life will just get complicated. Are you willing to give up your marriage for this man? After all, what do you really know about this Travis?"

"I know that he turns me on. I also know that I can talk to him about anything and he listens and understands."

"Maybe it's an act. Your husband listens and understands your needs."

"You are right. He did do that and many other things when we first got married, but after so many years together, I believe things have changed. After all, couples get used to each other and become less sympathetic and less understanding during the course of their marriage. Right now, I think that is exactly what has happened in my marriage."

"You know what, Malika? Getting involved with another man will only make matters worse in your marriage. Trust me, I know."

"I knew that you had stepped out before! When did this happen and who was it with?"

"It doesn't matter the who or what, but it was last year and things did not work out. I met this guy named Jonathan. I fell hard for him, but he wanted only sex. At first, I could deal with that because the sex was great. But you know what? I really did fall hard and wanted more, but he just kicked me to the curb."

"Well, that happened with you and I can't live by your experiences. I have to live by my own."

"You know, Malika, nothing I say will change your mind. All I have to say is, this is your life and there is nothing I can do to stop you. But I want you to consider this one thing: when you are with Travis, think about his wife and children. Think how you would feel if you were in her place and some hot professional woman had her sights set on stealing your husband."

"Actually, I don't know if that's what's happening. But I'm going to send him back home. I just want to spend time with him. I am not giving up my marriage and my son. I do love my husband. I love them both."

"Well, I'm not sure you can be in love with two men at the same time."

"I'm not sure either, but I am. So for right now, I just want you to be here for me and to listen."

"I can do that for you, but I just don't want you to make the same mistakes I did. It was very painful for me."

"Are you over him?"

"Yes. But it took a long time."

"He really hurt you?"

"Yes."

"I have to follow my heart and right now, it craves two men."

Pamela and I sat there at that table, by the huge picture window, staring at the cars that passed. We were deep in thought. I was thinking about Travis and how this happened to me. Yes, I needed counseling.

After we finished our lunch, we hugged and parted ways. She assured me she would always be my friend and be there whenever I needed her and I assured her the same. I was so glad we had lunch, because I knew she cared a lot about me and my happiness, and she wanted the best for me. That gave me the strength and the will to try again to talk to my husband. I had to make him listen. It was the only way I would be able to resist temptation. Dexter had to understand my needs.

I drove back to the office and asked my secretary, Ingrid, for Sarah's files. I was ready to audit to see what she had been doing with her clients. I could not continue to battle with a subordinate every day. I felt if the other staff continued to witness this without Sarah receiving some type of repercussions, they would eventually begin to try me and that was not going to happen. So I was on a mission. I was going to let this woman go and move forward with our program's mission.

As I read Sarah's files, I immediately noticed that she had not made visits in the last six weeks with 60 percent of her clients. This was a major no-no as our contract specifically stated that we had to make biweekly visits. That was strike one. Strike two occurred when I contacted 10 percent of her clients, surveyed our services with them, and was told by the clients that they were not satisfied with Sarah. Other complaints against Sarah ranged from never returning calls to losing their important paperwork. Others said Sarah was not dependable. She promised to return with things they had requested and she never did. I assured the program participants that I would look into their complaints and would get back to each of them. I planned to meet with her the next day after I documented everything and figured out my plan of action.

As I documented information on Sarah, my phone rang.

"Hello?"

"Are we still on for today?"

"Yes, Travis, we are."

"I'll see you at four."

I hung up the phone and I knew a smile stretched across my face because I could feel it almost touching my ears. Boy, I loved me some Travis. As I sat there, thinking and smiling, the phone rang again.

"Hey, Karen, how are you?"

"Girl, I'm fine. How's the family?"

"Everyone here is fine. How are Tim and Shannon?"

"They are all fine. I talked to Mom and she said that you lost some weight. I want to know how much and what did you do to lose it?"

"I'm not sure, but I may have dropped about two dress sizes."

"Girl, that is good. But you know it is not enough. You need to lose about thirty more pounds. You know men don't want fat women. You could lose your husband if you don't get all that weight off you."

"Karen, it seems to me that you are the only one who is worried about my weight. Dexter isn't complaining."

"Men usually don't. They just walk out on you when you least expect it. Trust me, I work with nothing but men and I hear them discussing this all the time. Yeah, they want to have sex with a fat woman, but they don't take them home for keeps."

"Karen, you have two seconds before I slam this phone in your ear."

"Why do you get so upset when I try to help you? I am your sister and if I don't tell you stuff, who will? You should trust your own sister enough to listen. After all, I do love you."

"You sure have a funny way of showing it. You don't do anything but piss folks off because you talk too much. There are some things you should keep to yourself. Be glad that I'm your sister because anybody else would beat your ass."

"This conversation is over."

I was shocked. Karen actually slammed the phone in my ear. That really surprised me. Karen was the type of person who everyone feared. No one wanted to hear anything bad about themselves from her. She was beautiful.

She had perfect features and was the perfect dress size, about a size four. Her bad qualities were that she knew it and treated others as if they should all bow down to be in her presence. Her husband was so in love with her that he could see no wrong in her. But others dreaded her coming around. It was too much trouble. You had to clean your home from top to bottom and purchase new things, because she would be so critical of everything in your house. You either let her think you were doing poorly financially or put on a big façade and pray her stay with you would be short.

Karen would hurt your feelings and would actually think you were the one with a problem if you fought back. She would be pissed if you said something to hurt her feelings. She could dish it out, but she couldn't take it.

I, on the other hand, was fed up with her and her fat jokes. I was ready to battle, but Mom begged me to keep peace in the family. Karen had one more time and it was on.

I quickly finished documenting my notes on Sarah's files. Now I had to write a corrective plan of action. This would be the first step in forcing her out. The corrective plan would be for thirty days and I would make it too difficult for her to meet her goals. After I wrote up what I needed her to accomplish, I put the plan in a manila folder, locked it in my desk drawer, and cleaned off most of my desk. Everyone had left the office except for Felicia, who was organizing her things before she left. The social workers and the nurse were out on home visits, seeing their clients. Ingrid left earlier to attend her daughters' teacher and parent meeting. I could hear Felicia locking her file cabinets. It just happened to work out that the office was nearly empty. Most days were like this because it was flexible since we were a home visiting program and we arranged our schedules around the families. Travis would be there in thirty minutes and I preferred that Felicia would not be in the office.

Felicia finally came to my office and said she was leaving.

"Come on, Malika. Let's go. You know I don't want to leave you here alone."

"That's okay. I have a lot of work to finish. You can leave. I will not stay late."

"All right. You be safe and call me on my cell if you need me."

"I'll call you if I need you, but really, I will be okay." Felicia was finally gone. Hopefully, she would not bump into Travis on her way out. But he wasn't due for another twenty minutes. In the meantime, I decided to read my e-mail.

Around 4:00 P.M., I heard someone knocking on the door. I waited a minute before opening it. I didn't want him to think I was just sitting there waiting for him. When I opened the door, my smile felt like it had expanded across my face and was as wide as the Mississippi River. I hated that shit. I knew he could read my feelings because how I felt about him was all over my face.

"Hi, Travis, how are you?"

"I'm fine. Can I come in?"

Travis walked over to the network center and began to fiddle with the system. I walked into my office. Sitting at my desk, I had a clear view of him. Occasionally, I would look up and he would be staring at me and smiling. Damn, he was handsome. I would smile back and continue to work. When I looked up the fifth time, he was not at the network. I peeped around and he suddenly appeared in my office.

"I see you are working hard," he said.

"Yes, you can say that," I replied. "Come in, I can spare a minute."

Travis took a seat in front of me. We began to talk about the network system. "Your network is fine, but I wanted to make some suggestions on increasing your hard drive."

"Do we need to do that?"

"Yes. With the amount of data your staff is entering into the system it is slowing down how the commands are responding."

"Will that be costly?"

"Not really, I can check around and give you three bids for the things you'll need."

"Okay, then do that and we'll look at the best bid and go from there."

I had a black horoscope book on my desk. He picked it up and found his sign. He was a Scorpio. From what I had read and heard from so many folks, the Scorpio was a total freak. Hell, that turned me on even more, knowing that was his sign. I told him I was a Capricorn and we looked each other's signs up and read them. We were compatible. That was good. Though I really didn't believe in horoscopes, it was good to know that even that book made us a possibility.

"Travis, how do you get men to listen, you know, to hear what is really being said?"

"To get a man or a woman to listen to you, remove all interruptions; or take them out of what is familiar to them. This way they will pay attention to what you have to say." Then he turned back to look at the book he was holding in his hand. Travis lifted the book up high in the air, he asked, " How often do you look at this book?"

"Pretty much never. It's the first time I opened it while you and I looked through it."

"Why?" He shifted in his chair and turned to face me directly, waiting on my response.

"I get too many interruptions at the office and the book is always here. There was no rush to read it."

I thought he was through with our conversation about getting a man to listen because he was so focused on that book. But he quickly returned back to our initial conversation.

"To get a man to listen, remove him from his comfort zone. Take him away from his regular patterns. It's like this. You expect your significant other to be there for you. Usually they are unless they are working or shopping, but they always return. You expect your spouse to return because they always do. So there is nothing new. You have these patterns and basically, folks keep to them. It doesn't mean you don't love the person, it's just that you know they will always be there."

"But you shouldn't bank on that," I said. "If you ignore your spouse, eventually, someone else will pay attention, then there's trouble. People want to be noticed, touched, and loved. If their spouse doesn't do it, somebody else will."

"That's why it is so important to take a person out of their normal comfort zone. It's like a breath of fresh air. It's like this book on your desk; it becomes useless if you never read it. Same thing with relationships! You have to keep talking to make things happen. If they don't hear you in a familiar place, do something different." He used the book to demonstrate it couldn't help you if you never read it, similar to a man not being able to hear your concerns if you couldn't get his full attention. So to fix the problem, he needed to know there was one.

"Well, my friend is thinking about having an affair because her husband doesn't pay attention to her and she feels insignificant."

"Maybe she needs to talk to her husband about her feelings. I'm talking about really giving examples, removing all interruptions like the TV and get him to listen."

"Trust me, she did. But he told her that he was happy and she should be too."

"She needs to keep talking. Men are hardheaded. You have to make them see things your way."

"My friend is almost there. She is very interested in this man. All he needs to do is say the word and it's on."

"She needs to take a vacation with him. I'm sure that will help."

Suddenly a smile rushed across my face. It felt like a light bulb was turned on. "You know that's a good idea."

Travis sat there smiling. A couple of times I noticed him staring at the picture of my husband. Maybe he knew it was me I was referring to. I could tell by the way that he looked at me. Even if he wasn't sure it was me, his face showed hopefulness.

We talked a long time about relationships. He didn't divulge any additional information about himself. I still did not know much about him. But I didn't really care. All I knew was we were together, smiling in each other's face for almost three hours. I was glad Dexter was picking up our son or the school would have been calling me more than an hour ago. It was almost seven o'clock and I was still not ready to leave.

"Let's get ready to go," Travis said.

"All right, Travis, let me shut down my computer."

As I walked over to get my purse out of my file cabinet, I could feel his eyes on my ass. I sort of bent over, so he could get a better look. *Come on, Travis, go after this ass.*

We walked out the door together, almost touching each other. He smelled so good. I couldn't keep it to myself.

"What are you wearing? You smell good."

"I'm not sure. Something my wife bought me."

Why the hell you bring her up? You are confusing me. You sit your ass in my face for three hours and now you mention her? Stop playing with my heart. We talked all the way down to our cars. He opened my door and I got in. We talked for another thirty minutes. He put his head through my window, and said, "We better get going."

"I know. I don't know where we get so much to talk about."

"Malika, we have a lot in common."

I smiled. I wanted to kiss him. Our faces were so close, but I didn't know what to do. I had been married so long, I was clueless. He was staring deep into my eyes with his head inside my window. He was in my personal space. I could tell he wanted to kiss me, but he too seemed afraid. Why couldn't I just pucker up and kiss him?

"Be safe and I'll call you for lunch."

"All right," I said as I started my car and left. As I pulled out of the parking lot, my phone rang. It was Travis.

"Malika, let's go to lunch Friday."

"All right, Travis, I'll see you then. Call me."

"I will. Good-bye."

"Bye."

I dialed my friend, Pamela. She picked up on the second ring.

"Girl, I have been with Travis for more than three hours."

"You didn't fuck him, did you?"

"I wish."

"Tell me what the hell you were doing for three hours?"

"We were talking. But I wish we did more. I'm tired of waiting. I want that man extremely bad."

"You need to take your ass home and fuck Dexter. Stay your butt out of trouble."

"Yeah, right! I am taking my butt to my family, but that will not stop what I want to do."

"I have one question, Malika. Does this man know you have fallen for him?"

"He must know. Why else would he sit around me like that?"

"Maybe he is trying to keep his marriage intact."

"You know what, Pamela? I don't want to break up his home. Like I told you, I love Dexter. I just want some excitement in my life. I'm attracted to this man. I have never stepped out on my relationship. This would be a first."

"That's why you should not partake in that sin because you will only fall in love with him."

"I know you're right. I'm basically there now. I know this is trouble, but I feel like I'm riding on a fast-moving train and soon it's going to slow down and something is going to happen."

We chatted about twenty minutes before I turned into my subdivision. "I'll call you tomorrow and we'll talk more," I said as I pulled into my garage. "I'm at home in the garage now."

"Go give Dexter some and forget about Travis."

"Oh, I am going to give Dexter some, but it's not going to stop me from wanting Travis."

"Bye, girl."

"Bye."

Chapter 14

Decisions Are for the Weak at Heart

I drove to the office bright and early. It was a cold but sunny Wednesday morning and I was scheduled to do battle with Sarah at 10:00. This was going to be a no-brainier for me. I would read her the riot act and she could do what I stated in her corrective plan or get to stepping.

As I pulled into the office lot, I saw Travis's black Mercedes. *Damn, I can't keep going through this. Why is he here so early? I feel so jumbled in my mind with him. Why is he here now? It's like he is torturing me. I feel like I'm out of control. Like I'm topsy-turvy! I can't work or think when he is around me. Yet we are not moving forward or backward. We are at a standstill. How did I get here?* I hit my steering wheel in frustration. *I have to go in. Something has to give soon. I'm tired of this back and forth.* I freshened up my lipstick, grabbed my briefcase, and walked into the office building. I spoke to several other tenants before getting on the elevator. When the elevator arrived, I stepped on and rode to the second floor.

I had a great night with Dexter the night before. I asked him to go to counseling and he said he would think about it. We also planned a trip for the summer. We briefly discussed some family issues and talked about our son and his achievements. He was proud of

Li'l Dexter and that made me feel really good. When we went to bed, he went after me. I had an explosive orgasm. True, I was thinking about Travis, but Dexter did all the work and did he whip it on me. I was huffing and puffing all over the bed. He was stroking me with that thick, fat, pretty dick. Dexter had a pretty dick. I hadn't seen many others except in magazines, but my man had a nice one and he knew exactly how to use it. That was why I had never stepped out. I was satisfied sexually, but emotionally I was missing so much that it increased my sexual appetite. Because I was so emotionally hungry, I started believing that maybe that was why I wanted Travis. He fed me emotionally.

I walked into the office, satisfied and ready to do battle. But first things first, I needed to know why Travis was at the office so early. As I put my key in the door and walked into the office, I heard Felicia's big mouth, laughing and playing around with Travis.

"Good morning, Malika," Felicia said with a huge smile on her face.

"Good morning, Felicia. Hi, Travis, how are you?"

"I'm fine. Sorry to be here so early, but I checked the system before I left this morning from my house and saw that you were having problems. As you know I can check everything from my office or home. Since I live so close to the office, I wanted to check everything out, because my staff and I are scheduled out at other offices and it would be difficult to get in touch with us today."

Yeah, right. It's not the system. Sarah said he was the worst IT man she'd ever seen, but the truth was becoming clear. Travis and I were having the same problems and he was infatuated with me too. *There is no way we are having these kinds of problems and my staff or I are not affected. I know things are coming to a conclusion soon because this is getting old.* Travis needed to admit he wanted to be around me, just like I enjoyed his presence.

"Thanks. I'm glad you checked. I have too much work to do today and I need access to my computer."

Felicia and I walked into my office. She wanted to know if I needed anything from her, because she was going to work in the field most of the day. I told her I needed her to stay around until 11:00 A.M., and then I too would be leaving. She went to work at her desk. I wanted her around while I met with Sarah. She would be able to call the leasing office to summon the police who worked in the building should things go wrong.

Travis stuck his head through my door. "Everything is fine. System is working. I'll see you Friday. I'll pick you up at noon."

"Okay, and thanks so much for coming by."

He waved his hand up in the air as if to say it was nothing and then he was gone. I worked on two letters before Sarah appeared at my door. It was 10:00 and I guessed she couldn't wait to see what the meeting was about.

Before we could get started, she asked me about Travis. I wanted to knock the shit out of her, but I kept thinking that soon she would be gone. She was wearing down my patience.

"Travis was here so early. I think he likes you, Malika. He finds things wrong with the system just to give him a reason to come see you."

"I'm not here to hear your thoughts on the IT person. I just want to meet with you about your level of work." *Sarah even noticed that he was lying about our system. I'm sure the other staff knew too.*

"Dang, Malika, are you mad because I asked you about Travis? Everybody knows he likes you."

"I can't believe you. I call you into my office to talk about your work performance and you talk to me about the contractor. What is wrong with you?"

"Ain't nothing wrong with me. You don't like me and you never did. That is why you are always writing me up. I don't see you writing up the other workers."

"Is it possible that I am writing you up because of your level of work? This is about you, not anyone else. I am speaking to you about your attitude, your work performance, and your clients."

After I went over everything with Sarah, she sat there stung. She knew her job was gone. I made it damn near impossible to meet the corrective action plan and all she could say was, "I want to meet with Mrs. Connors."

"No problem. I will contact her and let her know you want to meet with her. But right now I need you to get back to work and start on that plan."

Sarah huffed out of my office. I later called Samantha and told her Sarah was requesting a meeting with her. She gave her an appointment for Friday at 11:00 A.M. I gave the appointment time to Sarah. The rest of the day went by fine. Sarah stayed to herself and scheduled appointments with her clients. The other workers were busy in the field. Felicia changed her appointments to stay in the office since Sarah told her what was going on. Ingrid, my secretary, stayed in the office until the end of the day. They had heard Sarah complaining loudly about that bitch, which was me, and how she was going to tell the big boss on me.

Chapter 15

All Hell Breaks Loose

Samantha met with me about Sarah. She was concerned that I had gone from fall to winter with so many activities and soon it would be spring and I had not taken a vacation. She was, however, in agreement with me about Sarah. She felt she must go, because she said some very unprofessional things about me when meeting with my boss. First, she showed her an e-mail I had sent her and said I was sexually harassing her. I had to admit, Sarah was good.

I had sent her an e-mail sometime back in October around Halloween. Someone sent it to me and I was sitting at my desk, laughing, when she passed my office. She walked in and asked what I was laughing at. I told her and she looked at the e-mail and laughed. She pleaded for me to send it to her and I did. It was about a man who was walking past a hotel. A maid had tossed out some dirty white sheets, which were stained. The sheets went over the head of the man and they scared him to death, because he thought it was a ghost flying out of the sky. In the window of the hotel stood two half-dressed couples, looking out to see who was screaming.

She gave a copy to Samantha and accused me of sending an e-mail that she didn't want. So in essence, since the couples were in a hotel and partly dressed, she said I was sexually harassing her. Samantha was a smart woman though and she asked her if she had ever asked me to stop sending her e-mails and she said no. Samantha told her if she never told me my e-mails bothered her, it was not sexual harassment. You had to let someone know that something was bothering you, so they could stop.

She then told Samantha I made her type up my church work and showed her labels that I had her make when my secretary was out. Some church members' names were on the form, because they had donated money, services, and other goods to the program and we were sending thank-you letters to them. So she took something that had some truth to it and expanded it. But what she didn't know was I had written in my monthly reports to Samantha and the board of directors about the contributions to our program from my church and other churches throughout the community. So they knew my church had participated in our program. So this made Sarah's complaints not valid.

She also said I made her burn R&B compact discs for the office staff and families. Again, that was a lie. I allowed her to burn a Mary Mary CD in my office for all the staff at her request. In essence, none of her complaints were valid. So her grievances against me were basically bogus. For a solid week, instead of working on her plan, she plotted to get me, thus, potentially firing herself.

The following week, I scheduled an appointment with Sarah, but instead of meeting at the designated time, she walked into my office and handed me her resignation. I simply read it and walked her to her desk. I asked her to get her personal belongings and leave the building immediately.

"I can't believe you! Why are you harassing me?" She threw up her hands in exasperation and raised her voice loud so that others could hear. She reacted over-dramatically.

"Sarah, just get your personal belongings and leave. Whatever is left I will have couriered to you."

She stuck her foot out, put her hands on her hips, and smacked her lips. "In case you didn't read my resignation, it is for three weeks from this day. So basically, I don't understand why you are making me leave now."

Raising my hands up in the air to demonstrate that I had given up I said, "No more talking. Give me the company-issued cell phone, the Palm Pilot, and the office keys." I tossed aside my hair that flung over my eye. "As I said previously, your personal items will be sent to you by week's end."

Sarah huffed and puffed. She grabbed her desk drawer and roughly pulled it open. Clutching a folder, she violently flung her cell phone onto her desk. She puffed out air from her mouth, giving the appearance of defeat, like she couldn't believe she was beat at her own game. She snatched her purse and pointed to the other office equipment on her desk. Then she gripped her little jacket and stormed out of the office.

"Thanks, Felicia and Ingrid," I said to the two women as they stood by and witnessed what happened. "I appreciate your support. Ingrid, please clear out the rest of Sarah's personal items. Felicia, if you don't mind, would you help her? Just place the items on the desk and I will contact security to come and secure everything."

As I walked away, I felt refreshed. No more would I have to argue with Sarah over her work or her lack of respect for me. No more would I have to worry about her spreading dirty rumors about me around the office. If rumors were going to be spread, it wouldn't be her doing the spreading. I laughed because I had won.

"Malika, Samantha is on the phone for you. She is on line one."

"Thanks, Ingrid, please put the call through to my office."

I informed Samantha of Sarah's resignation and my actions. I told her I was securing our computer data and office files. She thanked me for thinking ahead and asked me to fax her copies of the corrective action plan, Sarah's resignation, and any other written documentation I had. We then scheduled a meeting together for Friday at 8:00 A.M. to prepare for Sarah should she keep the prescheduled meeting with Samantha.

On Friday morning, I met with Samantha. She came to my office. She had informed Sarah the meeting would be held in my conference room. We met about the budget and about Sarah's resignation. She wanted to know what happened and why Sarah had suddenly changed. I made sure she knew and understood that I had no clue. It really was sudden. Other than me thinking that she was jealous, I really never understood how quickly she changed to the person she became. Samantha and I worked over some program implementation plans and before we realized it, it was noon. Sarah never showed up for her meeting with Samantha. We worked right past the noon hour.

Around 12:10, Ingrid informed me that Travis was waiting. I asked her to let him know that I would be with him shortly.

"Malika, why don't you ask Travis to join us. I would like to chat with him about the network system."

I walked out and as soon as I saw him, that stupid smile crossed my face. Immediately, I became moist between the legs. Was the devil in my pussy? What was he trying to do to me?

Travis and I walked back into my office and Samantha stood to shake his hand. We all chatted for about an hour. I tried desperately to hide my smile and the glow in my eyes. Travis could not hide his feelings either. Whenever he talked or responded to a question, he would look at me and smile. Even though Samantha asked the question he would answer while staring at me.

"Travis, Malika told me that you had submitted three bids to increase the hardware on the network. Do you think anything else will be needed to enhance the system? We have some additional funds in our equipment line, so it would be a good time to do some improvements."

"Malika has been extremely helpful in keeping me informed about the work flow and the increase in client reporting of goals. I think because of the increase in clients and their activities, it would be wise to invest in a good backup system. You have an adequate one now, but because Malika and her staff are doing such a good job here, the backup system needs to be larger and more backup tapes are needed." He reached over and touched my hands while never taking his eyes off me. *Dang, that boy's feelings are obvious.*

"Okay that's good. Please add the cost to the bids and resubmit it to Malika."

"I'll do that."

Samantha and Travis proceeded to discuss the new program design for the MASK program. It seemed as if she would never leave. Finally, as our conversation ended, Travis made a blooper.

"Travis, it has been so wonderful talking to you. As I stated, if you can design this program for me, I would certainly appreciate it. Just submit the proposal to Malika and once I receive it, I will schedule another meeting with the three of us. Malika told me you have done an outstanding job with her system by making it virtually trouble-free. Continue to take care of her."

"No problem," Travis said. "Anything for my baby."

"Thank you. I'll see you and Malika next week. Malika, would you walk me to the elevator?"

As Samantha and I walked, I could sense something was heavy on her mind. Samantha and I were extremely close. When we met each other, we immediately clicked. She could read me too.

"Malika, are you and Travis seeing each other?"

"No, Samantha. Why did you ask me that?"

"I don't think you realized that when I asked him to take care of you, he said he would take care of his baby."

"No, he didn't say that. Did he?"

"Malika, he did. I don't know why you didn't hear it."

"I briefly looked down and reviewed the bids. I didn't hear him say that."

"Well, he did say it."

"Trust me, Samantha, I am not seeing him."

"Be careful. You and he are both married. Don't bring trouble to your life. It is obvious that he is into you. Just tread lightly."

"Samantha, did you really hear him call me baby?"

"Yes, and as I said, please be careful. Both of you are wearing your feelings on your faces. Your attraction for each other is written clearly across your faces."

I briefly thought back to what Sarah was saying. Maybe she was right. Our faces told the story. But I was angry at Sarah because of my controlling issues and felt that rather than serve our clients and do what I hired her to do, she was worried about what I was doing with a man. I didn't pay her to probe my life and to treat me badly because she liked the same man I did. I could honestly say I was angrier at the way Sarah treated me and the disrespect she showed. Plus, I had caught her on several occasions calling me a bitch and other names. But with Samantha she was showing she cared about me and wanted me to be careful. Sarah also spent time spreading rumors about what she thought she knew.

The elevator arrived and Samantha walked forward to get on it. She rubbed her left temple, and closed her eyes." I better be leaving, my head is throbbing."

"Have you been to the doctor? Because you have been complaining for two weeks about your headaches."

"I think it is my blood pressure. I've been rather stressed lately."

"Whatever it is, please let it go."

We hugged and she waved at me as the doors of the elevator closed.

I walked to the office and asked Travis if he wanted to reschedule, and he said no. "Let's go."

"All right. Bye, Ingrid. I'll be back soon."

"Have a good lunch."

"Thanks," Travis and I both said at the same time.

Travis and I had a wonderful lunch. He took me to this really private and very intimate restaurant. I had never heard of it.

As we talked, I imagined him sucking my breasts. I couldn't understand his words. Everything was fuzzy. I imagined his dick in my mouth. *As our eyes met, I sucked harder. I could swear that he moaned.* He brought me quickly back to the present.

"How are you and your husband doing?"

"We are fine. Why did you ask?"

"I don't know. I guess I was thinking about your friend."

"Oh, yeah, she and her husband are going to go for counseling and she said they are going to plan a trip for the early summer,"

"That's good."

He put his hand under the table and I thought I saw him press down on his dick. I gazed at him and he did the same. I thought, *Lord, please let me have one night with him. Let him ask me to go with him. Grant this, Lord.*

Now, I had it bad when I was begging God to let me have my lustful ways with a man who was not my husband. This was something God would not approve of and here I was begging Him. I had this man in my thoughts so bad that I was begging God who said that we should not lust. I was asking Him to let me break His law. Was I a damn fool or what?

When we got back into his car, he gently held my hand as we talked. Then he quickly moved his as if he did not realize what he was doing. We were heading for trouble and we were about to crash, but it was a crash I was looking happily to have.

When he pulled up to the building, he jumped out of the car and opened my door. We walked and smiled to the elevator and rode it to the second floor. We got off and sat on the brick-like bench. We stayed there laughing and talking until Felicia happened to walk to the restroom and saw us. That was my clue to go into the office. But before I left, I stopped. "How would you feel if a friend was falling for you?"

He reached up and rubbed his left eyebrow like he was grooming himself. He smiled, and then giggled as he stood up. He scratched his right ear. The elevator arrived and he actually strutted quickly and jumped on. He waved to me as the door closed.

Okay, I thought. *He's more scared of me than I am of him. He didn't even answer the question. Dang that was weird.*

I shook my head and proceeded to the office. I met with the staff to parcel off Sarah's clients and to thank the staff for supporting me. Felicia was twisting in her seat like it was burning her butt and she couldn't stand the heat. She kept grunting. I could tell she wanted to say something. Finally, she jumped in.

"Sarah deserves what she got. She kept disrespecting you. I don't know why you took so long to fire her."

Gwen, the other social worker, said, "She had to follow policy and procedures."

"I realize that, but that heifer should have been long gone." Felicia finally stopped fidgeting.

The others laughed and we chatted about having a program for our mothers that focused on Sudden Infant Death Syndrome. We selected a date and staffed the activity. Afterward, I went to my office to read my e-mail and instant messages.

The first instant message was from Travis. It read: Who is the friend who likes me? That was the only thing the message said.

I wrote back: What if I told you it was me. What would you say?

Five minutes later, I received this e-mail: That wouldn't be good. I work for you.

I responded: So what! No one would know. I hit send.

He responded: Have you ever done anything like this before? I mean, have an affair?

I replied: Have you?

He responded: No. What's next?

This whole conversation was tripping me out. I couldn't believe that after all these months we were flnally discussing this. So I responded: You tell me. This is a first for me. I nervously hit send.

His next e-mail read: Let's meet and talk. Malika, once you cross the line, there is no turning back.

I became anxious, almost upset. I replied: What do you mean? I have never done this before. What are you saying? I thought you had never done this either.

His next e-mail read: Hold your horses. I'm just saying we are taking a big step and once we do this, we can't take it back. When can I see you?

I got scared. Suddenly, I didn't want to have sex. I wanted to talk and let that lead to it. This entire conversation had me terrified. I was a grown-ass woman who wanted this man's dick so bad, I couldn't concentrate. Now that it looked like I might be getting it, I totally freaked out. I was too nervous to type a response. I was sweating and my knee was bouncing up and down so hard it was slamming against my desk. The shit was about to hit the fan, and I couldn't breathe. I hesitated before I typed again.

I sent another instant message: Dang, I just can't jump in bed with you. I need time to talk and to get to know you.

"Okay, how stupid was that," I whispered. I bit my lip until it bled. I was shaking. I was so nervous the words in my head became jumbled. I wanted him badly. Hell, I needed this. For months I'd been fantasizing and desiring this. I even prayed for this and, now, I was a mess. *Please, Lord, don't let me push him away.*

Travis replied: I need to see you just to talk, okay? We just need to talk.

"Calm down, girl." I was talking to myself and hyperventilating. *You about to get this dick! Stop tripping. Be calm. Let this shit play out. Okay!* I shook both my hands and flexed my fingers in and out. I stood up and paced the floor. I felt like a dumb teenager who had gotten herself into something much bigger than she could handle. I responded: What about Monday at five when my staff is long gone?

Travis's last e-mail read: Fine, I'll see you then. Have a good weekend.

I signed off: You do the same.

After I signed off my e-mail, I felt excited. *Finally! Now what?* I started panicking. I couldn't let another man see me naked. Oh my, I needed to diet. Suddenly, my anxieties were kicking in. I was terrified.

After I collected my thoughts and reread the instant messages over and over, I went home. As I pulled into the garage, I got out of the car and walked into the front yard to speak to Li'l Dexter. He was playing with some neighborhood kids. I hugged him.

As I headed to the garage, I saw Zena's car coming into the subdivision and decided to wait for her to talk. I walked across the street and waited for her to get out of her car. "Hi, Zena. How are you?"

"Girl, I'm fine today."

"I have that book for you on depression. Do you still feel sad?"

"All the time. I am barely making it to work and back home. I find myself crying a lot."

"You should call your doctor. I know since you are in school for nursing you may think—"

She interrupted me quickly. "Oh, no, girl. I don't think I know everything. I am a student."

I unzipped my purse and reached in, pulling out the thin book. "I've been carrying this in my purse, waiting to see you." I handed it to her. She glanced at it.

"Thank you. The symptoms are listed here clearly."

"Good. Do you have any of those symptoms?"

"I do and I'm so glad you brought this. Sometimes you don't want to face your fears."

"Are you gonna call your doctor?"

"Yes."

Zena pulled out her cell phone and called her doctor's office. He wasn't in, but she left a message to set an appointment.

"Girl, thanks. I want to get better, because feeling in the dumps all the time is not much fun. Thanks for giving me the courage to seek help. I'll let you know what's going on."

"No problem. I'll check on you this weekend."

As I prepared to cross the street, my cell phone vibrated. I answered it while looking back and forth to cross the street, checking for oncoming traffic. Not that there were many cars driving through our neighborhood, but you never knew.

"Hi, this is Malika." I said as I crossed the street and walked up my driveway.

"Heifer, what are you up to this weekend?" Pamela asked.

"I'm going to spend time with my family." I stopped walking to concentrate on what I was saying.

"Cool. You talked to Dexter about your issues?"

"Yes, Pamela, I have and again he feels like there are no problems in our relationship. But he's willing to go to counseling with me."

"See, I told you he would do what he had to. All you needed to do was to keep talking to him." Pamela said as she smacked her lips together making a slurping sound like she was eating something.

"Well, maybe there are no major problems to him. But I'm glad he agreed to go." I shifted my purse to my left shoulder.

"Counseling will help. But in order to work on your relationship you need to let that other shit go and keep building your home with your family. Ain't shit out here in the streets." Pamela giggled.

"It ain't like I'm trying to get in the street. I just want something to stir my juices up."

"As I said before, get stirred up at home."

"Okay Pam, let me check with you this weekend, okay?"

"I'll holler this weekend, love you girl."

"I love too, Pam." I ended the call.

Walking through the garage door into the kitchen I was hit with the smell of baked chicken, which was my favorite. Dexter could actually cook better than trained chefs. We had decided long ago that the first one to arrive home should start the cooking. This was because I usually had training in the evening for the staff. Today, he was busy cooking baked chicken, green beans, and Li'l Dexter's favorite, spaghetti, which made me feel proud to be his lady. He topped that with a tossed salad. Honestly, I loved this man. He was a great husband, a tender sex partner, and a great provider. His weakness was he didn't like to talk. He was quiet and generally didn't like to be bothered. He wasn't interested in my job or day-to-day activities and I just didn't understand that. It pissed me off. How could I have a strong relationship when my partner only talked when he wanted to? That was our problem. I was being stimulated with conversation and Travis had that area of my life cornered.

Travis and I talked about everything. But one thing I couldn't change and that was my love for my husband. I really wanted my marriage to work, but I wanted one time with Travis. I needed to feel him; then I could go back to loving and taking care of Dexter. After all, he was a good man and I wasn't planning to lose him for anyone. Thinking about it, I was scared. What if I enjoyed sex with Travis and wanted to go back for more? *Is this the reason I panic?*

***

That night, as I lay next to my husband after having sizzling sex, I silently cried. I cried because I cared for another man. I cried because I had done something so stupid. My mother always said never to say out loud what you wanted, because the devil would try to make sure you got it, so you would follow him. Stupid-ass me! I said I wanted Travis out loud, so the devil would let me have him. I loved God. I had been pleading with Him to let Travis and me get together, but He didn't play that. So I said I wanted Travis out loud, so Satan himself would give me my desires. Now you know that was stupid. Now I lay in bed crying, ashamed of myself, because I was letting a man come between God and me. In my right mind I would never ever do something that stupid and crazy. *Help me, God, please help me,* I begged.

"Malika."

"Yes."

"Are you crying?"

"Yeah."

"Why?"

"I don't know. I'm scared of losing you."

Dexter sat up and put his arms around me. "I promise you. I'm not going anywhere. Whatever is bothering you, this counseling should help. I love you. I might not say it all the time but I pray my actions show you that."

"Thank you. I love you too." I kissed him and we lay in each other's arms until I fell asleep.

Saturday was our church day. We are Seventh-day Adventists. It is also our family day. We went to church and visited with my mom and several of my family members and close friends. While at Mom's, I saw my brother, Kurt. As usual, he was begging for money. This really pissed me off, so I avoided him until I spoke to my niece.

"Malika, your brother, Kurt, stole my daughter's Easter dresses, the ones you bought for her—the pink one with the jacket and the red and white one. He took them both," Olivia's mother, Nikina, said.

"Are you serious? Oh, my God, I am going to kill that boy."

"He is always over here searching for something to steal and your mama just lets him."

"Mother," I screamed through the house. "Where is that no-good son of yours? How dare he steal things that I bought? I want his head on a platter. That boy is a crackhead and he needs help. You have got to stop being an enabler."

Olivia stood there and asked, "Malika, what is an enabler?"

"It is a person who supports an addict. You support him because you provide for his illness. You give him money and allow him to steal from your home because he is your son. There are no penalties for him because he is your child. But guess what? If you don't let him hit rock bottom, he is going to continue to bring everyone else down with him."

"That boy will be all right. He said he doesn't use drugs anymore."

"Well, if he doesn't, who stole the baby's clothes and why is your buffet almost empty? Mom, where is your fine china and expensive crystal glasses?"

"I guess he took them."

"Okay, Mama, I am through with him. He better not ask me for a dime!" I screamed as I walked away.

Later that evening, after we had our weekly family

dinner at Ponderosa, Kurt showed up at Mama's.

"What's up, Malika? Got some change?"

"If you don't get out of my face and get some help . . . Something is wrong when you steal children's clothing to feed your habits. Go to treatment."

"Let me get out of here before you piss me off."

"Before I piss you off? You stole clothing I bought for a toddler. I'm the one who is pissed."

"Do you have a dolla'?"

"Yeah, I have one, but you will never see another penny from me until you bring back those dresses."

Just like that, he walked out of the house. I was left so angry and deep down I knew he was sick, but I could not understand why drug addicts would not seek help when they sank as low as Kurt did. I also knew Kurt was gonna have a more difficult life if Mother didn't stop enabling him. But I knew I had to stop worrying about folks who didn't worry first about themselves. I decided I was through with this situation. Kurt was an addict and my mother was his enabler. I gave them both information on treatment options and phone numbers to call treatment centers and I left them.

Chapter 16

My Best Friends and Chicken Wings

Early Sunday evening, I met Pamela and Zandra at Culpeppers Restaurant on Highway 67. We sat in a far corner of the restaurant, so we could have some privacy. We all ordered their hot famous chicken wings with blue cheese dressing. We laughed at Pamela as she described a sexual encounter she had years ago. As we ate our chicken wings and salads, she went on to tell the story about how she almost killed this man. As they were having sex, she would turn her butt to him and ask him to screw her from behind. Then she would flip over and offer her vagina to him. Seconds later, she would flip back over on her stomach and cock her legs to the side, so he could hit it from the back again. It was so funny how she was quickly turning over and giving instructions like a woman out of control. She said when she looked back, the man looked exhausted. She finally admitted she cried and apologized to him because she acted like an insatiable animal in heat.

"Girl, you are too silly," I said. "I can imagine your ass sticking up in the air. And you talk about me wanting Travis to dick me."

"Yeah, but I wasn't getting nothing at home. At least you are."

"Well, keep in mind that sex isn't everything and that you still need other stimuli to keep the fire burning."

Zandra joined the conversation. "You two are man hungry and crazy as hell. All y'all talk about is sex. You are both freaks."

"You got that right." Pamela laughed.

"So tell us, Ms. Thing, if you fuck Travis, what is going to stop you from falling in love?" Zandra asked.

"Zandra, you are too late. She is already in love with Mr. Computer Man," Pamela volunteered.

"That's not true," I replied. "I really like him. I enjoy talking to him and—"

Before I could finish my statement, Pamela said, "And you want to fuck him."

"Chill, Pamela," I said. "You are a little too loud, folks are staring."

"Let them stare. Who gives a fuck?" she responded. "Now, let's not get off track," Pamela added. "We are here to convince Mrs. Hot in the Pussy to not do anything she doesn't want to live to regret."

"Ladies, the only thing I am going to regret is not getting a chance to sample his dick."

"Look at you. You are getting too streetwise on us. Fantasizing about another woman's husband will make you act like that."

"It's not like I want to keep him."

"Yeah, that's what you say now," Zandra said "But guess what? Once you are with him, you are going to keep wanting more and that's how women get messed up and fall in love."

"Maybe that's true," I somewhat agreed. Zandra was looking intensely at me.

"Be careful," she added.

"So, you are not going to tell me not to do it with him?" I asked.

"You are a grown woman," Zandra said. "If you want to have sex with someone who is not your husband, that's your business, but as your friend I say don't do it. But you are going to do what you want anyway." Zandra steadily looked at me intensely. "I just wish that as my friend you will listen."

Pamela clapped her hands. "Bravo. Bravo. What a speech."

"Fuck you, Pamela." Zandra was getting upset.

"Okay, my friends. Let's call a truce. Let's stop talking about this. We have so much more to discuss. Plus, you all said clearly you didn't want me to do anything. So we need to move forward."

"Although we don't want you to get hurt, know that we love you and if you need to talk about anything about that situation, we are here for you."

"I know. Thank you, ladies!"

As the evening wore on, we enjoyed each other's company and talked about everything. The subject of Travis and me was closed, but not within my heart. I had a meeting at 5:00 P.M. on Monday with Travis. Tomorrow could not come soon enough. We were going to discuss our feelings.

Monday, I met with my staff. As we discussed the upcoming workshop, the door to the office opened and in walked Travis. I couldn't stop the smile that swept across my face if I wanted to. Several of the staff stared at me.

They knew. Both of our faces said it all. We were smiling and staring at each other as if we were hungry for each other. We were worse than a bear eating steaks. So I did the only thing I could to get my staff out of our business. "Ladies, I am so sorry. I forgot about my meeting with Travis. I need to speak to him about some bids on the computer. Can you all finish up for me?"

"Sure!" Felicia and Frances responded at the same time. I left the meeting, so I could see my baby.

Felicia and Ingrid typed out a schedule for the staff to make sure everybody knew what their roles were. Sadly, I was a little embarrassed that they had to take over because I was so smitten. But what could I do? You can't hide your feelings when they are all over your face. I tried to save face by making them think I had an emergency meeting I forgot about.

"Malika, we need to talk. Would you walk outside with me?"

"Yes, Travis."

I picked up my keys, locked the personnel cabinet, and walked out the door with him. As we walked to the elevator, I looked at him and he was staring at me.

"What's up?" I asked.

"You! I have been thinking about us a lot and getting involved with you is unprofessional and wrong. I work for you. You are my boss."

What the fuck! Here we go! Friday it was me, now it's him. I inhaled air into my lungs and blew it out like it was burning my chest. "I think we are adult enough to handle ourselves."

"It is the integrity of the matter. Plus, I think you might fall in love with me."

"Are you kidding me?" I felt the frowns form in my forehead and my eyes blinked several times. I got dizzy. "Yeah, right! What about you falling in love with me?"

"I think you might get in too deep."

I almost felt like I was begging him. "I will not fall in love with you. Trust me. I'm not trying to marry you."

"Well, if you are sure, then let's do something together this weekend."

"Like what? I am not jumping in bed with you."

Suddenly, those fears had returned. *He just said he didn't think we should do anything. Then he says, "let's get together this weekend."* Like Friday, I panicked again with that same stupid stuff about "I'm not giving him none" when that's all I thought about. Hell, this whole thing was about my getting some dick. The truth was staring me in the face. I was a scared-ass pussy. I was blowing this relationship with all this scatterbrained confusion. What's wrong with me?

"I didn't ask you to," Travis said, with a funny look on his face. I was confusing him too. This man knew I wanted to sex him. Hell, I backed my ass into him and grinded on his dick. Now I was saying I wasn't jumping in bed, when he was saying, "don't fall in love with me." *Damn, I have to get a grip on my feelings.*

"Call me on Friday and we'll set up something." He jammed his hands into his pockets and kicked a few rocks on the ground. He was having a hard time looking at me.

"Okay, Travis." I relaxed my arms. I smacked my lips because I felt I was looking stupid. He looked at me with raised eyebrows. I felt like he was thinking I was a confused mess and he was correct.

I walked back into the building, got on the elevator, and pushed the button to the second floor. I had this huge smile on my face. We were going to spend some time together outside the office on a real date. All our time together had been on company time. Now we were seeing each other as a potential love interest. Though I was scared, I was happy. I briskly walked down the hall and went into the office.

All through the week I analyzed the budget. Tuesday, during the day, I wrote a grant for books, finalized the bids for the new hardware for the network system, and met with staff to assure that their files had been updated. Tuesday night, Dexter and I watched a few criminal television shows. We had a great time. He claimed that he had never watched the shows before, but he enjoyed them. As we sat on the couch, I straddled him.

"Malika, get off me." He playfully lifted his leg up to try to insinuate I was putting too much weight on him. I bent down and kissed him.

"Why don't you kiss me like you used to?"

"I kiss you while you are sleeping."

"That doesn't help or prove anything, especially if I don't even know I'm being kissed."

"But I am kissing you." He kissed me. "Now move," he said with a laugh.

I really enjoyed my time with him.

Wednesday and Thursday came quickly. We finished up projects in the office. I hadn't heard from Travis. I assumed he was making plans for us. He had asked me to call him Friday so we could set something up. I had planned to look at what was playing at a movie theater, thirty miles away, so I could have an alternate plan.

After reviewing the schedule of activities for Friday, I met with my staff to make sure they knew what their roles would be. After confirmation, everyone busied themselves with other activities.

It was around 4:00 P.M. The staff placed their latest records in the file cabinets. We did that on a daily basis as we had to document all activities and face-to-face visits per our contracts. Near quitting time, Ingrid notified me that I had a call. It was Travis. When I picked up the phone, Travis blurted out, "I've been thinking and this is wrong. We shouldn't do this."

"Why are you playing with my feelings, Travis?" I blew out the air I was holding in my mouth. Frustrated, I held the phone tightly in the palm of my hand.

"I'm not. It's wrong. You are my boss. You are off-limits to me. I have never done this before and it is not wise to start now."

I hung up the phone on him. I wanted to cry. I was so close, but not close enough.

As each of the staff notified me that they were leaving for the day, Felicia walked in to inform me that Travis was in the office and wanted to meet with me. "You're in good hands, so I am leaving," she said.

"Okay, I will see you tomorrow. Has everyone left the office?"

Felicia walked out, checked everyone's office, came back, and said the entire staff was gone for the day. She left and I went to the conference room to meet with Travis. When I walked in, he had the sweetest smile on his face. He looked so concerned. He got up and walked over to me. He kissed me on my right cheek and then on my left. He pulled me closer to him and hugged me tighter.

"You're shaking," he said.

"Sorry."

"I told you that if we take this route, there is no turning back." He stood behind me and whispered in my ear, "Oh, Malika, I want you so badly."

Travis rubbed my stomach and kissed my neck. He even took my hand and guided it to his manhood. I felt his swollen manhood and I was shaking like a leaf on a tree. I didn't know why I was so scared, but I was. I had never stepped out on Dexter. Travis turned me around and hugged me, and just as he was about to kiss my lips, his phone rang. It was one of his business associates. As he talked, he blew kisses at me. I looked down and noticed he was still hard and bulging against the fly of his pants. But I still couldn't tell if he was packing. Once he hung up the phone, things changed. He took me by the hand. "I can't do this."

"Why?" I asked as I pulled away.

"This is too much work, trying to sneak around with you."

I wanted to beg him, but I stopped. I was not going to let him see me cry. "All right, Travis, if that is what you want."

"It is."

I grabbed my purse and keys and turned the lights out. We walked out of the building. No words were exchanged between us. The only sound I heard was the thumping of my broken heart. I quickly jumped into my car and drove off. As I drove, my emotions came to a head and I started crying, so much so that I had to pull to the side of the road. I angrily banged on the steering wheel. "Please, God, help me. Please stop me from wanting him. Please help me."

I was so hurt. I kept thinking I was fighting two losing relationships. Though Dexter had started spending a little more time with me, I still felt emotionally empty. Finally, I had Travis's arms wrapped around my body. He kissed each side of my face and all over my neck. He whispered his need for me and as soon as the call came he immediately retreated. How could he turn his feelings on and off like a water faucet. I couldn't do that. I tried and here I was in so much emotional trauma I felt lost. I kept feeling his arms snaked around my body. It felt so good. He was so strong and then nothing. I wasn't sure I could take any more of this. I had to do something to stop my confusion and pain. I was embarrassed.

***

On Friday, instead of meeting with staff, I opted to participate in the events with the staff and families. I didn't attend all the activities we had for the families, but I did attend those that were most important to our contracts, like the health events, and the educational ones. Surprisingly, Samantha showed up. I always gave her a monthly report with our activities planned out and made sure she had an open invitation to come to everything. I really enjoyed myself and it took my mind off Travis.

Chapter 17

Getting Away

The week went by so fast. I spent the weekend enjoying my family. On the following Monday, I spoke to Samantha about the workshop we had the previous Friday. She really enjoyed herself and was so impressed with the relationship the staff had with our clients. She spent her time kissing and hugging the babies and just having a great time. During our meeting, she told me she had met with Travis about the project they had discussed and that the next meeting would include me. She stated that Travis didn't seem like himself.

"What do you mean he didn't seem like himself?"

"Usually when I see Travis, he's happy and much friendlier. Honestly, I got the feeling that something happened between you two."

"How did you get that impression? I mean, what happened to make you think something went down with us?"

"I mentioned your name and he didn't even smile. To me, that is unusual."

"Well, maybe something was on his mind."

"Yeah, maybe," she said.

As Samantha and I talked about a conference that my social workers and I would be attending in three days in Jefferson City, Missouri, she bent her head down and rubbed her temples. She looked somewhat distressed.

"What's wrong, Samantha?"

"Just a headache."

"Aren't you having them too frequently?"

"Since two weeks ago, I have had my share. But I think my pressure might be up. Actually, I drank a little apple cider vinegar this morning to help control my blood pressure until I can get to the doctor."

"Well, everyone said that works. But still hurry and schedule an appointment."

"I have a doctor's appointment late Friday afternoon."

"You know we are leaving Wednesday morning and will return Friday afternoon."

"Okay," she said. "If you need me, just call."

"I will, but please get to the doctor."

Tuesday, my staff and I met and talked a lot about our upcoming trip. We were attending workshops on parenting issues, conflict management, and domestic violence. We were excited because we had not attended a conference in more than five months, so we were due for some training. I planned to drive my husband's SUV because it seated nine folks comfortably, plus we could use the other seats for luggage. Only five of us would be attending the conference while the other staff would stay and monitor the program.

The conference was very informative. On Friday, to avoid the rush-hour traffic, my staff and I decided to leave the conference around 2:00 P.M. We had one training left that didn't impact our program. We really bonded during this trip and the staff even went to a local party with other conference attendees. Even though we had a close staff, Sarah had tried her utmost to tear us apart by discrediting me. She had even told my staff I was fucking Travis, which I guessed might have looked like it by the way we acted around each other.

"Malika, did you see that lady in the conference with that blond and orange wig on?" Felicia asked.

"No, and you didn't either. I didn't see any orange."

"Who didn't? Yes, I did! She looked a horrible mess. Did anyone else see her? I know I'm not the only one who saw that blond and orange wig." Felicia said while holding her stomach and laughing.

Frances laughed. "Who in the world could miss that ghetto-fabulous hairdo?"

Everybody continued to laugh. All through the conference, we had a great time. We spent the whole conference bonding and really getting to know each other. In fact, we were pretty close as a staff before the conference and even closer after it.

I drove Interstate 70 East back to St. Louis in my husband's Eddie Bauer Ford SUV, which had a V-8 engine. I put the pedal to the metal and even though I was driving safely, I was driving a little over the speed limit. As we were laughing and talking, my cell phone rang.

Felicia answered it and passed it to me. "It's Johnny Walton."

"Hello, this is Malika."

"Hi, Malika, this is Johnny. Are you in a safe area for a conversation?"

"Yes, I am." I didn't know what he meant by safe, but I assumed he meant whether I was driving or standing in a stationary position. I wanted to hear what he had to say, so I lied.

Chapter 18

This Shit Is Unbelievable

Johnny Walton was the president of the board of directors for the National Infant & Toddlers Association, which was the parent company of the Pal Project. He was a part of the good ole' boy network that kept the organization supplied with money from their rich friends. He was a nice man with the cutest and brightest blue eyes I had ever seen.

"I'm stable. What's wrong?"

"It's Samantha."

"What about her?" My voice raised an octave. I looked over to my right and noticed that Felicia looked concerned. She saw the expression on my face. From her own facial gestures, I could tell she felt something wasn't right. "What?!" She asked. I whispered to Felicia to be quiet and mouthed the word Samantha.

"She was taken to the hospital this morning and I am sorry to say, she is in a coma." Johnny stated.

"Oh, my God, not Samantha!" I screamed. As I did, my foot left the accelerator and the SUV began to slow down. I was also losing control of the steering wheel. Frances began crying loudly in the back seat.

"Pull to the side of the road," shouted Pat, one of the intake social workers.

"What is that noise?" Johnny Walton asked.

I pulled to the side of the road and stared at Felicia, who I wanted to shout at and say, "Shut up, bitch!"

She was screaming and crying, "Oh, hell naw, motherfucker."

"Johnny," I said, "please tell me she is going to be all right. Please!" I was sobbing; Samantha was my friend as well as my boss.

"I can't tell you that. Only God knows. Her husband has called her brothers and sisters from out of town. They are flying in tonight. They are going to pray about taking the ventilators and other life support machines off tomorrow."

Whimpering at the side of the road, I laid my head on the steering wheel and cried.

"Are you going to be okay?"

I didn't respond. Johnny held the phone until I was ready to speak again.

"Do you know what happened?" I asked.

"Apparently, she had been complaining about a migraine headache that she had had for a while. So they are trying to relieve pressure off her brain. Please don't share this information with anyone other than your staff and ask them to do the same. We don't want our friends and competitors to know what is going on as of yet."

"I won't make an announcement until I receive your call."

"Call me when you arrive back in town."

My conversation, cries and facial gestures gave away what was wrong. Staff already knew Samantha was complaining about her blood pressure and those headaches. As I ended my call, Felicia cried out loud, "Is she dead?" I shook my head and said, "Brain-dead." Felicia jumped out of the SUV. Frances got out and tried to help her distraught coworker, though she was in worse shape than Felicia. I was so flustered I couldn't think straight, and we were more than seventy-five miles away from our office. So we remained on the side of the road, five of us, three in the car crying and two walking up and down on the side of the highway, all broken-hearted.

Finally, after thirty minutes of crying, the two workers got back into the SUV and I started the car. For the next hour and a half, all I heard were sniffles and dry heaves. Finally, after what seemed like hours, we pulled onto the office parking lot. We unpacked the SUV and put everyone's luggage into their waiting cars. Felicia and I walked into the building to contact the other workers. Once on the second floor, we hugged each other. Felicia and I had a special bond with Samantha. Samantha thought, as I did, that Felicia was a loyal, hard worker.

As we opened the door, Ingrid walked up and reached out and hugged us. Apparently, one of the other workers left at the office had heard from one of Samantha's family members about what was going on and she told the rest of the staff. We all locked the office up and left. We talked about Samantha and what had happened as we walked to the parking lot, got into our cars, and drove off.

I hadn't driven five miles when grief overtook me. I pulled into a parking lot, laid my head on the steering wheel, and cried for twenty minutes. Scared, I pulled out my cell. After I dialed that number, I waited until I heard that voice. "Travis." I paused, trying to stop crying.

"What's wrong?"

"It's Samantha."

"Is she okay?"

"No." I was nearly hysterical. "She is in a coma!"

"What do you mean?"

"I don't know. She is near death."

"Baby, don't say that. I need to get to you. Where are you?"

"Almost home."

"I was going to come to you. But go home and I will call you tomorrow."

I called Dexter and told him what was going on. He knew Samantha through some networking opportunities with his company. I needed him to hold me. I started the car and drove to my house. I jumped out of the car and ran to Dexter. Since I was trying to communicate more with him, I had told him before we left that I was worried about Samantha and that she was having very bad headaches. When he saw my face, he reached out and I collapsed in his arms. "Samantha is brain-dead!" I felt so safe in my husband's arms. He held me and kissed my face. "I'm so sorry about Samantha." I melted into his chest and allowed him to cradle me. I was home. I felt his love and strength.

I cried the entire weekend. I was brokenhearted. That Friday night, they took Samantha off the life support machines. I called her husband to offer my condolences. He made me feel a little better because he told me how she felt about me. He said she was impressed with me and often spoke highly of my professionalism, intelligence, and her trust for me. I did not know that. He said that although it was difficult losing a wife, he was happy that he had her for the three years they were married. I silently cried as he spoke of his love for her. He told me that she died of a blood clot to the brain.

When I returned to work on Monday, Travis was waiting for me. He waited until I greeted and was briefed by my staff, before he walked into my office, offering me a hug. His strong arms comforted me. He kissed my cheek and said he was sorry to hear about Samantha. But it felt different. It felt like a friend who cared about me, unlike my husband's loving arms where I felt deep affection and a deeper connection. I also felt cheated because Travis walked out on me and had only returned to comfort me because he too shared my pain, not that he wanted it to be eliminated as my husband's embrace did.

"She really thought well of you, Travis. She was impressed with your work and your high standards."

"She was so intelligent and down to earth for such a young woman. I worked on several contracts with her and was impressed with the way she handled the attorneys and accountants. Samantha was the real deal."

"I know, Travis. She was so special."

"When are the funeral services for her?"

"They are planned for later this week. I will give you more details later. Her husband said that maybe on Friday. He is working on it with her parents."

Looking concerned, Travis said, "Losing someone who was so special to me would be so devastating. I couldn't stand to lose my wife or my children." When he said that to me I had a light bulb moment! The call that day in the office when he was hugging and kissing me was his wife. Travis loved her as I did my husband. We were both hurting and were looking for something, not someone. It was too easy for him to spend time with me, yet neither of us could really move that forward. Weirdly, I didn't get jealous; his words didn't hurt me. I actually respected him for loving his family.

"Nor could I, Travis."

With that, he stood up, walked over to me, and hugged me. "Are you going to be all right?"

"Yes," I whispered as the tears rolled down my face. He squeezed me close to him. It felt good being in his arms. But I felt something had changed in him too. In the office that day, I felt the heat in his body for me. Now I just felt concern.

"I'll call you later."

"Okay, Travis."

Chapter 19

It's So Hard to Say Good-bye

Throughout the day, my staff and I reminisced about Samantha. We missed her so. It was so unbelievable that she was gone. She was a healthy woman who only suffered from high blood pressure. She was not overweight. This shit was so fucking wrong. Why did she have to die? I decided I would not question God because I knew from my teachings, in church, that God knew best. But I sure in the hell was going to miss my boss and friend.

We went through the week in a daze. Services were on Friday. My staff and I had to have a lot of support because we were so devastated. We were mourning the loss of a loved one. The corporate office offered us grief counseling. I accepted it for our staff. It was something to go through. This was my first time having a session such as this. There were plenty of tears and plenty of questions.

The counselor was good. She handled a staff of ten pitiful women who were suffering and were so broken-hearted. It took several hours for the counselor to get us to calm down. We felt better after the session, but she scheduled two more follow-up visits.

Travis did not attend the funeral services. He called me to say it was too difficult, but he had gone to view her body. He apparently had trouble with funerals. I fully understood this. He e-mailed me often for weeks after the funeral. I missed him so much. For almost a year he was in my office at least three to four days a week. Now I just received e-mails about computer issues. We never ventured outside of the business aspect of our relationship. There were days I felt sluggish. I couldn't find the energy to care about too much. I shut my feelings down and tried to forget him. But there were days when the staff was gone that I would stare out the window and cry. My heart was in so much pain. I felt like he had stabbed me in the heart and left me for dead. I found no comfort in his e-mails. I knew he stayed in touch because he didn't want me to have bad feelings. Emotionally, I was drained. I found the things I enjoyed in the past were just like a fading memory. My joy was gone. I settled back into my regular routine. I gravitated toward Dexter and because he felt all was well the appointment to see the counselor was never made. As a matter of fact, I felt worse than I did initially, but the difference was I didn't care. I didn't talk to my friends much because I didn't want them to know I was in so much pain. I didn't want them to say I told you so.

Then one day, out of the blue, he called me.

"You want to go to lunch?"

"Yes."

"I'm on my way to pick you up."

"Call me and I'll meet you downstairs."

We went to a quiet restaurant that was frequented by professional white folks. We were the only African Americans there. He ordered a house salad and a steak and potatoes, while I ordered baked chicken. He also ordered chocolate cake for dessert.

"Are you enjoying your food?"

"Yes, thank you, Travis. This is a quiet restaurant."

"I miss you."

I responded, "I miss you too."

Travis cut his steak and took a forkful. "I thought of you often over the past weeks."

"Why?" I needed to know since he decided it was unethical to be with me.

"I care a lot about you but we're both married with families and I don't want you to fall in love with me, complicating things."

"What would make you think I would?"

"The fact that you have been married for more than sixteen years and never stepped out on your husband. I believe you would fall and I don't want to hurt you."

"Maybe you will be the one to fall. You said you'd never had an affair."

"Honestly, I haven't, but men are different. We can do things without the emotional attachment. I care about you, but like I said I have a wife and children and I'm not about to lose my family."

"I have a husband and a child. I didn't plan on wanting to be with you. Hell, this happened suddenly. I see why men and women can't be friends. We get too close. We spent too much time together. But trust me, I am okay."

"Have a piece of my chocolate cake. It is quite tasty."

"No, thanks."

"No, come on, try it," he said, while handing me a fork. We sat there silently, eating his cake. It was so romantic. I wanted him badly. Every time I took a mouthful of cake, I imagined him inside of me. I wanted to feel him deep inside of me. Even if it was only one time, I had to have it.

"Malika, I want to take you to a movie this weekend."

"I'm not fucking you!" *I know I am the author of this confusion. Why is it that every time he takes a step to-*

ward me I sabotage it with the same stupid stuff about not wanting him when that is all I think about?

"I didn't ask you to." He looked at me like I was crazy. But I had to say it. I wanted him to romance me. I was so confused that I confused him. Why would he romance me when he didn't want me to fall in love with him? I was so mixed up.

"I know, but I was establishing ground rules," I said.

"Well, let's just go to a movie and we'll see what our next steps will be."

"All right."

"Meet me at the movie theater in Edwardsville. You know the one I'm talking about?"

"Yes, Travis, I know."

"The movie starts at three. It's an action movie. I can't remember the name, but you'll like it because I've heard you say you wanted to go see it."

All week long I thought about what I would do when I saw Travis over the weekend. As I planned what I wanted to wear, my mind kept telling me to dress to make him want me. I told my sister, Karen, what I was doing just in case something went wrong.

"You shouldn't do that. It is so not you."

"Well, I can't believe you are saying this, considering you are doing it yourself."

"Well, Malika, you are not me. Plus, you should try to keep your husband. Travis is going to use you. At least you know Dexter loves you for you. After all, when you gained all that weight, he stayed, didn't he?"

"Karen, what is wrong with you? Why are you such a complete asshole? Call me when you know how to talk to me." With that, I slammed the phone in her ear. That bitch was getting on my nerves. *Why does Karen have to make me feel so insecure about myself? I love my big beautiful body and Dexter has never complained about my weight. Why does my own sister try so hard to make me feel so bad?* I didn't understand that. But it made me think that maybe I was ashamed of my body and that was why I was so reluctant to jump in bed with Travis. Was that why I was sabotaging an opportunity to feel his body next to me, as I'd dreamed?

On Saturday, I drove over to Edwardsville to visit a friend. I left more than two hours before I was to meet Travis. While I was laughing and kicking it with my girlfriend, Shanice, who I graduated from college with, my cell phone rang.

"Hi, this is Malika."

"Hi, Malika, I have some bad news."

"What?"

"I can't come. My wife was suddenly called in to work."

"Oooh."

"We can try to get together next week. I hope you are not upset."

"No, I am not. I'll talk to you later."

I was so upset that I told Shanice I had to leave, but I would call her later. I had to leave quickly because I knew I was going to cry. I walked out and got into my SUV. As I drove toward home, the tears started to fall. My feelings were hurt so badly I had to pull to the side of the road for safety. As I sat there, I screamed and beat on the steering wheel. I was upset that I ever thought something would come of us. Why did this man have such an impact on me? I had been a good Christian and an upstanding citizen. Everyone who knew me deemed me a professional, but this man made me break every professional rule and ethic I had ever learned.

I sat there thinking about the many times I had an orgasm while dreaming of him thrusting into me. That had never happened to me. All I had to do was think of my legs wrapped tightly around his powerful legs, and my panties would become soaked. I could be in the grocery store and his face would run across my mind, and I would have to squeeze my legs while squeezing my vaginal muscles. I did this to stop myself from having an orgasm in public.

How many times had I gone to church and midway through the sermon, my thoughts would trail off and I would be fucking Travis right there in the church? Not just a little fucking, but the entire act from foreplay to penetration. The pastor would be preaching about God and His commandments, and suddenly, I could feel his breath while he was sucking and licking my nipples. I would squeeze my thighs together and fuck him in my head. I could feel myself become as moist as morning dew. Then after he and I would climax together, the guilt would set in. "Please forgive me, God," I would say loud enough for only my ears.

Every week for six months, I fucked Travis in my head while trying to hear the sermon. I became convinced that Satan had targeted me and I was his candidate for hell. Satan had taken that very important place where I could pray and talk to God, and replaced it with a dick in my mouth. How could God hear me if I was sitting in the sanctuary, sucking a man's dick in my head? I felt like a guilty whore. How could I allow the devil to make me imagine fucking someone who was not my husband while in church? Didn't the Bible say that lusting was a sin? Yet I sat in the church and had full-fledged adulterous sex in my head. Not only that, my panties were soaking wet, because I was so horny for this man. I had to do something, but what? I didn't want to die suddenly and go to hell. I wanted to get that man out of my head.

Now that I thought about it, I felt like Travis was using me. I thought he played this game with my head and won. When I met him, I didn't want him; our relationship was totally professional. I was satisfied at home, not 100 percent happy, but I had no plans of having an affair. I always felt that I had a wonderful husband. He was a good provider and was very good in bed. He had only one flaw: he was not a good communicator. Dexter had been that way from day one, but it never bothered me before. Now that we were getting older and we needed to work on many things for Little Dexter, my expectations were different.

Travis picked up on my insecurities and played me like a fiddle. He knew how to get me started and pushed the right buttons. I had started to believe that maybe he had done this before. Accept me, chase me, and then dump me before anything ever starts and then call me back and start the process over. Well, I was so tired of crying for him. I was letting go.

Chapter 20

How Do You Mend a Broken Heart?

My staff and I held a parent meeting to discuss issues they needed to know about getting their children immunized in a timely manner. There were twenty mothers present for the informational workshop. Many parents did not believe in immunizations for their children, and those who objected stated the shots were dangerous and they wanted no part of giving them to their children.

I asked, "Can someone tell me what would stop you from keeping your infant's medical appointment?"

Three people raised their hands to answer. "Paris, tell us what would stop you from making sure your child is okay."

"Ms. Williamson, I didn't say I wouldn't do anything to keep my baby healthy. But if I didn't have transportation, I would have to reschedule my appointment."

"But, Paris, by virtue of not taking your child to the doctor for a checkup, you are risking her health. You see, when doctors schedule monthly appointments to check on children, they are looking to see if the baby is thriving. Some babies don't eat enough and may be too small; others may be eating too much and are too heavy. Doctors check to see if the babies' eyes can follow objects, even to see if the babies are growing at the appropriate rate. So when you consistently miss your doctors' appointments, I would say, yes, you are putting your child at risk."

"I never thought about it like that, Ms. Williamson. You are not trying to hurt your child, but sometimes you don't have a way to take them or someone you asked to take you may back out."

"How many of you have heard of having a backup system?" No one raised their hands. "Surely, when you plan to wear an outfit to a party or somewhere else, you prepare a second outfit just in case that one doesn't look right. How many of you pack second outfits for you and your baby?"

Every hand in the class was raised high in the air. All twenty women were in agreement.

"It is the same thing you do with your child. You should always plan on a second ride to the doctor, just in case. You can map out the bus route, carry cab fare, or contact one of the local organizations that provide free rides. There are at least seven agencies in this area alone that provide these services. Also, the state provides insurance through their health insurance carrier."

"So, is that a backup system?" asked Janice.

"Yes, it is," I replied. "It is having something planned just in case your previous plan doesn't work out."

I continued to talk to the class, because I loved the young women and knew if they could do better, they would. I also believed that many of them wanted to learn, but their circumstances thwarted them from overcoming poor decision-making skills. Also, I knew all of the parents I had met wanted their children to be happy, healthy, and educated. In all my years, I had never met a parent who said, "I want my child to be the worst damn child you have ever met."

I turned the class back over to Frances. Unfortunately, for me, I was still craving Travis's dick. All the time I was talking to the class, I could feel him penetrating me. Actually, my panties were wet. So I walked into my office and shut the door. I laid my head on the desk and let my dream overcome me.

I was working late and he saw my car on the lot. He came up to my office and knocked. I didn't answer because I was the only person there and I had not expected anyone. Suddenly, my cell vibrated. I picked it up.

"Hi. Are you alone?"

"Yes, I am."

"Open the door, please."

I walked out of my office and opened the door. Though I was very happy to see him, I tried my damnedest not to show it.

"What brings you here?"

"You."

I didn't even waste my time with asking why. Suddenly, he grabbed and kissed me. Damn, that boy could kiss. My legs buckled and he lifted me up, so I wouldn't fall. He backed me up against the file cabinet. We were kissing as if we would stop our blood would have seeped out of our bodies. He gently caressed my breasts.

"Malika, I want you so badly. I can't stop thinking about you."

He started rubbing his hands down my stomach until he reached my vagina. He slipped his fingers inside of my panties and moaned. "You're so wet. You want me, Malika?"

"Yes!" I said, trying to catch my breath. But before I could say another word, his tongue was back in my

mouth. I was enjoying his tongue because he knew how to use it, which left me wanting more.

Suddenly, he snatched my panties off. He tore them off because he couldn't wait to get inside of me. I unbuckled his pants and they fell to the floor. He lifted my dress up and I struggled to get his briefs down. This man was built. Not only that, he had a very large, thick penis. I couldn't wait to have it inside me. Before I could ask him to put on a condom, because we had thousands in the office, he entered me hungrily. His penis stretched and filled me up. He was lightly thrusting in me, but I wanted it harder. While sucking on his tongue like I wanted to suck his dick, I pleaded with him to fuck me harder. He then began thrusting in me, harder and deeper.

"Malika, damn you feel so fucking good. Shit, girl."

"Oh, Travis, I want you." I was going out of my mind. He lifted me high off the floor and I wrapped my legs around him. We were out of control. I had never fucked like that. "Harder, Travis, please. Damn, boy, this shit is good." Ten minutes later, he kissed my neck and I buried my head into his chest as I had multiple orgasms. Before he could come, my selfish ass asked him to put on a condom.

"Malika, it's too late for that," he said as I felt his penis almost double inside of me and then he exploded. After he had climaxed, he continued to gently roll his dick inside of me. "Malika." He affectionately called my name.

"Malika."

I jumped. It was Felicia calling me. I stood up from my desk and my panties were soaked. I was so afraid my clothes were soiled. At that moment, I decided I had to change jobs. I could no longer think like a manager, because here I was in a building with twenty parents and my staff, and I was stuck in the office mind-fucking the IT man. This shit was stupid and I knew that like a drug addict, trying to kick the habit, I had to change the people I was around. To rid myself of Travis, I had to forget when I fell for him, change the places we went together, and forget about the things I did with him. To find myself again — the professional, down-to-earth, clear-headed Malika—I had to find another job. Sadly, I had ruined this perfect job because I feared my staff couldn't respect me, knowing I had feelings for a contractor. No matter how much I tried to deny how I felt, it was so clearly written on my face that a blind man could see it.

I could no longer work like this. Travis had not been to the office in two weeks, no phone calls, no anything. I found myself searching and staring out the window; most of the time I cried. Even though my staff never saw the tears, Felicia voluntarily told me she was afraid for me. "Malika, what's wrong with you? The spark is gone from your eyes. You don't talk and laugh as much as you used to. I want the old Malika back."

I just ignored her. But I smiled. I didn't respond directly to her question. However, I thanked her for working so hard on the projects.

I had changed. The truth was Travis wanted a professional relationship with me. We had made a serious mistake, one that I would have to live with or change jobs. I decided I would find another job. He and I would never be able to work with each other again.

Chapter 21

Strangers in the Midst

Two weeks after the workshop, the computers crashed. Felicia called Travis five times and he did not call back. That shit never happened before. In the past, before that broken date, he would call me back in two seconds flat. So I e-mailed him and he e-mailed me back.

> Good morning, Malika. I am in Washington, DC. I will not be back in the city until Friday. I will send an employee to your office to look at your computer system.
>
> Travis

That was how much our relationship had deteriorated. It was so professional now. His employee took over the account. He was a very young, scrawny-looking Caucasian. Though he was nice, he was not Travis. I guessed Travis made sure he wasn't sending another fine African American brother for me to fall over. Although his employee was nice, I felt empty and broken.

Twice during the month, Travis stopped by to check on the computer system. I swore he almost ran out of the office. What a slap in the face. That said, I still had the head fuck. I still craved his dick and I still needed to talk to him. But it was so over. So why couldn't I move on?

It was a hot day in May when I received a call from a large corporation that was interested in talking to me about working for them. I had been sending out resumes because I was having a difficult time forgetting Travis and letting go. I scheduled an interview for the following week.

All week long, we did paperwork and held parent meetings at various times, so all of our parents would be able to participate. By the weekend, I was happy to have the much-needed break. Saturday, I drove over to East St. Louis to see my parents and we had a good visit. Kurt told me he was going to treatment and that he was tired of begging. For some reason, I believed him. While I was talking to my mother, Karen called and apologized. She informed me that she had said negative things to me on purpose, because she was jealous that I had more opportunities than she. In her mind, she thought our parents favored me because I was smart. She told me she loved me and I wasn't fat, but she knew calling me that would hurt me. She further explained that although she was rich, her husband, Tim, was an asshole. He was a great provider, but awful in bed. But that's another story. I accepted her apology and told her I loved her.

Earlier that morning, while I was in church and the pastor was preaching, my mind began to see Travis fucking me hard and rough. But I whispered, "Satan get back." Three times during the services, Travis grabbed my breasts and sucked them. Twice, he finger-fucked me. But I closed my legs and asked God to help me.

I enjoyed the time with my family because it kept my mind occupied. When I was talking and laughing, thoughts of Travis had a more difficult time getting into my head. I was trying hard to let go, but I still had crying spells and I still saw his face when Dexter was inside me. If Dexter knew I had fallen for another man, he never showed it. He continued to love me and he was trying harder to communicate more.

Sunday, I met with my girls, Zandra and Pamela. We had lunch at Joe's Crab Shack. We asked for a corner table so we could have privacy. Zandra wanted to ask a lot of questions, but I was limited in my answers.

"How are you and the computer man?"

"Zandra, you know I gave that up. You told me it was unprofessional and not to cross those boundaries and I didn't."

"Girl, you did the right thing. That man could have fucked you fifty times and decided to sue you for sexual harassment. It was a bad situation."

Pamela had to throw her two cents in. "I know it was hard and he was fine, but shit like that doesn't work out. As I always said, never get your butter where you make your bread. That simply means, don't fuck someone on the job, because you could lose your income."

"Yeah, you are right about that. But both of you know that shit sneaked up on me. I have never found myself in a situation like that. Although I have had many men pursue me on the job, I have always discouraged it. But this was different. I wasn't looking for anything and I certainly didn't need anything. Yet, he found the one area in my life that was suffering and that was my need to have a man talking to me, sharing ideas and dreams with me. You all know Dexter isn't a talker and that he only wants to communicate when it suits him, but I needed more."

"Malika, did you tell your husband what you needed?" Zandra asked.

"Yes, Zandra. I talked to him. He listened, and he agreed to go to counseling to help me. Things improved and changed again. But I knew that he cared. Hell, he's always there for me, he cooks for me and Li'l Dexter, and he makes sure we are comfortable. I guess for my man, being a great provider was showing love. Yet, it wasn't enough. You all know that relationships survive when you are communicating. You can have the best sex in the world, but if that's all gone, what do you have to look forward to? Travis and I could talk about anything, anyplace and anytime. He understood my job and the people I worked with, while Dexter didn't want to hear about my life. So it was so easy to fall for Travis. But, ladies, I am getting better. I'm looking to make a job change. I'm going to change my surroundings and start anew. Also, I have started to get Dexter to talk more. We're not where we need to be, but it's slowly coming along. A new environment will help me to get over Travis and help me to work on my marriage. Right now I feel like a rain cloud is over my head and until I make a change, it's hard to find sunshine. If I don't leave, I'm like the walking dead. So I have to think about me. I have to move forward."

"Good for you. I was really worried about you," Pamela said.

"I fell hard."

"No, you just wanted to sample another dick."

We all laughed and continued talking about life and other issues that were affecting us. My girls fought for me. They never once encouraged me to have an affair. They cared about my happiness and my marriage. I wasn't used to women helping each other like that. Some women would encourage you to have affairs and would also provide you with an alibi. But my two best friends wanted me to work out my issues with Dexter. They knew not all that looked good was good for you.

As we left the restaurant, Pamela said, "If you had gotten that dick, you would have been disappointed. He probably had a little-ass dick anyway."

Zandra agreed, "That's right! Usually men you want that bad can't fuck worth a damn. Count your blessings because if you had fucked him, you would be pissed."

We all laughed in that parking lot. Even though I was feeling better, I still wanted Travis.

Chapter 22

So Alone

Life has a way of bumping your head up against the wall so hard that you can feel the lumps and bruises. You know they are all over your head even if you don't look into the mirror. I felt sore all over. I was not myself. Falling in lust was so emotional for me that Zandra told me that I was having a lustful and emotional affair with Travis. She further told me that getting over him would be just as hard as mending a broken heart.

She was right. I could not shake him out of my mind. I found myself sinking as if I were in sand, losing my grip on my lifeline. How did I become so into a man who was not mine anyway? Why did this happen in my life at a time I was progressing and seeing so much success in my life? I could not understand it.

I skipped church and family day on Saturday and lounged around the house. I really didn't feel like seeing and talking to anyone. I couldn't fathom pretending to be happy when I was feeling as if I had a hole in my heart. I spent the entire day in my pajamas. I called Mom to tell her I was sick and would see the family the following weekend.

Since it was Sunday and I was feeling so alone, I decided to get into my car and drive to visit an old supervisor. She was easy to talk to and I could say anything to her. I drove the fifty miles to her house. The last time I visited O'Fallon, Illinois was almost a year ago when I went to look at a new subdivision being built. I had thought about moving. Maybe I should have. Moving may have prevented me from going through so much pain.

I drove over many highways and enjoyed the peace and quiet of barren roads. Not too many cars were on Highway 255 South. I had time to think as I took in the fields of grass and large stalks of corn. I marveled at the sun as it beamed on me. I felt a little better as I wondered what I would say to Brenda.

Brenda was a beautiful lady in her sixties. I worked for her about ten years ago and stayed on her payroll for ten years. She was the one who taught me how to run a company and how to keep a staff happy. She always said a happy staff was a productive one. She was right.

Brenda was a beautiful brown-skinned African American who had been married for almost forty years. She and her husband acted as if they could not keep their hands off each other. They were still having sex in their sixties. I knew she could guide me.

As I drove, my mind slowly went into a dream state. *Travis was rubbing his hands gently up my thighs. He pulled my thong over to the side and began to gently massage my clitoris. While he was doing that, he took my right hand with his left one and started to lightly suck my fingers. He asked me to pull to the side of the highway and I did. Reaching over, he pulled me close and started to kiss me passionately as his fingers manipulated my vagina. Light moans seeped out of my mouth as he whispered, "This is what we both have been wanting."*

I took my left hand and pushed the button to lay my seat all the way back. My seat nearly lay flat enough to mimic a bed. Then I pushed the knob that lifted the steering wheel. I did all this, but Travis wasn't having it like that. He released himself from his pants as we kissed. His nearly ten-inch penis popped out of his jeans. I became wetter. Travis pulled me over the cup holder that sat between the seats. He tore my thong completely off and helped to position me on top of him. He gently pressed me down on his manhood. As he entered me I gasped. It was total pressure.

He pumped up into me while French kissing me as we allowed our tongues to dart in and out of each other's mouths. We were both breathless as he unbuttoned my blouse and removed my breasts from my bra. He sucked and kissed my nipples. "Malika!" he moaned. "You feel so fucking good to me. I knew your pussy would feel like this. Damn, baby, I love you. You know that, don't you?"

I whispered, "Yes," as I bounced up and down on his thick penis. I was near climax. "Fuck me, Travis, do it hard."

With that, he put both his arms under my armpits and pulled me tightly to him, forcing himself deeper up in me. I screamed from the thrusting he was putting on me. "Oh, baby, oh, baby. I've been missing this."

"Yeah, it's yours, baby. It's yours!" I screamed while trying to grit my teeth. He was growing in me, both of us humping like it was life or death for us. We pumped hard. Him into me and me onto him! Finally, I screamed, "I'm coming, baby." We came together. "Damn that was good," we both said at the same time, out of breath.

I opened my eyes and found I was parked on the side of the highway with my thong in my hand. I screamed loud and prayed. *Thank you, Lord, for not allowing me to kill myself.*

I was so overcome with lust and love that I was hurt and confused. *Please help me before I lose my life or kill an innocent person while having these blackouts. I don't want to hurt like this anymore. Please, Lord, let me love and lust for the man you blessed me with. And, thank you, Lord, for pulling my car off the road because I certainly don't remember doing it myself. Amen.*

I pulled back into the highway and arrived at Brenda's home safely. I got out of the car and rang the bell. Brenda opened the door widely. She was so excited to see me. Her smile was as wide as the opened door. She clapped her hands with excitement.

"Hey, lady, how are you?"

"I'm okay."

"I was so excited to get the call that you wanted to come by. Come on in. I made some tea for us." I followed her into the kitchen and we sat at her oak wood table with the countryside blue and white kitchen curtains and tablecloth. Her home was so beautiful and tastefully decorated.

"I love coming here. It is so beautiful. I love how you decorated the place."

"I had to find a place that was comfortable and homey. Since we retired, I am loving it."

"I can see you're so happy."

"And you're not. What's wrong?"

I told her everything about me wanting Travis and about our plans to date, and how I always blurted out, "I'm not getting into bed with you." Pushing him away every time by making it seem that all he wanted was sex from me.

Brenda told me about being emotionally involved with someone. She said that Travis and I were emotionally connected, which was pretty bad in itself.

"Malika, an emotional affair is any infidelity that occurs through feelings or thoughts. Now with technology the definition of cheating has been expanded to include the traditional definition, plus the feelings and/or thoughts that comprise emotional infidelity. Look at it this way: cheating now includes having intimate conversations with someone while on a cell phone, meeting someone over the Internet, and sending inappropriate e-mails while maintaining a close, personal relationship with someone other than your spouse."

"I'm not in love with Travis. I just needed him."

"There is a difference between a physical and emotional affair. While the emotional affair may include meetings, it usually does not include physical contact. These affairs are committed via e-mail, texting, and talking on the phone. However, the physical affair is face to face and involves physical touching and kissing. Trust that an emotional affair can definitely lead to a physical one. Emotional attachments are very difficult to let go of because they start within the mind."

"Why is it so difficult to let go?"

"It becomes psychological. The end result is that the unfaithful spouse is paying more emotional attention to someone other than their partner, and they are removing themselves from the commitment they made to their marriage. That's why it is so hard. You are actually mentally bonded with another."

"I see. How do I get myself back?" I asked as I twisted my hair into a circle.

"Stop seeing the person and pay more attention to your husband."

I agreed with her. We spent the next hour talking and laughing. We reminisced about the past and joked about other things. I enjoyed spending time with her. I felt uplifted.

Chapter 23

A Change is Coming!

It's been said that the mind is so strong and powerful that it can make itself do anything. Almost a week had passed since my visit with Brenda. Although I felt like I was getting stronger, I still had good and bad days. Often my mind flowed right back to sexing Travis. I found myself walking around with his dick imbedded in me. I realized that was a problem, but thinking about him stimulated me so. But really every day I became stronger. I didn't think about Travis every day, but so much reminded me of him. When I heard a man laugh or giggle, I remembered. When we ate certain foods, I remembered the lunches. When the computer crashed or something happened at work, Felicia called Travis and he sent another worker. Still though, Travis benefitted me. When feelings of Travis overcame me I'd go and talk to my husband. Really just doing that helped me.

I continued putting out to associates and friends that I was searching for another opportunity. Although I could've very well started my own company, I'd rather have worked with other folks' money. It would take a lot of worry away from me because I could always go home to my life if the bottom fell out.

Tonight, I prepared a special meal for Dexter. I sent my son to be with his granny while I tried to get my marriage back on target. I prepared a big seafood feast with oysters. When Dexter and I were dating we always ate oysters believing they stimulated sex. Today, they'd just serve as a good way to talk. I just wanted some quiet time with my husband. I wanted to strengthen our marriage. I planned to fuck my husband tonight. I wasn't interested in making love. Dexter had it coming.

Dexter watched the news and I made a big salad. I had fruit and carrots, which are supposed to stimulate you too. I had shrimp, clams, and lobsters. I could feel myself becoming aroused already.

"Dexter, please freshen up and come into the dining room." I decided to serve in that room because I wanted everything pretty and perfect with my best china.

As Dexter and I ate, we chatted. "How was your day?"

"I had a good day. I got a lot of contracts completed and made a lot of customers happy."

"That's good. I know you were concerned about meeting your timelines."

"How was your day? Why the big meal? Today is not Sunday."

I broke out laughing. "That's funny! I cook nice dinners for you during the week."

"I know, but a four-course? What's the occasion?"

"You are the occasion. I just want to please my man."

"I see with all this food that stimulates sex. You know me, I don't need no help."

We both started laughing.

"Thank you, Malika. This is nice."

"You're welcome."

With that, Dexter gave me the biggest smile ever. After we finished eating, we got up and he kissed me on the cheek and retreated to the TV room. I cleaned the kitchen and went to join him.

We watched a couple of TV shows while he read his e-mail. Finally, we went upstairs.

"Let's take a shower together," I requested as I began to strip out of my clothes.

"We haven't done that in years," he said.

I walked up to him and kissed him fully on his lips and rubbed his penis softly. It jumped to attention. I wanted to soap him and rub him down.

I turned the shower on and stepped in when the water was warm enough. "Dexter, the water is great!" I called out as I began to soak my body with the strawberry body wash he liked to smell on me.

He joined me and I took his towel and washed his body. I took good care to wash his private area.

As I soaped him up, his penis stood erect. Suddenly, I had the desire to put it in my mouth. I wanted to please him. I took the shower head and directed it to his penis to rinse all the suds off. While I sprayed him off, he gently cleaned my private area. There was a place in our shower to sit down. I took the seat, which put me in direct line to face to his penis. I took his love tool and sucked him. He was moaning and gently pumping into my mouth. It felt good to please him. He was so aroused that he pulled me off the seat and began to kiss me with so much passion I nearly lost my balance. Then he turned me around and entered me from the back. I was bent over, holding onto the seat of the shower as he thrust himself deep within me. He was so into what he was doing. He was rubbing my back and massaging my shoulders. It was feeling so good that my legs began to shake as I began to feel trembles starting from my feet. "Oh, Dexter, that feels so good. Hit it hard," I pleaded. He did.

"Malika, damn, girl, you feel so good," he said as he pumped hard in me. Suddenly, my legs started to give out on me as the strongest orgasm I'd had in a while shot off. I began to pump into Dexter harder and faster and he returned the favor. He was holding my waist and hitting my love spot so hard, yet gentle, when he groaned and squeezed my waist as he came inside of me.

He held me in that position as both of our bodies settled down.

Finally, I stood up and turned to face him. "That was so damn good," I said as I tilted my head up and kissed him. We finished washing each other, dried off, and took act two to the bed.

Chapter 24

Changing for the Better

The third Monday in May, I called a meeting with my staff. I had to tell them I had accepted another job. My passion was gone. Even though I was getting better, I sometimes thought of him. Habits are so hard to break. I wanted to call and say the computer was down. But I knew he could check that anywhere. So rather than lie, I walked the office floors and stared out the windows. I was a mess. I missed Samantha so much that sometimes I couldn't determine if I was hurting because I missed her. If any of my staff noticed I had changed, they had not said anything. They worked harder to make our program stronger. Plus, they were still grieving over the loss of Samantha too.

Samantha's death had left a gaping hole in all of our hearts. I believed we were all in mourning, except I was mourning for two. Leaving had been my only option, even though my sister said I should stay and face my demons. I just couldn't. My strength to fight was gone. Plus, twice during the week I had pulled over while driving and begged God to tell me why this had happened. I asked Him to heal my heart. I wanted to stop hurting so badly.

I was tired of crying and feeling bad. I wanted my husband to be my one and only and I never dreamed that I would fall for someone else. I was broken and feeling exposed. I had always been professional. Never crossing the line, never cursing out a worker (until Sarah) because I never had to, but this thing with Travis had brought me to another level; one I wasn't proud of. It made perfect sense for me to leave, to abandon that which I loved dearly to save myself, to save my soul. I was lusting all over the place—in meetings, church, restaurants, and anytime I had a minute of silence. My mind craved to be stimulated the way Travis did to me.

I had tried to make Dexter understand my need, but he was at a comfortable stage in his life. He thought I should be satisfied he was providing for me and our son, and that he was with us. I found that even though I was satisfied and loved my husband, I wanted him to give to me what I felt Travis gave me. As I stood here, looking out the second-floor window, I saw all the lessons I had learned from my experiences at this company. I learned if I wanted something to happen, I had to make it happen.

I was going to make sure Dexter loved me mentally as much as he did physically. He was going to talk to me and I was going to make sure he did. I had to fight for happiness, and I was going to do that. Li'l Dexter was a happy child and I intended for him to stay that way. Dexter and I had a good solid foundation and I wasn't going to allow anything to crumble it. So I had to shape up or ship out, but I had the courage to do it.

I also learned that friends came and went, but real friends stayed and fought for you. Like Zandra and Pamela did. My girls knew I was going through a rough period. We had worked hard for our friendship and they were not willing to let me do something that they felt was out of character for me. They didn't badger me. Well, maybe a little bit, but I understood why. Marriages like mine were hard to find and keep, and we were all trying to keep our families intact. I appreciated Pamela and Zandra for sticking by me and making sure I made the right decisions.

I also learned there was always a reason for people to hurt you if you just looked. Karen loved me, but she had to remove those bad feelings about me from our childhood. My parents never favored me. Karen forgot she never showed love for school and my parents were focused on providing for those children who wanted an education. She just needed to be reminded, that was all.

Mostly, I learned God really did put people in my life for a reason. Brenda was a woman I respected both professionally as well as personally. She was also spiritual. Her conversations were important to me. Samantha was there to remind me how quickly my life could end and how I had to keep everything in check. She taught me how to see things with a clearer mind. In Travis's case, she picked up immediately on his feelings for me and warned me to be careful. I appreciated how she didn't make me feel guilty about Travis. Her approach wasn't like my former employee who seemed to harass me to find out information. I was very uncomfortable with Sarah, whom I felt I couldn't trust. But Samantha was careful and knew how to handle sensitive subjects. Had I listened, I wouldn't have such a heavy heart now. But mainly, I learned that time was so short and I couldn't stand around moaning and crying about things. You changed, you grew, and you went on. That was why I decided to leave. I could no longer grow at this company. It was time to go and I was about to meet with my staff to say good-bye.

Chapter 25

Don't Want To Go, But Have To

The staff was sick about my leaving. They were hurt, but after I explained why I was leaving and the opportunities that awaited me, Felicia supported me. Once she did, others did too. We shared so much at this company and all of us had grown, Frances probably the most. We had shared birthdays, weddings, baby showers, new cars, new homes, a college graduation, and so much more. So leaving was really hard.

On the last Friday in June, I walked into the office for the last time. I had already met with the board and completed my exit interview. They were devastated about my leaving, but could not match the additional $20,000 I was receiving on the new job. They gave me a crystal picture frame and a gold-plated business card holder for services rendered.

As I prepared to say good-bye, Felicia grabbed my hand and pulled me into the large conference room.

"Malika, we want to talk to you," she said as she pulled me toward the room.

Once she opened the door, the staff shouted, "Surprise!"

I really was surprised. There were balloons everywhere, gifts on a table in a far corner, food for days, and Travis. He stood tall in the corner with a huge smile on his face. I was shocked to see him.

"Malika, I invited Travis," Felicia whispered to me. "He stopped by to say good-bye. He can't stay long. But first we want to talk to you." I walked to the conference room table and sat down.

"Malika," Frances said, "I want you to know that you have really been a great boss. There was never a day I didn't want to come to work. You made our office exciting, happy, and stress-free. I want to tell you that you are a strong, talented black woman and I am proud to have worked for you. You are who I strive to be. So many women who make it don't know how to be humble and pull others along the way, but you had that down pat. You are unique, beautiful and I love you. Don't be a stranger, I want to keep in touch with you."

I stood and hugged her tightly. Felicia sat there crying. Finally, she said, "I love you, Malika. You are the best," she said as her tears rolled down her face. It got so emotional with them crying that I dropped some tears. Travis walked over, shook my hand, and said he was going to call me for lunch. It got to be too much in that room for him. I felt like he had abandoned me again. I remembered his tall, sleek body and I could feel his robust arms around my waist. I could feel his soft kisses on my face and neck. I felt like it was a love that could have been, but wasn't and would never be. I felt hurt that a man who had sat with me for months, held my hand, caressed my arm, shared himself with me couldn't stay for my entire party before saying good-bye to me forever. I cried for what I had with him, a good friendship, and I cried for the conversations I was missing. But I also knew that I needed to treat this as a growing experience and, like him, I simply needed to let go and continue to grow and sprout my wings. For the lessons I learned, I was so grateful. When he walked out I was so glad I hadn't given myself to him.

I knew that had I not been so resistant to quick sex, or acted so spacey about us, we would have had sex and still lost each other.

After all the testimonies, good-byes, and good food, we all did a huge group hug and they all helped to take the gifts to my car. I hugged the staff again and waved to them as I drove off. We had planned to have lunch the following week. For us, it wasn't good-bye, I could truly feel that. I knew I would definitely have positive contact with all of them.

It was going to be a new day. Although Travis ran out of my going-away party, I understood. It was awkward with him being there. I was going to miss all the things that happened in that second-floor office, both real and unreal. But for the better, I learned I had real needs and I was going to make sure they were being met.

Although I wasn't over Travis, I was getting stronger and realized that nothing good came without pain. In life, you take the good and make it better, and also, you take the bad with the good. That's what I planned to do.

Chapter 26

Face to Face with My Past

"Ms. Williamson, you have a call on line three." It was my new secretary, Maria.

"Thank you," I said as I picked up the phone. "Hi, this is Ms. Williamson, how may I help you?"

"Hey, Malika, this is Felicia. How are you?"

"I am fine. How are you, girl?"

"I'm doing good, but I called to tell you about Sarah Lee Gee. She filed an appeal with the company because she was turned down for unemployment. They said she acted a fool on that phone. She was cursing and saying you were cursing her out on the job and that you had fired her. She accused you of all kinds of things. But the new supervisor told her it seemed as if she was the problem and since they had recorded her conversation, the employment counselor told her the same thing. They rejected her appeal because they had documentation that she resigned, while you were trying to help her keep her job."

"Wow," I said. "I guess she couldn't even keep her attitude in check long enough to get her money, and that is such a shame."

"She acts like she has some mental issues."

"Felicia, let's not spend our time discussing her. How is the rest of the staff?" Felicia told me five people resigned within two months of my leaving.

"The office changed," she said. "You know when you were here, we were all happy, but the new supervisor doesn't have the same passion to help folks as you did. The staff picked up on that and many of them are leaving."

"That's too bad," I stated. We chatted for about twenty minutes until my secretary notified me of another call.

After hanging up line three, I picked up the next line. "Hello?"

"Please go to lunch with me." Travis surprised me. I paused. I couldn't breathe. *Why is he doing this to me? What does he want?* I didn't know how to act. *Oh, God, I can't go through this anymore.* I laid my head on the desk. *I'm just getting over him. I just can't do this anymore.*

"Malika, are you there?"

"Travis, how are you?"

"I guess I am fine. How's the new job?"

"Everything is fine here."

"Go to lunch with me. I want to see you and I am not taking no for an answer."

"Maybe next time."

"No, this time or I am coming there."

"Travis. I can't do this. Please!"

"Malika, I just want to make sure you're okay."

"I'm okay."

"That's great! But I still want to see you."

I hesitated again as I wondered if I was strong enough. Finally, I said okay. "When?"

"Today. Meet me at Friday's."

I met Travis shortly after 12:00. When I walked through the door, my heart started beating rapidly. He was standing there, waiting for me. He walked up to me and we hugged. Then the hostess seated us.

Our lunch that day was awkward. It was obvious that whatever we had was still there. But things had changed. We were reluctant to say too much, not knowing what the other was thinking or feeling. I could tell this was the real good-bye.

We laughed a lot about nothing. Then it was time to go. We never broached questions about feelings or about our families. I thought he just wanted to be with me. It was nice, but it was time to say good-bye. I still had those same feelings about him though. They were much more controlled now.

As we both prepared to leave, he grabbed my hand. "Malika, if things were different—"

"You don't have to say anything. I already know."

"I really miss our talks."

"Me, too."

We smiled and stood up to leave. He left a tip on the table and we walked out. He walked me to my car and we hugged one last time. It felt so good in his arms, but so wrong. We would have had a powerful love, hot sex, and passionate kisses. I could feel it in the heat of his hands. But things that were not meant to be were simply not meant to be.

I drove back to the office and before getting out of my car, I cried. I cried for the pure love I could have had that may not have taken as much work as I was going to have to put into making my marriage solid. I cried because I missed my friend. I cried because I really did love him. For the first time, I could say that I, Malika Williamson, fell deeply in love with Travis Ingram. Though, if he had returned those same feelings, I was sure it would have caused big problems in our marriages.

What we shared on the second floor strengthened me. I was a better person and much more sensitive. I was much more observant. Mostly, I was more professional and stronger because I did not cross that line. What happened on the second floor, in my past, was over and done. It was for the best.

I picked up my cell phone and pressed the Google application. I typed Dr. Hosea Penelton, a marriage counselor who was on the office resource list, retrieved the phone number, and pressed call. The phone rang twice and a woman answered.

"Hi, this is Malika Williamson. I would like to make an appointment for my husband, Dexter, and me. We need marriage counseling."

Two weeks later, after my lunch with Travis, I was requested by the company's owners to sit in on a meeting with two board members. As the executive director, they wanted my opinion on a new computer center that they were building in our building. Apparently, they had written a proposal and received a grant for five million to teach low-income people computer skills. They wanted me to meet the new contractors and offer my opinion, because I had worked in vocational training before.

As I walked into the conference room, I heard the receptionist whisper to my secretary that the owner of the company was a fine, pretty-ass brother. They were giggling like little girls who had just noticed they had a crush on a little boy. As I walked past, they stopped talking.

I walked up to the door and as I entered, the owner, Mr. Jerome Hathaway, smiled and turned my way. He was talking to someone, but I could not see his face. As I walked closer, Mr. Hathaway said, "Hi, Malika, please come here and meet the new contractor."

I smiled and watched as the group of executives opened up and exposed the man they had crowded around and was talking to. He looked me straight in the eyes. My heart dropped. It was my chocolate temptation.

"Hi, I am Travis Ingram."

"Malika Williamson. It is nice meeting you." I was trying to stay professional and not let on that I knew Travis. I was flabbergasted. All I could think about was lusting and coveting. I refused to go back there. It was a major struggle and I was simply not strong enough. Dexter and I were in counseling. I refused to go backward. Life was good! I looked at him.

He didn't take his eyes off me. He stared at me as if I was the most beautiful woman he had ever seen. I turned and walked to the table. I felt exposed again. I felt defeated, weak almost. I couldn't go through this again. This little voice inside my head kept saying, *whatever will happen, will happen, and whatever is meant to be, will be.*

ORDER FORM
URBAN BOOKS, LLC
78 E. Industry Ct
Deer Park, NY 11729

Name: (please print):_______________________________

Address: _______________________________

City/State: _______________________________

Zip: _______________________________

QTY	TITLES	PRICE
	16 On The Block	$14.95
	A Girl From Flint	$14.95
	A Pimp's Life	$14.95
	Baltimore Chronicles	$14.95
	Baltimore Chronicles 2	$14.95
	Betrayal	$14.95
	Black Diamond	$14.95
	Black Diamond 2	$14.95
	Black Friday	$14.95
	Both Sides Of The Fence	$14.95
	Both Sides Of The Fence 2	$14.95
	California Connection	$14.95

Shipping and handling-add $3.50 for 1st book, then $1.75 for each additional book.
Please send a check payable to:

Urban Books, LLC

Please allow 4-6 weeks for delivery

ORDER FORM
URBAN BOOKS, LLC
78 E. Industry Ct
Deer Park, NY 11729

Name: (please print): ___________________________

Address: ___________________________

City/State: ___________________________

Zip: ___________________________

QTY	TITLES	PRICE
	California Connection 2	$14.95
	Cheesecake And Teardrops	$14.95
	Congratulations	$14.95
	Crazy In Love	$14.95
	Cyber Case	$14.95
	Denim Diaries	$14.95
	Diary Of A Mad First Lady	$14.95
	Diary Of A Stalker	$14.95
	Diary Of A Street Diva	$14.95
	Diary Of A Young Girl	$14.95
	Dirty Money	$14.95
	Dirty To The Grave	$14.95

Shipping and handling-add $3.50 for 1st book, then $1.75 for each additional book.

Please send a check payable to:

Urban Books, LLC

Please allow 4-6 weeks for delivery

ORDER FORM
URBAN BOOKS, LLC
78 E. Industry Ct
Deer Park, NY 11729

Name: (please print): ______________________________

Address: ______________________________

City/State: ______________________________

Zip: ______________________________

QTY	TITLES	PRICE

Shipping and handling-add $3.50 for 1st book, then $1.75 for each additional book.
Please send a check payable to:
Urban Books, LLC
Please allow 4-6 weeks for delivery